MISSISSIPPI

N I G H T S

MISSISSIPPI
N I G H T S

D. M. WEBB

AMBASSADOR INTERNATIONAL
GREENVILLE, SOUTH CAROLINA & BELFAST, NORTHERN IRELAND

www.ambassador-international.com

MISSISSIPPI NIGHTS

Printed in the United States of America

ISBN: 9781935507918
eISBN: 9781935507949

Unless otherwise indicated all Scripture quotations are taken from NKJV

NEW KING JAMES VERSION, © Copyright 1982 by Thomas Nelson, Inc. Used by permission. All rights reserved.

Cover Design by Matthew Mulder
Page Layout by Kelley Moore of Points & Picas

AMBASSADOR INTERNATIONAL
Emerald House
427 Wade Hampton Blvd.
Greenville, SC 29609, USA
www.ambassador-international.com

AMBASSADOR BOOKS
The Mount
2 Woodstock Link
Belfast, BT6 8DD, Northern Ireland, UK
www.ambassador-international.com

The colophon is a trademark of Ambassador

DEDICATIONS:

First and foremost, I thank my Lord
for His grace and inspiration.

To my sons, Caleb and Blake: your encouragement
pushed me to "The End," and y'all really
understood your mamma's quirky ways.

To Mom: you listened to my rambles about the
story and inserted your "two cents'" worth.

To my Scribes who Scribble (scribes 236), Jo Walker, Susan
Tuttle, Kenneth Briggs, Linda Hanna, Carole Towriss,
and Jean Huffman: y'all helped make this possible.

To ACFW loopers: you're a great group that answers a
truckload of questions and loves to give helpful advice.

To Rip Copeland, Willie Wilson, and Tracy Shaw: thank you
for information on firefighting protocol and situations.

To Sgt. Gary Morris: thank you for the
crash course in police procedure.

To Mr. John Kilpatrick: you nurtured the
dream of writing within me.

To Sean: for dreams, for ideas, for being there

PROLOGUE

The squad car radio blared its announcement and caused Sergeant Jeremy Boyette to dribble coffee down the front of his uniform. Nine o'clock at night with four more hours to his shift, Jeremy needed the extra caffeine kick to stay awake. He swiped at the wet spots and scowled.

The radio blared again, asking for J forty-three to contact dispatch. Jeremy reached over to turn it down. Same-o, same-o. A quiet May night. The flickering neon light from the movie theater's sign beat a tempo against the hood of his car. He had parked his Jasper City squad car by the building and decided to enjoy his rare Jack's Express coffee, taking a much deserved break. His only battle was the one he waged against the jumbo jet mosquitoes.

His phone belted out Journey's *Don't Stop Believin'*. "Yo, little brother."

"You sleeping in the squad car again?"

Jeremy grinned at his brother's teasing. "Naw, just taking a break. It's quiet tonight. Where are you?"

"Fire Station Three."

"Thought you were off tonight."

"I am. Figured I would play a hand with Sam and Toby before heading home. Oh, Rebecca wanted me to give you a message."

Jeremy leaned against the headrest. "And that would be?"

"She doesn't care if you are on duty or not. You cannot weasel your way out of a fitting." David's laughter boomed across the phone. "She said you better show up at Mike's for the final fitting tomorrow because she will not have an ill-fitted best man at her wedding. Her words."

"You told her I was working?"

"Yup. But she said, and I quote, 'I don't care. It only takes five minutes, and if he wants my cheesecake on Sunday, then he'd better show up tomorrow.' End quote."

Jeremy laughed. "Okay, I'll go. I'll go."

"I know you will. Sarah said she would drag you in there by your nonexistent hair."

"Hey, hey. Low blow." Jeremy removed his cap and ran his hand over the stubble. "I didn't mean to lose the bet."

"Yeah. I told Rebecca that I would probably need to shave my head so you wouldn't feel like a total fool."

"I bet she liked that."

A crash sounded in the background. "Hey, the boys got the table down from the attic. I'll call you later."

"Later." Jeremy closed his phone and slipped it back into the holster on his belt. "Yup. A quiet night."

Another announcement squawked. "All units, a report of a two-vehicle accident at intersection of Fifth and Terrence Drive. All units respond."

Jeremy cast the dregs of his coffee out the window and threw the empty cup to the floorboard. He grabbed his mike. "Dispatch, show four nine responding."

He hit his lights.

The blue strobes battled with the flickering neon sign as he pulled away from the sidewalk.

"Forty-nine, be advised there is entrapment. Fire and Rescue are responding."

"Copy that, dispatch."

Jeremy peeled around the corner and zoomed past the brightly lit strip malls. A couple of blasts from his siren edged vehicles out of the way. Up ahead, a thin line of smoke climbed into the air. Not good.

Jeremy raced down Terrence Drive. His tires squealed as he jammed the brakes. He jumped out of the car, leaving the engine running. Onlookers stood on the sidewalks and gazed in morbid fascination as he ran to the scene. A man sat doubled over on the opposite curb. Blood at his feet.

The twisted remains of a Chevy Silverado meshed into a silver Ford Taurus greeted him. Oh, no. Rebecca's car.

Jeremy hurried to the side of the car and peered in. Her head lolled against the headrest. Her hands still gripped the steering wheel. Blood flowed from a deep laceration to her forehead.

"Rebecca? Can you hear me?" Jeremy reached through the smashed window. He detected a faint and thready pulse through the sticky warmth of blood.

Damage assessment. The truck had wedged the steering column against her legs. He tried the door, but it was crushed in at all angles like an empty beer can.

He hit his mike. "Dispatch, one victim. Single, white female. Trauma to head and legs. ETA on Rescue?"

"ETA three minutes."

Jeremy leaned in as far as he could and gripped her hand. The edge of the door pressed against his mike. "Rebecca? Listen to me. You will be fine. Stay with me now. You have a wedding next week."

Dispatch came back. "All units mike check. Open mike on the channel."

Jeremy cursed under his breath. Maybe David wasn't listening to the radio chatter. He removed his mike from the vest and attached it at his collar. Then, he sniffed.

The ozone stench of an electrical burn wafted through the car. Panic beat at his chest. Rescue needed to hurry.

"Rebecca, you hang in there."

More squad cars arrived. Two officers leapt from a car and cordoned off the area. Two men from the other cars rushed to him. Jeremy released Rebecca's clammy hand.

"Markston, the other driver is over there on the curb. I want his statement. Baers, with me. We got to find a way to get her out."

They tugged at the passenger door. It refused to budge.

Jeremy crawled onto the hood. Heat emanated from under the buckled metal. He took the glass punch from Baers and attacked the windshield. It spider-webbed from the impact. He and Baers folded it away from the dashboard.

Head first, he climbed into the car. Sirens wailed in the distance.

"Rescue Two en route."

Jeremy wormed his way over the steering wheel, keeping his right hand on the dashboard for balance. Smoke burned his nose and eyes. Heat seared his hands.

Her eyes fluttered opened. Thick clouds billowed up from the dashboard and choked him.

Baers tugged at his uniform's vest. "Boyette, get off! Engine's on fire!"

Jeremy stretched further. His fingers fumbled at the belt's catch. "I almost got her."

"Get off!"

Rebecca's eyes, cloudy and vibrant blue, gazed into his, but then he slid away. Jeremy struggled as Baers dragged him off the hood.

Baers spoke into his mike as he pushed him away from the car. "Dispatch, we can't reach her!"

"All units, stand down and await Fire and Rescue." The calm voice contrasted against the chaos of the scene.

Orange flames licked out from underneath the hood. Oh, please, no! No! Rescue wouldn't arrive fast enough. Baers latched on to his vest and pulled him away from the car.

Jeremy grabbed his mike. "Dispatch, please advise! Victim is still trapped! Car is fully involved."

Seconds ticked by. "All units are commanded to stand down."

Jeremy cursed. Orders were orders, but not this time. He strained against Baers. "I have to get her, Thad!"

Baers' arm wrapped around his neck. "Stop, Boyette. You can't get to her! Chief ordered us to stand down."

Jeremy bucked against his friend. His vision reddened as Baers tightened his hold.

"Jeremy, you can't reach her, man! Stop."

The fire truck arrived. Firefighters vaulted to the pavement and pulled hoses. A smaller truck barreled onto the scene. A man heaved a large, heavy tool out of the truck's side panel. The jaws of life, made to rip apart doors.

A black '65 Mustang slid to a stop behind the fire trucks.

David didn't need to be here. Jeremy strained against Baers' hold. "David's here. Let me go!"

Baers released him, and he hurried to his brother's side.

David's terror-widened eyes absorbed the scene. He plowed past the officer at the yellow tape. "That's Rebecca."

Jeremy pressed his hands against his brother's chest. Veins popped up along his arms as he strained to hold him at bay. "They're getting her."

David pushed past him. His long legs ate up the pavement as he raced to the fire. "You left her there? You left her!"

"David! Stop!" Jeremy caught his arm and spun him around. "We were ordered to stand down until Rescue puts out the fire."

Wild, unbridled anger lanced from David's face, and his voice broke. "You left her?"

His hands slammed into Jeremy's chest. Jeremy stumbled, then righted himself and dove after his brother as David whirled around.

Jeremy grabbed a fistful of David's shirt. Fabric ripped out of his hands. "Baers! Stop him."

His mind catalogued every action like frames of a film. He tackled his brother around the waist, halting David's flight and bringing him to his knees. Firemen ducked back as orange flames shot into the night sky. He heard a strangled scream be-side him.

The heat from the blast seared into him. The weight of the impact pushed at his chest. He fought and struggled to contain his brother's crazed flight.

David's arms and legs clawed and crawled across the pave-ment, dragging them both closer to the inferno. The fire's deaf-ening roar filled his ears. Heat radiated against his face.

A fist pummeled into him.

Pain exploded inside his head.

Other hands came to his aid. Markston and Baers hauled David to the curb. His brother fell to his knees. Sobs racked his body. Jeremy staggered and knelt beside David. Pain from his brother's eyes bored into him. Tears streaked both of their faces.

In the distance, men shouted. Water sizzled as it fell down onto the burning car.

But nothing would ever erase the scream, erase the howl, that poured forth from his little brother's soul.

CHAPTER 1

The white gravel drive, with its mailbox reading *Dean and Leigh Boyette*, wound down to the stately brick Georgian house. David had never driven the familiar ride with such apprehension. He was the prodigal son returning home—minus the guilt.

Rocks crunched beneath the tires as he brought his old, beat-up Chevy truck to a stop. He sat there, hands on the wheel, taking deep breaths. Sweat coated his palms. It had been three years since he last sat in this drive. Letters, phone calls, and e-mails had kept him in touch, but now he was back in Jasper City for good. He was an adult, for crying out loud, and he did not need to be running home like a small child.

The door creaked, testimony of the truck's age, as he opened it and stepped out onto the driveway. His boots, like the truck, had seen better days. So had he.

Old possessions. Old clothes. Old beyond his thirty-five years. Just plain old.

David grabbed his duffel bag from the bed of the truck and trudged the few steps to the front door. He sidestepped the fat tomcat asleep on the porch's step. Fat Tom, big, yellow, and lazy.

"Mornin', Fat Tom," David whispered.

Fat Tom opened one eye in greeting and then rolled over, perfecting cat arrogance.

David cocked his head. The door knocker was new, outlandish, and bulky. Mom's idea. He lifted the clown and let it fall against the metal plating. Yep, that heavy clank would get someone's attention.

So he did it again. And again. And again.

Someone yelled. "Coming!"

The clown went up and then down.

"I said I'm coming!"

Again David lifted the clown and let it plummet.

"Coming!" This time the voice screeched.

The door jerked open, and the woman, plump, beautiful, and smelling of jasmine, screeched again. This time in delight. "David!"

His feet practically left the porch as his mother pulled his tall frame down to her, enveloping him in a strong hug. "Oh my goodness! You said next week, David! Oh my goodness!"

The mantra nearly brought him to tears as she kept him in a bear hug, rocking gently.

"I couldn't wait, Mamma." Her gray streaked hair muffled his voice. "I had to see you."

She finally pulled back. "Oh, I have missed you. You look tired. And shaggy. Look at that hair. You would think it was the 70's again." She pulled at him. "Come in, silly! Go put your stuff up and get to the kitchen. I got to fatten you up again."

David bent to kiss his mother's cheek. "I've missed you, Mamma. And your cooking."

"Your sister will be here in a little while, along with Marty Junior. She will be so surprised to see you."

His mom practically skipped back to the kitchen as David climbed the stairs. Once again the familiar felt strange. Same pictures still hung on the wall. The handrail still wiggled. New rosy carpet covered the floor.

He turned right and stood in front of his bedroom. His dad had painted over the green stripes that he put on the door so long ago. He peered inside. A wave of sadness surged over him.

Same full size bed. Same curtains. Same old furniture. But none of his life before remained. When he left, he had screamed, shouted, hurled curses, and said he would never return. Now his room was a guest room. His things must have been packed away in the attic or the storage building out back–his things that had once occupied the new home that he would have shared with Rebecca, things that David had moved into this room before he left it all behind. He forced a swallow past his dry throat and blocked those thoughts.

The duffel bag bounced once when he threw it on the bed. He sat beside it and buried his head in his hands. Weariness, that old cliché, washed over him and entered his bones.

He was too tired and too empty.

As exhilarated as his mother was to see him, and his father and Darlene probably would be also, he doubted Jeremy would welcome him back. Resentment, borderline hate, still flowed between them.

"Your things are in the attic."

That deep, melodic voice had never changed. It commanded attention and brimmed with affection.

David smiled at his father, who leaned against the door frame. "Hey, Dad."

"Come here, Son." His dad took two long strides and pulled David into a tight embrace. "It's so good to see you home, Son. Let me look at you." His dad held him at arm's length. "You look tired. Beat up."

"I am tired."

"What happened in St. Louis?"

David shook his head. "Nothing, Dad. Nothing at all."

"You needed home." His dad could read him just as well as that well-worn Bible of his.

"Yeah. I needed home."

═══

Things in the house might have changed in small degrees, but David found the kitchen in the same state as he remembered. Decorative plates hung on the wall above the sink. The walls still bore the neutral khaki color his mother preferred. The old black cat clock hung by the old wall phone jack. Neither worked, but his mother refused to throw away the cat.

Magnets littered the refrigerator, holding up pictures made by the grandchildren. The counters still held the black and silver coffee pot, the silver canisters, and the fat chef cookie jar. The bar was the same. The painted bar stools that David designed as a Mother's Day present were still there, mended in many places. Even the aroma of the kitchen was the same. Bread, cinnamon, and the faint hint of coffee told him he was home.

David sat with his father at the bar and accepted a cup of coffee from his mother. She bustled about, fixing a thick sandwich and a thick wedge of apple pie for each of her men.

His dad picked up his cup. "Did the chief give you a hard time? I know he didn't want you to leave."

David leaned back as his mother set a plate in front of him and kissed the side of his head. "No. He just said to let him know if I ever wanna come back." David shoveled a forkful into his mouth. "Mmm . . . this pie is delicious, Mom."

His mom beamed and went about cleaning the countertops.

"Would you want to go back?"

"I don't really know, Dad. When I got to St. Louis, I loved it. But the bustle of city life was wearing me thin. Got to where a man couldn't hear himself think." David paused and swallowed the last bit of his coffee. He set his cup down, and his mom whisked it away. "A man could lose himself, Dad."

His cup of coffee reappeared, and then his mom was gone, leaving the two men alone.

"Were you afraid that was happening?" His dad pushed his half-eaten sandwich aside and leaned forward onto his elbows.

"Sort of." David took the last bite of his sandwich and talked around a mouthful. "I had everything I needed or wanted. Everything seemed right, but then it all got old. Bright lights. Steady hum of vehicles. I just got this gnawing in my gut."

His dad stood and put his dishes in the sink. "You needed home. No shame in that, David."

"I know, Dad. But I am a grown man. It feels weird to run home, tail between legs."

"Is that how you feel?"

David shrugged and pushed aside his empty-again cup. "Not really. Just sometimes."

His dad leaned against the sink. "Son, sometimes a man just needs to be around family to remind him that there is still something solid out there."

"Ever the wise man."

"Only wise because of many mistakes." His dad hesitated slightly. "Jeremy is still here, and you know you can't avoid him. He's your brother."

A wall slammed down around his heart. "Three years is a long time, but not long enough. I don't know how I feel anymore. Hurt, angry, I don't know." He looked up. His father studied him. He looked away. "Empty, Dad. Mainly empty."

The front door slammed open, and a tall, ungainly body came hurtling through the doorway. All feet and legs, Marty Sanderson skidded to a stop.

"Oof!" A woman maneuvered around the teenager. "Marty! You're like a walking wall. One minute running, the next– wham! You stop."

David watched the small, lithe figure search for the cause of her son's immobility. Her green eyes locked onto David. A dimpled smile spread across her face. Darlene Boyette Sanderson launched herself into his waiting arms, her red flannel shirt flying out behind her. Same Darlene.

"David! Oh my goodness! You said next week. Oh my goodness! David!"

David laughed over the repeat of words. Like mother, like daughter.

"I couldn't wait."

"I'd say not." Darlene pulled back and looked him up and down. "You need to fatten up. You're about as skinny as Marty."

David looked over at the bashful teen and pulled him into a hug. "Marty, you've grown."

Red-faced, Marty grinned. "Hi, Uncle David."

"Hi, yourself. What grade are you in now?"

"Tenth." Marty shuffled his feet, unaccustomed to the attention. "Mostly like it."

David sat back down at the bar. "Any girlfriends?"

"David!"

"What?" He cast an innocent look at his sister.

"He's only fifteen. Leave him be." Darlene perched at the bar and stared at her brother. "Why so early?"

David glanced at Marty as the teenager walked over to the refrigerator and opened it. The kid's head disappeared within. "I was already packed and nothing to do except read old letters I had gotten in the mail."

At his statement, Marty peeked over the door and quickly ducked back. Marty grabbed some deli meat and constructed a sandwich, pointedly ignoring David.

"Letters?" Darlene grabbed David's cup and joined her mother at the counter. "I didn't send any. Did you, Mom?"

His mom smiled and refilled the cups. "Of course I did. I hate e-mails." She ambled over to Marty and started putting the sandwich fixings back into the refrigerator. Marty grabbed his sandwich. David made room for him at the bar.

A pickle hung over the edge of Marty's sandwich. David plucked it out and popped it in his mouth. "Your grandmamma's letters weren't the only ones. Were they?"

Marty buried his face into his sandwich.

Darlene laughed. "I sent you a couple of cards."

"I read those too. And Sarah's." David nudged Marty. "And yours."

"So, David, tell me about the big city life of St. Louis." Darlene sidled up close to him. "What was it like?"

David smiled. "Busy. Very, very busy."

CHAPTER 2

David stood at the kitchen window, empty cup in hand, and gazed out. Thoughts rambled through his head, not allowing him to focus. An old, restless feeling decided to revisit, and he would need to find something to do soon.

He dropped his cup into the sink on his way to the back door. Just past the hedgerow in his parents' backyard stood the small pond. If his dad held true to form, then the old fishing rods would still be in the back of the storage building.

Outside, the faint morning sun washed everything in its soft light. Soon his parents would rise and start their day, but David did not welcome the day of restarting his life—not yet anyway.

Fat Tom left his place on the back porch step and followed him to the building at the back corner of the yard. The door stuck slightly as David pushed it open and felt for the light switch.

The bare bulb flickered and lit the small area in a harsh light. David pushed aside a chair that was apparently in the process of being reupholstered. There on the back wall stood his catfish pole next to a crafting table full of his mom's scrapbooking items.

He reached for the fishing pole and knocked it over. The rod crashed into a small box and scattered its contents. He bit back a curse and squatted to pick up the photographs that littered the concrete floor. He paused over one picture.

His nostrils flared at the sight of the photo. He and his brother, arm in arm, smiled as they posed in their tuxedos. He fought the urge to crumple the photo. Instead, David replaced it inside the box and noticed there were no pictures of Rebecca. His mom must have them stuffed in a separate container.

David snatched up his pole and the nearby tackle box. He nudged Fat Tom outside with his foot and made his way to the pond. A glorious morning of silence awaited. His steps slowed. He underestimated his father.

His dad sat on the wooden bench, leg crossed over knee and arms stretched along the back. He smiled at David as he made his way down to the bank.

"Morning, son. You sleep well?"

David ruffled his dad's hair as he passed by. "Morning, Dad. I slept all right."

A few mockingbirds were up and about. One perched on a hedge and watched the men at the water's edge. David picked up a pebble and chucked it at the bird. It flew off the twigs and landed nearby on the ground. It casually started pecking at the dirt. Pesky birds. He chucked another pebble at it. Didn't need them to hamper his fishing.

"Tomorrow's Sunday."

"Um-hmm." David cut the old hook off the line and opened his tackle box. He pushed aside some lures and flies and found his bag of catfish hooks. As he tied one onto the line, his Dad spoke again.

"You going to church?" His dad shifted on the bench. "You know the rules of the house."

David threaded the plastic worm onto the hook. "I know. So, why even bother asking if you know the answer?" With a flick of his wrist, the line flew out into the air, arced with perfect grace, and plopped into the water.

"I just want to make sure. It'll be good for you. But . . ."

David slowly reeled the line in a bit and then let it rest. "But what?"

"Jeremy is still attending. He and Sarah returned last year. He teaches Sunday School for the teen boys."

David felt his dad's eyes on him and refused to look over. He reeled in his line and cast it out again. His throat burned. His knuckles turned white as he held the rod in a death grip.

"David?"

"What, Dad?" He yanked the fishing rod, bringing in the line before turning to his father. "What do you want me to say? How about, how could Sarah still stand to be with the coward? How can I forgive the–"

"Enough!" His dad bellowed. He uncrossed his legs and stood.

David held back a snarl and recast the line. A few heavy moments hung between them. His father placed a hand on his shoulder, and David felt some of his anger abate. How did his father do that?

"David, son, Sarah doesn't see him as a coward. Neither do we. I know it still hurts, but you will be around your brother more often than not."

"I know that." David nudged the tackle box over with his foot and shifted his stance. His father's hand fell away. He turned to go back to the house, but David stopped him.

"Dad?"

"Yes?"

David let the fishing rod droop. "I don't think I am ready to forgive him yet. How can I forgive him, knowing that he could've saved Rebecca?"

His father took a few steps toward him and gripped his shoulders. He squeezed them. "You forgive as Christ forgave. It will come, David. Open your heart."

David watched as his dad walked away and disappeared beyond the hedgerow. He heaved a deep sigh and turned back to his fruitless fishing. Repetition calmed him, so David cast out the line again.

Maybe later he could finish the chair in the storage building or maybe get that old Harley going again. Anything to stay busy.

Anything to keep the craving at bay.

═══════

Jeremy Boyette leaned against the hood of his Jasper City squad car. He cupped his hand around the Zippo lighter, careful that the flame didn't touch his gloves, and lit his second cigarette in a row. This stress was going to kill him. He shoved the lighter back into his cargo pocket and inhaled the tobacco smoke. Nicotine raced throughout his body. Jeremy raised his face to the setting sun that glinted behind the old downtown buildings.

He had an hour left to his shift, and he felt dog-tired. This morning did him in, but it was worth it. Now they had an informant. Jeremy inhaled another long drag. This one had better work out. That drug ring would go down this time, and he'd make those Memphis gangster wannabes think twice about entering his town.

Another draw on the cigarette, but no closer to relaxation.

"Jer!" Baers' voice yelled from the back door of the police station. "Captain wants ya."

Couldn't the guy ever just come and get him like a normal person? Jeremy inhaled one last time and crushed the cigarette under his heel.

Baers, the tallest, biggest, and darkest officer on the force, stood at the door when Jeremy entered. "How many does that make today?"

"What?" Jeremy grimaced and pushed past the giant.

"Thought you told Sarah you were trying to quit."

"I did. Down to a pack a week."

"You just smoked a pack out there."

Jeremy ignored him and continued down the gray hall. Why did they always use gray? He felt antsy tonight. And in a foul mood. He turned the corner and entered the police captain's office on the right. Captain Conners' lanky build was hunched over his desk with a cell phone plastered to his ear. He motioned for Jeremy to sit and then rubbed at his head. If he rubbed too hard, he would rub away what was left of his hair.

"I'm right on it. We should have information by the end of the weekend. Yes, I understand. Goodbye." He all but chucked the phone down and rubbed at his eyes.

Jeremy sat patiently in the chair and waited until his boss turned his gaze to him before asking, "Wanted to see me, Captain?"

"What's the situation on the drug ring? That was the Chief. Mayor wants an update by the end of the weekend. The bubble head doesn't realize that's tomorrow."

"We got a pretty good source this time." Jeremy crossed his ankle over a knee. "This one is more reliable. Not affiliated with the gang, but he's in the area where they meet."

"We know that location yet?"

"No. Not yet." He shrugged. "I'll give it until next week at least."

"Good. Next week then." Conners shuffled some papers around, lifted a few, and then pulled a sheet from under his blotter. "Dang mess in here."

Jeremy accepted the print-out Conners handed him. "Oh, you got to be joking!"

"Sorry. Budget came in, and we got slashed. As of now, I'm pulling you off the morning shift and back onto mid shift. And that's where you need to be. Chief's orders."

"Do you know how long it has taken me to get to morning shift? Three long years! And now because of some pencil head, d–" He stopped and stared at the ceiling a moment. He was too tired to argue, as if it would've done any good, anyway. "So, start tomorrow?"

"Yup. Go home, and I'll see you here tomorrow evening. You could do with a good night's sleep. Oh, and send in Baers."

Jeremy shook his head and walked to the door. "He ain't gonna take it quietly."

Conners picked up a set of ear plugs and smiled. "Oh, I came prepared."

Jeremy found Baers in the breakroom, filling in paperwork. "Captain wants you."

Jeremy felt his gaze as he removed his tactical vest and hung it in his locker. He slammed the locker door and turned to Baers. "Did you hear me?"

"Yeah. I'll get there. Where you heading to?"

Jeremy let out a heavy sigh. "I'm back on mid shift starting tomorrow, so I get to go home."

"That sucks." Baers' hands paused and dropped the pen. "Ah, man. You mean to tell me—"

"Yup." Jeremy clapped Baers on the back as he walked by. "See ya tomorrow night, big fella." He hurried down the hall to the door. True to form, Baers barreled out of the breakroom, bellowing a string of oaths, and disappeared down the hall to the captain's office. The door slam echoed down the hall. He swore Baers made the cinder blocks shake.

Jeremy slipped outside. He reached for his pack and shook out a cigarette. The lighter made its customary scratch as he opened it and lit the tobacco. He needed the reinforcement before he told Sarah the news. Just when he thought things were going to be better, enter the politicians. Barely enough brain cells among the lot to create an amoeba.

Jeremy puffed on his cigarette as his walked to his Ford F-250. He climbed in and sat back, intent on finishing at least one cigarette before heading home. He gazed out at the lights of downtown. Such a small town and yet so close to the big city that they were beginning to see their share of urban crime. Jeremy snarled and took another drag on his cigarette. He needed to stop thinking about work.

A few cars zipped by. Teenagers joyriding the downtown lanes on a balmy March night. Jeremy smiled as he watched them. He remembered doing that with Sarah. Once he graduated school and the police academy, he found himself the one chasing after those teenagers.

His brother was one of them. Seventeen and a license to drive, especially a Mustang Fastback, was a bad combination. David always upped the ante on everything.

He took the last drag from his cigarette and snuffed the butt out in the ashtray. Boy, was Sarah going to be surprised . . . or angered . . . or both. Chief Johnson had better stay out of her hair for the next few days. Or better yet, that pansy mayor of theirs.

The phone beside him belted out Styx's *Babe*.

"Hey, babe. I was just thinking about you." Jeremy pulled his truck onto the street.

"Really? About what?"

"About who you would like to roast over a pit. The chief or the mayor?" He flipped his blinker on and took the left turn onto the main strip of town.

"Bad news?"

"You could say that."

"I've got news for you too. But you first."

Jeremy shook his head. "Nah. Better to tell you in person."

"I see."

Pots rattled and clanged. She was preparing supper, and he was hungry. "Look. I'm actually on my way home. I got the rest of the night off."

"How'd you get that?"

"Chief decided I needed to work tomorrow instead." He stopped at the red light and waited. "I'll be there in about five."

"Okay. See ya when you get here. Love you."

"Love you too, babe." Jeremy closed his phone. No sooner had he set it down than it played Mozart's Fifth. "Hey, Mom. What's up?"

"Nothing really. We're having Sunday dinner tomorrow, and I wanted to make sure you didn't forget."

Jeremy groaned. The light turned green, and he drove straight. "I didn't forget. But I've been moved back to mid shift. Starting tomorrow night."

"Oh." He pictured his mom slumped in disappointment. "I was so hoping you could come."

"Look, if I got the time, I'll swing by. But I probably won't be able to stay long."

Her voice was chipper when she spoke. "Wonderful. There's something else I need to tell you."

Jeremy pulled into his subdivision. "What's that?"

"David's home."

He swerved to miss the neighbor's mailbox. "Home? I didn't think he was coming until next week."

"He came early."

"Why?" Jeremy pulled into his drive and stopped in front of the garage. His small brick home that sat farther back from the street than the others loomed before him.

"Why? Because he did." He could hear muffled laughter in the background.

"He's there now?"

"No. Think he said something about the fire station. Anyway, I wanted you to know." Jeremy heard his dad call out to his mom. "Gotta go. I'll see you tomorrow, honey. Love you."

The phone went dead. Jeremy sat there. David home? What happened to a week to prepare? His brother couldn't even give him that. Talk about upping the ante.

He pulled off his gloves. The pink and puckered burn scars stared up at him. What a mockery that he carried scars from doing something David believed he hadn't done. He had tried. Only he'd failed. Jeremy sighed and opened the door. He needed another cigarette, but Sarah would kill him if he lit up at home.

Sarah, her dark velvet hair pulled into a ponytail, met him at the door with a kiss. "I choose the mayor."

Jeremy laughed and wrapped his arms around her. "Right choice. Tofu for brains slashed our budget. Now I'm back on nights."

She sagged against him. "Oh, Jeremy. After all that time to get on days."

He held her tall and slender frame to his. "It might be for the best. Who knows? Things happen for a reason."

"Hmm. They do, but we don't always have to like it."

He let her go and followed her past the living room and into the brightly lit kitchen. "Where's Dennis and Sophie?"

"Dennis is at Marty's for the night. Sophie is at Amy's house. I told her she had to be home by eight." She opened the refrigerator and bent to seek out food.

"You mean we got the night alone?" He twirled her around and backed her up until she was pressed against the sink. "See, things happen for a reason."

Sarah giggled and wrapped her arms behind his head. "Yeah, they do. Don't you want to hear my news?"

"Later."

"But your mom called and told me."

He lifted his wife into his arms and whisked her out of the kitchen and down the hall. He buried his head against her neck. "I heard. Don't repeat it."

He pushed the bedroom door closed with his booted foot and lowered her onto the plush bed. "Tonight. Right now." He placed a kiss on her forehead. "No mayor." Another kiss on her nose. "No chief." He placed another kiss on her lips. "And definitely no brother."

Sarah smiled up at him, and her brown eyes softened. "Things happen for a reason?"

"Yeah. Like finally having a night to ourselves. No children." He lowered his head and kissed her deeply. Her arms latched around his back and pulled him closer. Nothing like the love of a wife to take away your worries.

The front door slammed. "Mom! Amy decided to come over here tonight! Mom?"

Jeremy rolled off of his wife. Sarah sat up and leaned over him, giggling. Oh, how cruel. She kissed his cheek and purred into his ear. "There's always tonight when they go to bed. Go take a shower. You reek of cigarettes."

With a smack to his chest, she hopped off the bed and disappeared out of the room. He pulled a frilly pillow over his face and groaned. Things happen for a reason. Like his craving for another cigarette.

CHAPTER 3

Linkin Park played in the background. The music bounced off the walls and shelves in the garage, drowning all other sounds and thoughts. David pushed aside the toolbox and turned up the volume on the radio. He needed his thoughts buried this morning.

Early morning rays filtered in from the opened garage door. Fat Tom lazed on an old tire at the corner. David glanced at the cat and grunted. Fat Tom dogged, or more accurately catted, his every step. David either tripped over the danged feline or stepped on his tail.

The wrench slipped. His knuckle grazed the motor of the '85 Harley. He bit back a curse and sucked at his scraped knuckle. It was Sunday. The least he could do was curb his language. He picked up the wrench and tried again.

No matter how much force he applied, the nut refused to turn. David stood and clutched the wrench, ready to chuck it at the bike, but he didn't want to nick the beautiful red paint. He dropped the wrench back into the toolbox. Somewhere on the shelf had to be some lubricant. He pushed containers aside, pulled boxes out, and cast them to the floor as they turned up no results. If they clattered, who knew? Linkin Park belted out *In the End* at high decibels.

There was no can anywhere. Dad's supplies sure were lacking. David turned and scowled at the covered hulk sleeping on the other side of the garage. He had resisted touching that part of his history, but he remembered a can lying in the glove box.

He growled and stalked to the car. His hands shook as they grabbed the canvas. With a forceful yank, it soared into the air and floated down to the cement floor. His black beauty. The paint gleamed beneath a faint smattering of dust along the hood. He opened the door, and the smell of polished leather greeted him.

David swallowed. The last time he drove his Fastback was at the funeral. His fists clenched as the memory flooded his mind. Rebecca's closed silver casket and those horrible carnations. Rain. Why did it always rain at a funeral? And thunder.

He cleared his throat and blew out a breath. That was the past. Get over it.

David ducked his head and slid into the seat. It cupped his long frame. He ran his hand along the steering wheel and dashboard. She was so pretty with her black interior, sculpted bucket seats, and gleaming panels. He shook his head. Enough of this.

He hit the button on the glove box and pulled out the small can of lubricant. Keys jingled as they hit the floorboard. He leaned over and picked them up. Without a pause, he inserted the key and turned the ignition. It whined and coughed, but wouldn't catch. He tried again. The starter chattered but then fell silent. Absolutely great. It sat too long.

He unfolded his long frame out of the car, pocketed the keys, and went back to his Harley. First things first; he wanted to get the Harley going. He squatted back down and used the lubricant to loosen the nut.

The music plummeted to a soft level. David slipped the wrench, and his knuckle connected again. A curse slipped out.

He turned, knuckle at his lips, and found his father standing by the radio, eyes narrowed. Yeah. It wasn't a very good curse. David picked the wrench back up. "Sorry, Dad."

"You're up early. Couldn't sleep?" His father, cup in hand, perched on the edge of the metal tool cabinet. The smell of coffee wafted over to David.

"No. I slept fine. Just woke up early is all." His dad watched him as he sipped his coffee. "Really, Dad. I slept just fine."

"Well, I wondered. Knew you came in late."

"Met Sam and Toby at the station is all. Stayed talking until late." David finally loosened the nut and had it off. He was no child.

"Did you speak with Thomas?" Another sip of coffee.

"Yeah. I start tomorrow. C shift."

His father raised an eyebrow. "C shift? I thought you were going to do A?"

David shrugged. "I prefer the C shift. And I asked the chief for it."

"I see. Well," his father slapped him on the shoulder, "breakfast is ready. Clean up and come eat."

David laid the nut and wrench to the side. The Harley was almost ready. He could finish it after breakfast.

"If you don't mind, I'll skip out on early service and Sunday School. I'll be there for the main worship service." He rubbed at his hands with a grease rag.

His dad pursed his lips and turned to the door. "Come on. Your mom whipped up a big breakfast, so I hope you got an appetite this morning."

David grimaced. "If she keeps on, I won't be able to keep off the weight. I swear, why she got to cook so much?"

His father held the door open and waited for David. "Because she cooks when she is worried."

David pushed past his father to the utility sink in the laundry room. He popped the lid off the Fast Orange and scooped out a glob of the gritty cleaner. "What's she got to be worried about?"

"You."

David paused, warm water pouring over his lathered hands. Him? Surely no one knew. He swallowed the lump in his throat and dried his hands. His dad still stared at him. He stared back. He'd perfected the act of nonchalance long ago. "Why worry about me? I'm fine."

"Hmm. So you say." His dad turned away. David followed him into the kitchen and opened the cabinet door to retrieve a coffee cup as his dad spoke again. "Jeremy will be here tonight for dinner."

David banged his head with the door. Ow. "And?" His hands didn't shake as he poured the coffee. That was a plus.

"Your mother is just worried how you two will behave toward each other. That's all."

David smiled. He reached out and ruffled his dad's hair as he walked past him. "Nothing to worry about, Dad. Nothing to worry about."

A lot to worry about. Like he told his dad yesterday, sometimes three years just wasn't long enough.

Margaret Allison Goddard waited for the children to seat themselves along the Zion Baptist Church's pew. Two of the three-year-olds bounced around on the red cushion, anxious for their mamma and daddy to arrive, while the other children from class wiggled and squirmed. She placed her hands on their heads and leaned down.

"Max, Lilly, be still for just a little while longer. Your mamma will be out in a moment."

Max's little cherub face smiled. "But I gotta go."

"To the bathroom?"

"No. Outside."

She laughed and knelt down in front of him. "We don't go outside yet."

He squirmed and tugged at his overalls. "But I gotta wewease him."

"Release who?"

His smile brightened. Max's chubby little hands reached down the bib of his overalls and pulled out a brown, warty toad. A ripple effect coursed down the pew. Lilly, his twin sister, stood up on the pew, her high-pitched squeal filling the sanctuary. One by one, the other girls caught a glimpse of Max's prize and started shrieking. The boys had to see, and they crowded around Miss Maggie and Max. Oh my.

"How long have you had him?"

"Since breakfast. Mamma dinna know, Miss Maggie."

"Well," she held out her hand, "let me have him now. I'll put him outside."

She grimaced as tiny amphibian feet touched her palm. Quickly, she cupped the toad in her hand to prevent it from hopping away. Last thing she needed was Jasper City's own version of the Pascagoula squirrel.

"Sit down, guys. Girls, hush. I got the toad now, so sit and be quiet. How are we supposed to behave in the Lord's house?"

Amber, a pixie faced five-year-old, raised her hand. "Quiet and with good behaveness."

Maggie's mouth twitched. Behaveness? That was a new one. The door opened behind her. The youth filed into the sanctuary. Relief at last; her cousin had arrived. The toad hopped around in her hand and felt really quite disgusting.

Sarah followed behind the teenagers and came to stand beside Maggie. "What you got there?"

Max jumped up. "She got a horny toad."

The youth snickered. Maggie turned to Max. "This isn't a horny toad. I think you caught a regular toad."

"But I wanna horny toad, like Papa said he caught." Max's lip pushed out, and he plopped back against the pew, arms crossed.

"Well, horny toads don't hop near churches, Max. Got to find them in the desert."

"Or the zoo, Miss Maggie." A redheaded, ten-year-old girl chimed in. She smacked her gum and propped her elbows on the back of the front pew. Her skinny body half plopped over the top as she teetered along its edge.

"Yes. And the zoo. Which, Max, we will get to see next weekend, right?" At his nod of assent, she turned to the red head. "And Poppy, go spit out the gum."

Poppy screwed her face up in a puckered snarl and left the pew. She clomped her way out of the sanctuary. Maggie turned to Sarah. "Mind watching my group while I go release the hopping prisoner?"

"You really got a toad in there?"

Maggie picked it up between her forefinger and thumb and held it out. Little girls squealed again, and the little boys jumped up shouting "cool." She held the droopy-legged toad out to Sarah. "Pretty big, isn't he? And to think Max had him in his pants during the entire Sunday School."

Sarah shook her head and waved Maggie away. "Go on. I got them."

Maggie pushed past the double swinging doors and met Poppy in the large, cream carpeted, split level foyer. "Stop. Open."

Poppy rolled her eyes but complied and showed a mouth full of teeth and no chewing gum.

"Okay." Maggie leaned down and dropped a peck on top of her head. "Don't bring gum to church again."

"But I forgot to brush my teeth this morning. I didn't want someone to call me garbage breath again."

Maggie stopped short. She cupped her captive in her hands a littler tighter and knelt down in front of Poppy. "Who called you that?"

"Just some of the boys." Poppy looked down at her black, shiny Mary Janes and scuffed at the carpet. "But it was only once."

Maggie sighed. This little girl had no one. Her grandmamma was her only relative, and she was lucky if the woman brought Poppy to church on an irregular basis. She started to reach out and hug the girl but stopped. She almost forgot about the toad.

"How about if I keep a toothbrush here for you? In the office? That way, if you forget again, it will be there for you. Okay?"

Poppy's smile lit her face. "Really? Oh, thank you, Miss Maggie."

She threw her arms around Maggie's neck. A small oomph escaped her. She teetered. Heels didn't help. With Poppy around her neck and the toad cupped in her hands, she couldn't catch herself as she toppled. Poppy landed on top of her, and the toad escaped.

"Quick, Poppy! Catch him!" On hands and knees, Maggie and Poppy tried to catch the elusive toad. "There!"

She and Poppy dove under the water fountain, but the toad hopped away. Across the hallway and down the steps they scuttled. Maggie lost a high heel somewhere on the steps. Poppy missed the dratted creature and slid the rest of the way down. Five steps at most, but it seemed like Mt. Everest as Maggie chased after the creature.

The toad made it close to the welcome table, and Maggie stood and hobbled after it. She fell to her knees. Her hand slapped down. And missed. Good gracious, that thing was hard to catch.

"Where did it go, Poppy?"

"Um. He's got it."

He? Maggie pushed away from under the table and looked up. A very handsome, very tall man in a white shirt and dark denim stood in front of the full-length stained glass that bordered the front door. Light from the windows lit his body in an aura of red and white. His hair, long enough to brush against his ears, glowed like a halo about his head. He stepped away from the door. Green eyes met her gaze head-on. A wide, beautiful smile spread across his sad face.

"Is this yours?" The velvet timbre of his voice caressed her ears.

Wow. Nothing but wow. Even Poppy was speechless.

Maggie rose to her feet, feeling off balance with one shoe missing. What she must've looked like. A grown woman in a pink sundress on hands and knees chasing a toad in church.

"Thanks." Maggie started to reach for the toad, but he pulled it away and held it up in front of his face.

"Doesn't seem like your kind of pet."

Maggie laughed. "He isn't. One of the kids had him during Sunday School. He escaped from me before I could throw him out."

He laughed, turned to the door, and opened it. With a gentleness she didn't expect, he placed the toad on the doorstep and pushed it with his finger. The smell of freedom sent the toad into a frenzy, and he hopped off lickety-split.

"Thank you." She started to hold out her hand but then thought better of it. "I don't know if the old saying is true about toads and warts, but to be safe I better not shake your hand."

He laughed as he closed the door. "Well, I held the toad too. So I see no problem." He held out his hand.

Maggie hesitated a second and then slid hers into his. A working man's hand, callused and hard. "Maggie Goddard."

His eyebrow quirked up. "Ah, related to Bro. Johnny?"

"Yeah. He's my father. This is Poppy Littleton."

He gave the little girl a smile. "Poppy, that's a very beautiful dress."

The girl blushed and twirled around in the black and white checkered dress. "Thanks," she mumbled and dashed back into the sanctuary.

"She's shy around strangers." Maggie limped to the steps to retrieve her shoe. Two big steps had him there before her.

He scooped up her pink high heel and held it out to her. "Cinderella, your shoe."

He was a charmer, indeed. "Thank you. New in town?" She propped against the wall with one hand and replaced her shoe.

"No. Used to live here. Name's David Boyette."

So this was the elusive brother. "Jeremy's brother. Sarah's my cousin."

"Figured that out. Sarah told me her uncle took over the church a couple of years ago. You like it here?"

"I do." She held her hands out. "If you don't mind, I need to wash my hands just in case there is toad pee on them."

A chuckle shook his chest. "Sure. See you around, Maggie Goddard."

She watched him push through the double doors. He threw a smile over his shoulder at her, and then the doors swung closed. Charmer, indeed. Well, with Jeremy's bad boy brother back in town, life just got spicier.

Maggie ducked into the restroom and turned on the water to wash her hands. She glanced in the mirror. A small smudge of dirt ran across her forehead. Great. Guess he was smiling at that and not at her.

Oh, well. Who could say her life was boring and needed more spice? Garden snake last week. Toad and a sad Prince Charming today. What would happen next week? A squirrel or a lizard, maybe? Who knew? She smoothed her dark blonde locks back into place and checked to make sure no other smudges existed before she returned to the sanctuary and the Disney kids.

=========

Sophie had spied David when he came in and had launched herself into his arms. Three years had changed her from a scrawny girl to the dark curly-headed teenager dressed in a lacy white dress beside him. She had the face of a classic beauty for a thirteen year old. Someday hearts would break because of her.

David pulled his niece's pen out of her hand and responded to her note.

No Girlfriend. Your friends are too young.

She smothered her giggle behind her hand and took back the pen. David felt a thump on his ear and turned to see Darlene pursing her lips at him.

"What?" he mouthed.

"Listen. To. Sermon," she mouthed back.

Sermon? It was just the announcements.

He winked at his sister as Sophie handed him another note. Such beautiful handwriting.

Will you be at Grandma's?

David accepted the pink pen back and started to reply. A hand lashed out from behind him, and the pen and paper were ripped from his hands. He turned around and glared at a furious Sarah. Oops. An irritated Darlene was okay. An angry Jeremy or Dad was tolerable. But a furious Sarah was a tsunami of pain.

David gave Sophie a lop-sided smile. He leaned down and whispered, "Yes, I'll be there, but we better pay attention now."

He sat back up and settled against the inside corner of the pew. Sisters and sister-in-laws. The know-it-alls of the world. He propped his arm along the back and crossed an ankle over his knee. David smiled down at Sophie as she sidled up closer to him. At least someone truly missed him.

Bro. Johnny closed down the last of the announcements. Something about a zoo trip for the little children, some picnic thingy at the river, and a love offering for Ms. Phyllis Wardlaw and family. David cast a glance at the last pew on the far side. Yeah, there sat Ms. Better-than-thou. He wondered how Bro. Johnny handled her, or if she handled him like she did the last preacher.

A flash of color in the corner of his vision caught his attention. He returned his gaze to the front. Maggie and her little protégé sat three pews in front of him. Poppy squirmed around. Maggie bent her head and whispered. The girl quieted.

David gazed at Maggie. Her hair glistened in the light from the windows. He noticed earlier that she wore no make-up. She didn't need it. Those freckles were absolutely gorgeous on her. And that pink dress and shoes made him think of cotton candy. Bet she was just as sweet.

A sharp elbow stabbed him in the side. The congregation had stood. Sophie handed him the hymnal. He stood beside her. Dread ate at him. He hated these old, grandma songs. The pianist, someone he didn't recognize, strung the notes together in a smooth form. It might not be so bad after all.

Sophie sang beside him. He glanced down at her. Where did she get those vocals? The beautiful sound of an angel. Once the song was over, they sat. A man he didn't know stood, led them in prayer, and then they sang another grandma song.

David closed the book and slid it back into its holder.

Sophie stood. "I need by, Uncle David."

He angled his knees to let her by and then turned around to Sarah. "She's singing the special?"

Sarah held her finger to her lips. David faced forward. Already he could feel eyes on him. Now that Sophie was up on the platform, his mom and dad were in his line of sight. His dad sported a slightly amused expression. His mom raised an eyebrow at him, so David turned his face away. He felt Sarah's stare dig into his back. Sheesh. He just asked a question.

The lights dimmed. David watched with apprehension as Darlene's husband came down from the choir and picked up an acoustic guitar from its stand. At Sophie's nod, he picked at the strings. David's eyebrows rose. He had forgotten how good Marty was with the guitar.

Entranced, David listened as his niece sang the popular Casting Crowns song *Who Am I?* No CD. No accompaniment other than the guitar.

Her voice wove through the congregation. It was more than her voice. It was the words. He hadn't heard that song in so long. A lump crawled up his throat. David gulped in a heavy breath. The words drove into him.

"Who am I that the voice that calms the sea. . ."

Could the storm within him be calmed? The image of a voice calling through the pounding and hated rain as he bobbed in the raging sea reached out to him. It wasn't possible. Nothing would quiet the storm in him. They were just words.

Who am I? That question again.

Who was he?

His chest heaved.

His fists balled.

A hand landed on his arm a second before he bolted. His dad had reached across the small space that Sophie vacated and patted him on the arm. David relaxed.

What was wrong with him? What was he running from? He nearly embarrassed himself.

In moments, Sophie finished. A few shouts of amen rose from the back. Marty hugged her and returned to the choir loft. David lifted his eyes to the choir. He had been ignoring it, knowing that Jeremy sat up there in the baritone section, but he had to see Jeremy's reaction to his daughter's song.

A soft smile played across his brother's face, and his eyes glinted. Jeremy watched Sophie as she returned to the pew. David locked gazes with him.

For one brief second the three years of estrangement fell away. They smiled at each other. Then the wall returned. David looked away. He wouldn't give in that easily. No way.

He leaned over to Sophie as she sat down. "Beautiful, So-so." She beamed at the old nickname.

Bro. Johnny stood up and removed his jacket. Not a good sign. When a pastor removed his jacket, that was when the Bible beating began. Hellfire and brimstone would be cast amongst them.

"Sophie, thank you for the blessing. Let's hear another amen for such an angelic voice bringing us the message of salvation in song."

Amen echoed around him.

"Let's get to business, shall we? Open your Bibles, and if you didn't bring your Bible today, then people, let's share God's Word out there."

David swore the preacher looked at him. He couldn't help it that his Bible was still in the moving truck and hadn't made it here yet. A voice inside his head told him that wasn't true.

Sophie held her white Bible open and placed it on his knee. "We'll share, Uncle David."

David gave a half-smile. She was an angel. And he was the devil.

"Open to Ecclesiastes chapter three. Everything has its time . . ."

David leaned down with Sophie, heads touching, and followed Bro. Johnny as he read the Scriptures. Before long, David lost himself in the words.

———

Jeremy ushered his teenagers out the church door. Service was great, and now he looked forward to watching his baseball game before his shift started at four o'clock. His teens took off in different directions as they passed the threshold. He stopped by Bro. Johnny and held out his hand.

"As always, Bro. Johnny, great sermon."

The preacher gripped Jeremy's hand and slapped his shoulder with the other. "Thanks. Heard you were starting mid shift again."

"Yeah. Tonight. Going to be rough the next few days making the change over." He watched as Sophie bounded like a gazelle across the paved parking lot.

"How's things going with David back home?"

Jeremy gave a half-smile. Bro. Johnny had never been one to hold back a question. "Don't know. Haven't talked to him yet."

"There's always now." He gave Jeremy a pointed stare and then looked across the lot.

"Subtle, Preacher. Subtle."

Bro. Johnny smiled and greeted the next person in line as Jeremy took the short brick steps down to the lot.

Across the parking area, Sophie launched herself at David, who staggered under the assault. Jeremy heard his brother's laugh mingle with his daughter's as they stood by the red Harley. So David got it going.

Jeremy raised his eyebrows and eased his way across the pavement. His brother hadn't seen him yet, and Jeremy watched as David bent his head down to hear whatever it was that Sophie was saying. His steps faltered, and he stopped behind the Parker family's van.

He knew David and that stupid hard-headedness of his. Jeremy cast a look back at the steps. Sarah and Darlene stood at the bottom of the steps, involved in conversation with one of the women on the activities committee. Sarah looked up and met his eyes. She gave him a small nod towards David and then turned back to her conversation. He blew out his breath and advanced, swinging wide around his brother. Better to flank him than to go straight in.

As he neared, he overheard some of the conversation.

"Why won't you sing with me, Uncle David? Your voice is pretty."

"Men don't have pretty voices, So-so. We have nice or booming voices." David threw a leg over the Harley and settled down onto its seat. "I'll catch you later, okay?"

"When will you take me for a ride on the motorcycle?"

"When your mamma says you can. I'm sure your dad would be okay with it, but it's your mamma who scares me." David put his finger to his lips. "Shh. Don't tell anyone I said so."

Sophie hid her smile behind her hands and smothered her giggle. David looked up, and the laughter died from his eyes. Jeremy tried to smile. This wasn't going to be as easy as he thought.

"David."

"Jeremy."

Jeremy stopped by Sophie and ruffled her hair, ignoring her protest. "I see you got the Harley running."

"Yeah. Decided to ride it today, test it out. She's a little rough. Needs more work." David slumped, looked at his hands, brushed imaginary dust from the gauges, anything to avoid meeting his gaze. Typical.

"Sophie, go tell your mom it's time to go. And round up your brother, please."

"Yes, sir. Bye, Uncle David. See you later." She whirled and half ran back to the church.

Jeremy turned back to his brother. David spoke first. "She's turned into a beautiful little woman."

"Yes, but she's got Sarah's temper."

David snorted. "I bet."

The conversation lagged. Jeremy cleared his throat. David's eyes narrowed as Jeremy set a hand on the handlebar. "Dad said you took C shift at the station."

His brother sniffed and looked away. "Yeah. C Shift Captain."

"That's a downgrade from Battalion Chief, isn't it?"

David gave a heartless laugh and shook his head. "You come over here to bust me about my position?"

Jeremy sighed. Leave it to David to get confrontational for no reason. "No. I just came to say 'glad to have you home.'"

"Okay. You said it." He brushed Jeremy's hand off the handlebar.

His brother wasn't getting away that quickly. Jeremy gripped his brother's arm and leaned in close. "I meant it, David. I'm glad you're home. Can't we make amends this time?"

He watched his brother stare off into the distance toward the cemetery for a moment, and then he peered down at Jeremy's hand and turned a raised brow to him.

"What's with the glove?"

Jeremy let go and shrugged. "Nothing. Just wear it out of habit." He stepped back as David started the bike. "David?"

"Look, I didn't come here to make amends. I didn't come here to forgive. My reasons for returning are my own." David's mouth clamped shut, white lines forming around the edges. His nostril flared a couple of times. "I won't talk about it, Jeremy."

"Fair enough." What else was there to say? "I'll see you around then. I might drop by Mom's for dinner tonight. Will you be there?"

David's face was a closed book again, but Jeremy knew his brother. Three years didn't make that much difference. Something swam on the surface moments before.

Another shrug. "I probably will. Staying there for the time being."

"Plan on moving out soon?"

"Yeah, Mr. Inquisitive. Going to check out a prospect right now." He revved the motor.

"Whoa!" Jeremy stopped him. He met his brother's cold green eyes. "Where's the helmet?"

"Not wearing it." David smirked and threw him a wink. "Arrest me."

Jeremy grimaced as his brother peeled out of the parking lot. Stupid idiot. David didn't even check both ways before tearing off down the country road. The Harley's rumble faded, and Jeremy stood there, tapping his thigh with a fist. For a first talk, it didn't go so bad. Although, he detected a roiling storm underneath David's cold demeanor.

"Jeremy!" Sarah called from the car, passenger door opened. "Ready?"

Yeah, he was ready for home. Ready to put his brother out of his mind for the time being. He walked to the car and slid into the driver's seat.

Sarah kissed his cheek and then gripped his gloved hand. "How did it go with David?"

So much for putting his brother out of his mind. "Better than I thought. Probably because we were in the church's parking lot this time." Jeremy started the car and backed up. His kids were in the backseat already listening to their iPods. "I just don't know how to speak with him, Sarah."

She stroked his knee with a light touch. "It'll happen in time, sweetie. From what I understand from Mom, he's not the same. You think he's on something?"

"Sarah!"

"I'm just asking." She shrugged as he pulled out of the parking lot and turned for town. "He doesn't even look the same."

She fell into silence, and Jeremy considered her words as he drove in the same direction as David. She was right about David not looking the same. His brother looked angrier, like a man fighting and burning in his own inferno.

"It wouldn't be drugs, Sarah. David would never risk popping positive on a drug test." Jeremy took the right turn onto Abrams Street leading to his subdivision. "I'll keep tabs on him."

"I know you will." She pulled out a notebook and flipped it open. "Let me tell you what we came up with for the picnic in a couple of weeks. Give me your insight."

Jeremy listened with half an ear as she spoke about the church's riverside picnic. The other half lingered on David. He missed those late night conversations while on duty, the crazy practical jokes, even the good-natured rivalry. Something was wrong, and he would find out what.

———

David rode the motorcycle into the opened garage. The aroma of charcoal reached him as he dismounted. That and burnt meat. Dad was grilling.

He glanced at his watch. After six o'clock. He was late. Mom would just have to get over it. At least he was here. He grabbed the small package out of the side bag and slipped it into his back pocket. Then he pulled his shirttail from his waistband to hide the bulge.

He entered the house, bypassing the laundry room, and peeked around the corner into the kitchen. So far, so good. Apparently everyone was out back. He darted through the kitchen and rounded the corner into the living room. He stopped suddenly as Jeremy's voice reached him. His brother found time to stop by, after all.

Jeremy lounged on the sofa, ankle across his knee. "I'm telling you, Marty, that was a bad call on the Braves this afternoon."

"You're just saying that 'cause your precious Braves are only two games ahead. You just wait until the next game. Cardinals'll wipe them–David!" Marty Sr., his balding head gleaming in the light, jumped up from the couch opposite Jeremy and approached him. "Glad you're home."

Marty's arms wrapped him in a bear hug. David pounded the big man on the back. "How ya doing, Marty? Seems like you gained even more from Darlene's cooking!"

The man's laugh was as big as his belly. "What can I say? Your sister took after her mom." He backslapped David across the abdomen. "Looks like you could stand a few more home-cooked meals."

David laughed and shoved his hands into his pockets. "Probably so. Lost about thirty pounds. Can still take you down, though, big man." He leaned back against the wall. "How's the suing business?" He ducked the swipe Marty took at him.

"I don't sue people, man. I only help them relieve themselves of 'burdens.'" Marty walked back to the couch and settled down with a grunt. "It's good. Took on a few more clients. Mainly civil stuff."

Jeremy chimed in. "Yeah, and the mayor is furious about it too."

That struck his interest. The old mayor was latched onto the town like a cancerous barnacle. "You've got to tell me about that in a moment."

Marty laughed. "Oh, you will love it."

"I bet." David nodded at the stairs. "I'll be back."

He left Marty and Jeremy haggling over politics as he scurried up the stairs. He slid inside his room and closed the door gently. The wood was smooth against his forehead as he leaned against it. He didn't expect to find Jeremy here so soon. Hopefully Jeremy didn't read him this time.

With a sigh, he pushed off the door and walked to his window. He peered past the white curtain and watched his family. Marty Jr. and Dennis tossed a Nerf football around, just out of Sophie's reach. She jumped and leapt around, trying to grab it. Monkey in the Middle. He remembered playing that game a lot as a child. That was a long time ago.

He let the curtain fall back into place and reached behind him to extract the small, brown-papered package from his back pocket, thankful for small miracles of passed laws and ordinances. A couple of years ago, he couldn't have bought it on a Sunday. He slid it inside the nightstand drawer and left his room.

Time to deal with Jeremy.

Neither his brother nor Marty were in the living room. Must have made it outside, then. David padded through the kitchen and pushed aside the patio door. His mom turned at the sound and smiled.

"David, you finally got here. Where've you been, sweetheart? Everyone's been asking for you."

David placed a kiss on his mother's temple. "Everyone?"

"Well, the kids mostly."

"I bet. Well, I see Jeremy made it."

His mom set the stack of plastic plates on top of the table. "He said he happened to be in the neighborhood and decided to swing by since he was out this way."

David rolled his eyes and swiped a cucumber slice off the platter in front of his sister. "Mom, that's Jer-speak for 'it's a slow day—might as well do the family thing.'"

"Well, even so, at least he's here long enough to have supper." She patted David's cheek before retreating into the kitchen.

Darlene rose from her chair and gave him a hug. He fought the urge to roll his eyes again. This was the huggiest family he'd ever seen. "Glad you got here. Save our burgers, please. Dad and Marty are determined to turn them into meteorites."

Sarah laughed. She sat at the wrought iron patio table, peeling and dicing tomatoes for the salad. "I prefer well done, but not burnt. At least, not like Marty's burnt."

"I'll go rescue the beef." David looked around the yard. Jeremy wasn't out here, either. Must have gone back to work. He trotted over to his father. "Move over, Dad. You're killing them."

His dad waved the spatula at him and pointed to his pink frilly apron. "I got the King of the Grill armor on!"

David playfully shoved his father over and took the tongs off the rack. "I want mine still mooing, please. Darlene needs hers in a coma. And you know Mom likes hers with a little pink. Only Marty and you want burnt rocks of flesh." He flipped three burgers over and slid another onto a platter, then rolled the hot dogs around to sear evenly.

His dad smacked his bottom with the spatula. "I got the apron. Move it."

David refused to budge. He added two more burgers to the platter. "And I am the grilling expert."

"You don't grill. You lightly toast." His dad smacked him again, this time across the back. "Move it, motor head."

David shook his head. "My, my. You still get mean over the grill."

His dad laughed and gave him a shove. "My grill. My burgers."

"My stomach." David grabbed the platter and bowed. "I'll bring the platter back for your meteorites, Mr. Grill King."

Darlene looked up with a smile as he set the platter down in front of her. "The burgers are saved. One for you, one for mom, and one for me."

She slid them into a covered dish. "Thank you, little brother."

"Did he smack you?" Sarah looked up from the cucumbers she was slicing.

"Yeah. Why?"

She twirled her finger in the air. "Turn around."

David complied. "What? Wait, did he leave a mark?"

Darlene giggled. "A good and nice black spot on your bottom! But you can barely see it."

"Dang it, Dad!" He dusted his pants but only succeeded in smearing the charcoal soot. "My best bleeding pants!"

His dad looked up and waved the spatula at him with a smirk on his face.

"Haven't you learned yet?" Jeremy's voice spoke from the patio door. Obviously, he had not gone back to work yet. "You know he'll leave a mark somewhere whenever someone tries to save the beef."

"Well," David growled, "at least it wasn't the shirt."

Sarah giggled. "You sure about that?"

"Oh, you've got to be–" He broke off at his mother's raised eyebrow. "–kidding me." He twisted and tried to view his shirt in the reflection of the patio glass.

Jeremy smirked and leaned against the chair Sarah sat in. "Between the shoulder blades."

"Perfect."

"Oh, just take it off." His mom set a bowl of potato salad on the table. "I'll wash it."

David mumbled under his breath as Jeremy laughed and went to join their dad and Marty at the grill. He unbuttoned the shirt. "Fine. Did you wash my red t-shirt, Mom? I didn't see it in the hamper this morning."

"In the laundry room. On the dryer. I'll go get it for you in a moment." She bustled back into the kitchen.

David slid the shirt off and balled it into his hands. Darlene squealed as he turned around to walk inside.

"Oh, my gosh. Sarah, he's got a tattoo!"

Sarah looked up and giggled. "You better not let your mom see that! Jeremy!"

David scowled. "It's just a tattoo. What's the fuss?" He placed his hand over his navel to hide the red and yellow artwork.

He pushed the patio door open, but Darlene's hands latched onto him, pulling him back onto the patio. "Let us see!"

She and Sarah wrestled with him, trying to make him remove his hand. Sisters and sister-in-laws, the world's worst irritations.

"Dang it, Darlene! Sarah!" David hunched over and clasped his other hand, still holding his shirt, over his stomach. "Jeremy! Marty! Get a handle on your wives!"

Jeremy and Marty looked up from their conversation at the grill. The kids ventured closer to see the commotion. Darlene and Sarah were relentless. He pushed them away and leapt off the stone patio and onto the ground. They followed and ganged up on him again. Their hands pulled and pinched at him. He fought down the laugh.

"Stop it!" They wouldn't listen. Jeremy and Marty made it to them and pulled their giggling wives back.

"He's got a tattoo and won't let us see!" Darlene pounced on him again.

"Cool! Let us see, Uncle David." Dennis, his blue eyes gleaming, bounced around the huddle.

"No." David was losing his battle. Sarah jumped back into the foray. "Jeremy, get your wife off me." He pulled his shirt out of her grasp and held it over his stomach.

"Oh, I'm sure you can handle her." Jeremy walked back to the patio and pulled a chair out. He sat down and watched as Marty Sr. stood chortling over the ruckus. "This is great entertainment."

David choked back his laughter. Darlene had him on the ribs now. Smaller hands grabbed at him. "Oh, not you, too, So-so."

Sophie giggled and pushed at him. "I want to see it, too. Come on, guys!"

Dennis and Marty Jr. fell upon him. David collapsed onto the soft grass. He strained against them, but it was too much. Sophie's and Darlene's fingers dug into his ribs. Sarah pushed at his hands, and the boys held his feet down.

"Stop!" Tears ran down his face as he laughed. "Oh, please, stop. I can't breathe."

"Show us!" they chorused.

He shook his head. The poking resumed. It was torture. "Okay, okay."

He couldn't stand it anymore. He had to breathe, and no one could win against this family.

He let his hands fall away.

Dennis high-fived Marty Jr. "Check it out. That is cool. Mom, I want one!"

"Absolutely not!" Sarah sat down on the ground beside him and smacked his stomach. "A flaming sun? What are you, a rock star? Jeremy, check it out!"

"Oh, no." David started to push up from the ground, but Darlene pushed him down again, her fingers posed over his ribs. The evil sister.

Jeremy and Marty peered over the women's heads. Jeremy nodded. "That's different. What are you, a rock star?"

The kids burst out laughing. Dennis hooted. "That's what Mom said!"

They each slapped David on the stomach and took off back to their game. Man, they took too much after their parents.

"What made you decide to get that?" Jeremy waved the women away and held out his hand.

David accepted it. Jeremy helped pull him to his feet. "A dare one night. Last man at the scene kind of deal."

Marty cocked his head and stared at David's stomach. "That had to hurt."

"Not if you had enough beers with it." David rubbed at the tattoo. "I lost, by the way."

"No kidding." Jeremy shook his head. "Why didn't you just shave your head instead? Less painful."

David's smile faded as did Jeremy's. His fists clenched and his nostrils flared. Jeremy looked away.

Marty slapped them both hard on the back before David uttered a word. They winced. "Let's go eat! Dad's got the food ready."

The spell broke. Jeremy walked off with Marty. David followed. His dad was placing the burnt beef on the table. He stepped up on the patio as Dennis breezed by.

"Grandma! Check out Uncle David's tat!"

Loud mouth.

His mom turned around. She raised an eyebrow and squinted at the flaming tattoo. "Hmm. I think I would have gone with a little more yellow."

His dad's laugh bellowed as she handed David his red t-shirt and pulled the soiled one out of his hand.

David smiled and pulled the shirt on. "Funny, Mom."

He smacked Dennis on the head as he walked by and sat down at the table. His sides ached from the torture session. Marty lit the citronella buckets on the table as Sarah uncovered the dishes.

Jeremy gazed at the platter. "Dad, are you sure you got the burgers? Or are these the briquettes?"

David chuckled as his dad threw an ice cube at Jeremy. His stomach growled at the smell of the food, even his dad's burnt rocks. He placed his napkin in his lap as the rest of the family noisily settled into their chairs.

"Let's ask grace." His dad held out his hand, and one by one around the table everyone's hands joined.

Sophie slid her hand into David's right, and Marty Jr. grabbed his left. They bowed their heads.

"Lord, bless this time in our lives. Wonderful food and family with which to celebrate your glorious day. Thank you for bringing David safely home to us . . ."

Sophie's hand tightened in his. The rest of the prayer flowed past him. Safely home? If they only knew, they wouldn't think he was safe. Not at all safe.

CHAPTER 4

Maggie closed the door to her Second to None consignment shop and locked it. She shuffled the folders in her hand and sighed. Even on a half-day Wednesday, she tired quickly as if it were a full day of selling. She really needed to reorganize her time.

"Maggie!"

She turned at the shout and grinned as Mrs. Turner from city hall hurried down the sidewalk toward her. "Hey, Mrs. Turner. Did you jog all the way from the courthouse?"

The plump woman huffed, fanning her red-splotched face with a well-manicured hand. "I had to catch you before you started the door-to-door."

"Oh. Yeah, I was about to start." Maggie looked down at the folders in her hand. "Is there something wrong?"

"Mayor Wellington needs the forms for McKay's Jewelry Shop and Johansen Art Gallery." She propped her hands on her wide hips, still fighting for breath. "He wants to deliver them personally. I told him you always close shop early on Wednesdays and you did the rounds before heading to church. He had me run all the way to tell you."

Maggie chuckled. "You could have called."

"I did." Mrs. Turner shook her head with a laugh. "Maggie, you forget to turn your phone back on every Wednesday."

Maggie's face flamed. She ducked her head and flipped through the files for the mayor's request. "I know. I meant call me before I closed shop."

"He didn't tell me in time." Mrs. Turner took the files and huffed one last time. "Why do you keep turning it off?"

"Why do you, during lunch?" Maggie raised her eyebrow at the woman. "Because of the mayor!"

They laughed. Mrs. Turner fanned her face with the files. "Oh, my. Let me get these to him. I'll see you tomorrow, Maggie."

"Okay. Bye, Mrs. Turner." Maggie watched the woman plod down the sidewalk at a more sedate pace. She looked both ways before crossing to the courthouse that stood in the middle of the downtown square. Maggie heaved a sigh of relief.

That was two less for her to contend with. She snorted. She needed to be shot next time she agreed to help with the festival planning. It was too stressful, especially with the mayor constantly sticking his pointy nose into everything.

She turned the corner to the small parking lot she shared with the neighboring store, Mike's Formal Wear. Her little store used to be a small storage area for Mike's, and she really needed to talk to Mike about the renovations. And maybe renegotiate her rental fee.

The folders threatened to fall out of her hands as she opened her truck's passenger door. She had to take a look at her map and change into her walking shoes before she started her rounds. Standing like a flamingo, she pulled a flat off, chucked it into the truck, and struggled to pull her neon pink striped shoe onto her foot. Now the other. She stamped a few times to settle them more comfortably on her feet and then opened the glove box for her map. The layout of Jasper City unfolded in her hands, and she counted the green spots compared to the red.

She ran her finger along the downtown area. Next to Mike's was the flower shop. Check. Cross the small street and then there were five more shops. Mrs. Turner had those. Cross another street and there was the dairy treat shop, a gift shop, and the downtown bank. She already had their commitments. Except for the dairy treat shop, which opted not to participate. May their milk curdle.

On the other side of the square was a funeral home, the jewelry store, and an old post office building that was now the art gallery. The mayor had those now. She pulled a yellow marker from the console and marked the buildings. Standing on each corner was a gas station. Check, and each was a no. She searched for her black marker and found it lying on the floorboard. She popped the top off and marked the gas stations with an X. Maggie followed the path back around to her shop, skipping over the large red brick building. That was her first stop. Then she would go from there to the large brown building behind it.

She stuffed the map back into the glove box and grabbed the folders. Now on to the Jasper City Fire Department and Jasper City Police Department. She bit her lip. The bad boy brother should be there. A small part of her felt silly. She was too old to crush on a man.

 She'd go to the police department first.

The truck rocked as she slammed the door. She walked down the sidewalk in front of her store and crossed the two-lane street to the other side of the square. She gave a quick wave to Jason Martin, who stood at the rolled-up gates of the firehouse. He paused from washing the ladder truck for a moment and waved back. He motioned for her to come over, but she shook her head and held up a finger.

He would want to talk, and she didn't have time for him. Two dates were enough to know he wasn't the one for her. She hurried down the sidewalk and up the police department's steps.

The air inside rushed past her as she opened the door. A large counter with a glass partition stood in front of her, with two doors on either side. An elderly woman's voice reached her. "Jasper City Police Department." That was Betty handling an incoming call.

The echoing sounds of phones beeping and radio chatter from the patrol cars created a symphony of sorts. Maggie crossed the small lounge area and approached the desk.

"Hey, Sandra!"

The petite black woman looked up and flashed a smile. "Hey, Maggie. Festival time?"

"Yup. Chief in?"

"No. But Captain Conners is here." Sandra screwed up her face. "But he's on the phone at the moment."

Conners' voice echoed through the building. "I said I don't care! If you think you can do better, then be my guest!"

Sandra shrugged. "You don't want to know. He's been on a rampage since Monday." She stood and disappeared past the glass partition. The door to the right clicked, and Sandra peered around it. "Come on."

Maggie slipped through the door. "If he's in that terrible of a mood, I can always come back later."

Sandra shook her head, the little, tight ringlets in her hair bouncing. "No. He becomes so mellow when you're around, and we sure could use the respite. Even Baers is on edge. Captain is out-shouting him."

Maggie grinned at the officer's name. "And how is that coming along?"

"Slow. For a smart, handsome fellow, he sure is dumb about women." She paused at the corner of the hall. "Go on in. I gotta get back to the desk. Betty can't handle the calls all by herself."

"Okay." She stopped Sandra before she turned around to leave. "You should just ask him out for coffee. Take him to Jack's. Thaddeus Baers is not a man who will make the first move. Trust me. That guy is one shy bear."

Sandra's white grin flashed. "I think I will. Tomorrow. From what I heard, he and Jeremy are going to be pretty busy tonight. I'll talk to you later."

"Thanks, Sandra." She turned around and tiptoed to the captain's office. Her knuckles barely rapped the door when his voice caused her to jump.

"I said next week. Sergeant Boyette has assured me that the informant will have the information we need for the bust." There was a pause. "I know. Yes, sir, I know." A crash echoed in the room.

Maggie pushed at the door and cleared her voice. "Ahem. Captain?"

Conners looked up from the overturned metal mail tray. "Ah, Maggie. You are a pleasant surprise."

She snorted. "Surprise? You knew I was coming."

"Not this early."

"Well, I thought I would see if my favorite police captain was ready with the donation list and the signup roster for the game."

He waved to a chair. "Sit. And yeah, I got it somewhere." He looked under a stack and then opened a drawer and shuffled papers.

Maggie sat down and surveyed the top of his desk. She spied a spreadsheet on his mail tray and picked up the light blue paper. "Is this it?"

He pulled his half-submerged head out of the drawer. "Oh, that it is."

Maggie laughed and read the list. "I see you got Jeremy on the list. Playing second base? You know the game is at five. He's not working that night?"

Conners shook his head and opened the other drawer, pushing folders aside. "Yes and no. I put the men on half shifts; that way they can all participate at the festival. Caused a major headache juggling all those schedules, but it's a once-a-year thing. Anything for my boys."

Maggie accepted the white folder he pulled out and handed to her. "Are these the donations?"

"Yes. I have them at the house. You can have them picked up anytime. Just call Martha so she'll know when to expect you or whoever."

"Okay. I don't see you on the roster."

"I'm not playing." He leaned back and tapped his knee. "Too many injuries, hence the reason I am behind a desk."

"You can be the umpire."

"No way." He chuckled. "Every year a hothead from each department gets in a fight during the game, and the umpire gets stuck in the middle of it. Nah. I leave it to the younger men now."

Maggie laughed with him. "Remember last year? I didn't think anyone was going to be able to take Baers down, but Toby gave it a good try."

"Well, it's all in good fun. Wouldn't be a ball game if there wasn't at least one officer and firefighter to get benched."

Maggie shook her head. "I just don't understand y'all." She stood to go, but Conners waved her back into the chair.

"I ordered a pizza, and it should be here. Keep me company, please. That way Sandra doesn't have to lie when she tells the bonehead in city hall that I'm busy with someone. For some reason he keeps bypassing the chief and harassing me."

His pleading look convinced her. She settled back down with a dramatic sigh. "Anything for my boys."

His laugh shook his body and scattered a few more papers about his desk.

========

David pulled into the firehouse and parked the motorcycle in the corner. The smell of grease and oil in the bay greeted him. He breathed in deeply. This felt more like home.

He dismounted and hooked the helmet on the handlebars. The new flaming sun shone in the fluorescent lights. The design cost him a pretty penny but was worth every bit of it.

"David, you're finally here, man!" Jason walked past with a roll of hose.

"Had a meeting. Now I gotta get my paperwork caught up."

"Yeah, I heard about the wreck. Horrible way to go."

David frowned. "No one died. What are you talking about?"

Toby Jones, his blond hair gleaming, came in from the side door. "He's talking about the Fusion."

David laughed. "Oh, that. Yeah, it's heading for the scrap yard. No way they are fixing that car." He slapped Toby's shoulder as he walked past and rounded the corner.

Wet hoses lay stretched out in the small hallway. Sam Tennyson and Mark Fowler, on their knees, ran their hands slowly over the hoses.

"Why the hall?" David stepped carefully over the snaky apparatuses.

Sam ran his hands under one of the lines as he spoke. "You're in late. Was in the bay, but finished those. Chief had these short ones stretched out in here. Don't ask. Been a hectic day."

"How many leaks?"

Sam looked up. "Two so far. Y'all really did a number on them."

"That's why you're still here?"

"Yeah. Thomas had me on hose duty. Just about finished. You won't like what he's got you on. Sucks being a captain," Sam added with a grin.

David pushed open the door to the office. He peered in and greeted the chief. "Thomas. Thanks for allowing me to take care of business."

"Any luck?"

"Yeah. I'll move in by next week." David rounded the desk and peeked through the blind slats. "Need to catch up on paperwork. How's the day going?"

Thomas Dearborn snuffed out his cigarette. "Been a quiet day, but the mayor is sending someone over to get the roster sign-up and donation list. And I need an inventory list of the medical equipment."

"Sure thing." David accepted the folders and frowned. "You leaving early?"

"As of now. C shift is on, and since you're finally here, might as well call it a day." Thomas stood and stretched. "I have to run over to PD for a moment. Oh, and we got three rookies coming in at the end of the week. I have two of them on your shift. Think you can handle the training?"

David shrugged and hid his scowl behind his hand. "Sure thing."

"Good." Thomas flung his jacket over his shoulder, and David followed him out of the office. "Two wrecks, a brush fire, and a medical call. That was a busy shift for you."

"Wouldn't be so bad if we weren't so undermanned."

"Working on it, David. We're not the big city."

David snorted. "Big city politics were worse. Believe me, this small town stuff is nothing compared to what goes on in the city."

He followed the chief out the back and behind the firehouse. Thomas opened his car door and then looked over at David. "Miss the city any?"

"No way. Glad to be home."

"Even if it was a step down?"

David stuffed his hands in his pockets and bit his lip. Was it worth it? "Yeah. Even if it was a step down."

Thomas shook his head with a laugh. "If you say so. Oh, glad you cut that mop off."

David ran his hand over his head, the short bristles tickling his hand. "Yeah."

He stepped back as the chief pulled away from the curb and drove off. Thomas' question played in his mind. Was it worth it? St. Louis offered more money. He was Battalion Chief there. Here he was only C Shift Captain. Fourth man on the totem pole.

Worth it? Yeah. St. Louis would have eventually killed him.

He opened the side door and weaved his way through the fire engines in the bay. A small piece of red caught his eye. He bent down and picked up a small plastic shard. Great.

"Toby!"

"Yeah?"

"We need to change out the right brake cover on Engine Two." He rounded the corner of the truck, tossing the plastic shard into the garbage pail as he passed by. "Looks like we busted it the other night pulling it in."

"Okay!"

David looked around. He didn't see the man anywhere. "Where are you, dude?"

"Oh, here." Toby popped his head from around the opened bay. "Got a visitor."

He watched as a vision in white floated inside his firehouse bay. She smiled at him, a pile of folders pressed against her chest. Her hair was pulled into a ponytail with golden ribbons shooting out around it. Her white blouse billowed around her hand as she pushed at a wayward lock of hair. His eyes traveled down her pink-clad legs and lazily back up. The woman must have an affection for pink.

"Maggie Goddard."

"David Boyette." She mimicked his tone.

He swallowed against his dry throat. "What brings you here?"

"The mayor. Festival time will be here in three weeks. Thomas said he had the roster ready, and I'm here to pick it up."

David nodded. "Oh, yeah, yeah. Come on. I'll get it for you." He led her to the hallway, silently cursing himself for acting like a school boy. Idiot. "Watch your step. Boys are checking hoses."

She tiptoed over the stretched hoses, waved to the men on the floor, and brushed past him as he held the door open. He breathed in her scent as she passed. Oh, man. She smelled of cotton candy.

He didn't realize he'd closed his eyes until he heard Sam hoot. A few catcalls echoed down the hall from Jason. David glared before he shut the door. They were making something out of nothing.

"I think Thomas left them on the desk somewhere." David eased past her and rounded the lump of scarred metal. Run reports and folders covered the surface. He picked up a red one and looked inside. "Yeah. Here you go."

Maggie browsed through them. "Oh, you're going to be the catcher."

David perched on the corner of the desk, his knee lightly brushing against her leg. Maybe she wouldn't think that was intentional. "Yeah. Position I used to play before I left." He watched as she read the lists.

She flipped to the donations spreadsheet and raised her eyebrow. Puzzlement etched across her face, creasing her forehead.

"It shows that there's a collection of vintage Hot Wheels toy cars to be auctioned off and a stack of old records?" Maggie looked up. "We only asked for a few not-too-valuable things. Like lamps or paintings or such."

David shook his head. "It's only valuable to the person who bids."

"Who owned the old records?"

"Don't know."

"Oh my, did you see the list?"

"No. Why?"

She handed him the paper. He took it from her and looked at it. Wow. Whoever did this was donating a bundle of money. "These records have to be priceless."

Maggie set her handful of folders on the table. She stood on tiptoe to read over his arm. "See that one?" She reached up to point at one of the entries.

David gave her the paper and read over her shoulder instead. Short stuff would need a step ladder to read over his. He propped a hand behind her on the desk, bringing himself a little closer to her. "Which one?"

"Here. That's a 1958 Elvis album. And look here, Kenny Rogers, Eagles--"

"Live version at that." David dipped his head closer to the paper. "A Conway Twitty. Oh, Mom would love that one. Queen and Twisted Sister."

Maggie ran her finger down the list. "This is a small treasure find. I've got this retro player at home."

David scooted further up on the desk, bringing himself even closer. Her arm now brushed against his uniform's sleeve. "The one that plays records, CDs, cassettes, and iPods?"

"Yeah. Dad got it for my birthday last year. Oh, what I wouldn't give to have these." She heaved a sigh and blinked away the dreamy look.

He shrugged. "Bid on them."

"I can't. Festival volunteers cannot bid on items. Mayor's rules."

"Get someone else to bid on them."

Maggie smiled and collected her folders. She backed up a step to look at him. "That's a good idea. Dad might, but I don't know if he'll be free to do the bidding. But Sarah probably can for me."

"Hey, yeah, get Sarah. Everyone would be too afraid to bid against Satan Sarah."

Maggie squealed and covered her mouth with a hand. "How did you find out her nickname? She hates that name."

David grinned. "Can you keep a secret?"

Her eyes brightened, and she leaned in closer to him. Her tantalizing scent reached his nose. Intoxicating.

"Yes. I can keep a secret."

He bent down even closer to her, his lips bare centimeters from her ear. "So can I."

"Oh." She screwed up her face and whacked him in the chest with the folders.

David laughed. She had definitely been spending too much time with his family. "No, really. Jeremy told it to me a long, long time ago. While he and Sarah were dating."

"She was a terror back then." Maggie placed the sheets in her file and then opened the door and stepped out into the hall. "Well, thanks for the files. Will you be able to stop at church tonight?"

David leaned against the door jamb, his hands stuffed into his pockets. "Doubtful. But I can catch you later if you want. Maybe tomorrow morning for coffee?"

Maggie smiled and shook her head. "No. Sorry, I can't. I have two appointments in the morning."

He narrowed his eyes. She wouldn't get away that easily. He never took no for an answer. "Then I'll come to the shop."

She cocked her head at him, a little puppy dog with blue eyes. "There's no need." Her feet danced past the hoses as she walked away.

David smiled and pushed away from the door. "Maybe no need. But where's the harm?"

He followed her through the bay. Toby was busy with the back of Engine Two, and he paused to watch them. David scowled at his friend as he passed by. He didn't need Toby watching him.

Maggie stopped at the opened bay and turned to him. "There's no harm, David. But I prefer to have no interruptions at my store."

"Then I'll buy something. Be a customer." He crossed his arms over his chest and dared her to say no this time. The sun, lower in the sky now, cast a golden ray across her face. "It's just coffee. Nothing more." He smiled, fighting the impulse to push away a lock of hair that fell across her brow.

She huffed at the strand, blowing it away from her eyes. "Just coffee?"

David took a step closer, staring into her bright blue eyes and tracing the sprinkle of freckles along her nose and cheeks with his gaze. "Just coffee."

She squinted and pursed her pink lips at him. His thoughts went from good intentions to where it had no business being, especially with a preacher's daughter.

Her voice brought him back around to reality. " . . . winning with you, is there?"

Huh? He took a gamble on what she had said. "Not really. I'm a determined man."

Maggie huffed once more and turned around. She called over her shoulder. "Creamer and two sugars. Strong."

David smiled. Yup, he always won. She crossed the two-lane and disappeared beyond the corner. Definitely a sweet confection. David licked his lips and turned back into the firehouse. Score one for him. Toby stood by the truck.

"She's out of your league, man."

David stared at his friend. "What do you mean? She 's a woman. Any woman is in my league."

Toby bent down and started polishing the taillight. "She is way too good for you and any of us. Jason went out with her twice. Nothing came of it. He said she was way too classy."

"I don't plan—"

Toby rose and stood nose to nose with him. His friend's reaction caught David off guard. "I'm only saying this once. You are my boss and my friend. We've known each other since high school. That said, I know what you were like before and now. You hurt her, I hurt you."

David's nostrils flared. He thrust his chin up and stared Toby down. "As I was saying, I don't plan to do anything. I just want to know her a little better, as in find out more about her. She's the preacher's daughter, for crying out loud."

"Exactly." Toby walked away and left him standing alone in the bay.

A muscle in his jaw twitched. He relaxed his posture and forced out a sigh.

She was the preacher's daughter, but she was also a beautiful woman. Her freckles captivated him. Her breathy little voice drew him in like a moth to a flame. He laughed quietly. If he kept on thinking like that, she would have him reciting poetic endearments.

He ran a hand over his face. Snap out of it. Women were trouble. And he had to deal with too much paperwork.

The boys were rolling the hoses as he walked past to the office. He slammed the door and sat down at the desk. His run reports glared at him. David picked up a pen and started filling out the forms. He sniffed. The scent of cotton candy lingered in the air.

CHAPTER 5

Jeremy quietly shut the car door and popped the tab off his holster. He touched his radio. "Dispatch. 10-23."

He rapped on the front door. A small scuffling sound reached his ears. The curtain in the window to his left moved slightly. He rapped again. The door creaked open a fraction, and haunted eyes peered out.

"Yes?"

"Mrs. Pearson?"

"Yes?"

Jeremy angled his body to let the light from inside shine on him. "I'm looking for your grandson Bobby. Is he here, ma'am?"

She eased the door open a little wider. Jeremy fought the impulse to recoil. Bloodshot and bruised eyes stared from sunken holes. Her teeth, what remained, hung by pieces of skin. She feebly worked at the chain on the door as she spoke past her broken teeth.

"He's not here. Not anymore."

Jeremy pushed at the door and stepped inside. He took in her appearance. Clothes hung on a bony frame, white hair matted with blood, and bare feet. The left foot's little toe jutted out at an odd angle. He reached out for her, and she shrank back. Fear poured from her. He let his hand fall to his side.

"You called 911, ma'am?"

"I was mistaken." She brought her right hand up to her face and pushed at a strand of hair that fell forward.

Jeremy peered outside. A few neighbors stood at their doors, watching. He gently shut the ragged door. She shrank even farther away from him. "Mrs. Pearson, don't be afraid. I'm here to help. Let me call this in, okay? Let us help you."

She shook her head, eyes darting around the room. "He'll be back. I shouldn't have called. He'll be mad."

Jeremy pushed his disgust deep down. Her grandson did this. Lowlife scum. He held out his gloved hand and implored her to take it. "I'm just going to lead you to the sofa, okay? Nothing else."

She hesitated briefly before sliding her right hand into his. Her left hand stayed curled around her chest. She hunched her shoulders even more as she shuffled over to the couch to sit. Jeremy sat down, keeping his eyes on the window.

"Tell me what happened, ma'am."

She shook her head. Her whisper barely reached him. "I can't. He'll be back soon. He always comes back."

"Did he say that?"

She stared at him. No. Her eyes said it all. He was gone for good this time.

"Did he take anything with him?"

She nodded. "He needed some cash. I only had a hundred twenty dollars. He took it because he needed it." She twisted the hem of her threadbare sweater in her fingers.

"Mrs. Pearson, I need to call and have you checked out." He reached forward and held his hand out again. "Let us take care of you now."

Her willpower gave way, and she collapsed, folding in on herself. He sank to his knees and held her fragile frame as she shivered. Her words were incomprehensible. He reached up to his mike.

"Dispatch."

"Go ahead."

"J forty-nine. Request EMS at 16 Woods Street. Radio forty-three."

"Copy, forty-nine."

He held Mrs. Pearson, waiting for the ambulance. His anger at her grandson grew and festered as he comforted the poor woman. Bones of her spine poked through. How long had she gone without food? The poor woman was a withered sack of bones. She looked eighty, but her DMV record had her at sixty-two. Jeremy sighed and fought his anger down. Let it rest in the pit of his stomach along with his disgust.

He offered a prayer for her, asking for protection from her lowlife grandson. Red lights flickered outside, followed by a set of blue.

"Mrs. Pearson, the ambulance is here now. They're going to take you to the hospital, okay?"

She started shaking. "I don't have money. Bobby will be back. He'll find me." Her lips trembled. Blood pooled at the edges.

He pulled out his handkerchief and dabbed her mouth as the door opened. "Here. Hold this. When you get to the hospital, there will be a woman there. She will help you, okay? You just worry about getting well."

Two paramedics hurried to Mrs. Pearson's side. Jeremy sidestepped their stretcher and looked up to see Baers enter the house.

"Not here?"

Jeremy motioned him outside. Once on the porch, he shook his head. "Took off, but not before beating the mess out of her. He's after Franklin. I know he is."

"Where's Franklin at? And how did he figure Franklin was giving us the info?"

Jeremy shrugged. "I don't know. But Franklin's got a big mouth. I'll call in Detective Sparrow. He'll want to know." He shuffled out of the way as the paramedics wheeled Mrs. Pearson down the small, bare yard to the ambulance.

"Sure no one is here?" Baers peered inside. "Small home."

"Yeah. She had the door latched—a chain. That's a joke." Jeremy followed Baers inside and down the tiny hall. "I don't think he stayed here often. Ripped a hundred and twenty dollars off dear old gran."

Baers pushed open a door on their right. "Grandma's room."

Jeremy pushed open the opposite door. "Bobby's room. Practically bare." He stepped inside. No pictures or posters on the walls. Closet with no door. A few jeans and a shirt hung inside. He turned on the closet light. Nothing on the shelf.

Baers grunted. "Nothing under the bed. This place is empty."

"Yeah. He's not doing business here." Jeremy shut the door behind them. "I'll have the place taped off and get the crew out here in the morning. There's got to be something to lead us to the lab."

Baers peered into the miniature kitchen. "Smaller than my sister's trailer."

"Poor side of Jasper City. Old houses. Guarantee the plumbing's never been updated." He flipped through some of the magazines lying on the wobbly coffee table: *Reader's Digest, Woman's Day,* and a Sunday school book. He paused over that. It was the same kind his church used. He read the date. Last quarter's lesson book. He thumbed through the stacks. Two more lesson books were buried, but there was no recent publication.

"Find something, Jer?" Baers peered out the window.

"Not really. Sunday school lesson books. Three old ones but not a new one."

"Thinking donations?"

"Probably." Jeremy replaced the old lesson book. "I'll check it out. Call a few of the churches and see if they donate the old books."

Baers stepped out onto the porch. Jeremy paused in the doorway and cocked his head. A slight sound, like that of breaking glass, sounded from one of the bedrooms.

"Baers. Someone's back." He pulled his gun and started to reenter. A sudden whoosh of hot air swept down the hall. He dove for cover. "We got a fire!"

Baers, haloed by his car's blue strobe lights, jumped off the porch and into the yard. Jeremy stumbled to his feet and onto the porch. The fire consumed its way down the hallway, eating at the walls and wooden floor.

"Call it–" Something hit his chest. Pain blasted into him. His body flew back into the opened doorway. His breath left him. The door's threshold dug into his neck.

Two more popping sounds echoed in the air.

Baers shouted into the radio. "Shots fired! Man down!"

Behind him, the fire roared. Baers shouted a curse. Then, hands pulled at Jeremy, dragging him away from the fire and heat.

Jeremy struggled to breathe and to keep his eyes open. His arms refused to move. He wasn't ready. Oh, please, not yet. He blinked against the fading darkness.

═══════════

"Engine Two en route!" David replaced the radio in its slot and held on as Toby shifted the gears. "Slow it, Toby!"

Toby downshifted and hung a sharp left. David gripped the dashboard tighter and shouted a string of curses at him.

Toby laughed. "Lighten up, dude. I am one with the truck."

"You're gonna be one with my fist if you kill us before we get there."

A strained voice, staccato-like, sounded over the radio. "Dispatch, show Engine Three on scene. Calling scene command. Single residence. Fully involved."

David banged his fist against the dashboard. He spit out a hard oath. Again, Station Two beat them to the scene. "That's two, Toby. We gotta get our boys moving faster."

Toby shook his head and laughed. Ahead a single, small house lit the neighborhood in an orange glow. Engine Three's lines stretched and belched water. Toby jammed the brakes, and their truck hissed to a stop. David grabbed his mike. "Dispatch. Engine Two on scene."

David vaulted out onto the pavement. He waved to Jake Patterson, Station Two's lieutenant–his scene command competition.

"Jason, grab the cross lays! John, grab a plug!" David strode to Jake's side. "Situation?"

Toby yelled from the pump. "Water's coming!"

A sudden hiss erupted as Jason's line belched water onto the fire.

"Just containment. The house is shot." Jake motioned towards the side. "Propane's been out for months. We were lucky enough to get the gas off before the flashover pushed us out."

"What happened?" He motioned for Toby to raise the pressure and touched his mike. "John, catch the left side. Got a flare-up."

"Some hood torched the back room." Jake jabbed a thumb over at the ambulance. "Cop was hit by the person who set the fire. I called Inspector Dawson. He'll be here in the morning. As usual."

"Cop?" David peered over Jake's shoulder. Two uniforms stood at the back of the ambulance. He recognized Markston, who nodded, slapped Baers on the shoulder, and walked off. Baers moved away from the ambulance's back door. David's eyes widened. Jeremy sat on the edge, a pretty little paramedic working on him.

He bit back his curse. "That's Jeremy. Hold the line. I'll be right back."

"No hurry, man. Fire ain't going anywhere." Jake strode forward and guided the second hose's aim to the roof.

David hurried to the ambulance. He slowed a few steps away and removed his helmet. "Jeremy?"

His brother, leaning heavily upon his hands, looked up. Pain laced his eyes. His words slurred. "Yo, little brother."

David looked at Baers. "They doped him?"

Baers nodded. "Got hit. Check it out." He held up Jeremy's vest encased in a plastic bag.

David let out a low whistle. The hole was the size of his fingertip. He took it from Baers and studied it. "That was an impact. What? A forty-five?"

"Looks like."

David knelt in front of his brother. "Hey, Jer? You awake, man?"

Jeremy raised his head again and smiled a dopey smile. "Yeah. See the bruise?" Jeremy pointed to his bare chest and at the red blotch above his heart.

David ran his fingertips across it, pressing lightly, and Jeremy cringed. Nothing seemed broken. "Yeah, that's a big one." He looked at the paramedic. "Vitals?"

"All good. The vest took the impact. No obvious sign of trauma." She handed Jeremy his shirt and pack of cigarettes. "Hold on to these." Then she looked up at the other officer. "Officer Baers, he's good to go. He'll be at Jasper Medical."

"I got him." David gripped his brother under his right arm and helped him into the back of the ambulance. "Come on. Let's get you onto the stretcher, okay?"

"Sure." Jeremy fell against the white-covered foam. "I don't think my eyes are working very well."

David laughed. "They're fine. You're just doped up. Get your feet up there." He pulled at Jeremy's legs, sliding his feet onto the stretcher.

Jeremy's head lolled around, eyes hidden behind a hand. David laid his helmet to the side and turned to the paramedic. "I need you to call his home."

She nodded and wrote down the number David recited.

Jeremy called out to him. "Hey, little brother, look at this. My pack's totaled." He waved his pack of cigarettes in the air.

Morphine was some good stuff.

David, with a roll of his eyes, grabbed the pack from his brother's hand. He studied the package. The center had caved at such a depth that the cigarettes had expelled strands of tobacco out their tops. David pulled out a few. They crumbled to the floor of the ambulance.

"Where'd you have them?"

Jeremy tapped his chest and winced. "Top pocket. Behind my vest." He reached below him and pulled out another pack from his cargo pants. His fingers shook as he tried to slip a cigarette between his lips.

The paramedic ripped it out of his mouth and threw it in the biohazard bag. "No smoking."

"I'll take those." David snatched the second package from his brother's hands. "I thought you were quitting."

Jeremy laughed. "I am." He closed his eyes and belted out a song. "It's lonely tonight! All the stars are bright! But you didn't tell me you were leaving me . . ."

The little woman secured Jeremy to the stretcher. "He's going to be a little out of it for a while."

"I'll say. He's serenading an ambulance."

She climbed back in front and nodded to her partner before turning to David. "Either you go with us or you hop out. Which is it?"

David gave his brother one last look. Jeremy would be okay. He hopped out the back. Baers slammed the doors shut. The ambulance pulled away, and David watched his brother disappear around the curve.

"He's fine, David. They just have to check him out." Baers slapped his back, but David didn't respond. "He's fine. Bruised is all. This is just procedure."

"I know." David held up the destroyed package. "Did you know he carried a pack in his shirt?"

Baers took the crumpled package and turned it over and over in his hands. His meaty finger traced the depression. "God works in mysterious ways. This helped absorb the impact."

"Yeah. Lucky him." David took the package back and slid it inside his turnouts alongside the other one. "I gotta get back to the fire."

He slammed his helmet on his head. He had a job to do. He'd worry about his brother later. As he trudged to the fire, he noticed most of the flames were dead.

He met Jake at the edge of the house. Jake looked over at him. "How's he doing?"

"Banged up. Vest caught the bullet. Nice big bruise." David touched his mike. "Jason, hose the left-side window one more time." The wind blew a mist of water his way and onto his face. A cool spray against the fire building within him. David stood there, watching the water run off the roof and onto the ground.

He nudged Jake. "Well, you got scene command. So, what's next?"

He listened as Jake rattled off tasks, but his mind was on his brother, who could have been killed tonight. David heaved a big sigh. He pushed that thought from his mind and followed Jake to the trucks. There wasn't much left to do other than clean up. He radioed for Toby to shut the pumps down. Repetition. Fight the fire. Clean up after the fire. No thinking allowed.

―――――――

David leaned his head against the seat as Toby backed the engine into the bay. The air brakes whooshed. He threw open his door and hopped down onto the cement floor. No thoughts. Not yet. On autopilot, he pressed the button to lower the bay doors. They settled against the floor with a grinding hiss.

He tore his helmet from his head and strode past the red truck, leaving Toby to the engine check. John was stripping off his turnouts. Jason had the side panels opened, stowing away the loose equipment. Pent-up energy pushed him past them to the corner, where he pulled off his own turnouts. He unhooked his jacket, and Jeremy's packs fell to the floor. He eyed them as he stepped out of his boots, pushing the bunker pants down over them and draping the suspenders to the side.

His jacket fell across the bench behind him. The smell of soot and ash wafted up his nose as he leaned down to fasten his work boots. Sweat trickled a cold trail down his spine. He grabbed up the cigarettes. The first of the body tremors worked their way through his gut.

"Toby! I'm in the office. Handle the engine, will ya?"

He didn't wait for Toby's reply. The door to the office opened at his kick. He pushed it to with his foot and plopped down on the chair. His cell phone lay by the run reports. Its angry red light flashed at him. His hand shook as he reached for it.

With a snarl, he opened it. Three missed calls: one from his mom and two from Sarah. He dialed Sarah's number.

She answered on the first ring. "Where are you?"

"At the station. I just got back from the scene." He lowered his head into his hands, balancing the phone at his left ear with his thumb.

"You should've been here with him."

David gritted his teeth. Anger burned a thin line next to self control. "He's fine. I made sure of that. I couldn't leave the scene."

"Since when are you so rule oriented?" Sarah snapped. "Don't bother to come. He's checking out right now."

The phone went silent. David scrubbed at his face. Now he was the bad guy. What did they want from him? He dialed his mom's number.

A cacophony greeted him. Sarah's upset voice, his dad's placating tones, and the beeps, intercom, and alarms of a busy hospital almost drowned out his mom's voice.

"David. Are you okay, sweetie? Sarah's in a rile about you."

"I know. I couldn't leave the scene, Mom, but Jeremy was okay. I made sure of it."

"I know. You wouldn't have left him if it was serious. How are you doing?"

David shrugged. "I'm fine. Scared me at first. Just coming down from the adrenaline rush." He slumped in his chair and twirled it to look out the window. His feet propped against the windowsill, pushing at the half-closed blinds.

"You'll be fine. Take a breather." Her voice faded away and then came back. "Jeremy's discharged. We're heading home now. He's perfectly fine. No broken ribs, but plenty sore."

"I bet. That was a hard impact." David fiddled with his brother's pack of cigarettes with a shaky hand. "I'll call him in the morning. After Satan Sarah cools."

His mom laughed softly. "She'll calm down, you know that. Call me if you need to."

"I will, Mom." He closed his phone and stared up at the ceiling. Too bad he was on duty. He really needed a drink. A knock sounded at the door.

Toby peered in as David turned around. "Got the engine prepped. You doing the run report?"

"About to start it."

"I'll do it. You go take a break, get some rest. Jeremy doing okay?" Toby rounded the desk and picked up the paperwork.

David stood. He rolled his shoulders, loosening the tension. "Yeah. Bruised. Nothing broken." The phone slipped into his pocket along with the pack. "I'm going to step out for a moment."

"Okay." Toby sat at the desk. He pulled the report to him as David opened the door.

"Hey, Toby." His friend looked up at him. "Thanks."

"No problem, dude." He lowered his sweat-matted head back to the paperwork as David slipped out of the office.

He walked the length of the small hall. He peeked inside the dayroom to his left. John and Jason sat on the sofa, a platter of fries in front of them, watching the flat screen. He had no desire to join them yet. Later he'd head over to Station Two and check on those guys. Station Three could wait until the morning.

The cold air met him as he pushed through the back door. Typical March weather. Never could make up its mind if it wanted to be hot or cold. He stuffed his hands deep into his pockets and leaned against the brick wall. His fingers fondled the plastic pack.

The security light gleamed on the plastic when he pulled it out of his pocket. Marlboro Reds, strong stuff. He pulled one out and twirled it around his fingers. It'd been a long time since he'd smoked one. He breathed enough smoke from the fires to never smoke a cigarette again; but, this might be strong enough to kill his craving for a drink.

He shrugged. Nothing to lose for trying. The cigarette slid between his lips. He opened the door. By the doorway, a box of matches lay on top of the shelf next to the charcoal and lighter fluid. David grabbed the box. He squatted, his back propped against the wall, and lit one of the matches. With a shaky hand, he shielded the light and held it to the cigarette.

Its tip glowed. He inhaled. The smoke burned a path into his lungs, which spasmed once. A hard cough threatened to rip his bronchial tubes out. Sheesh, that was strong! He coughed again. Soon his body adjusted to the old, familiar friend. He took another drag and sank down to the ground. Through the lightheadedness, he smoked one more hit, dragging the noxious cloud deep into his lungs.

His head hung between his knees as the nicotine rushed through his system. The call of a drink slowly diminished until it was a faint cry in the dark.

He held the cigarette to his lips. From one extreme to another. He took one last pull and flicked the cigarette away. The nasty thing did its job. The shaking stopped. He looked up and watched the stars burn in the night sky. Now, if he could only hold out until morning.

CHAPTER 6

Jeremy stared at the ceiling in the dark gloom. Morning had come, and his aching body decided to wake up before anyone else. Outside the window, the haze of sunrise barely lit the sky. Beside him, Sarah breathed deeply, her hand resting on his stomach. He propped his arms behind his head. Sleep eluded him. His body craved a cigarette, but it also didn't want to move.

He couldn't stay in bed, no matter how inviting it felt.

He rubbed at his eyes and reached down to remove Sarah's arm. She could sleep through a tornado. The only thing that would wake her was the obnoxious alarm. He struggled to sit, his right hand gently holding his shoulder.

The clock showed another five minutes before the alarm would wake his wife. He eased to his feet and shuffled across the bedroom to their bathroom. He quietly closed the door behind him.

The light flickered to life. His eyes squinted against the harsh onslaught. In the mirror, the bruise taunted him. He ran his finger across the angry red that blossomed over his chest.

He sank against the cool edge of the sink. It could have been his heart. His body shook and shivered. Oh, man, what if he'd died last night? He buried his head in his hands. His prayer of thanks shot to heaven. Only the hand of God kept that bullet from completely penetrating his vest.

The door clicked. He bolted upright as Sarah stepped up to him. She stared back at him in the mirror.

"You'll be okay, honey." She kissed his shoulder, her hand rubbing up and down his back.

"I know." He tried to smile at her. A small knot lodged in his throat, and he swallowed it. "I was blessed to survive. Thinking back on it, I can't shake the feeling how close I came to dying. And I realized I wasn't ready yet."

Sarah wrapped her arms around his waist. He pulled her closer, watching her in the mirror as she kissed the red bruise with gentle lips. "You might not have been ready, and neither was I. God kept you safe." She met his reflection. "I pray for you every night, when you leave for work, when you call me, before I go to bed. I pray for you when I'm cooking dinner."

Tears spilled from his eyes. He brushed at them and looked up, his chin trembling. His dear and wonderful wife. He brought her to him, pressing his lips against her wild, tangled hair. His beautiful wife.

"I don't know what's wrong with me."

Her voice was muffled. "You just had a brush with death. It's expected." She pulled away and reached up to caress his cheek. "Your training taught you this. Go speak with your dad or Uncle Johnny, if you have to. You are fine now." She rose on tiptoes and kissed the corner of his mouth. "Take a shower while I get breakfast ready. I'll let Dennis drive the car to school today. We'll just curl up, watch old movies, eat popcorn."

Jeremy smiled and pressed his forehead against hers. "That's all?"

Her eyes gleamed. "Or whatever else you may think of." She gave him a small pat on his bottom as she left the bathroom.

He leaned his elbows against the sink. It would take a while, but he'd manage to get past the feeling that death had a hand on him. He would have to.

He turned on the cold water and splashed his face, scrubbing away the grit and sticky morning feeling. His toothbrush clattered as he dropped it into the sink. He needed to get a grip. With fingers that danced with a mind of their own, he managed to get the toothpaste on the bristles. Man, what he wouldn't give to be able to find his cigarettes.

———

David walked out of Jack's Express Cafe and headed across the small street to the shop with the little pink awning. He promised Maggie the coffee—creamer, two sugars, strong. Not him. Black and strong or nothing.

The bell above the door clanged twice as he entered. Smells of sugary confection drifted around the store. The musty odor of books mingled with the oily residue of paint. Clothes hung on racks throughout the store. To his right was the register and the glass casing holding vintage jewelry and sparkling baubles.

He bumped into an old Wonder Horse with one spring gleaming brightly in contrast with the other three black-coated ones. She must've repaired it. A small black stool with a painted espresso cup on it stood near the counter. He settled on its varnished surface and waited.

Her voice spoke at the back of the store. "I got the first three, but the fourth and fifth of the series are not here. I have yet to be able to find them on the Internet."

An older woman's voice spoke next. "I'll still take them. I love this series, and I know my granddaughter will love it for her birthday. Do you think you might be able to find the other books?"

Her voice drifted closer. "I am not sure. I'll check a few online auctions and see. If I do, I'll give you a call." When she reached the front of the store, her eyes met his, and a smile drifted across her face.

He raised his brows at her clothes. A light pink tunic shirt flowed over a pair of patchwork pants. His eyes traveled to her feet and found a pair of pink jelly sandals. This woman definitely didn't belong in this decade.

"Thank you, Maggie. Can you hold these for me until tomorrow? I'll have my daughter swing by to pick them up."

"I will."

David greeted the older lady as she went by. Maggie slipped behind her counter and set the books on the shelf behind her. She pulled a sticky note off a pad and labeled the stack. Once done, she turned to him and leaned against the counter. The scent of cotton candy drifted over to him.

"So, you came."

"I came." He pushed her coffee toward her. "Hot and strong."

She grinned again, her eyes sparkling brighter than the baubles under her elbows. "Thank you."

He took a sip and grimaced. "Ugh. Hold on, this one is yours."

She laughed as he switched the cups. "What's wrong with mine?"

"Cream and sugar." He took a sip. A sigh escaped him. "I don't know if this is going to work or not."

She sipped her coffee and wiped her lip. "What do you mean?"

Her fingers pushed a wayward lock of hair behind her ear. He could have done that for her.

David shrugged and leaned back against the wall. Weariness had seeped into him. He ran on sheer willpower now. "Long shift."

"Lots of fires?"

"Just one. Last night." David twirled his coffee around. He didn't know her. Not by a long shot, but he needed to speak to someone. "Got there and found out that a suspect that Jeremy had been chasing burnt the place. After, apparently, beating the sh—" He coughed. "—stuffing out of his grandmother."

Maggie sat down on her stool. Her eyebrows rose. "The poor woman. Is she okay?"

"She's in the hospital, but that wasn't the worst." He took another sip of his coffee. It left a small, foggy ring on her counter, and he trailed his finger through it as he spoke. "Jeremy was shot. Found out when I got there."

He held up his hand to halt her question. "He's fine. The bullet didn't penetrate. But. . ." His voice faltered. His brother could've died, yes. What if . . . he pushed away that thought. A harsh laugh escaped him. "Actually, I wasn't planning on saying anything. I really don't know what to think about it."

Maggie placed her hand over his, her cool, soft skin soothing against his. "It doesn't hurt to tell a sympathetic ear. And mine are the most sympathetic in this town. At least, that's what my dad always says." She smiled. "Have you had breakfast yet?"

David shook his head. A yawn threatened to escape him. "But I'm not hungry. Actually, as much as I want to stay here and talk to you, I find that it's taking everything I have to stay awake. I think I only got in about four hours of sleep."

Maggie rounded the counter and stood in front of him, her legs barely brushing against his knees. Her eyes stared deeply into his. Somewhere in those blue pools, he saw a chance. She liked him. "Then go home. I'll take a rain check, if you want."

He rose to his feet, coffee in hand. Was she asking him out? "A rain check? Like a date?"

She shook her head. "No. Like a friendly coffee or breakfast."

David bit at the inside of his lip. Apparently, she drove in the slow lane. He could play that game. "Okay. I'm actually off come Saturday. Breakfast?"

"Don't you remember? Saturday is the zoo day for the children at church."

He didn't remember. He thought a moment. "Monday, then? Can't promise I'll be good company. I work Sunday, so I can't do breakfast. And I'm filling in for the B shift captain Monday. I can make time for dinner Monday evening."

Maggie smiled as she walked him to the door. "Okay. Jack's?"

David nodded. "Jack's it is. About six." He held the door slightly open and gazed at her. The freckles were out in force today. He wanted to touch them. He wanted to lean in and kiss her, to feel those shiny pink lips against his. It would make all the worries go away, at least for a short time.

She reached up and patted his chest. The spell broke. "About six, then. Sorry you have to work Sunday."

He bit back a groan. "No choice." He smiled. "But it's usually only two Sundays a month. You can always drop by for a visit."

The door opened under his hand, and he stood to the side to allow a dark-haired woman and her child inside. Maggie greeted them before turning to him. "I just might. Then, dinner Monday."

His heart skipped a beat at her smile. He beamed at her as he pushed past the door, the bell once again clanging above his head. His smile stayed plastered to his face as he retrieved his motorcycle from the firehouse and rode out of the bay.

He turned onto the main road, zipping through the traffic. Buildings blurred. He weaved through the four green lights along the main strip. His bike banked dangerously around the last right turn past town and flew five miles down the old country road.

He stopped at the stop sign and then shot straight. Soon his parents' mailbox loomed ahead. Gravel flew up from the driveway as he sped down it. He skidded to a stop inside the garage, his tires leaving a black mark. The exhilaration of the ride boosted his energy. It had to be enough to make it up the stairs. He stretched as he stood. The aroma of cinnamon greeted him as he entered the house.

His dad sat in the kitchen at the bar.

"Morning, Dad."

"Morning, Son. You look beat. You okay?" His dad set his paper down and stared at him.

"Yes." David barely made it past when his father reached out and laid a hand on his sleeve.

"You sure?"

David sighed. "Yeah. I'm fine. Exhausted." He leaned against the counter. Whatever energy he had rushed out of him. His legs wobbled. He jutted his jaw forward. "Seeing Jeremy like that, then Sarah yelling, plus there were two more calls last night. It's taken its toll, is all."

His dad squeezed his shoulder. "Have you called your brother?"

"Not yet. I need sleep first. I'm dead tired." David pushed away from the bar. He called over his shoulder as he walked to the stairs. "Tell Jeremy I'll bring him his cigarettes later."

He heard his dad chuckle.

The shower hummed as he topped the stairs. Great. He'd have to wait until his Mom finished before he could get clean. He slipped into his bedroom and locked the door. His feet almost sighed in relief as he pushed off his work boots. Clothes fell to the floor until he was clad only in his boxers.

The room darkened as he shut the blinds and pulled the curtains close. He sat heavily upon the edge of his bed. Fine time for sleep to elude him. He scrubbed at his face.

The sight of Jeremy in the ambulance popped into his mind.

It needed to go away.

He yanked open the nightstand drawer. The bottle of Glen Livet stared up at him. Pain throbbed in his head. His gut churned with anger, anxiety, and fear. The shaking returned. He twisted the cork out and upended the bottle. It burned. It flooded his bloodstream.

He fought down his rebellious stomach.

Another drink, and the image of Jeremy and the fire faded. One more swallow. The pain in his head receded. David held the bottle in his hands. Only a couple more mouthfuls were left. He shrugged. The liquid rode the fiery trail into his gut. He needed the sleep, and this was the perfect aid.

He replaced the empty bottle in the drawer and closed it. Cool sheets caressed his hot skin as he rolled over and pulled a pillow to his chest. He grinned. Slowly, the room disappeared into a black haze. His mind drifted away. A dreamless sleep would be his sanctuary soon.

CHAPTER 7

The truck driver unloaded the last of the boxes into the garage. The head mover held out the clipboard. David scanned the paperwork, scrawled his signature on the paper, and turned to his meager possessions.

Only ten boxes, one green plastic tub, and a blue plastic tub stood in the garage with him. His headboard and bed frame leaned against the wall. He'd have to buy another mattress. A large, brown leather recliner that had seen better days was the only other furniture he had. Less to move, less he had to pay, less he had to remember.

As the moving van rumbled out of the driveway, he pulled a few boxes to him and rummaged through them. His clothes, a few books, movies, CDs, and other small items. He pushed the box to the side with his foot and grabbed the blue tub. Maybe it was in this one.

The lid popped off easily, and a stack of albums greeted him. His grandfather's old vinyls. He flipped through them, looking for that certain record. His fingers paused over the Moody Blues before he pulled it out. It wasn't the one he was looking for, but it would do. He flipped through some more and found an old Foreigner album. He slid it out of the tub.

Laying them to the side, he spied a red Bible lying on top of the covered knick-knacks. His hands shook as he picked it up. His fingers traced the embossed cross on the smooth leather cover. A lump lodged deep in his throat. He swallowed against it. His hand shook even more violently as he opened it. Get a grip!

"That's not very many boxes." Jeremy's voice echoed in the garage.

David dropped the Bible into the box. With a flick of his wrist, he flipped a pillowcase over the book and stood.

"No. Just packed the essentials. Sold the rest." He kicked another box to the side. His pots and pans, by the sound of it. "What are you doing here?"

Jeremy raised an eyebrow. "Parents live here." He side-stepped Fat Tom and fingered one of the boxes open to peer inside. David hopped over a larger box and slapped the flaps closed. Jeremy laughed. "Porno? Seriously?"

David moved the box to the side. "Bother someone else."

Jeremy lowered himself into the recliner and sighed. "Wow, now this is comfortable. Broken-in in just the right places."

David glared at him as he stacked another box to the side. Did the man not have somewhere else to go? "Why are you really here? Thought you were cleared to go back to work."

"I am. Go back tomorrow. No more pain. Nice, ugly green bruise." He crossed an ankle over his knee. "Dad told me that your stuff from St. Louis was arriving today and that you broke the news to them that you were moving out come Wednesday."

"Yeah?" He pushed the last box to the side. Jeremy sat in his chair, eyes narrowed, waiting for more of a reply. Well, he wasn't going to get one.

"Why? You're welcome here. Surely it couldn't be the rule about church." His brother wiggled farther down in the chair, the leather squeaking under his weight.

David picked up his albums and walked out of the garage. "My reasons are my own."

The bright sunlight hammered into him. Finally, the weather had agreed to give them spring. He opened his truck door and laid the albums on the bench seat. Old albums, old Chevy truck. When he turned around, Jeremy stood behind him, arms crossed.

David flinched. "Sheesh, don't you ever make a sound?"

"Guilty conscience?"

"Nothing to be guilty of." He pushed past his brother and headed for the house. "Dad ask you here to talk me out of it?"

"No. Mom did."

His steps faltered. Figures. He altered his direction, heading for the pond. Jeremy followed. No one would know his reason. No one could be allowed to know his reason. Jeremy still hounded his heels.

"David, come on! Stop and at least talk."

David lengthened his steps. The hedgerow needed clipping. Sprigs stuck out at odd lengths. The grass was ankle deep now. It would need cutting soon. Jeremy grabbed at his arm and pushed him around.

Anger flared within David. He lashed out, his hands hitting Jeremy full force in the chest. Jeremy winced and staggered back a step.

Jeremy snarled. "Hot headed—"

"I told you, my reasons are my own. Can't a man just make a decision and not be questioned?" David stepped up to Jeremy, meeting him straight in the eyes. "I don't care if Mom or Dad or God himself tells you to find out why. You will not know. You will never know."

Jeremy's blue eyes flashed. Red anger whirled around in them. Fury rose within David. He clenched his hands and jutted his jaw forward. "I'm only ten minutes away. Not to mention closer to the station. Works out for the best." His control was slipping. The shaking was returning. David backed up a step. "Just go away."

Jeremy's scowl burned into him. "What's your problem? I only came to placate Mom and Dad. Why are you so worked up?"

David headed for the pond. He had to distance himself. It had been too long. For the past few days, his family had bragged on his brother. Jeremy this. Jeremy that. So what if he caught a bullet in the chest? He didn't die. It didn't permanently hurt him.

David tried to control his breathing. What was wrong with him? He needed a drink. His chest heaved. Sweat trickled down his back and into his waistband.

His brother needed to just leave. Disappear back to his happy little family.

Jeremy slid in front of him. David skidded to a stop and turned his face away. "Get out of my face."

"Not until you listen." Jeremy stepped closer. A muscle worked in the corner of his jaw. "I'm not here to change your mind. Mom wanted an answer. One that you refused to give her."

"I told you. Closer to the station."

"Not that answer. Wrong question."

David narrowed his gaze. He shoved his fists into his pockets to keep them still. "What question?"

"Why are you suddenly behaving like this? She said Thursday you locked yourself inside your room. You skipped out on a family lunch today, claiming exhaustion. And now you inform them you have an apartment." Jeremy looked away and pressed his lips together. Heavy moments hung between them before he spoke again. "She asked me to come and find out what's wrong. You won't talk to anyone."

David refused to retreat. He stared hard at Jeremy. Jeremy's condemnation sent waves of anger through his gut. The perfect son.

David lashed out. "Good little Jeremy. Grow up. Can't be a mamma's boy forever."

Quicker than a cobra, Jeremy snatched a fistful of his shirt and brought him closer, his nose bare inches from his own. "Let's get this straight right now. I don't care what you do with your life. Mom is worried, and it's her life I care about. So, whatever is eating at you, then good riddance to you. You don't need to be around her."

Anger boiled over. He rammed his hands up and broke Jeremy's hold. His elbow contacted with Jeremy's cheek, sending him a step back.

Jeremy spat at the ground. "I ain't fighting you. Be bullheaded if you want." He walked away.

"Just like you. Coward as always."

Jeremy paused, back ramrod straight. His head cocked to the side. His fists clenched in their gloves.

David scrubbed at his face. He moved too soon. Jeremy would be relentless now. Couldn't let him know. He hurried to his brother's side and laid a shaky hand on his shoulder.

"Look. I'm sorry, really. I've been totally exhausted lately." The sun hid behind some clouds, and shadows danced over them. Jeremy's muscles relaxed under his hand. It had to work. Even if he didn't mean it. "The apartment puts me closer to work. I won't have to risk waking Mom and Dad when I do come in."

Jeremy slowly turned back to him. His eyes were cautious, calculating. David worked a smile, burying his anger deep within. That fire had to stay hidden.

Jeremy shook his head. "No. Look, I'm sorry. I know you've been filling in for B shift. You didn't need me baiting you."

David shrugged. "No harm. It's just a bad time for me to talk, that's all."

He trudged back to the house beside his brother. As they rounded the corner, his parents pulled into the drive in their black Dodge 300. The smile didn't seem to want to stay in place, but he had to keep his game face. For just a while longer. Soon, he'd be in his own apartment.

Jeremy glanced at him as they neared the garage. "Why a bad time?"

David sighed. "Just drop it, please."

"Dropped, then." Jeremy leaned against the brick column outside the garage. "For now."

Their mom and dad entered the garage. Mom looked around. "I thought you had more stuff?"

"Sold most of it. Less to worry about." David set a box on top of the box that held the porn magazines. Didn't need his mom finding that one. "Mom, look, I'm sorry that I haven't been talking lately. I'm just tired."

She brushed at a wayward curl near her face. "But why leave?"

David leaned against the boxes. His dad and Jeremy had disappeared around the front of the house. The creaking of the front porch rocker floated across the air toward him. He ran a thumb over his lip. He hated lying, no matter how easy it came to him lately. "It puts me nearer the station. And I'm out and about so much that it's better that I stay near town."

"What about church?"

Her eyes worried him. She would eventually be able to read him if he stayed.

David dropped a kiss on top of her head. "I'll still come. On the days I ain't working, maybe not for Sunday school every morning, but I promise I will try for services. Will that help?"

She smiled and patted his hand. "For a while. I just worry about you, sweetheart."

"Nothing to worry about, Mom. Nothing at all."

"Well, come on in for lunch."

David shook his head. "I'll be there in a bit."

She walked away. The hand he had shoved in his pocket unclenched. Guilt ate at his heart. He had lied. David hung his head. He was never going to drag himself out of this hell he created.

He kicked the box. Why even try? Pointless anyway. He took a deep breath, quieting his thoughts. Can't let Jeremy and his dad read him. He needed to move into that apartment soon. The sooner the better.

———————

Maggie pulled her truck into the side parking lot at the firehouse. If David had to work on a Sunday and couldn't make it to church, then she would bring church to him. And a plate of fried chicken, potato salad, corn, and a huge wedge of apple pie. She smiled as she climbed out of the truck, her gifts balanced in her hands. Hiding a plate of food from hungry Baptists wasn't easy. She grabbed the mason jar of sweet tea and hoped he liked it. Even it was hard to hide.

She stuffed the CD that had been lying on the console into her denim jacket pocket. With a kick from her foot, the door slammed shut. Now that she was here, she wanted to bolt. This was stupid. This was insane. Good gracious, what was he going to think of her?

She squared her shoulders. As gracefully as she could manage, she crossed the pavement toward the door. Jason emerged. His face broke into a grin as he saw her.

"Maggie! Hey." He eyed the plate and tea. "Who's that for?"

Her face heated like a furnace. "Um. For David. He couldn't make it to church this morning."

"That's from this morning?"

"No. We had fellowship tonight. Thought I would bring him something to eat." She gave him a weak smile. "Guess I should have thought about you guys too, huh?"

He chuckled. "That's okay. Believe me, it'll be appreciated. David's in a foul mood tonight. Got us all busy with stuff. Three hours straight with no break. So, if you could distract him for even a small bit, that would give us a breather."

He held the door open, and she stepped into the well-lit bay. A clatter echoed from the far side, followed by a string of curses. David's voice rose above the shout.

"I said the other way!"

"I am. Hold on, I think I got it."

There was another clatter. Then another round of shouts and curses spilled forth.

"Stay here. We've been working on the downed engine, and it ain't going well. Let me go get him." Jason hurried off into the direction of the shouted curses.

The voices suddenly quieted. A sudden crash boomed, causing her to jump, and then David's voice. "What the—"

"David! Visitor!" Jason's voice drowned out the rest of David's shout.

"What? Who?"

A murmur of voices drifted her way, and then David rounded the back of the first engine, wiping at his hands with a rag. Pink tinged the tips of his ears. "Sorry about the language. Aggravating engine."

Maggie grinned at him. He stumbled over something.

"So, what's up? Why are you here?—although it's a pleasant surprise, don't get me wrong." His green eyes bored into her. Even with the grease lining his face and neck, even with the sweat matting those short little strands on his head, he made her heart thud.

Why was she here? Good gracious, she almost forgot. Grow up.

She cleared her throat. "I brought you something. I thought it wasn't totally fair that you had to work while we had fellowship tonight. And potluck dinner."

His eyes brightened. "Ms. Edie make her fried chicken?"

She held her tongue between her lips as she removed the foil off the top. The aroma of the chicken drifted around them. "And I added a big wedge of your mamma's apple pie."

His eyes traveled over the food. He practically salivated over the plate. She covered it back up.

"Have you got a place to put it?"

David blinked. "Yeah. Come on. We'll go to the office." He led her toward the back.

She looked over at the group of firemen as she passed. Jason gave her a thumb's up. She shook her head with a smile and hoped they took advantage of the respite. From what she had seen, the Boyette boys ate fast.

No hoses to sidestep this time. Maggie slipped into the office and set the plate on the desk. "I also brought something else for you."

He pulled a small folding chair up for her and then sat down in the office chair behind the desk. "What's that?" He ripped the foil off the food.

She stopped him. "Your hands are dirty."

"I . . ." He glanced down at them and sighed. "We're used to grabbing food whenever, dirty hands or not. Be right back."

The door shut behind him. She reached over, folded the foil, and pulled the napkins out from under the plate. Condensation trailed little rivers down the outside of the tea glass as she un-screwed the lid from the mason jar. The door opened. David came in with not only clean hands but also a clean face.

He reached for the chicken, but she stopped him with a hand on his. Wow. Three years had made him forget a lot. "Prayer?"

He sighed. A rumble filled the room, and his ears turned pink again. Apparently he was extremely hungry, but he bowed his head. "Gracious Father, for what I am about to receive, let it fill and nourish my body as You fill and nourish my soul. Amen."

"Amen."

"Can I eat now?" His voice was almost childlike.

She laughed. "Yeah."

He picked up a piece of chicken and bit into it. A pleasurable moan escaped him as he chewed. He spoke past the bite. "I've missed Ms. Edie's fried chicken."

She watched him as he took a sip of the tea, not sure by his expression if he liked it or not. He held it out in front of himself and then took another long drink from it, almost downing the whole glass in one gulp. Guess she should have brought more than one pint glass.

"Who made the tea? It's delicious."

"I did."

"Really?" He smiled.

Her insides turned to pudding. Oh boy, he had such a beautiful smile. "Yeah. One of the few things that I do well."

He took another bite of the chicken. "I'm sure you can do a lot of things very well." The chicken bone fell to the plate, and he picked up another piece.

Maybe she should have put three pieces on the plate. "Did I fix enough?"

David nodded. "Oh, yeah. Believe me, even if it was only apple pie, it would have been enough." The pink on his ears traveled farther down as he slid his gaze over to her. "I'm pigging out, ain't I?"

She laughed and propped up on her elbows. "You just look like a hungry man to me."

The bone landed on the Styrofoam plate, and he dug into the potato salad. The corn went next. She shook her head. He was a human vacuum filling a bottomless cave. He drained his tea. A belch rumbled from him, and the pink ears turned red.

"Excuse me." He smiled sheepishly. "I'm too used to eating fast. Never know when we might get toned out."

"Been busy tonight?" She held a napkin out to him and tapped the corner of her mouth. "You got a little bit right there."

"Oh, thanks." He wiped at the errant piece of potato. "It's been pretty quiet tonight. Just a lot of chores. Fixing the engine. Inventory. Cleaning. The last few days I've had were hopping, though."

"Want me to refill the glass? Just point me to the fridge."

"Oh, no. I'll get it in a minute." He picked up the fork. "Thank you very much for this."

She reached over and patted his arm, the starchy feel of his uniform shirt stiff against her fingers. That had to be hot on him. "You're welcome. Oh, like I was saying before, I also brought something—"

The building became a living intercom. "Station One, Station Two. Field on fire at Buccaneer and Sesser Road. District four and five toned for mutual aid."

David leapt from his chair. "Sorry, Maggie. I got to go." He rounded the desk but then suddenly turned and dipped down toward her. "Thank you."

Then he was gone. The ghostly warmth of his lips on her cheek lingered.

Oh, wow—

Sirens screamed. The radio in the office hummed to life. "Dispatch show Station One, Engine Two responding!" David's disembodied voice echoed in the room.

Maggie peered out the window. The red trucks barreled down the road out of sight. The sirens faded, but the radio continued its blaring as dispatch and the trucks chattered. She reached over and covered the apple pie with the foil.

A yellow legal pad lay near the edge. After searching in the desk, she found a black ballpoint pen. She read aloud as she scribbled a small message to him.

"David. Here is a copy of the sermon from this morning. I thought of you as Daddy preached it. Mr. Jacobs dubbed an extra copy for me. Hope you enjoy it. Love . . ." She stopped. Love? She blackened the word. "Sincerely, Maggie." Well, it would have to do.

The jewel-colored case rested on the note. With a sigh, she turned off the light and left the office. Quiet haunted the bay as she walked out the opened gates. Her steps sounded hollow. Fascinating how it all seemed deathly still without the guys.

Even the parking lot seemed lonely now. She opened her truck and climbed in. It rumbled to life when she turned the ignition, but she paused. She touched her cheek. He had kissed her. Oh, wow.

CHAPTER 8

David hung his turnouts in the locker and sank down onto the bench. He was bone tired. Again. Thomas walked by and thumped his shoulder.

"I've got C shift scheduled for Thursday. Tony's out again for knee surgery, so I need you to pull a double. Work with A shift on Wednesday." Thomas stood in front of him, waiting.

David looked up at his boss. "Yes, sir. No problem. When's the rookies coming?"

"Thursday. They'll be here at noon." With that, Thomas walked away, shouting at a couple of the boys on the back of the rig.

David's bones ached as he stood. Even with the shower he had taken earlier, nothing seemed to wash away the grime he felt against his skin. For a small town, this one was hopping at night. He stretched. His spine crackled like a log in a fire. As much as he wanted to go to sleep, he had a shift to run. He'd get some sleep later.

Toby met him at the back of Engine One. "How's it going, dude?"

"What are you doing here?"

"Filling in, like you. Bret is out, and B Shift is down a driver-operator." Toby leaned against the rails on the truck. "So, I ask again, how's it going, dude?"

David lowered himself down on the diamond-plated bumper. "Tired. This town is too much like St. Louis. Too busy at night."

"Maybe tonight will be better. Kids are back at school and gone back to college. Really, the only thing we have to worry about are the grass fires started by the farmers." Toby scanned the bay. "Nothing really pressing tonight; why don't you get a few z's?"

David shook his head. "I got a date."

"Oh, really?"

"Yeah. Actually, she won't call it a date." David stood. "Eating with Maggie at Jack's."

"When?"

A breathy voice echoed behind them. "Now."

They both turned. David's heart slammed, closing off his airways. Could she look any more delicious? Her hair, highlighted by the bay's lights, flowed around her face. He sought out her freckles as she approached them. She had been in the sun today. Her cheeks matched her dark pink, gauzy-looking shirt. He checked her jeans. Plain old jeans this time. And plain old black sandals. But as she reached to push back a strand of hair, her earrings flashed.

She didn't disappoint. Little pink butterflies hung from delicate lobes.

David flicked a butterfly. "Cute. I like them."

Now her face matched her shirt. "Thanks. How are you doing, Toby?"

The big guy smiled and shrugged. "Good enough." He slapped David on the shoulder. "I'll go take care of the chores, then. Have a good da– I mean, dinner."

David arched his eyebrow. That wasn't a slip of the tongue. He'd make Toby pay for that.

"So," he turned back to his little heart stopper, "hungry?"

"Am I ever." She walked with him out of the bay.

The sun left a thin line of dusky red in the sky, barely visible beyond the downtown buildings. A hum penetrated the silence as they walked across the street and onto the sidewalk in front of her shop, and then the streetlamps blossomed to life. The sight of her doorway decorated with Easter decorations made him smile.

"How was shop today?"

"Slow." She kicked a pebble. It skittered across the sidewalk and down the small steps. "But that's a Monday for me."

David laughed. "I almost forgot it was Monday. Been so busy, I've lost track of time."

"You didn't forget about our dinner."

His stomach answered for him. "Yeah. Well, I apparently have a reminder about that." Heat touched his ears as she giggled.

They crossed the small street and ambled their way toward Jack's Express Cafe. David was in no hurry, despite his stomach's determination to rub a blister on his backbone. Maggie apparently wasn't in a hurry, either. Every other step, she bumped lightly against his arm, sending that delectable scent up to him.

She broke the awkward silence. "Sarah told me you've gotten an apartment. Where?"

The door chimed as he opened it and ushered her inside. Clattering dishes and talking customers mingled with the aroma of good cooking in the small building. "The Lake Grove Apartments."

She chose the nearest booth and slid onto the purple vinyl, her back to the door. "That's pretty ritzy, isn't it?"

"Not really that much. Mainly studio apartments. I like it, and it's close enough to work, yet far enough away that I don't hear work."

Maggie smiled at his statement. "Hear work? I never thought about it that way, but I guess that would apply. So," she opened a menu, "what are you ordering?"

David left his menu on the table. "Deluxe country fried steak plate. The best there is."

Maggie put hers aside. "Okay. I'll match you."

He raised his eyebrow. The little woman dared to eat as much as him? "Dessert?"

"Of course. Double decker chocolate fudge banana split."

She planned to kill him with sugar. "Bring it on, then."

A teenage waitress came by. "Need to hear the specials?"

"Nope. Two orders of the deluxe country fried. Sweet teas. And load the mashed potatoes." He regarded Maggie. "Too much?"

"Nope." She waved her hand at him. "Never too much."

"Good." He reached to his side and shifted his radio over. The dang thing kept poking him in the side. "I don't like having dinner with a picky eater."

"Oh? Then you've had lots of dinners with picky eaters before?"

"Too many. All disasters." He accepted the cold glasses of sweet tea from the waitress, giving her a smile that made her blush. "But those are stories for another time."

"You do that a lot, don't you?"

He pushed her glass of tea toward her as he sipped his. "What?"

"Smile at the girls." She leaned forward on her elbows. "You send them all into a twitter. Even Poppy was speechless when you smiled at her that day in church."

"Blame my dad. Inherited his charm." He gave her his brightest smile. "Is it working?"

Maggie giggled. "No. Boyish charms don't work on me."

He leaned forward, his elbows resting on the table. The noise of the café dimmed as he stared deep into her eyes, watching a flood of emotions swirl in their depths. What was she thinking?

Her lips parted as he asked, "How about my appeal?"

She rose slightly, bringing her eyes level with his. Her tongue peeked out and wet her bottom lip. Somewhere he had lungs, but they had left him.

Her voice was soft as she asked, "How about mine?"

Slam. Her eyes twinkled like a dozen sapphires as she leaned back in the booth. David shook his head. The sounds of the café sang into his ears with their noise. Silverware was back with their symphony of clattering dishes. Quiet voices echoed.

"Touché." He sat back with a smile. "At least I know that you're here because of me and not because of my smile."

Maggie toyed with her straw. "Oh, I wouldn't say that."

He laughed again and looked away. "Well, at least—"

His radio squawked. He hung his head with a sigh as it sounded off in the café. "Station One, Station Two, report of a two car accident, possible injuries, Thomas Drive. Please respond."

Maggie waved at him. "Go. Go. I'll see you again."

David forced a tight smile. "May I call you?"

Her response was lost as his radio blared again. "Station One, request from PD, Rescue One needed."

No time to waste. He jumped to his feet and bolted, leaving Maggie at the booth. He hightailed it across the street to the firehouse, his lungs burning as the adrenaline pulsed through him. His mind replayed her look. She seemed to have been expecting something.

Rescue One barreled out of the bay, barely slowing as he hopped up on the running board and pulled open the passenger door. Toby never spared a glance as he pulled out onto the road heading for Main Street.

David gripped the radio as he settled onto the captain's seat. "Dispatch. Rescue One en route times two."

With Engine One behind them, sirens screamed as they flew down the main strip heading for Thomas Drive, taking David farther and farther away from Maggie.

———————

Maggie sat there. It was there on his face, his desire to kiss her again. She smiled. She'd let him, eventually.

The waitress came to her table. "Do I need to cancel the orders?"

Maggie shook her head. "No. Make them to go, please. And can you get me some to-go cups for the tea?"

"Yes, ma'am." The girl bounded away, her ponytail swinging. Within moments, the girl had two large cups for the tea, the to-go containers steaming with the dinners, and a plastic carry bag. She gave Maggie the ticket.

"Wait." Maggie held the ticket out. "This is two meals. I'm only charged for one."

The girl shrugged. "Jack said to charge half price."

"Tell Jack I said thank you. And here." Maggie held out a ten and five. "Keep the change."

A smile spread across the teen's face. "Thank you."

As she fairly skipped away with the ticket and payment, Maggie bagged her items and left. The night turned a little chilly as the wind picked up. She could smell rain on the wind. For once, the forecasters actually got the weather report correct.

Same as last night, the gates stood gaping wide open. She entered the quiet bay and tiptoed her way to the office. A fat ceramic pig, dressed in red fire gear, propped open the door. She chuckled as she passed it.

The container almost tipped open as she pulled it out of the bag. Oops. She would hate for him to have to eat it off the desk. Hopefully, it would not cool off too much before he made it back. She dug through her bag and found her butterfly notepad. At the bottom was her pink sparkly pen.

"David. Here's your dinner. Guess it'll be another rain check. See you Saturday at the riverside picnic. Maggie." She slid it between the flaps of the container so that David couldn't miss seeing it. "At least I didn't put love on this one."

As she left the firehouse, her phone chimed. She pulled it from her pocket. "Hello?"

"Miss Maggie?"

"Poppy? What's wrong?"

She could hear the little girl sniffle. "Grandmamma's not home."

Maggie held back her sigh. Poor girl. Third time this month. "Okay. Keep the doors locked. Don't open for anyone but me. I'll be there in a few minutes."

"Okay, Miss Maggie." The line clicked.

She hurried across the street and around the corner to her truck. Anger ate at her. What kind of woman would leave a ten-year-old home alone? That woman didn't deserve to have her granddaughter. At least Poppy had Maggie. She set the bag of food on the bench seat and started the truck.

With a rumble, she pulled away from the small parking area, calling her dad as she drove. Agitation tangoed with her anger. She had to find some kind of balance before she picked up Poppy.

He answered on the third ring. "Maggie, how's the dinner?"

"David got called out. But that's not why I called, Dad. Josephine went off again."

His heavy sigh hissed across the phone. "You going to get her?"

"Yeah. If it would do any good, I would have DHS out there, but you know they'll just take her away. Poppy doesn't need that." Maggie bit back her tears. "How could the woman be like that?"

"Honey, not everyone can love like you. Just pick up Poppy. I'll get the couch prepared."

"Thanks, Dad." She closed her phone. Ahead, she could see the flashing red lights of emergency vehicles. Lights from cars and the streetlamps reflected off the firefighters' gear and the police officers' jackets. She sighed. And her night had seemed so hopeful.

She took the right turn, leading her away from the rescue scene and farther into the poor side of town. Neglected houses stood in ragged formation along the street. Some yards sported clean, if not empty, yards, while others sported weeds, bare spots of ground, and junk as decorations. She shook her head; there was a difference between living in poverty and wallowing in it. Josephine Littleton wallowed in it.

She pulled her truck into the narrow driveway and regarded the yellow stone house. Paint peeled at the window sills. Duct tape ran a spider web pattern across one of the living room windows. There was barely any grass to talk about. A long time ago, the chain link fence had fallen away, but no one had bothered to fix it or remove the sections that slumped to the ground.

A curtain in the living room moved as Maggie exited her truck. Broken concrete jutted up from the sidewalk. Maggie sidestepped it and stumbled as her foot sank in the soft dirt. Her ankle popped.

She hobbled up the steps. Poppy had the door opened before Maggie could knock. The little girl threw herself into Maggie's arms. Her body trembled.

Poppy's voice spoke through Maggie's shirt. "Thank you, Miss Maggie. I asked God to help me remember the number you gave me. Then I remembered it was in the little pink Bible. Then I couldn't find my little Bible. Then I remembered I had to hide it from Grandmamma, so I put it in my toy box."

Maggie closed her eyes against Poppy's litany. Oh, Lord, she needed strength and calmness. She pulled the girl's little, thin frame to her, holding tight.

"God answered you, Poppy. Come on. Let's get your clothes."

Poppy shook her head and hiccupped, tears brimming in her blue eyes. "I don't have any clean. Grandmamma didn't wash any. And the others, she took to sell." She slipped from Maggie's arms and rushed to the back door. "I've got my bag. Toothbrush, hair brush, and Sorta."

"Sorta?" Maggie followed her. Nestled against the small canvas bag was a black and white kitten.

"Yeah. It's a sorta cute kitten. I found her yesterday in the backyard. But, Miss Maggie, I don't have any milk for it."

Two little outcasts. Maggie scooped up the kitten, cradling it in her hands. Fleas crawled over the poor creature. It mewled softly, nosing around. Maggie fought back another heavy sigh. The poor thing was barely even weaned.

She stood. "Come on. Have you eaten yet?"

Poppy picked up her bag. "Grandmamma left yesterday. I ate the last of the cereal this morning."

Heaven help her!

Maggie bumped the door open with her hip and ushered Poppy outside. "Use the passenger side, Poppy. And there's food on the seat."

The little girl ran to the side of the truck and climbed in. By the time Maggie made it to the truck, Poppy had the container opened and was digging into the mashed potatoes. She looked up with a big smile, her innocent eyes beaming as she shoveled the food into her mouth. So much for Maggie's meal, but the little girl needed it more.

Maggie set the kitten on the floorboard.

Mashed potatoes flashed in Poppy's mouth as she asked, "Will Sorta be okay down there?"

"She'll be fine. She can eat some of Samson and Delilah's food when we get to the house. After we give her a bath."

Maggie backed out of the driveway and headed home. Poppy smacked away at her food, her bony, jean-clad legs swinging back and forth over the edge of the seat. Maggie fought the impulse to hold her nose. The poor girl must have been too afraid to take a bath while alone. Bet she didn't go to school today, either.

When she paused at the stop sign, she turned on her right blinker and prayed that the wreck wasn't gruesome. As they pulled out onto the main strip, Maggie glanced over at the rescue trucks. Only a few remained. David was still there. She knew that stance. The red and blue flashing lights silhouetted his body. An officer directed them past the wreckage.

Poppy, like all children, sat transfixed by the scene. She gasped and pointed. "Look, Miss Maggie! There's Mr. David. Isn't he handsome? You think he's the boss? He seems like the boss. See, he's pointing at the other man. What's he saying? Can I hear what he's saying?"

Maggie laughed. From the look on David's face, it was better she not hear his words. "No. And yes, he's the boss tonight."

"Can we stop to say hi?" Poppy stuck another mouthful of potatoes in her mouth.

"No. He's too busy at the moment. It was a terrible wreck."

"Should we pray for them?"

Maggie eased over to the other lane and sped up, away from the wreck. Away from David. "Yes. Prayer is always good."

She took a deep breath and drove home. Prayer was always good, but was it a sin to pray for someone's punishment? She stole a quick glance at the little girl, now happily munching on the steak. Such a beautiful child to have such a horrible grandmother. She didn't deserve to be alone.

———————

Jeremy pulled his squad car up to the front parking space at Second to None. The lights were on, and there was movement inside the shop.

He touched his radio. "J forty-nine. Ten-six at Second to None."

"Copy, J forty-nine."

He stepped out. The humid air of the night stuck to him. He glanced around. No one was about this time of night. His eyes traveled to the firehouse. The bay doors were closed. Guys were probably sleeping after that last call.

A movement by the window caught his eye. He climbed the steps to the door and rapped on it, peering through the glass. The movement stilled. He shielded his eyes from the glare of the streetlamps and squinted. A shadowy figure made its way to the front.

He pushed the tab off his holster and rested his hand on the butt of his gun. Relief surged through him as Maggie stepped into the light. Her body slumped in apparent relief.

She turned the lock and opened the door. "Jeremy. You gave me a fright."

He smiled at her as he eased into the store. "What are you doing here so late?"

Maggie relocked her door. She waved for him to follow as she retreated to the back. "I'm trying to find Poppy some clothes. She's so skinny, and it's hard to find something that fits properly, especially pants."

"Poppy?" He peeked into the box that she piled pants and shirts into. "What's happening now?"

"Josephine is in Memphis. I finally reached her an hour ago. She said she wouldn't be back home until Sunday. Can you believe that?" A pair of pants shot into the box, rocking it back with its force. "The woman supposedly had a baby sitter for Poppy, and supposedly the baby sitter called and said she couldn't make it."

Maggie threw another set of pants into the box. Jeremy took her hands and held them. "She left Poppy alone?"

Maggie nodded. Tears brimmed her eyes. "I won't call DHS, Jeremy. They will take Poppy away to some home or whatever. Josephine asked me to keep her 'til Sunday. I'll do it for Poppy, not for that hateful, old woman."

Jeremy put his arms around her shaking shoulders and held her. Tears soaked his uniform as she cried against his shoulder. He could think of nothing to say to her. There wasn't anything to say. Some people were just like that. Never a thought about anyone else. "You have Poppy at your house?"

Maggie pushed away, wiped her eyes, and continued packing. "Yeah. The stupid woman took her clothes to sell. So, here I am, finding–or at least trying to find–something for her. All I got at the house for her is the black and white dress. I keep it there for Poppy to wear to church. Too afraid to let that horrid woman get her hands on it."

Jeremy propped himself against a clothes rack. "What size is she?"

"Oh, about an eight. And that's with a belt. Sevens are too short. Unless we find a capri."

Jeremy held up his hand. "Stop. I have no idea what a capri is. Have you called Sarah?"

Maggie stopped. "No. I didn't want to bother her. It's so late."

He pulled out his cell phone. "I think she still has a few of Sophie's old clothes. Let me see."

"Oh, thank you, Jeremy!" She turned to her box and started closing the lid.

Sarah answered. "Hey, baby." A yawn escaped her. "You on your way home?"

"Just about. Had one more stop to make." He walked toward the front door. "Listen, Maggie has Poppy for a while, but Poppy's grandmother took her clothes. Do you still have any of Sophie's old ones?"

"Yeah. I have them in the garage. They probably need washing. I've been meaning to give them to Goodwill. Just been forgetting to grab them."

"A reason for everything." He nodded to Maggie as she approached with her box. "Sarah's got Sophie's clothes."

"Are you at Maggie's?"

"At the shop. Saw the lights on."

"Hand her the phone."

Jeremy held out his phone. "Here. Sarah wants you."

Maggie took it from him. She strolled toward the back of the store as she talked with her cousin. Jeremy sighed. What a night. First the wreck. Then his meeting with the informant. And now this.

"Maggie, I'll be at the car." He slipped out. There had to be something on that woman. He opened his car and leaned in, pulling his terminal closer. He typed in Josephine's name and address and glanced around the quiet and dark downtown square. Nothing moved. All was quiet. The terminal beeped. He looked at the screen and sighed. Nothing.

He leaned back. At least it was a blessing that Poppy had Maggie.

She exited the building with her box. Jeremy unfolded his frame out of the car and accepted his cell phone. "Sarah said she'll bring the clothes to the parsonage tomorrow. They should fit. If not, I can alter them enough."

Jeremy nodded. "You okay?"

"Yeah. I will be. Sarah said she'll pick Poppy up from school. That helps since I only have one helper at the store. Ms. Axelbury only works on Fridays and Saturdays."

He took the box from her hands. "Where's your truck?"

She waved at the side facing the firehouse. "Over there."

He followed her. When she opened the door, he slid the box onto the seat. "You call us if you need anyone?"

"I will, Jeremy." She glanced at the firehouse. Her face creased in a frown before turning to him and forcing a smile. "I'd better let you get home before Sarah starts to think I'm trying to steal her man."

Jeremy laughed. "Okay. Come here, man stealer." He wrapped her into a hug. She sniffed once and pulled back. "We're here if you need us."

She climbed up into her truck.

Jeremy walked back to his car and fell into the seat. Poor Poppy. He shook his head. He'd make sure that his routes carried him past the Littleton house from now on. It was the least he could do for the little red-headed sweetheart.

He backed up his car, waved at Maggie as he drove by, and pulled into the station. He touched his mike. "Dispatch. J forty-nine at station."

He ignored their reply and pulled his gear from the side seat. Home was calling him. All he wanted was to curl up next to his wife and sleep for a thousand years. The cool interior greeted him. Five more minutes and he'd be out of here.

———————————

David parked the company car by the building. He rubbed at his eyes. B shift was not a well-oiled machine, especially Station Two. He dragged his body out of the car and rounded the corner.

A flash pierced dark. The light at Maggie's store flickered off. He frowned. She walked down the steps, carrying a box to a squad car sitting at the curb. Jeremy.

David slinked back into the shadows, leaned against the brick wall, and watched. After a little bit, she and Jeremy walked to her truck. He slid the box inside. They talked for a moment, and then Jeremy reached out and pulled her to him.

He narrowed his eyes. Surely his brother wasn't messing around. The squad car pulled away, and Maggie sat in her truck. Another minute passed, and she didn't move.

David crossed the two-lane and approached her truck. She had the window down and her head hung. Was she praying? He tapped the truck bed as he walked up to her window.

She looked up at him. Not a drop of surprise in her eyes, but they lit up. That was a good sign. "I was wondering how long it was going to take for you to come over here."

David frowned. "How'd you mean?"

She laughed. "I saw you. You were watching." She pushed open her door and turned around to face him.

He propped against the door and shrugged. "Yeah. Saw you leave the store. Saw Jeremy."

"And you thought something was going on."

"I . . ." Was he that transparent? He gripped the truck's cab. "Yeah. It did cross my mind."

She smiled at him. "Such a suspicious mind." She leaned her head against the headrest. "I had to find some clothes for Poppy."

"For Poppy? Why?"

"Long story."

He grasped her hand. "Come on."

She followed him, limping on her left foot, to the back of her truck. He lowered the tailgate, hopped up, and patted beside him. "Tell me what's going on."

She wiggled up by him. Her cotton candy scent barely reached him. The smell of honeysuckle floated through the air. She pushed her hair behind her ear, and the smell reached him again.

"I really don't even know where to begin."

David shrugged. He held her hand. His thumb stroked her soft skin. "Just start talking. I get the feeling you take care of Poppy a lot."

"I do. Her grandmother, Josephine, just up and leaves whenever. Leaving Poppy alone. Poppy only has her grandmother. Her mom died seven years ago. Drug overdose. The father is an unknown. There's no other family. When Dad and I came here, I took a liking to her. Soon I found myself tending to Poppy on several occasions."

"Ever call it in?"

"No." She shook her head. Her hand left his, and she turned around until she was facing him. "I can't. Poppy would be taken away. It took two years to pull her out of her shell. And I love her too much to let some state employee say they know what is better for her welfare. Poppy doesn't need strangers."

He brushed her hair away from her eyes. "Okay. Bad idea. So, you have Poppy now?"

She nodded. "Right after you had to leave from Jack's, she called. There wasn't even any food in the house. So I gave her my food."

That sounded like his Maggie. "Oh, thanks for the food you brought me. You didn't have to do that."

Maggie shrugged, avoiding his eyes. "Well, I knew you would be hungry. Anyway, I picked her up. Wrenched my ankle on the sidewalk."

He reached for her leg. "Let me see that. I wondered why you were limping."

"No. It's fine now." She pushed at his hands.

"Just relax. Put your leg up here." She raised her leg into his lap. He rolled up her pants leg and slid his fingers under her butterfly anklet to press the joint. She winced. "Sorry."

"That's okay. It's tender. It hurts if I put too much pressure on it."

"What did it sound like when you hurt it?"

"A popping sound."

He ran his hand up her shin and then down the foot. Nothing seemed out of place. Goosebumps formed on her flesh underneath his touch. "You probably have a torn ligament. Put some ice on it tonight and take some naproxen sodium for the inflammation."

She smiled, swatting his hand away, and pushed her pant leg down. Her leg left his lap to dangle over the tailgate. "Thank you."

"So. You got Poppy, popped your ankle, had your food eaten, and. . .?" He leaned back on his hands, watching her fiddle with the seam of her pants. The desire to touch her overwhelmed him.

"I took her and Sorta home."

That was a weird name. "Sorta?"

"A kitten she found. We gave the kitten a bath. Samson and Delilah weren't too thrilled to have a newcomer in the house."

He arched a brow. "Samson and Delilah? Should I be writing this down so I can keep it all straight?"

She smiled. "My cats. I got Samson two years ago. Then I adopted a female kitten. Had to have Samson cut because of the new female, so I named her Delilah."

David chuckled. He sat up. A strand of hair fell between her eyes. He reached out and brushed it back as he replied, "I had a dog named King Saul. Best friend, but that dang mutt would bite my hand at least every other day. So what happened after you got Poppy home?"

She waved a hand in front of her nose. "I gave Poppy a bath. Oh my word, she stunk. I finally contacted Josephine." Her brow creased, and her mouth turned down. She bit out her words. "The woman won't be back until Sunday! Can you believe that? So here I am, trying to find Poppy some clothes because the woman took her other ones to sell."

David pushed his anger down. To abandon a child and take her clothes? If he ever saw the woman, Lord help her. Maggie's hands shook. He covered them, her skin cool and soft beneath his hands.

"You have her now. Don't think about that old hag."

"Oh, David, I don't know if you understand. I feel like . . . I don't know what."

"Angry."

She hissed. "Yes. And . . ."

"And sad." He brushed a thumb across her cheek, tracing a row of freckles. Tears pooled in her eyes. "I've seen a lot of that in St. Louis. But Poppy is fortunate to have you. They had no one."

Maggie sighed. She pressed her cheek against his palm as a couple of tears escaped. "I would do anything for her."

"I understand. I feel that way about my nephews and niece. Come here." She came willingly and melted into his arms.

Her arms encircled his chest. Her head tucked neatly under his chin, wayward locks tickling his lips. His breath caught. This felt so right. She fit so perfectly against him.

Their breathing synchronized. Somewhere in the distance, a whippoorwill sang. The scent of the blooming dogwoods mingled with her honeysuckle shampoo. The wind blew a few of the petals across the air in front of them.

His heart pounded against his ribs as her hand crept across his chest.

He looked down at her as she rubbed her nose. "I smell, don't I?"

She blushed and giggled. "Just a little. Like an overcooked grill."

"Great."

"It's okay . . . just charcoal-y . . ." She pushed at him, straightening up. "I really need to go. It's late. Poppy has school tomorrow. I have work."

David caught her hands and pressed them between his. They were so small, so slender. He didn't want her to leave, not yet. "You'll find me if ever you need to talk?"

"I will." Her eyes traveled back and forth as she watched him. Her face softened.

What did she want?

He traced a finger over her brow and down the side of her face. She was beautiful. Sapphire eyes. Pink lips. He leaned forward. Her eyes fluttered closed. Just a touch. That was all he wanted. Just one touch.

Her cool lips met his. Soft and yielding. His fingers buried themselves in her silky hair and cupped the back of her head. She didn't pull back. Her arms circled his chest, pressing him closer.

He couldn't get enough. She tasted like cotton candy. He wrapped his other arm around her waist. His hand fell to her hip–

Hot, humid air rushed between them.

Through hazy vision, he watched the cloudy, soft look disappear from her face. Her hand pushed at his chest.

"I'm sorry. I shouldn't have let that happen." She jumped from the tailgate, staggering once under her bad ankle.

For a second or two, he sat there. He blinked and pushed back the red heat of desire. She was already in the cab. He slammed the tailgate shut, barely missing his finger. He hurried to the front of the truck. Another near miss as he caught the cab door before she closed it.

"Maggie—"

"No. Look. Let's just forget it, please." She struggled with her seatbelt.

He jerked the door from her hand. "No. I won't forget it. I . . ." He took a breath. "I'm sorry. I thought that's what you wanted."

She slumped. A hurt expression crossed her face. "No. That's what you wanted, David." Her hand closed around the door handle and pulled.

He allowed her to close the door, but he stopped her with a hand on the steering wheel before she cranked the truck. "That's not all I want."

Cool gemstones stared at him. Passion no longer swam in her eyes, but her lips were still swollen from their kiss. "Prove it, then. I've heard enough to know that you play fast and loose—"

"Not true." He clenched his jaw. Funny how lies of the past haunted him. "I never did."

"What would have happened just then, huh? Don't tell me that was just an innocent little kiss."

He snarled. "Don't tell me you didn't want something more." Women. They all promised but never delivered. He could do without that kind.

Her hand covered his, and his anger receded at the cool touch.

"Maybe what they say isn't true, but I see in you a man who doesn't want anything more than a physical relationship. I can't be in another relationship like that." She stroked his hand with a finger. "Prove to me that you want me beyond the physical."

David leaned inside, inches from her lips. "Be careful of what you ask for."

She patted his cheek and leaned forward. Her lips were soft against his flesh. The cotton candy scent invaded his senses. "Be careful of what you promise. Good night, David."

She smiled and then backed up into the street. He watched as her truck disappeared down the street. Then he glanced around the deserted square.

He had just been snookered. The woman was determined to make him fall for her. Well, she asked for it. He'd prove to her that it wasn't just physical. Yeah. Two could play that game. Only after a cold shower, of course.

CHAPTER 9

David pushed the door open. Chaos greeted him. Boxes littered the floor of his studio apartment. Sunlight poured through the windows. Way too bright. One of these days, he would have to buy some blinds or curtains. But not today.

He shoved a box to the side with a foot. That box needed to go live in the dumpster. Two more opened boxes, contents glaring at him, stood in the way. He stepped over them. One of these days, he'd finish unpacking. Wednesday had given him enough time to move into the apartment but not to unpack.

He set the bag he carried on the counter and unloaded the few items: milk, eggs, bread, bacon, cereal, chips, beer, and frozen dinners.

He stuffed the food away and placed a frozen dinner into the microwave. The six pack rattled as he slid it onto the shelf and grabbed one of the bottles. The top to the beer bottle flew across the kitchenette as he wandered to the small flat screen across the room. The cold malt soothed his parched throat as he searched through a box full of movies. He needed a good shoot'em up. Especially after his horrible night. A few choice words about the rookies escaped his mind. Apparently, the academy had lowered its standards.

The microwave dinged.

He slipped the DVD into the slot on the Xbox console. One of these days, he'd buy a nice Blu-ray player. He padded to the kitchenette and retrieved his cardboard meal.

The last few drops of his Heineken increased his thirst for more. He chucked his empty beer bottle into the garbage can, and it rattled against the bottom. He grabbed two more beers and settled into his leather chair with his meager fare.

Man, what he wouldn't give for his mom's home-cooked meal. Price he had to pay for moving out. Oh, well.

He played the movie. Time to enjoy the mind-numbing action of zombies being mutilated. After a couple of stale bites, he set the tray on the floor. Tasted exactly as it smelled, cardboard and plastic. He drained his bottle and set it on the floor. The top of the next one sailed across the room and bounced against the door. He'd find it later. His chair was way too comfortable at the moment.

Halfway through the beginning of the movie, he drifted away with the sounds of the film and a pleasant buzz in his head. Gunfire, yells, and the movie's background music merged with the collage of scenes in his mind. A weeks' worth of work and stress interspersed with a smiling, freckled-faced pixie danced behind his closed eyelids. The image of her blue eyes, sparkling and laughing, faded into a red haze. In the distance, fire crept closer, beating out a tempo—one, two, three. Repeat. It advanced closer and louder, yelling his name.

He jerked awake, spilling some beer across his stomach. His curse echoed in the room, competing with the loud knocking at his door.

"In a minute!" His heart rate slowed, and his body protested as he levered himself out of the chair. He drained the rest of the lukewarm beer and threw the bottle into an empty box as he passed by.

"David?" The muffled voice called from behind the door.

He rolled his eyes. Darlene. He forgot she was going to visit today. He pulled open the door and leaned against the frame. Her green eyes stared up at him, deep dimples forming on both sides of her face. "You're early," he told her.

She pushed past him, carrying a covered dish. The scent of chicken and melted cheese floated up to him. "Yup. And I would have told you if you had answered your phone."

"What is that?" He kicked the door closed. The metal top from the beer gleamed from the corner. He scooped it up and threw it into the box holding the bottle.

"Chicken casserole." She slid it across his counter and uncovered it. "I thought you could probably use a good meal."

"Yeah, I could. Thanks. Tried a microwave meal, but it was nasty." He picked up the empty bottle and half-eaten meal. They joined the other Heineken in the can.

Darlene eyed his shirt, pushing her brown locks back under her red headband. "What's on you?"

"My drink. I was dozing when you knocked. Spilled my beer."

"Well, go change, and I'll fix you a plate."

He sighed. She wasn't going to leave anytime soon, so he might as well settle in for a chat. His new mattress squeaked as he sat on its edge and pulled a green plastic tub to him. Somewhere in the pile of clothes was his black t-shirt. Darlene started talking as he stripped off his beer-soaked garment.

"I told Marty that we need to have a bash next month. It'll be Marty Junior's birthday. Of course, Marty Junior didn't want a birthday bash until I told him that he could pick the place. So far, he is still thinking . . ." She turned from the counter with a full plate as he sent the dirty shirt sailing toward the bathroom door. "You know, I still can't get over that tattoo. Whatever made you decide on that design? I see you as more of a phoenix or dragon."

He smiled and pulled the clean, black AC/DC shirt over his head. She walked toward him as he looked around for a chair or box for her to sit on. "I like it. Figured flames suited me."

She shrugged. "Well, I guess it does. Anyway, the boys are still going on about it. Sarah is livid because Dennis already said that he's getting one once he turns eighteen. You really like to start a riot in the family." She waved him to the leather chair. "Sit. I'm fine. Actually, seeing your place now, and the mess it is in, is driving me nuts."

He accepted the plate and sampled the food. Cheese, onions, and moist chicken melted in his mouth. His eyes closed in pure pleasure. "Um. So good."

She kissed his head. "Enjoy. I'll only make you something every once in a while, Mr. Bachelor."

"Darlene," he spoke around his mouthful, "you don't need to clean my place."

"It's a pigsty, little brother." She scooped up a handful of magazines and stacked them on top of an overturned box. "And knowing you, you'll put it off until you're keeping company with rats and roaches."

"Now, that's disgusting. I'm not that bad." He shoveled another bite into his mouth and ignored her pointed stare. When she leaned down and opened a box, he jumped from his chair, sliding the plate onto the cushion. He should have thrown that box away earlier. "No! Wait."

She pulled out a magazine. Her hand flew to her mouth. "David!"

He reached over her head and ripped it from her hands. She bent down and pulled another one out of the box. "Darlene! Come on, that's—"

"Porno? Seriously?" She dodged his hand and opened it. The centerfold page unfolded.

Heat flooded his face as his sister stared at the nude photograph of the blonde model. He dumped the one he held back into the box.

She danced away from him, keeping the magazine out of his reach, and flipped through the pages.

She laughed. "Don't tell me you are reading them for the articles."

He held back his growl. "There are good articles in them. Give me that!"

"No." She hopped over a box and waved the magazine at him. "You know they're airbrushed, right? No woman is that toned or that tanned." She gazed intently at the centerfold again. "Definitely not real."

He snatched it from her hand and threw the crumpled magazine back in the box. "And the point being? I know they ain't real."

She shook her head. "You can't really be into that, can you?"

"I bought them last year. Haven't bought any since." He closed the box and shoved it toward the door. His face still flamed. "I'm not addicted to it."

"I would hope not. I mean, those models are like what? Eighteen or nineteen at most? What would you think if Sophie was in it?"

He grimaced. His niece in a porno magazine? What did she think? That he was some sort of pervert? "Not cool." He ignored her gaze. "I was planning on taking that box to the dumpster."

She bounded across the floor. "Great! I'll do it. And if you even try to remove the box from the trash, I'll set the dumpster on fire!"

"You're such a fire bug." He shook his head as his sister picked up the box and left the apartment. Leave it to his nosy and bossy big sister to take matters into her own hands.

He took his empty plate into the kitchen. Placed the casserole in the refrigerator and started to reach for another beer. His hand paused. Darlene would question him drinking another bottle. Better not chance drinking brew number four.

She slipped back inside. "So? You got a broom?"

He shut the refrigerator door. "You can't be serious about cleaning my apartment, can you?" He opened his small pantry and pulled out a skinny, cheap broom.

"Yup. But, you aren't to do anything. Sit back. Watch your movie and let me clean." She took the broom from him and started sweeping his kitchenette.

"I can't do that while you're here. Let me help."

"You worked five, twenty-four-hour shifts with no day off until now. And even if you did manage to get some sleep at the station, those bunks can't be that comfortable." She shoved him away and towards his chair. "Sit. I'll clean this up once. Unpack a few things for you. Oh, and I got Marty bringing you a small table and shelf. It used to be in my study, but I bought new ones a few months ago. Might as well make use of it. They were only collecting dust in my garage."

David sank into his chair. Still feeling like a bum, he watched as she quickly worked the floor. "You don't have to do this. And it feels weird watching a movie and watching you clean."

"Then don't watch. Tell me about your days. How's the new job going for you?"

He sighed and lowered the chair back. With a flick of his thumb across his game controller, he turned off the Xbox console. "Not bad. A little bit of a change from St. Louis, but a welcome change. Oh, did I tell you the other day about the new grant application?"

"No." She moved into his living area and started unpacking a box of dishes. "You think y'all going to get it?"

"Hope so. We could use new sets of turnouts and new medical equipment." He crossed his ankles. With a full belly, drowsiness descended upon him. His words slurred. His eyes became heavy. Maybe it was a full belly and the three beers. Bumps and thuds echoed from Darlene's direction. "Anyway, I got Thomas looking over what I wrote."

"You know how to write grant applications?"

"Took the course two years ago. Chief at the St. Louis station requested it." He yawned. Darlene had to be bored with him talking about work. "I don't need to bore you."

"Oh, it's not a bore. But you can tell me about Maggie."

He opened an eye and glared at her. She cast him an overly bright smile as she lined up his CDs, stacking them on the floor.

His small stereo sat against the wall on top of a small box, the subwoofers and speakers stretched out around it. Must have been the bump he heard.

"There's nothing to tell. Tried to have dinner but got called out. Nothing to tell."

An REO Speedwagon CD started playing. "Would you tell me if there was?"

He smiled and let the music surround him. Maybe some day there would be something to tell. "Probably not. Probably not, big sister."

"Yeah, I kinda figured that." Another thump and metal scraping sounded from her corner. That had to be his small shelving unit. "Besides, I can get more info from Maggie herself. Learn nice little tidbits about you."

"Yeah, right. Can't goad me today, Darl-ling." She snorted at the nickname. He resisted the urge to snort back.

Darlene would be out of luck. Maggie would never kiss-and-tell, and neither would he. Man, what a kiss that was.

The song switched over to a softer ballad. His head grew heavy. Darlene's voice buzzed on and on. Something about Jeremy and the river, but it was all mush. The music drifted with him until he floated away. Somewhere in that hazy fog, his name echoed.

———————

Jeremy waited for Darlene to answer the phone. He pulled his truck up to the station and hopped out.

He slung his duffel bag over his shoulder as she picked up on the fifth ring.

"Hey! I couldn't find my phone for a second."

He rolled his eyes. Darlene and her phone. "You should get a flashing neon one. Then you wouldn't misplace it."

"Hmm. I don't think they make sparkly, neon green ones." A small crash came through the line. "Oops. Sorry about that. This shelving unit isn't quite easy to put together."

"You need more shelves? Your house is practically a book shelf in itself." He slipped into the cool interior of the station. No one occupied the locker room as he entered.

"Oh, I'm at David's. Brought him a casserole. And decided to unpack his stuff for him."

Jeremy shook his head as he pulled his tactical vest out of his locker. "Hold on while I put you on speaker. I gotta get dressed for work." He set the phone on the nearby table.

"I thought you had the night off." Her voice echoed in the small room.

"No. That's next weekend. But never fear, I do have tomorrow off." He smiled at her sigh of relief. "So, why are you unpacking dear little brother's things? And where is our troublemaker?"

"He's asleep in his chair. I was talking to him and the next minute—boom! Out like the proverbial light." Another bump. "I found something interesting while unpacking."

Jeremy snapped his uniform shirt. "Let me guess. The porn."

"You knew!"

He laughed as he buckled his belt, shifting his paraphernalia in place. Stupid baton kept smacking him where it had no business smacking him. "Yeah. Saw it last Saturday. What did he do when you found it?"

"Oh, jumped around like a monkey. Said, 'I bought them last year,' 'the articles are good,' and 'I was planning on throwing them away.'"

Jeremy chuckled at Darlene's fine rendition of David's voice and scooped up the phone. He perched on the bench near the lockers. "Did he throw them away?"

"Oh, no. I did. Anyway, why would any man look at those? I mean, the models have fake assets, for crying out loud!"

Jeremy choked. The things that came out of his sister's mouth. "Most single men look at them. I did when I was younger."

"Too much info!"

"Hey, that was a long time ago. Before airbrushing. Before marriage. Before common sense. Before God."

"Still. What would you say if you found Dennis with the magazine or worse yet, Sophie with one?"

Jeremy pinched the bridge of his nose. "I don't even want to harbor that idea."

"Or worse, like I told dear little brother, what if he bought one and there was Sophie on the centerfold?"

Jeremy fumbled with the phone, catching it before it hit the floor. No way would his little girl ever be that stupid. "Not cool, Darlene."

"Yup, that's what he said. Anyway, I threw them out. He didn't seem to mind."

"He was probably just too lazy to make the effort to do it himself. Who knows what he was up to while in the big city."

"Drinking and partying? Chasing women? Who knows." She grunted a couple of times. "Whew! I don't know what he has in this foot locker, but it's heavy. Been trying to push it to his bed."

"You are actually cleaning his place?" He scowled. His confounded brother got all the special treatment.

"Only this once. He's worked five days straight, Jer. It'll make him feel better. Although I thought he would keep me company instead of falling asleep like he did. Made it. Footlocker is now at the foot of the bed."

Jeremy rose from the bench, nodded a greeting to Baers, and slipped outside. He needed a cigarette before the shift started. "He must have been tired."

"Either that or the three beers. I found the empty bottles as I was cleaning."

"Hey, can't fault a man for wanting a beer. I drink them too. Especially after a hard day." His Zippo scratched and sent a small flame upwards. The tip of his Marlboro glowed as he inhaled.

"Yuck. Don't know how y'all stand the stuff. Anyway, I'm almost through. Gonna make his bed. Are you and Sarah still bringing the floats? I know the water will still be cold, but it's gonna be a hot day tomorrow. I think they forecasted the lower nineties or somewhere along that line. I think the weather forgot what month this was."

He inhaled another drag. "Yeah. Still bringing them. I'll see you tomorrow. And stop pampering David so much."

"Jealous." She giggled. "I'll talk to you tomorrow. Love ya, big brother."

"Love you, Darl-ling." He closed his phone and leaned against the brick wall. So Darlene found the pornography magazines. Hope it embarrassed the fool out of David. Served him right.

He flicked the butt to the ground and stepped inside. Another long night waited for him. He didn't have the luxury of thinking about his bullheaded brother. Let alone think about his secrets.

Baers handed him a stack of paperwork. "You look deep in thought."

Jeremy shook his head. "Nah. Not really. Just wondering what it would take to get my sister to clean up my house too."

Baers arched his brow.

Jeremy ignored him and handed him the last sheet. "Here. Give this one to Markston. Let him take that route tonight. I'll take the inner streets." Like he said, he had no time to think about his brother. Not tonight.

CHAPTER 10

"Miss Maggie, are you sure I can't take my seahorse? Grandmamma bought it last year. I think the duck tape is still on it. I—"

"No. There will be floats there. Come on, hop up into the truck." Maggie ushered Poppy's still chatting form into the cab. She shook her head at the child as she closed the passenger door and rounded the front. Poppy's voice greeted her as she opened the driver's door. She smiled. The kid never hushed.

"—and I told Sophie yesterday that I was happy to be able to go. It'll be so much fun. Will Mr. David be there, Miss Maggie? He's so nice. Sophie said he was, and Sophie is always right, you know. She knows a lot."

Maggie put the truck in reverse and backed out of the parsonage's driveway. Within moments, interspersed with a few of Poppy's praises for Sophie, she arrived at the riverside picnic site. Cars and trucks littered the edges of the road. She peered through her lashes as she got out of the truck and pulled her covered dish from the seat. No sign of the red motorcycle. Not yet. She held back her sigh.

"Miss Maggie, can I go on down to the pier? I see Sophie there."

Maggie ruffled Poppy's hair. "Go ahead, sweetie. And stay out of the water. You can't swim, and I don't feel like getting wet today." But she was talking to thin air as Poppy's skinny body hurled itself in reckless abandon down to the water's edge. Maggie shook her head and kicked the door closed. Three days of constant badgering about the picnic from the excited child. Amazing that Poppy restrained herself this long.

Maggie navigated the worn dirt path that led to the wooden pier. At the base of the path, the women of the church had tables erected and covered with food and drinks.

Maggie slid through a throng of teenagers.

"Hey, Miss Maggie!"

"Is that your cinnamon bites?"

"Love your sandals!"

"Miss Maggie, glad you made it."

The chorus of their voices worked a smile out of her.

Two of the boys followed her as she set her largest casserole dish on the table by the pies and cakes.

"Hey, not now." She slapped their hands as they snagged the small cinnamon and sugar coated biscuit bites.

They laughed and took off, each with a handful of the treats. She rolled her eyes. Doubtful there would be any left by the time they sat down to eat.

"Maggie, I was afraid you wouldn't make it." Sarah rounded the corner of the table and wrapped her into a hug.

Maggie returned the embrace. "I had a tough time convincing Poppy that she didn't need her seahorse float. She seems to think the duct tape would keep it afloat."

"Poor child. Where is she now?"

Maggie pointed to the pier where Poppy stood next to the raven-haired Sophie and her friend Amy Myers. "She has determined that Sophie is her new best friend."

Sarah laughed and squeezed the dishes closer together as another woman set her items on the table. "Sophie adores her. She told me last night that she is going to make sure Poppy is happy. She even went through her closet to choose some shirts for her."

Maggie closed her eyes to hold back the tears that threatened to pour forth. She pressed her fingertips against her trembling lips. Never had she thought another person could care for Poppy like she herself could.

"Oh, Maggie, sweetheart, what's wrong?" Sarah pulled at her arm, leading her away from the table and over to an empty area near the water's edge.

The tall blades of grass swayed in the gentle wind. Children squealed and laughed. Poppy and Sophie threatened the older boys who splashed water at them. People milled around the pier or the tables laden with food, or they lounged on the chairs and chaises dotting the small bank. These were her church family. Poppy's church family.

Sarah rubbed her hand up and down Maggie's upper arm. "What's wrong?"

"Nothing." Maggie brushed at her eyes, swiping the tears away. "It just hit me suddenly that I don't have to do this alone. For the last year or so, I kept believing that I was alone in taking care of Poppy. Until now." She motioned at the people. "Poppy has a family. And look at her. She's so happy with Sophie. But it won't last. Josephine comes home, and then Poppy will be back in that miserable house."

"Oh, sweetie." Her cousin pulled her into a tight embrace. "Even though she'll be back there, we'll always be here for Poppy and for you." Sarah held her at arm's length and peered at her. "Jeremy told me the other day that he'll make sure he drives by Poppy's home on his route to make sure she's okay."

Maggie sank down to the ground and wrapped her arms around her knees. "But why? Strike that. I know why, but I don't understand the reasoning. Poppy isn't yours or anyone's responsibility."

Sarah's shoulder brushed against her as she sat beside her, her flip-flops sliding slightly in the mud. "You love Poppy. And through that, we have come to love her. Look at them. Even the boys care about her."

Maggie watched as Dennis held Poppy's hand as she negotiated the slippery bank to the water's edge. Marty Jr. stood ankle deep in the water, his hand held out as Poppy was transferred to him. With an easy lunge, she hopped up onto Marty's back as he gave her a piggy back ride into waist-deep water. Her high-pitched laughter echoed over to Maggie.

Maggie sniffled. "I never thought I would be so blessed to know such a sweet child. And she talks incessantly about David."

Sarah laughed. "He has that charm over ladies, that's for sure."

Maggie plucked at a grass blade. Embarrassment stole over her. "Can I ask you something?"

"Hmm. Let me guess. About that darling, troublemaker brother-in-law of mine?"

Maggie giggled and immediately clamped her hand over her mouth. Good gracious, she sounded like a schoolgirl. "Yeah. I talked to him the night when I picked up Poppy."

"And?" Sarah leaned back on her hands and watched the children's horseplay.

"And. . .we talked. And. . ." She plucked another blade of grass and twisted it around her finger. "And we kissed."

Sarah gasped and turned so fast that her ponytail slapped her across the chin. "No! You waited until now to tell me?" She sat up, practically bouncing. "Do tell. How was it? What happened?"

Heat spread across Maggie's face. Oh, boy. She should have kept her mouth shut, but she had to tell someone. A shadow fell across her. She looked up as Darlene plopped down beside her.

"Hey. What's up? What's the gossip?"

Sarah leaned forward, motioning Darlene closer. "Maggie was just about to tell me about her kiss with David."

Darlene covered her mouth with her hands. Her muffled voice held a hint of glee. "No!" She dropped her hands and gripped Maggie's. "Do tell, do tell. I knew something was up when I was at his apartment yesterday."

Maggie squinted at Darlene. "What do you mean?"

Darlene waved a hand. "Oh, I asked about you, and he had this little smile. But he wouldn't tell me. So . . ."

Another blush worked its way across her cheeks. The heat flowed down her neck, or maybe that was the sun. "Well, we were talking about Poppy. Sitting on my tailgate."

"Oh, I like the tailgate talks."

"Hush, Sarah. Let her speak."

Maggie smiled at Darlene. Another blade of grass fell victim to her fingers. "It wasn't planned or anything, but he leaned in and kissed me. But . . ."

"But?" Sarah frowned. "That doesn't sound good."

"Well, that's what I wanted to speak to you about. And you, Darlene. He . . ." She bit at her lip. How should she word this?

"Did he try to coerce you? Or get you to do something you didn't want to?" Darlene's eyes narrowed.

"No." Maggie patted at Darlene's hand. "No. Nothing like that. I mean, it got a little carried away. Oh, boy, what a kiss." Heat flamed through her again. "But I broke away. It scared me. You know how my last relationship ended. I was afraid I was about to go down that road again."

Darlene put her arm around Maggie's shoulders. "Smart girl. As much as I love my brother, I know how he is."

Maggie shrugged. "What if he isn't ready for a serious relationship? I mean, I heard the rumors about him and his conquests. Is that true?"

Sarah laughed. "No. Not at all. Of course, his attitude back then didn't help dispel any of those rumors."

"I agree." Darlene shielded her eyes with a hand. "He racked up quite a reputation in school and out. Everyone believed he was this bad boy when, in fact, he was quite shy. He had a few girlfriends, but nothing serious until Rebecca."

"So, he wasn't this 'wham, bam, thank you, ma'am' kind of guy?"

Sarah shook her head. "Jeremy was the bad boy. I know, kind of hard to believe, isn't it? The tales I could tell you about him. But David was more daring and reckless. Ever since high school, he has lived life on the edge."

Darlene nodded. "I think that is where the rumors started. David liked the fast crowd. But now. . ." She glanced over at the tables.

Maggie followed her gaze. Coming down the small dirt path was the object of their discussion. His sandaled feet displayed confidence with every step. His shirt, tight across his strong shoulders, flapped in the breeze. Maggie smiled. His legs, long and muscular but definitely white, showed beneath his shorts.

"He's different," Darlene finished.

Sarah murmured her agreement. "He's quieter. And sad."

"I know." Maggie sighed. "I see that in him. And I think that is what draws me to him. He's so sad, but yet I see so much life inside him."

Darlene's hand fell on her arm. "Give it time, Maggie. We can tell you're in love with him. He'll come around if it's meant to be." She motioned for them to lean in closer. "And I don't think God would mind if we start pushing him your way."

Sarah laughed again. "Definitely not. How cool that would be . . . not only my cousin but also my sister-in-law."

Darlene hugged Maggie. "And I wouldn't mind having you as a sister."

Maggie pushed at them and glanced back at David, who was making a bee-line for the tables. "I think it's too soon to talk about that."

"Never." Sarah checked on the children at the water and then yelled. "Dennis! I said not to do that."

Maggie ducked the mud that flew up from Sarah's flip-flops as she dashed to the children. Darlene chuckled and helped Maggie to her feet. "Let's go save the kids from Sarah. I told her it was unreasonable to expect the kids to stay out of the deep water."

====================

David watched Darlene and Sarah surround Maggie. Up to no good, they were. Maggie's hair, pulled into a low braid, glistened under the sun. Bet the freckles were even darker today. Would she smell like cotton candy? Or something different?

He raised a brow, dodged a protruding root, and headed for the tables. The trio's eyes burned into him, but he ignored them.

Sarah's yell cut across the air as he rounded the edge of the table. He smiled as his sister-in-law took off after Dennis and Sophie. Now what was the problem?

He shielded his eyes from the sun and watched as Dennis and Sophie pulled Poppy back out of the water. He scoffed. The kids didn't go in too deep. Darlene and Maggie reached her side. Looked as though Maggie was scolding Poppy. He smiled at the déjà vu feeling. A long time ago he stood where Poppy stood. He turned away from the scene.

An elderly woman stepped up to the table. His heart lifted at the sight of his old Sunday school teacher. The aroma of fried chicken floated on the air. He stepped up to Ms. Edie as she set her dish down on the table.

She gasped when he wrapped his arms around her waist. "Oh!"

"Ah, Ms. Edie." David dropped his cheek down to hers and held her little frame to his. "You get prettier every day. When are you going to marry me?"

"Oh." She giggled and swatted at his hands and then turned in his arms. When he let go, she patted his cheek. "You only say that because you want my chicken."

David grinned and pressed her hands between his. "Ms. Edie, you wound me. You don't look a day over sixty, and I have always had a thing for older women."

"Oh, posh." A soft blush crept across her face. "You say that every time I make your favorite fried chicken. And I'm eighty-one." She patted his cheek again and handed him a chicken leg. "Here. Don't tell anyone."

David kissed her cheek. "I knew there was a reason you're my favorite lady."

"Oh, posh. Go on now." She swatted at him again and nudged him away from the table. "Go on, now."

He bit into the juicy and spicy chicken. Ms. Edie could put Colonel Sanders out of a job. He glanced over at the water. Satan Sarah had finally freed the children from her wrath, but she stood nearby, guarding them. The woman needed to lighten up. He took the last bite and dropped the bone in the large trash can near the trail.

A few of the men walked by and greeted him. David nodded back. He spotted Jeremy at the far edge, talking with Marty Sr. and Bro. Johnny. A bobbing redhead at the corner of his vision caught his attention. Poppy chatted beside Maggie. No. She was begging, pleading. Her bony little arm kept pointing at the water where the older kids horse played and splashed. Maggie shook her head. Her own arm motioned at the floats near the edge. Poppy stomped her foot and then walked away, sulking.

David grinned. So, Maggie wouldn't allow her in the water. He'd fix that.

He scanned the water. There were his two lackeys. How to get their attention?

"What are you up to?"

He jumped at Jeremy's voice. Sheesh, the man moved too quietly. "Nothing." He looked down and spotted a tell-tale bulge in Jeremy's back pocket. "Hand me your Zippo, will ya?"

"Oh, now you smoke?" Jeremy passed him the silver lighter.

"No. That's your crutch." David traced the police emblem on the front. "Nice. Present?"

"Yeah. For Christmas. What do you need it for?"

"For this." He angled the Zippo, allowing the sun to glint across it. The beam danced across Dennis' face. When the boy looked up, David motioned for him and Marty Jr. to come to him.

"What are you up to that you need the boys?" Jeremy accepted his lighter back.

"You'll see." David started climbing the overgrown trail behind him that led to a group of trees whose branches reached over the river. A few brier bushes grabbed at his shorts. He skirted around another clump and looked over his shoulder.

Jeremy's oath hung in the air as he ran into the briers. His brother must have forgotten about them. David circled the tree, peering up into its branches.

"You think it's still there?"

David shrugged. "Has to be. That was a good rope I snitched from Mr. Daniels' barn. Man, I remember he was mad when he found out."

"I remember that Dad made us work to pay for it." Jeremy pointed at a branch. "There it is." The thick, yellow rope hung in loops around the huge branch.

A rustle from below produced a red-faced Marty Jr. and Dennis.

Marty squinted. "What's up, Uncle David, Uncle Jeremy?"

Jeremy shook his head, still staring into the tree. "I don't think it'll hold your weight. It's been years since it was used."

"We'll see. You game?" He narrowed his eyes at his brother. See if he was too cowardly to try.

Jeremy narrowed his own eyes, mouth set in a thin line. "Fine. But you first."

David snorted. "Figures. Dennis, Marty, see that rope up there? Think one of you could shimmy up there and throw it down?"

They looked at each other, grinning, before Marty stepped forward. "I can."

David gave him a leg up. The teen gripped a branch and, like a monkey, leapt from branch to branch until he reached the one with the rope.

Jeremy stood under it. "Yeah. Just unwrap it right there. Hold up. You got it tangled on the small limb there." He turned to Dennis. "Is anyone looking?"

Dennis peered past the tall weeds and bushes. "No, sir. Coast is clear. This is so cool."

David smacked his head. "You are sworn to secrecy. Only your granddad knows where this rope came from."

Jeremy snorted. "And Mr. Daniels."

"Don't think he'll be telling anyone unless you got a direct line to God." David caught the rope as it dropped to the ground. "Hold up, Marty. Can you reach the tie-off?"

Marty scooted farther down the branch. "Yeah. Whatcha need?"

"See any marks or cuts?"

"No, sir. Looks fine to me."

Jeremy looked over at David. "Think we can trust him?"

David smiled and looped the rope into a foothold. "We'll see. Come on down, Marty!" He finished tying the rope as Marty dropped down from the overhead branch.

"Dad, Mom looks like she's looking for you." Dennis let the bush fall back into place.

"Go distract her. And don't mention this to anyone." Jeremy glanced at David. "Who's the victim?"

"Victim?" Marty paused. Dennis looked back.

David stripped off his shirt and threw it at Dennis. "Hold on to this for me. And you see that piece of driftwood next to Darlene and Maggie?"

Marty smiled. "That long piece by Mom?"

"Yeah. See if you can get Poppy over there. I need a clear shot. Way too many briers up here now."

Jeremy grinned. "Oh, you are asking for trouble. Maggie had explicit instructions that Poppy not go into the deep water, only along the edge. She can't swim, David."

"No worry. I won't let go of her." He winked at his brother as he stepped into the loop and lined up his path. "Sure you don't want to go first?"

"No way."

"Pansy." Jeremy's reply was lost as David jumped off the small ledge, yelling in his best imitation of Tarzan.

———————

Maggie turned from Darlene as Poppy passed her in a rush. She narrowed her eyes. Those boys were up to something.

Dennis and Marty Jr. had Poppy to stand by the bank. They glanced up at the trees and stepped back.

Poppy screwed up her face, but she didn't move from her spot.

"What are they doing?" She tapped Darlene on the shoulder. "Is that David's shirt that Dennis has?"

Darlene looked over at the boys and then at Poppy. "Oh, great. Sarah!" She took a step towards Poppy.

Maggie grabbed her arm. "What? What's going on?"

A Tarzan yell penetrated the air. Everyone paused in their activities, except for the older ladies, as a bare-chested man swooped upon the gathering. Air swooshed as David flew past, scooping up Poppy with an outstretched arm.

Maggie gasped. She pressed her hands to her mouth.

Poppy's scream echoed against the water as they soared overhead. Red pigtails flew out as the rope reached its zenith. David, with Poppy clinging to him, gracefully arced over the water, feet pointing down. His arm wrapped around the child, and they plummeted into the dark river.

Maggie's breath slammed back into her chest as the rope came to rest against the bushes at the water's edge. Dennis and Marty Jr. grabbed it and took off. Maggie rushed into the water. Its coldness enveloped her as she waded in waist deep.

Stupid man! Where were they?

In front of her, two forms popped up. David yelped and shook the water from his eyes. Poppy cried and laughed. She clung to him, her eyes wide. She spotted Maggie.

"Miss Maggie! Did you see me? That was so much fun. I want to do it again."

Maggie waded further out. Water lapped at her chest. She clutched at her heart. "David James! You scared me to death doing that. And look at me. I got my clothes all wet now."

David grinned and treaded towards her, Poppy clinging to his back. "Loosen up, Margaret Allison."

She scowled. "Oh." Infuriating man. "Poppy, you okay?"

"Oh, yes. It was so much fun."

David stopped in front of her. He tweaked her nose with his fingers as Poppy wrapped her legs around his chest. "She's fine. I wouldn't let anything happen to her." His arm grabbed at Poppy as she slid around until she dangled from his neck.

"I can't believe you did that." Maggie reached up. Her fingers brushed at a trickle of water by his brow. "When did you tie the rope there?"

"Long time ago. Jeremy and I use to come rope swinging." His green eyes glinted as he looked over her head. "Uh oh, hold on. Here comes Jer now."

Maggie turned as another yell echoed. Jeremy swooped down. He kicked out his feet. The rope snapped as it arced and fell into the water. Jeremy splashed down without the grace David had.

Within seconds, his head popped up, yelping. "Whoa! It's freezing."

David laughed. He cupped his hands around his mouth. "Pansy!"

Jeremy responded with a rude gesture.

"Jeremy Dean!" Sarah's voice shot out, and Maggie laughed at the furious scowl on her cousin's face. "You're in front of the church, you idiot."

Jeremy cast her an innocent look.

Dennis collected the rope from the bank. "You broke it, Dad."

Jeremy smiled at his son and swam towards Maggie and David. "Well, I think we can safely say that Marty Jr. was wrong."

"Apparently."

Sarah's voice yelled out to him. Jeremy sported a lop-sided grin. "Well, I'm being summoned. How much would it be worth to push her in?"

David smiled. "Priceless, but I dare you to do so."

Jeremy shook his head. "I value my life too much." Poppy's squeal filled Maggie's heart as he splashed Poppy once before he swam to the bank.

Such a joyful sound. She gasped as David's hand latched onto her arm. Cold water engulfed her. She pushed against the muddy bottom and surfaced, only to find David treading towards the pier with Poppy on his back. Oh, she'd get him for that.

She struck out, gaining on his leisure pace. He laughed at her as she neared.

"Don't do it. I've got Poppy."

"Do it, Miss Maggie! Do it!"

David feigned an injured look. "Oh, little flower, you're supposed to be my friend."

Poppy giggled and splashed a handful of river water into his face. He sputtered. Maggie cast her own handful. "Hurry, Poppy. To me."

Poppy jumped from his hold and into her arms. She sank a little from the weight, but quickly swam to the pier. David followed in her wake. When she grabbed the wooden planks of the pier, Poppy scampered up. Maggie started to follow, but her laughter weakened her. She managed to get a leg up on the deck.

Poppy bounced on her feet. "Oh, hurry, Miss Maggie! He's here."

She let out a yelp as David's hands gripped her around the waist and threw her backwards into the water. Again dark, murky water surrounded her. She reached out. Fabric met her fingers, and she grabbed the hem of his shorts, tugging him under. Air bubbles escaped as she laughed underwater.

Poppy squealed as she surfaced. "He's behind you!"

Maggie ducked back under and felt for the pier's beams. She pulled herself along until she was under the wooden deck. When she broke the water's surface, David was turning circles, looking for her.

"Where'd she go, Poppy?"

"I ain't telling, Mr. David."

"Ah, now, little flower. Didn't I just give you an adventure?" He treaded the water and turned. His eyes locked onto hers. "Ah ha!"

Maggie squealed and swam away from the pier, heading further out into the river. The current pulled at her, tugging her slightly downstream. David grinned and broke through the water. She gasped. Goodness, he was fast. With as big of a leap as she could muster, she struck for the bank, trying to outdistance him.

His hand latched onto her shirt and pulled her underwater. She twirled and tried to kick up to the surface, but his arms wrapped around her, bringing her to him. They surfaced in a big splash.

He grinned at her. "Can't get away from me, Maggie Goddard."

Maggie gazed into his eyes, his arms holding her in the frigid water. Her chin trembled with the cold, but heat emanated between their bodies. His eyes softened. Oh, boy. He was way too charming for her health. "What if I don't want to, David Boyette?"

He pushed a wet lock of hair away from her brow. "Really mean that?"

Poppy's voice interrupted them. "Can I jump back in?"

"No!" Their voices shouted in unison.

They laughed and swam towards the little girl dangling her feet in the water. A small bit of disappointment flooded Maggie. Poppy had lousy timing, for sure.

When they reached the pier, David gave her a boost onto the deck and then hoisted himself up beside her. Poppy slid between them, her body shivering.

"By any chance, did you bring any towels?" Goosebumps pimpled the skin along his chest and arms.

"Yeah. In my truck. Good thing I had the foresight to bring clothes too." She nudged Poppy. "Let's go grab them, shall we?"

David lumbered to his feet and helped them stand. Maggie smiled at him as they walked down the pier. Her gaze fell to his stomach. She raised her brow at the tattoo.

"Sarah told me you had a tat. How long have you had that?"

He touched his stomach. His shoulders rose in a shrug. "Not long. A drunken dare."

Maggie tore her eyes away from the muscled abs. "It's nice. The tattoo, I mean." Dennis saved her from further embarrassment as he ran past.

"Here's your shirt, Uncle David. Can't stay long. Fellas found a box turtle down the path."

He took off but came back and grabbed Poppy's hand. "Come on, Poppy. You got to see this."

Maggie nodded at her. "Go on. I'll bring you the towel."
Poppy took off with Dennis, her little feet flying across the
muddy bank.

"You're great with her, you know."

She shrugged as they crossed the road to her truck. "I guess
so." The truck door creaked as she pulled it open. Two small
beach towels lay on the seat. She handed David the pink one.

He opened it. "Princess?"

Maggie smiled. "It's either that or Dora the Explorer."

His face screwed up. "Not much of a choice, but beggars
can't be choosey." He wrapped the towel over his shoulders,
scrubbing at his head.

She dried her own hair and turned towards the stack of
clothes. Her long blue tunic shirt was draped over the back of
the seat. She grabbed it. "Think you can stay put while I go to
the other side to change my shirt?"

David grinned. "That's asking a lot of me. Tell you what.
Make you a deal."

Maggie cocked her head at him. "Yeah? And what would
that be?"

Her breath stilled as he bent closer. His hand propped against
the door frame, reminding her of the other night. His other
hand traced the outline of her jaw. His finger gently touched her
bottom lip. Oh, boy.

"I promise not to peek–mind you, I'll be tempted–if, Maggie,
you will go out with me Monday night."

She dared to look up into his eyes. The green had become
a living pool of light. Her own face reflected back at her from
those depths. His head dipped closer. Maggie pressed her back
against the truck. She wanted this, didn't she? He kissed so well

the other night. She would like another. Oh, wow. She was a female version of Oliver Twist. Please, may I have some more?

His lips barely touched Maggie's when Sarah's voice called out. David growled and pushed away.

Maggie heaved a sigh. Of relief or regret?

"Maggie, Poppy is looking for you. David, the men need your help with the tables. We're trying to fit them closer together." Sarah crossed the road to them.

David looked longingly at Maggie and then nodded. "I'll talk to you later."

She snagged his wrist. Heat from his body warred with the cool water that coated his arm and ran under her palm. He looked down at her fingers before lifting his eyes to hers. She smiled and rose up on tiptoes to kiss his cheek. "Six o'clock?"

His eyes sparkled. Oh, my, how bright they were. Gleaming emeralds. "Six."

She watched as he crossed the road, a bounce to his steps. Ignoring Sarah's questioning gaze, Maggie pulled an over shirt out of the cab for Poppy and shut the door. Oh, boy. She had a date Monday night.

———

Jeremy sucked a breath through clenched teeth as he shifted in his seat, waiting for Dennis to bring him some water. His damp shorts rubbed a raw spot against his inner thighs. He plucked at the hem of his shorts and shifted again in the lawn chair.

Cold water dribbled down his back. He glared at Dennis, who grinned down at him. "Give me that, goofball." He took the water bottle from the teen's hand. "You and Marty Jr. heading to the movies?"

"Yes, sir." Dennis plunked down on the grass beside him. "We're supposed to meet Angela and Mike there, but Mike backed out at the last moment."

"So, it's gonna be just Angela?"

Dennis squinted. "Well, no. She invited two of her friends with her. Marcy and Sasha."

Jeremy raised his brow. "I thought Sasha was in reform."

"She was. But she's been going to counseling." He placed a hand on Jeremy's forearm. "We are only doing movies, Dad. And who knows, maybe I or Marty can make a difference in the girl's life."

Jeremy sipped at his bottle and gazed across the river. Few people were left. Most of the food was gone. He sighed. It was a great day, despite his embarrassing plunge from the rope. His gaze settled on the pier and the couple who sat with a little red-head between them.

Dennis's gaze bored into him. He didn't want to think about his son out with girls. Man, he wasn't ready for this. It made him feel old.

"Dad?"

He took a deep breath. "Okay. No later than eleven. And I expect an update by nine."

Dennis jumped up. "Taking the truck or Mom's car?"

Jeremy smiled. "The car. Especially since she has the back seat full of boxes for Goodwill."

Dennis grimaced. "I ain't planning on doing anything, Dad."

Jeremy handed him his set of car keys. "That's the reason I'm letting you have the car. No room in case you decide to be stupid."

His son rolled his eyes and, with a huff, stood and motioned to Marty Jr. "See ya, Dad. And thanks."

"Nine!"

"Nine. In at eleven. Gotcha."

Jeremy watched his son hightail it to the car with Marty Jr., who shouted reassurances over his shoulder to Marty Sr.

"Growing up too soon. Before long, it'll be Sophie." Sarah dropped into his lap. Her weight pressed his semi-wet shorts deeper into him. "I don't think I'm ready for that."

Jeremy nuzzled her neck. Sunshine and cinnamon flooded his senses. "I ain't ready for Dennis to be out there. Lord knows what he's up to when we allow him out."

Sarah chuckled. "Same as you when you were that age?"

He bit back a groan and leaned his head back. "Oh, I hope not. Amazing that my dad never found out half of what I done."

"Well, it just made you a better officer." She leaned against him, pulling his arms tighter around her. "Did you notice that David hasn't left Maggie's side all afternoon?"

"Yeah." His brother rose to his feet. Poppy followed him to the table, where they collected a plate full of sweets. Jeremy snickered. Maggie would have her hands full with a hyper child tonight.

"She's in love with him."

"I feel sorry for her."

"Jeremy!" She smacked his hand. "Don't be so callous. David deserves to be happy, and Maggie would be good for him."

He frowned at his wife. Why did everyone in the family pamper and defend the man? "I don't think he's ready. In case you haven't noticed, the man is hiding something."

"He's hiding pain." Sarah wiggled around until she faced him. "He needs family and church."

"He needs a butt-kicking."

She rolled her eyes and hopped up. "You are so obstinate sometimes."

A cold wind picked up and whipped her ponytail around her face. Jeremy stood and wrapped his arms around her, pressing his forehead to hers. Tonight was not a night to deal with Sarah's ire. "Sorry, sweetie. The man just gets my back up. But I promise that I'll be there for him."

"Promise? Darlene and I know that something is wrong, well, according to your mom, anyway."

"You've been talking to Mom about David?"

"And you." Another blast of wind hit them. She looked up, holding her ponytail still. "That's coming in fast."

Jeremy peered up at the sky. Dark clouds, with a tint of green, rolled across the horizon. That wasn't good. He pushed at Sarah. "Go and start packing the stuff up."

She took off to the tables. He spotted Maggie herding Poppy to the tables. David stood on the edge of the pier, watching the clouds. Jeremy jogged to his brother.

The boards creaked under his weight. Water lapped against the banks, rising with each surge. The cold wind buffeted his body. He stood beside David.

"Bad?"

David grunted, staring into the sky. "Got your phone? Left mine in the truck."

Jeremy pulled out his cell and handed it to him. While David dialed, Jeremy walked over to Sarah. "Call Dennis and tell him to cancel the movies. By the looks of this, it isn't gonna be a quiet night."

Sarah nodded. "Okay." She turned to Sophie. "Go put those in the truck. Poppy, take the cloths and help Sophie."

The girls hurried off, following Maggie as she lugged baskets up the trail for some of the church women. Jeremy turned back to his wife.

"Can you hitch a ride with Darlene or Maggie? I'm going to head to the station. If it is as bad as it seems like it will be, they're going to call me in, anyway."

"Jeremy!" David hurried to his side and handed him the phone back. "Thomas requested everybody to the station. National Weather Service has us under a tornado warning. Tunica was hit ten minutes ago. It's heading this way."

David flew up the trail, pausing long enough to drop a small peck on Maggie's forehead as he passed her. Jeremy looked to Sarah. "You heard him. Call Mom and Dad, make sure they made it back from Memphis."

"Jeremy, be careful, sweetie."

He brushed his lips against hers. "I will. Love you." Her prayers, he was sure, were already being sent upwards as he climbed the trail back to the road.

David's ratty pick-up barreled past as he headed for his Ford truck. His phone buzzed.

"Thad?" He hopped onto the seat. "We being called in?"

"Just all of mid shift. Captain says this is going to be a bad night. How soon before you make it here?"

Jeremy cranked the truck and pulled away. "About fifteen minutes out."

"See ya then."

A heavy sigh escaped him. So much for a pleasant night. He fought his truck as a strong gust battered against it. The sky darkened. He craned his neck to look up at the sky. He should have gotten the truck with the moon roof.

Trees bowed as low as possible as the wind whipped down the highway. Veins popped along Jeremy's arm as he fought to keep the truck on the highway.

He jumped as a rock slammed against his windshield. No, it wasn't a rock. Hail. Marble-sized ice balls bounced against the hood and windshield. His heart raced as he shot a quiet prayer heavenward. He needed his family kept safe tonight.

———

David picked up the last piece of burnt metal from the road and cast it onto the truck's flatbed. Rain pelted him and his turnouts. Black sooty rivers ran down his legs and onto the pavement. He waved to the chief.

"That's the last."

Thomas nodded and motioned to the wrecker. It puffed and lumbered away, carrying the warped metal hunk, formerly known as a Dodge Charger.

Thomas turned to David. "How's the boys holding up?"

David pulled off his helmet. Rainwater was preferable to sweat. "They're hanging in there. Storm's letting up, so we'll be able to rest for a little while. That is, if no other idiots decide to joyride in this mess."

He followed Thomas past Engine One. The bumper invited him to sit down on its shiny, wet surface, but if he gave in, he wouldn't have the energy to last the night.

"It's not over yet. We have another wave heading our way. Vortex indications on radar, but no sightings."

David dragged a hand across his eyes. "It isn't tornados that worry me. The river's currents are strong, and the water's high enough to wash out some of the lower roads. Volunteer stations are working at clearing most of the debris from them, but they already had two of their trucks stall in the low dips."

Thomas opened the door to his car, shrugging out of his jacket before falling into the seat. "Jackson still chief at District Eight?"

"Yeah. And Pete James is still at District Seven. They got most of the roads covered. Toby's playing message bearer tonight."

"Good. I'm heading over to Station Three—"

Dispatch broke in. "Station One, PD requesting rescue at Bokushi River."

David took a deep breath. He needed strength to make it through this one. Thomas slammed the door to the car as David whirled around. He trotted to Engine One, yanking at his turnout jacket.

Toby called into the mike as he jerked open the door. "Engine One en route, dispatch. Advise type of rescue."

David dropped into the captain's seat and slung his turnout jacket into the jump seats, narrowly missing the rookie. He unbuckled his bunker pants and fought to slide them off. Between the sweat and the rain, his body was soaked clear through.

"Engine One, please be advised, one victim trapped in Bokushi River at Little Black Point. PD requesting water rescue."

Toby grimaced. "Copy, dispatch. Engine One ETA three minutes."

David wiggled his feet out of the boots. "Who's on call for water rescue?"

"Besides you? Sam is the only one. And he's at a barn fire on Dublin Road."

Great. He turned to the rookie. "Chuck, when we get there, I want you to grab the PFDs from the side panel. You know what they are, right?"

Eyes wide, Chuck nodded. "Personal floatation devices."

"Yeah. There's a throw bag in there, also. Grab it." He turned back around and flashed a smile at Toby. "At least I'm already soaked."

Toby chuckled and turned the engine onto the country road. "Well, well. That's a lot of cars for a trapped swimmer." He pulled the engine to the side, behind the flashing blue strobes of the police cars. "What fool would venture to Little Black Point in this weather at this time of night?"

"Suicidal fool?" The engine lumbered to a stop. David threw open the door. His feet slipped against the slick running board as his hand missed the door handle. Pain stabbed his lower back as it met the metal. He grimaced. This night needed to end soon. He was not going to last much longer.

Chuck threw him the PFD. Toby came around with a heavy-looking bag. David nodded toward it. "Is that the rescue rope and stuff?"

"Yeah. You ready?"

No.

"Sure." Toby passed him the harness.

He navigated the overgrown trail to the river's edge and struggled to slip the harness over his shoulders. Wet grass slapped and tangled at his feet. Chuck appeared beside him.

"What do I do?"

David spared a glance at the rookie. "Help out Toby. I'll need strong hands on the rope."

A small smiled tugged at his mouth as the young man hurried ahead of them to the scene. Of the rookies who arrived, Chuck was by far the best. He was actually the fastest learner. If Toby wasn't careful, Chuck would be vying for a driver-operator position.

Officers stood near the edge. He spotted Jeremy on his stomach leaning over the edge of the steep drop-off. Little Black Point, perfect for swimming in the deepest part of the river on a calm day. A death trap during a storm.

David shook his head. Job to do. Couldn't let his tired mind drift away.

Toby reached over. "Hold still. The back clasp isn't fastened."

A harsh tug had the harness biting against his chest. He pulled at the front straps. "Latch the rope on."

Toby snagged the end of the rope from Chuck, snapping the carabiner to the harness. He yanked it. "Good to go."

Chuck handed him the throw bag. He slung the strap over his shoulder, settling the red bag under his arm.

David approached the edge and peered over. "What you got?"

Jeremy looked up, taking in his gear. "You do water rescue?"

"Two years now." He fell to his hands and knees beside his brother. Below them, a small form fought against the current, hands gripping an outcropping of rock.

"It's Franklin. He slipped. Managed to call 911 before he lost his phone."

David nodded. "Toby! Going over. Got a good descent path."

"Gotcha, man."

He took a deep breath and lowered himself to his stomach. With slow movements, he pivoted until his legs hung over the edge. Inch by inch, he slid his legs off solid ground. Easy. "Toby, start lowering me down."

Franklin's voice broke through the rain that lashed against them. "I can't hold on!"

David looked over his shoulder. Terror filled the teen's eyes. "I'm coming, Franklin. I need you to hold on a little bit longer, okay."

"I can't!"

"You can, Frankie. Tell me about yourself. What grade are you in?" He dug his fingers into a muddy handhold. The edge gave way. His body slammed against the river wall.

Jeremy, eyes wide, snatched at him. "David!"

"I'm fine, I'm fine. Give me some slack!" He took another breath. His heart ricocheted in his chest. Man, he hated it when that happened. "Frankie? You still there?"

A weak reply answered. "Yes. I'm in ninth. Failed a year."

David sought a foothold. His foot slipped. Another cascade of mud plopped into the raging river. "How are you doing now, Frankie?"

"Okay enough. Mainly B's."

"Hey. That's good. I made mainly B's. A few C's too." Another foot down. He looked over his shoulder at the teen. "I'll tell you something, Frankie. You're strong, man. You keep holding on to that rock, okay. I'll be down in no time."

A sudden yell penetrated the air. Franklin had lost his grip. The river swept his body down a few feet before slamming him

against a muddy protrusion of river wall. Franklin's hands clawed
at it, his fingers digging into the mud.

"Toby! Slack!"

"David, don't do it." Jeremy's terrified face watched from
above. His hands clutched at the grass tufts along the edge.

The wind whipped against David. His clothes molded him
in a wet cocoon. Franklin held on only a few feet downstream.

David tugged at the rope. "Toby!" Franklin couldn't hold on
much longer. "I can make it. Give me slack."

Toby refused to release the rope. David spouted an oath.
Fine time to obey protocol. He'd take care of that.

Jeremy's voice issued orders. "Bring him up. Franklin's too
far away for him to reach. We'll try down there."

David ripped the red bag from his shoulder and pulled out the
rope. His numb fingers fumbled, refusing to bend when needed.
He latched the rope onto his harness. His body rose slowly to
the top. Working quickly, he threaded the rope through his fingers until he found the carabiner at the end. He latched it to the
rescue rope's loop and unlatched the rescue rope from his harness. His hands strained to hold on.

Jeremy peered over the edge and cursed. David gave his brother
one last look and pushed off the wall. Cold water grasped at him.
He rolled, letting the current drag him down. The PFD brought
him quickly to the surface, and he gasped in water and air.

He spotted the boy a few feet away. Franklin struggled to
hold on, his fingers buried deep into the wall of clay mud.

David rode the current toward the teen. He grimaced as
the water rammed him against the point. Jagged rocks bit into
him. His hands latched onto Franklin, and he wrapped one arm
around the boy's chest and under his chin.

"Relax. I got you." David fought against the pull of the current as it tried to drag him away from the wall. "Listen to my voice. I need you to grab my harness and hold on."

Good thing that the boy had enough sense to listen. The teen grabbed the harness in a death grip. David looped extra rope around the boy and fastened it to the carabiner. Franklin gasped as a yank pulled them away from the wall. David kept one hand around the teen and treaded water with the other, struggling against the current. He had to stay as close as possible to the river's edge.

The current grabbed at his body, tugging it downward. He raised his chin, gasping at the air. He wasn't going to make it. The water was too fast.

The muddy wall greeted them again. He flattened against it, pinning Franklin between him and it. "Now, we have to help these guys a little. Start climbing. Dig your fingers into the mud."

David had to give it the boy. Fatigue leeched into his own body. No telling how weary the teen was, but he obeyed. Foot by foot, the guys up top pulled them up. David dug his feet and hands into the wall.

Mud coated their bodies. Run-off from the ledge coursed over David's face and into his eyes.

Suddenly, grass tickled his palm. Weeds cut into his skin.

Hands grabbed at the pair, pulling them away from the edge. David fell back onto the ground. Rain bombarded his face.

He coughed, and his chest rattled. Great. He rolled over and staggered to his feet.

Paramedics led Franklin to the ambulance. Officers circled around him, including Jeremy. David fumbled with the carabiners.

Toby reached forward and helped him. "That was risky, man. That rope wasn't rated for that much weight."

David shook his head. "Had to be done. Franklin wouldn't have lasted much longer." He shrugged out of the harness. It hit the ground with a thunk. Chuck collected the rope and equipment.

"You okay, man?"

"No." He leaned heavily against Toby's shoulder. "That was a river from hell. I didn't think it was going to let me go."

Toby slapped his back. "Come on. Let's get you back to the station. You made it free and clear."

He forced his weak legs to follow Toby through the tall grass. Lights from the vehicles blinded him. He held a hand to his face, blocking the bright lights. Voices shouted. Many giving directions, some. . . he paused. He blinked against the harsh glare.

A news van from Memphis parked near the police tape. They spouted off about a daring rescue of a drug ring informant. The tall, shapely news anchor listed off the names of the officers involved. She didn't bother to tamp down her excitement. David scowled at the mention of Jeremy's name.

He turned away from the spectacle. Newscasters. They rated up there with wedgies and moldy cheese.

Another cough racked his body. Not good. He reached Engine One and propped his hand against the grill as the cough tortured him. His body doubled over from the hacking. He waved off Toby's concerned expression as he and Chuck carried the equipment back to its home in the side panel.

He spat phlegm onto the ground as the cough eased.

A tap against his shoulder brought his attention around.

Jeremy glared at him. "That was stupid. You could have been killed. First rule for us: personal safety first."

David narrowed his eyes. Leave it to his brother to fuss about obeying rules. "I was fine. Attached another rope."

"And it could have snapped. Stupid!" Jeremy growled and looked away. His mouth curled up into a snarl as he turned back around. "You don't think, do you? You just do it."

Another cough threatened to consume him as anger boiled, matching the heat that flooded his face. "You would have lost your precious informant if I hadn't done that."

"We had another spot to try." Jeremy ran his hands over his face. "What if you had missed? What if the rope snapped?"

"It didn't." David shoved away from the grill. Jeremy needed to leave well enough alone. All he wanted at this moment was to finish his shift, go home, get a drink, and get some sleep. "Leave it alone, Jeremy. The boy's safe, y'all get the info he has, and all is well with the world."

The engine rumbled. Toby sat in the cab, waiting. David turned away from his brother.

A hand on his arm pushed him back around. "You don't care about rules, do you? You never do. Don't you realize that you could have been killed?"

David stared hard at his brother. Yeah, he could have died. Death came suddenly. What difference did it make if it came during a rescue or in his sleep? "So? Then you wouldn't have to be bothered with me anymore."

Jeremy pressed his lips into a thin line. "That's not it, David. You have to stop taking so many risks."

"Like you would know? You never risked anything in your life. I save people. Whether I know them or not." David pointed at him. His body trembled. "You? If it meant breaking protocol, then you would just watch them die."

Jeremy's hand slammed against his chest, driving another lung rattling cough from him. The grill pressed against his sore back as Jeremy held him against the truck.

Spittle flew from Jeremy's lips and hit him on the cheek. "I have never left a person to die! Never!"

David broke Jeremy's hold. His fist connected with his brother's lips. Jeremy staggered back. His gloved hand touched his mouth. Blood glinted darkly in the headlights.

"Tell that to Rebecca." For once, David loved the rain. It hid the tears.

He turned his back on his brother and climbed into the truck. The door slam echoed in the quiet cab. Ignoring Toby and Chuck's wide-eyed stares, he picked up the mike. "Dispatch, show Engine One returning to station."

"Copy, Engine One. Time oh-two-hundred."

He leaned his head against the seat. It didn't feel like two in the morning. "Drive, Toby. And shut up."

His heart thudded heavily against his ribs. His face and eyes burned. He turned up the heat in the cab as he shivered uncontrollably. Man, he needed a drink right now.

CHAPTER 11

The light blue painted ceiling stared back at Jeremy as he lay in the bed, hands behind his head. He'd donate his left kidney for a chance to sleep a little longer, but his body refused to allow him that luxury.

The red numbers on the clock glowed twelve fifteen.

It was time that he made an effort to rouse himself from the soft, cool sheets. Thanks to his wonderful wife, who allowed him to sleep in after the all-nighter he pulled, he had enough rest to be able to deal with the day. He hoped.

He rolled over and smoothed his hand across Sarah's empty side of the bed. Her flowery scent drifted up to him. Man, he needed her by his side right now. Buck up. She'd be home soon from church.

He kicked at the covers, sending them sailing to the foot of the bed. His skin crawled with a gritty film. He needed a hot shower. Or maybe a cold shower. At this moment, he would take whatever was dealt.

He stumbled into the bathroom, made use of its amenities, and then reached in to turn on the shower. Clean water burst from the shower head. He'd have to apologize to Sarah for not taking a shower when he came in early this morning. Weariness had eaten at him, and the call of the bed had been too strong to ignore. He remembered only shedding his clothes and falling between the sheets.

Steam rose from the water. He undressed and stepped inside.

"Now, this is heaven." His voice echoed in the blue tiled stall.

He pressed his hands against the tiles and leaned in until his forehead touched. Cool ceramic contrasted with the hot steam. Sore muscles turned to butter as the hot water streamed across his shoulders and back. He raised his face, allowing the water to wash away the grimy feel. His bottom lip throbbed with a sharp pain.

He brought a finger to the sore. Blood washed away in the stream and down the drain. Crazy brother. He should have landed his own punch on the hotheaded ingrate.

The bar of soap squished as he pried it from the clam shell dish. Foam and bubbles spilled over his fingers as he ground it between his hands. He scrubbed at his body, willing his anger at David to subside.

No such luck.

The bar of soap clattered to the shower's floor. He stood under the stream until the water ran cold. Even that didn't cool his fury.

He slid back the door. Small hands with slender fingers greeted him, holding out a towel. "Hey, baby."

Sarah ran a hand over his back as he wrapped the towel around his waist. "How's the lip?"

Jeremy faced her. Her dark hair against her head highlighted her gorgeous eyes. He cupped her face in his hands. She melted against him as he placed a light kiss on her supple lips.

He broke away and tried not to smile at her. "Hurts a little."

She reached up and traced it with her forefinger. "I've got some balm for it. Going to tell me how you got it?"

Her floral perfume clung to the steam in the bathroom. He breathed deep, pressing his forehead against hers. "Just an on-the-job accident."

"Uh huh." With feathery touches, her fingers traced the water trails over his chest. "You know the grapevine is fruitful. Want to rethink that statement, Officer Boyette?"

He groaned and captured her hands. "Trust me, hazards of my job. It was just a scuffle."

Sarah snorted and pulled her hands out of his grip. Her fingers traced an old scar across his right side. "This came from a scuffle."

She followed the water trail down his stomach with a fingernail. He closed his eyes. His lovely vixen. Her body rose to tiptoes, pressing herself to him.

She purred against his ear. "Just a scuffle, my dear?"

Jeremy buried his hand in her hair. Sarah's eyes darkened as she peered up at him. "A scuffle with David. But let's not talk about him and his many problems. Right now, I just want my horrible night erased from my head."

"I can do that for you." She brought his face down to hers.

Her arms wrapped around him, pulling him closer. Sarah could always make him forget his troubles.

———————

"So, do you want leftover pot roast or a hoagie sandwich? I can shred the roast if you want a roast beef sandwich." Sarah brought her head out of the refrigerator and looked back at him. "Well?"

Jeremy lowered his newspaper. "Whichever. I really don't care."

"Then hoagie it is. I don't feel like roast beef today." She pulled a handful of the sandwich makings from the shelf and dumped them on the table where he sat. "The bread's behind you. Start decorating it while I get the meat."

He reached behind him and snagged the bag. She placed a handful of meat packages on the wooden surface and pulled up a chair. Together, they smeared condiments and piled meat on the hoagie rolls.

Dennis bounded into the kitchen. "Mom, is it okay if I head to the park?"

Jeremy looked up. Why did they always ask her? Suddenly, he had become the invisible parent. "No. It's Sunday. No one goes anywhere today, other than church."

Dennis rolled his eyes at him. "Except for you."

"Watch it, bub." Jeremy held up the butter knife. "I didn't get in until six. You get a job like mine and see how it feels to you. Until then, you shut it."

"Yeah, well, because of you, I had to miss out on a date last night."

Sarah lowered her spoon with a thwack against the table. "Dennis! You watch your tone."

Jeremy let his son simmer a little in Sarah's glare. Was this his penitence for the problems he gave his parents?

Jeremy cocked an eyebrow at Dennis. "I thought it was just movies?"

Yeah, let the boy weasel out of that lie.

Dennis bit at his bottom lip. "It was. I mean, it was going to be, but Sasha was there. I was going to ask her out for a milk-shake afterward." He turned to leave.

"Don't leave. Sit." Jeremy pushed the chair across from him with his foot. "I want to talk to you."

With a harrumph, Dennis plopped down, arms crossed. Jeremy frowned. Briefly, with his arms crossed, Dennis resembled David. Defiance must run in his family.

"This girl, Sasha. She's been in reform school, a step away from jail. Do you honestly believe that she would be a good girlfriend?" Jeremy placed a finished sandwich on the platter in front of him and pushed it toward his son. "Honestly, now, Dennis. The Bible teaches us about being unevenly yoked. Is Sasha a believer?"

Dennis shrugged. "But she might become one if she's around me."

Sarah opened her mouth, but Jeremy waved her into silence. He leaned toward Dennis. "Whether she's a believer or not, with you being one and the lifestyle she leads, it will lead you into a world that you are not ready for. Trust me, son, there are things that you do not need to be involved in or know about at your age."

Dennis's voice pleaded. "But, Dad, she's great. Beautiful. Funny."

"Then invite her along for a youth outing." He turned to Sarah. "When's the next one?"

"End of May. Out-of-school celebration." She spread some mustard on the bread. "Then Maggie is hosting an all-night game night at the parsonage in June."

"See?" Jeremy shrugged. "There's plenty to do with her."

"Yeah, but–"

"But you won't be alone with her. Which is exactly my point." Jeremy pointed the knife in Dennis's direction as his son tried to leave the table. "Sit."

A growl came from Dennis's area.

"And eat."

Sarah placed another sandwich on a platter and called out. "Sophie!"

Jeremy shook his head at the footsteps that thudded down the hallway. Sophie hurled herself into the kitchen, raven hair flying out behind her. She skidded into the chair.

"Dad! Guess what I just heard."

"That John Masterson finally looked at you?"

She rolled her eyes. Did his kids ever do anything else besides eye rolling?

"No. I gave up on him. Jackson Taylor is much more interesting, and he doesn't burp at the table."

Dennis let out a loud belch and smirked at Sophie.

"Dennis." Sarah cut him with a piercing stare.

Jeremy smiled as he passed Sophie the chip bag. "So, what was so interesting that doesn't involve boys?"

"Men."

His sandwich plopped down onto his platter, the tomato sliding out. "Come again?" He tucked the red slices back in the folds.

Sarah passed him a napkin. "She's yanking your chain, baby."

"Actually, Mom, I just heard something about Daddy." Sophie stuffed a chip in her mouth. "I heard it from Mary, who heard it from her dad when he was talking to Mr. Tennyson, and she told me."

Jeremy cocked his brow at her. What would Sam Tennyson say that would be so interesting to his daughter? "And? So Sam told Mark, and Mary overheard what?"

Sophie grinned, her swinging feet bouncing her petite frame up and down in the chair. "She said that Uncle David gave you a busted lip last night. What did you do, Daddy? Why did he get mad at you?"

Jeremy's hand stilled over his pile of chips. A hush fell around the table. Dennis glared at Sophie and then turned to him. An expectant expression plastered itself across his son's face. Sarah placed her hand on his.

Sometimes, he really hated living in a small town. "Nothing that should concern you two. And Sophie, no more gossip."

Dennis scowled and pushed at his plate. "But, Dad, you always say that there should be no secrets in this house. You want me to be honest with what I do, but how can I when you show us otherwise?"

Sarah pushed Dennis's plate back in front of him. "Finish your lunch. And there are some things that you shouldn't worry about. Things are different when you're an adult."

Sophie fiddled with her lettuce. "Should we worry, then? Is something wrong with Uncle David, Dad?"

Jeremy sighed. He pushed away from the table, crossed the kitchen, and opened a cabinet. Three sets of eyes watched him as he poured his tea. A pop-hiss came from the table as the kids opened their soft drinks.

Their eyes followed his every move, waiting for him to answer. How could he explain this? Even he didn't know what his brother's problem was.

Sarah cleared her throat. She twirled a piece of bread in a dot of mustard on her plate. "Your Uncle David is. . . well, he's having a hard time readjusting to being back home."

Dennis nodded. "Because of what happened to Rebecca?"

"Yeah." Jeremy sank into his chair in relief. Sarah's explanation would work. Maybe that really was the problem with his brother.

"So, we pray for him?" Sophie peered at him through her lashes. "I can still see him, can't I?"

"Of course, you can. On both accounts." Jeremy picked up his sandwich. "We all need to pray for him."

"And hope he doesn't bust your lip again?" Dennis gave him an innocent smile and bit into his sandwich.

Jeremy narrowed his eyes. "Yeah, that too."

He sat back, listening to Sarah and Sophie chat about their upcoming shopping date with Maggie. His mind blocked their chatter about clothes and resumed his worry about his brother. Sarah had to be right. David needed to readjust. But the thought didn't sit right with him. There had to be more.

———

David rolled over and glanced at his clock. Five o'clock. He slept the day away. Again. He pushed back the covers and stood. An hour until his date with Maggie. He needed to call her.

His hand lashed out and gripped the wall. An angry mob clashed behind his eyes. He groaned and staggered to the kitchen. The light from the refrigerator assaulted him. He squinted and pulled out a bottle of water. Oh, man, he should've stayed in the bed.

He shut the door with a barefoot kick and then rummaged in his cabinet. Didn't he put it there this morning? Great. He slammed the door. It rattled in protest. He turned and spotted the small bottles on the corner of the counter. Oh, there they were. Sneaky meds.

He popped off their tops and downed the doses. One for pain. Yeah, he had that. One for congestion. A definite on that. One for infection. Well, he didn't really need it, but he'd take it, anyway. A rumble ripped through his chest as he held back a cough. The doctor this morning assured him the meds would work within a few days. Yeah, right.

His body cried out for a drink. Something strong would work the gunk out of his chest. The warning labels on the bottles glared at him. Well, that solution was out of the question.

He needed a distraction. Something to keep the craving at bay.

Jeremy's smokes lay on the table in the kitchen. He could barely breathe as it was. Nicotine wouldn't be the answer tonight.

He picked up his phone and fell into his recliner.

Maybe she'd come by. No. He really didn't want the company. Besides, he needed her number.

David paused and then dialed Darlene's number.

She answered on the fifth ring. "David!"

"Hey, sis."

"You don't sound so good."

"I've got a bad case of bronchitis and a sinus infection, or so says Dr. Peterson." He pinched the bridge of his nose. Pressure built behind his eyes. "Look, I was supposed to go out with Maggie tonight."

"And now you can't."

"Yeah, and I don't have her number." He chuckled and then went into a bout of hacking. A groan escaped as he wilted into the chair. "Can't believe I forgot to ask for her number."

Darlene laughed. "I'll text it to you. You need anything?"

Yeah, a shot in the chest. Or maybe something to shut up the brass band in his head. The room swam. When was the last time he'd eaten? "You think you could see if Mom could whip up a batch of her soup? I could really use it."

"You shouldn't have moved out."

Oh, he hated that big sister superiority. "Don't go there."

He grimaced. The water he swigged threatened to travel back up from his stomach.

Her sigh hissed over the air. "Okay. Sure you don't need anything else?"

"No. Just soup." Oh, he was such a pansy. "And company?"

She laughed again. "Sure, little brother. Give me an hour."

David hung up and waited for the text to come through. His phone beeped, and the avatar he chose for Darlene smiled up at him. Finally, he had little Cotton Candy's number.

He dialed. She answered on the first ring.

"Hello?"

"Hey, beautiful."

He imagined her smile and those little freckles. "Hey, handsome."

"Wasn't someone supposed to be taking you out for dinner tonight?"

"Well, I think so. But he doesn't sound so good." Her end crackled and then cleared. "What's up?"

How he hated doing this. Would she forgive him? "I have to cancel. I feel like—" He stopped and started again. "—awful. Went to the doc this morning. Bronchitis and a nasty infection."

"Oh, I'm so sorry. You need anything?"

She was way too sweet for him. "Darlene's bringing me some food. I don't remember eating today. Or was that yesterday? I don't know. I feel too sick to think straight."

"You poor darling. Call me if you need anything, okay? And call me when you start feeling better."

"Thanks, beautiful."

"Not a problem, handsome. We've had a rain check before. I'll call and check on you tomorrow. You get some rest."

David waited until the line disconnected. Sweet and absolutely wonderful. He had looked forward to that cotton candy scent tonight. Maybe even another small kiss. One storm and a river, and now look at him. A pathetic, sick man lolling around in a recliner. Give him a gut and a muscle shirt, and he would look the part.

He let the phone hit the floor and pulled the small blanket around him. Oh, let him die now.

The doorbell chimed. David frowned. His clock flashed six nineteen. An hour passed already? Man, that was some strong medication.

He staggered to his feet and lurched to the door. Two pretty ladies stood, grinning up at him. One held a big bowl, and the other clutched a plastic pitcher. He blinked at the duo. His mind refused to focus.

Darlene reached up and touched his forehead. "You're burning up. Get back inside."

His mom pushed past his sister and gripped his arm, hugging
the pitcher of tea to her side. "Come on."

He allowed his mom to propel him to his bed. Did he really
need to be pampered? "Mom, I can sit in the chair."

"No. You lie down." She set the tea on his nightstand. "I
thought I taught you better. What a mess. You wait just a moment while I straighten the bed."

He stood swaying as his mom smoothed the sheets and folded
the blanket to the foot of the bed. "Here, lie down."

She pushed him into the bed. He fell among his high stack
of pillows, and she pulled the sheet to his chin. "Really, Mom. I
can do this myself. I just asked for soup."

"Well," she tucked the sheet around him, "you got me, instead. Plus some sweet tea and some yeast rolls."

His microwave dinged. Darlene rattled around in his cabinets until she found a bowl that apparently passed her inspection.
He doubled over as another cough ripped his lungs out of his
body.

"Oh, kill me, please." He rolled over to his side and sighed as
his mom joined Darlene.

Darlene chuckled as their mom poured tea in a glass. "Men.
Y'all are such babies when you get sick."

David made an obscene gesture.

"David James!" His mom set his tea down on the nightstand
and smacked his head. "Grow up. You boys have gotten so vul-
gar lately."

"Sorry, Mom." He reached for his tea. The cool liquid
soothed his parched throat.

"I wouldn't worry about it, Mom. We can chalk it up to illness." Darlene brought a steaming bowl to him. "Here, sit up and try this."

David struggled into a sitting position and accepted the bowl. His hand shook slightly as he held the spoon. The hot tomato soup slid down, warming his stomach. "Mmm, Mom. You make the best."

She leaned down and kissed his brow. "Don't you know it. Only the best for my children."

He frowned as Darlene plopped down at the foot of his bed with a deck of cards. Yeah, take advantage of a sick man.

"Here, Mom, pull up a spot and play." She patted the edge of the bed.

"Rummy?"

"What else? Since he's sick, we might actually win this time."

David rolled his eyes and took another bite of the creamy soup. "Yeah, wait until I'm sick and half out of it to play against me. The medicine will knock me out real soon, you know."

His mom squeezed his foot through the sheet. "And when you do fall asleep, we'll tally your points in with ours and let ourselves out."

"And people wonder where I get my conniving from."

His mom laughed. "Deal, Darlene. Let's see if he really is too sick to play."

David smiled and set his half-empty bowl to the side. He took another swallow of tea to clear his clogged throat.

His thoughts went to Maggie. She would have enjoyed this. He picked up his cards and snorted. If the hand life dealt him looked anything like this, then maybe things wouldn't be so bad after all.

═══════

Maggie held up a purple burnout t-shirt. The hollow echoes of shoppers in the small department store buzzed in her ear as she contemplated the shirt. "How about this one? I think it would look good with the capris."

Sarah pursed her lips and then shook her head. "Nah. Not with that design. Here, how about this one? Plus, it'll be a nice change from your usual pink."

Maggie regarded the baby blue tee with an Eiffel Tower graphic design. "Yeah. I like that one. Throw it in the buggy." Maggie replaced the purple shirt on the rack. "Sophie, how are you coming along?"

The teenager ambled over, holding a small stack folded over her arms. "I found three shirts, one dress, and two pants. What do you think, Mamma?"

Sarah reached out for a red and white striped shirt. "This one is good." She dropped it in the buggy and turned back to Sophie for the next top. "But this one . . ." She took it and threw it on top of the rack. "No. Too revealing, especially for your age."

Maggie smiled and picked it up. The yellow shirt's neckline dipped in a low vee, and the hem barely would have covered the girl's navel. "Yeah, I agree."

She walked over to the smaller rack and hung the garment as Sarah finished looking through Sophie's pile. The shirts and pants flew into the cart. Sarah handed the dress to Sophie. "Go try it on."

While Sophie hurried to the changing rooms with her dress, Sarah turned to Maggie. "So, you were saying?"

"What? Oh, earlier?" Maggie held up a pair of wild colored socks, inspecting them. "I called him for the next three days. He was getting better, I could tell. He sounded disappointed that we hadn't had a chance to truly go out yet. He did mention, if he felt better this Friday, going on a rowboat ride."

Sarah arched her brow. She took the socks from Maggie's hands and replaced them on the hook. "Not your style." She handed Maggie a pair with lollipop designs.

Maggie grinned and threw them in the cart. "Well, I told him I would have to see. Even though he said he felt well enough to go to work on Thursday, I still think he's overtaxing himself."

"He does that. He and Jeremy both." Sarah turned to Sophie's voice. The girl stood near the dressing rooms, modeling the dress. "That looks good. If you like, we'll get it."

Sophie squealed and hopped around in the slender yellow sundress. "And it'll look so great with my white sandals."

As she disappeared back into the changing room, Sarah resumed. "I really wanted to speak to you about David, though."

"Oh, about what?" Maggie fiddled with a selection of tights, looking for an opaque navy in her size. Petites were so hard to find.

"How much do you know about David? We told you about Rebecca, how she died, and that he left for St. Louis shortly afterward. Rebecca's parents moved away–"

"Oh, that reminds me!" Maggie exclaimed. "They'll be here next weekend. Their gallery generously donated a few local paintings."

Sarah frowned. "David and the Johansens haven't been on speaking terms since the funeral. Does he know?"

Maggie shook her head and leaned against the edge of the cart. "No. But then, the conversation never came up. I didn't realize there were bad feelings between them."

Sophie rushed out of the dressing room. "Here, Mamma. Can I go check out shoes now?"

Sarah grinned as she took the clothes from Sophie. "Yeah. We're right behind you."

Maggie fell in step as Sarah pushed the cart behind Sophie, who hurried to the shoe aisle. As much as she liked shoes, Maggie really didn't want to shop for any. The bright lights in the department store pounded into her head. Hopefully, they could make their way over to the food court soon.

Sarah turned down the women's section. "I need to find some good pumps for church. Mine are so old and scarred." She browsed over the size eights, and Maggie searched through the sevens for some sensible sandals.

"So," she glanced up at Sarah, "what happened between him and her parents?"

"No one really knows. Jeremy seems to think that it was a blame game that happened. They really didn't want her to marry David. Don't get me wrong." Sarah sat on the bench and slipped a pair of black low heels on her feet. "They're nice people, but they come from the 'upper' society. You know, cotillions and parties and balls. Rebecca was an alumnus from Ole Miss. Business and art degree. To them, she could have done better than a high school graduate firefighter."

Maggie frowned. How horrible to know that someone didn't approve of someone else simply because he didn't have a college degree. "He's not dumb. Actually, he's very smart. The things that he knows."

"Oh, I know that, and so do most people. But David never applies himself to his utmost potential. Not unless the situation warrants it."

Maggie smiled. "Naturally lazy?" She inspected a pair of pink leather sandals. Nah. She had enough pink shoes. Actually, she had enough pink everything.

"Yup." Sarah replaced the black shoes and pulled down a pair of red ones. "Oh, I like these."

Maggie shook her head. So like Sarah. "They'll match your new dress we bought from Kohl's."

Sarah smiled and slipped the box in with the clothes. Sophie came around the corner carrying her shoes and a box. The sparkly white Mary Janes shone on her feet. "How about these, Mamma? I love them. Not tight and not at all loose."

Sarah checked the price on the box. "If those are the ones you really want. No wearing a couple of times and then ignoring them."

Sophie beamed and plunked down on the floor to remove the shoes. "Okay." She threw the shoes in the box and handed them to her mother.

Sarah looked at Maggie. "You find anything?"

Maggie shook her head and replaced a blue sandal into its box. "Not really. Actually, I really want to go to the food court. My head is killing me."

"Oh, I didn't realize." Sarah put her arm around her. "Migraine?"

"No. Not yet. The fluorescent lights are too harsh." Maggie trailed after her cousin as they made their way to the check-out register. "You don't think there will be trouble, do you, when the Johansens arrive next weekend? Where are they now?"

"Jackson, I think. Or Canton. Somewhere down there." Sarah piled the clothes on the counter. "And I think it'll be okay. I'm more worried about the game."

Maggie curled up her lips in a lopsided scowl. "So am I, especially when you told me what happened after the rescue." She grabbed her clothes as Sarah paid for her purchase. "Surely, they won't be that stupid."

Sarah gave a small huff. "You would think, but they're Boyettes. Most times, they react without thinking. And with their attitudes toward each other lately, it might escalate on the field. Those two are so competitive."

Maggie filled out her check as the girl scanned her items and bagged them. "Why do they act that way? Doesn't David know that Jeremy tried to save Rebecca?"

The check-out girl looked at her and popped her gum. "That's ninety-six and seventeen cents."

Maggie wrote the amount in and handed the check to the cashier. She stuffed the receipt in the bag and followed Sarah and Sophie out into the mall's walkway. "I just can't imagine holding a grudge that long."

Sarah stopped. Her dark eyes flooded with compassion and worry. "You would think. David used to be so full of life. Now? Something is wrong. He can't still blame Jeremy for Rebecca's death. I've tried to get Jeremy to tell him that he tried, but my darling husband can be just as stubborn as his brother."

Maggie smiled and hooked her arm through her cousin's as they resumed following Sophie down to the food court. "Well, things will look up. Don't they always?"

Would they really? That sad face and haunted, green eyes had captivated her. But when she gazed into his eyes and saw—no, felt—the love and life buried deep within him, she realized that she loved him. She ducked her head so Sarah couldn't see her smile. She loved David. Just saying the words sent a pleasurable shiver down her back. Dang it all. The man had stolen her heart.

CHAPTER 12

David sidestepped a puddle of melted ice cream. The trees overhead created shade through most of the park. He stepped over a discarded bag of popcorn. People jostled him as he traveled the main fairway toward the gazebo.

Chairs arranged in gentle arcs offered a relaxing atmosphere. A local folk band played a rendition of an old hymn: *On Jordan's Stormy Bank*. The familiar tune drifted his way, along with the aroma of funnel cakes. And cotton candy. He smiled.

He would never find Maggie in this Saturday afternoon crowd. The auction was supposed to start in thirty minutes, and he wanted to sit beside her.

A hand landed on his shoulder. "David, you finally showed. Figured you wouldn't come until it was time for the ballgame." David turned around. Sam stood with his arm around a tall brunette sporting a splash of bright red across her lips. His friend sure loved the high-maintenance gals. "I wanted to see the auction. Couple of things caught my eye."

"It's been delayed. Heard the mayor had some announcement or whatnot, so the auction won't start until four thirty." Sam waved a hand at his date. "Hey, this is Tiffany. She's from Southaven. Tiff, this is David. Friend and boss man, at least, sometimes boss."

Tiffany held out a long, skinny, manicured hand. Some expensive, spicy scent reached him. "Hi, David. I've heard a lot about you."

David shook her hand and grimaced. "Coming from Sam, I don't know whether I should apologize and run the other way or what."

A childlike giggle grated against his ears as her blue eyes crinkled. "Oh, it was all good. He told me you just came back from St. Louis."

"I did."

Sam clapped him on the arm. "Why don't you swing by The Mudslide later this evening? Play a game of pool?"

"I might. Really depends." He looked over their shoulders. A little blonde head came into view and then disappeared. Should have known to look in the crafts section first. "It was a pleasure to meet you, Tiffany. Sam, I see someone. I'll catch you later before the game."

"It wouldn't happen to be someone blonde, would it?" Sam smiled and allowed him to pass. His small chuckle followed David through the throngs of people.

Amazing how many people actually lived in Jasper City. David angled his body to miss the flight of two preteens as they barreled past. The horde thinned somewhat, and David glimpsed the little woman, her pink sleeveless shirt billowing in the breeze around her. Maggie and her color pink. Too bad she wasn't wearing that little sundress she had on when they first met. Man, she was beautiful that day.

She ventured down to another booth. A bump against his back woke David from his spell. Sheesh. He'd get run over in this hoopla.

To his left was a small glass-blowing booth. He ducked underneath the tent and perused the items. He'd surprise her.

"How you doin', sir?" The vendor rose from his sports chair, pushing the legs of his overalls down over his boots. He grabbed his cane from nearby and tilted his straw hat back. "Looking for anything in particular?"

David smiled. "Yeah. Looking for something pink, delicate, and absolutely beautiful."

The older man huffed into his white mustache and smiled. "Well, I've got beautiful things. Lots of pink, and they're all delicate. All done by hand."

"Seriously?" David fingered a small hummingbird that hung on a string from the rail overhead. Light shot through it, casting rainbows over the inside of the tent. "That's amazing. Must take a lot of patience."

"Very much so." The man hobbled to the far end of the glass counter. "Here are some of the newer items I made. Anything among them you think would do? This for a lady friend?"

David smiled again. The old coot really knew how to drum up a sale. "Yeah. Actually. . ." He turned and spotted Maggie across the path at a tent selling totes. He pointed to her. "That's her in the pink."

"Oh, Maggie Goddard. She's a sweet woman." He held out his hand to David. "I'm Buster Fields. Funny name, I know. Maggie sells some of these items for me in her shop."

"David Boyette." David shook the man's hand. "Apparently, she is well known in the town."

Buster laughed, reminding David of thunder rumbling across the sky. "Don't know about that, but Maggie is a dear heart. Wonderful woman. But–" He eased away from the counter.

"Things on display won't do for your woman. A classy female like her needs something special."

Buster picked up a small cardboard box and set it on the counter. He opened the flaps. David peered in. Nestled inside was an array of colorful creations.

"May I make a suggestion?"

David nodded. "Sure. There's a lot to choose from."

"Go for the butterflies."

"Yeah, she likes those." He replayed the images of the butterflies that dangled from her earlobes and the anklet that wrapped around her soft, smooth ankle.

He reached forward and ran a finger over the smooth glass of a red and white butterfly, wings folded up above the body. Its neighbor gleamed at him. The pink and aqua colors flowed in a lazy swirl around the wings. "May I?"

Buster nodded. "Go ahead."

David pulled the delicate butterfly out of its foam bedding. A loop on its back allowed for a string to be threaded through it. Unlike the others, this butterfly's wings were fully spread open. Light shot through the glass, highlighting the masterpiece. Other colors danced among the pink and aqua. Red specks. Blue veins. Purple swirls. All mingled in a kaleidoscope of gems.

"I think you found the one."

David held it out to him. "Can you string it for me? It would be nice for her to be able to hang it up."

"I can." Buster took the small glass butterfly. "She's a mighty lucky lady to have someone like you."

"No." David smiled and glanced over at Maggie, who had moved down two more tents. No. She wasn't lucky to have him. "No. It's more like I'm blessed to have her."

Maggie handed the vendor a ten and thanked him. She smiled as she slung the pink flamingo motif tote over her shoulder. At this rate, she wouldn't have any money left. Good thing she was at the end of the line.

She stepped onto the straw-covered path as she stuffed her pocket book and keys into her new tote. She loved these events. Until the next day, when she would realize how much she spent.

A pair of well-worn boots stopped in front of her.

"I know those boots." She looked up into emerald eyes. "And I know you."

His eyes crinkled as he smiled his Cheshire cat grin. "Hey, beautiful."

"Hey back at you, handsome." Maggie brushed an eyelash from his cheek. "Thought you weren't going to be here until the ballgame."

Could the man not look any better with his white button down rolled up to reveal strong forearms and carpenter jeans that hugged him nicely? A pair of aviator glasses sat on top of his head where his short, blond strands glistened in the sun.

David offered her his arm. She rested her hand lightly in the crook of his elbow. "I decided to come a little early. See the sights. Listen to the music." He guided her along the outskirts of the crowd and through the picnic-table-strewn park.

"That I don't believe. Folk music isn't your kind of music, or did you forget what you said the other day?"

He snorted and ducked his head, hiding his face. "Well, I can listen to it for a little while. Besides, they're playing regular music now."

Maggie cocked her head. Sure enough, the band played eighties music. Talk about retro.

They ambled toward an empty picnic table not too far behind the gazebo seating. He hopped up on the surface and patted the top beside him. "Actually, Maggie, I thought I would sit with you during the auction."

"Did you now?" She slid beside him and nudged his shoulder with hers. "What if I told you that another man had asked me to sit with him?"

He sniffed. His mouth turned downward in a fake scowl. "Then I would tell him to buzz off. But not in those exact words."

Maggie laughed. "I would love for you to sit with me. Oh–" She clapped her hands together and bounced up and down. He would love to know this. "I got Sarah to agree to bid for those records."

A small light gleamed in his eyes. "Really? That's cool."

"Yeah. Maybe she'll be able to get them." She brushed at a piece of dirt that marred the knees of her capris. Heat from his body burned against her side. The man ran hot like a raging fire. She cleared her throat as her thoughts slipped into a place they had no business traveling. She glanced at him. "Anyway, I thought that if I got them, you might want to listen to them with me."

"Are you asking me out on a date, Miss Maggie?" Green fire danced in his eyes as he leaned closer to her, one hand on the table behind her.

She smiled. "Maybe. I put a down payment on a cottage by the river. Should close on it next week. I thought you might like to . . ." She shrugged. What was she doing?

"To what?" His hand reached for hers. Long, hard fingers intertwined with her small, short ones. "Dance in the moonlight?"

"Are you really that romantic?" Her body sighed in relief for the way out of the conversation. "I think you've been in the sun too long to talk about moonlight and dancing."

He chuckled. "Probably. Here, got something for you." His fingers left hers and dug a small package from the side cargo pocket of his jeans.

She held the small, brown paper gift in her hands. "Oh, David."

"Um . . ." He scratched his head and gave her a lopsided grin. "It's prettier than the wrapping. You might want to open it. But if brown paper wrapping floats your boat . . ."

A giggle escaped her. Her fingers shook as they pulled the wrapping away. A small gasp filled the air between them. She picked up the butterfly by its dark pink ribbon. The sunlight brought the glass figurine to life.

She held it higher. Rainbows danced across her lap. She followed the small specks of color over his lap, up his chest, and on his face.

"Do you like it?" His voice spoke in barely a whisper as he leaned closer to her.

Reds, yellows, and oranges played a complex game over his lips.

"I do." She cradled the butterfly in her hand, ending the light show. "It's absolutely gorgeous. Thank you."

His finger caressed her cheek. "I'm glad you like it." He lowered his head toward her.

Her breath caught. In public? He had to be crazy, but his lips drew nearer. The lure of his scent, a woodsy spice, pulled her closer. The yells, shouts, and laughter faded away. Music from the gazebo—some Kenny Rogers song—grew louder in her ears, competing with the drumming of her heartbeat.

His lips grazed hers for one split second before the world slammed down around her as someone called his name.

"David!"

Sarah.

"Dang it all!" Maggie clamped her hands over her mouth as David chuckled. Oh, Lord, she shouldn't have said that.

"My thoughts exactly."

Maggie smiled at him. "Although I don't think those were the words you were thinking."

"No. More R-rated than yours."

They turned as Sarah approached them, her long legs eating up the distance. "David, I thought I saw your motorcycle earlier. What are y'all doing over here? The family's over there."

She pointed across the park on the other side of the chairs. "I was heading over to the Lovejoy's tent for a bag—" She spied Maggie's tote. "Oh, I like that."

Maggie held it up. "They have another one over there."

"Nah. I'm going for the blue daisies." Sarah's glance slid between the two of them. "Did I interrupt something?"

Maggie smiled and cut her eyes toward David. His arms were crossed against his chest, and a dirty snarl twisted his lips as he stared Sarah down. She giggled. "No. Not really. We were just talking."

David rolled his eyes at her statement and leaned against his knees. "Yeah. Just 'talking.'"

She nudged her shoulder against him. He got the message and pulled her closer to his side. "Oh, let me show you what David bought me."

Sarah let out a small gasp as she held up the glass butterfly. "It's beautiful." She batted her eyes at David. "How romantic."

He rolled his eyes again and turned to Maggie. "You want to go with Sarah? I can meet you at the family table later."

She reached up and laid a hand against his cheek. "Okay. Save me a seat for the auction?"

"I will." He gave Sarah one last dirty look and hopped off the table. He threw Maggie a wink. "Try not to spend too much."

She watched as he stuck his hands in his pockets and disappeared into the crowd.

Sarah turned to her. "I did interrupt something, didn't I?"

Maggie scooted off the table with a sigh. "Sort of. But it's okay—oomph!"

She broke off as her world whirled about her. An arm wrapped around her waist as a hand cupped the back of her head. Soft, hot lips settled over hers in a bone-melting smooch. Just as quickly, she was set back on her feet.

David tipped a nonexistent hat, winked at Sarah, and disappeared again.

Maggie blew out a breath. Amazing she even had any left. Oh, boy, that man knew how to surprise her. She turned wide eyes onto Sarah.

Her cousin's face lit into a wide grin. "Like Jeremy said, David always upped the ante."

"I'll say." Maggie eased forward on trembling legs. "I don't know if he's good for my health or not, though."

Sarah's laughter floated through the crowd as she led Maggie back to the crafts.

———————

David flicked a bug off Maggie's leg and leaned over to whisper in her ear. "You think he'll shut up pretty soon? I'm getting pretty tired of his rattling on and on."

Maggie thumped his knee with a fist before letting her hand settle on his. "Hush. He's almost through."

David leaned back against the plastic chair and crossed an ankle over his knee. He scrubbed at his face and then let his arm fall onto the back of Maggie's chair. Most of the crowd had settled into the chairs, waiting for the auction. A motion at the front of the rows caught his attention.

Jeremy, decked out in full dress uniform, sat at the edge. That had to be hot. Even with the sun sinking below the horizon, the air hung over them in a hot, humid sheet.

Maggie was right. The mayor finally wound down.

". . .and this city is better for it. So it is with great pride and tremendous honor that we can award two fine officers of Jasper City. Please, let's give a warm welcome for Sergeant Thaddeus Baers and Sergeant Jeremy Boyette."

David narrowed his eyes as his brother climbed the short steps to stand beside the mayor. Baers' tall form dwarfed the two others. Mayor Wellington raised his hands to quiet the crowd.

"Sergeants Baers and Boyette, it is a privilege to award you both for a job performed above and beyond the call of duty. Because of your brave and fast action, this town is one step closer to ending its war on drugs. Please accept these plaques as Jasper City's appreciation. . ."

David turned away from the proceedings. Great. He risked his life to save the little twerp, and Jeremy gets the recognition. A burning knot built inside his stomach. Figures that the city would hail his brother as the hero. Always Jeremy. Never him.

He clenched his fists. The anger fought back, but he forced it down. Down past the pit of his stomach. Slowly the feeling receded, leaving in its wake a bitter taste on his tongue.

It didn't matter. It was just a piece of paper. His nostrils flared. He had to reign in his thoughts.

People stood around him. Maggie glanced down at him, questions burning in her eyes. He stood and clapped along with the others. Acting was like lying. Recently, he had gotten better and better at it.

They sat as the mayor reclaimed the microphone. "Now, what everyone had been waiting for, Jasper City's Charity Auction. Let's welcome Michael Dunbar as emcee."

David leaned over to Maggie. "I'll be back in a little bit."

Worry flooded her eyes. "Something wrong?"

He shook his head. "No. I'll be back." He patted her knee and then excused himself past the older couple seated next to him.

Eyes watched his every move, piercing him with their gazes, following his every step. He shook his head at his imaginings. No one watched. As fast as his legs allowed, David skirted past the assembly and through the throngs of people standing at the back.

He eased toward the parking lot. Once through the gates of the park, he sank down on the wooden fence rail along the sidewalk. What was wrong with him?

He needed a drink, that was it. He hadn't had one in almost a week.

He wiped the sweat off his lip and drew in a deep breath. His mom should have told him that Jeremy was getting an award tonight. He would have made sure to miss it.

Jeremy the hero. Jeremy the Great. David the–he cut off the thought.

Buck up. No revisiting that memory. He buried the thoughts back into the black depths of his mind. He could get through this. He had to get through this.

He stood and dried his hands on his jeans. He'd grab a drink and something to eat before rejoining Maggie. An excuse as to why he got up and left. He stuck his hands in his back pockets and leaned his head back.

A few stars peeked through the dusky sky. Streetlamps kept their bright glow at bay. The park scents of sugary confections, corn dogs, and popcorn drifted along the small breeze. A chill crept across his arms. The weather was turning again. Maybe it'd cool off by the time the ballgame started.

He blew out a breath. Calm replaced his turmoil. He turned and took a step, almost colliding with an older couple leaving the park.

He looked up to murmur his apology and stopped. Panic set in as Mrs. Johansen stumbled to a stop. Shock rooted him to the spot.

Rebecca's parents were here? They had moved. What–?

Mr. Johansen placed a steady hand on his wife's arm. They looked well. David brought his eyes to Mr. Johansen's watery blue eyes. They looked old.

"David." He held his hand out to him.

David automatically shook the man's hand. "Victor."

Mrs. Johansen stepped forward and wrapped him in a hug. Shock morphed into utter horror. Was she searching for a place to bury the knife?

She pulled back. Her eyes, so much like Rebecca's, searched his face. "Oh, David. I have been waiting for this day. I've been wanting to see you again."

"Come again?" He shook his head. Did he fall into another dimension? First Jeremy, and now this.

Mr. Johansen pulled his wife to his side, an arm around her waist. "We parted on horrible terms, David. We regret the things we said to you. We've prayed for a time to personally say that we're sorry."

David's voice croaked. "I don't know what to say." He buried his hands in his pockets. "I . . . I never thought I would run into you. Mom said you had moved to Canton."

Mrs. Johansen smiled, tears glistened in her eyes. A perfectly manicured hand with those French style nails brushed at her nose. "I heard you left for St. Louis. Did you like it there?"

"I did. For a while. But decided big city life wasn't for me." He swallowed against the lump in his throat. What was he supposed to say to them? What did they want from him? "Y'all opened a gallery down there?"

"We did. Showcasing a lot of Rebecca's work. Picked up a few more local artists." Mr. Johansen turned to his wife. Wariness leaked through his expression as he glanced at David. "Come on, Madeline, we'll be late for the dinner. It was good to see you, David."

They nodded to him and turned towards a line of parked cars at the end. David watched them. Nerves in his legs jumped around. His stomach jack hammered against his spine. He should go to them. He had forgiven them long ago. He needed to tell them that. They would have been family, and didn't family forgive?

He clenched his fists. He couldn't do it. It was asking too much of him. They approached a sleek, gray Jaguar.

He had to stop them before they got into the car. David bit back a curse and hurried to their side.

"Victor! Madeline! Wait."

Their surprised faces turned to him. He slowed to a more sedate walk.

Mrs. Johansen rounded the front of the car and met him halfway. Without thought, David wrapped her in a hug. Her pouf hairdo wobbled dangerously on her head. She buried her face into his chest.

"Thank you, David." Her whisper was a sweet balm to his ears.

She pulled away, patted his chest once, and hurried back to the car. Mr. Johansen squeezed David's shoulder as his wife slid into the passenger seat.

"That meant a lot to her."

David pressed his lips together for a second and then sniffed. "I couldn't let her think I hated her. I know we said awful things to each other. I won't ask you to forgive me. What I said was hateful, and I don't deserve your forgiveness."

Mr. Johansen gave him a sad smile. "No one deserves forgiveness, David. But we love you like a son and still care about you. I wish we could stay longer and at least have dinner, but we have to be back in Canton tomorrow." His hand slid from David's shoulder. "Maybe someday."

"Maybe." David waited until Mr. Johansen got into his car and backed up before turning toward the park.

What a night. He really needed that drink about now.

As he entered the park, the emcee's voice floated above the din. He hoped he hadn't missed the auction on the records yet. He stopped by a food cart and grabbed a large cola and some cotton candy.

He excused his way through the people again and fell into his seat.

"Where've you been?" Maggie's eyes sparkled as he handed her the sugary treat. "Never mind. You came bearing gifts!"

"For you. Sweet cotton candy for my sweet cotton candy girl." He plucked off a piece of the spun confection and let it melt on his tongue.

She leaned over and whispered. "I ain't your girl yet."

So she thought. He waited until she sat up before whispering back. "You're wrong."

She smiled and punched his knee. "The records are up! Oh, where's Sarah?"

━━━━━━

Jeremy peered through the chain link of the dugout. His wife sat beside Maggie on the wooden bleachers. Maggie clutched her small stack of records to her chest, chatting nonstop. Jeremy smiled. Sarah worked hard to make sure no one had outbid her on those vinyls.

"Jer! You're on deck, man."

Jeremy climbed the short set of steps and squinted against the bright ball field lights.

"Knock it outta the park." Baers smacked his rear as he passed by.

He picked up the bat and practiced a couple of swings as Dillon Ross batted. He glanced at the scoreboard. In the lead by one. That wouldn't last long. The Jasper City Polecats fought the JC Demons without either one gaining the advantage.

The metallic crack of the bat echoed as the ball flew high into the air in a foul behind home plate. Jeremy sighed. So much for Dillon at bat. Any pop foul in that area never got past his brother.

David knocked off his mask and scurried toward the fence, easily catching the softball.

"Good try, Dillon." Jeremy slapped the officer's shoulder as he shuffled past.

The man shook his head. "Watch those insides. Toby's killing us tonight."

Jeremy smiled and popped his gum. "Those are the ones I can hit, man." He stepped up into the batter's box.

Sarah's voice shouted over the crowd's roar. "Go, Jer!"

He gave her a one finger salute.

"Batter up!" The umpire bent over behind David's squatting form. His brother's green eyes flared behind the catcher's mask.

Jeremy sighed. Here they went again.

David stood. "Hold up." He motioned to the umpire. "Need a dusting."

Jeremy stepped back as the umpire dusted off the plate. Red dust floated into the air and tickled his nose. He snorted and rubbed his face against his sleeve. He would not give David the satisfaction of a sneeze.

The umpire resumed his place. Jeremy rocked into position and brought his bat back.

"Time."

Jeremy stepped back and glared at David. His brother winked and trotted out to Toby on the mound. Ingrate did that on purpose. Both of the men glanced in his direction. Toby nodded.

David ambled back to the plate and squatted. "Getting tired, old man?"

"No. You?" Jeremy spat in front of his brother's spot, barely missing David's left foot. David sneered at him.

He readied himself in position. Without warning, David hopped up and held out his glove to the side. The ball sailed into David's hand.

They were walking him. Figured. He'd hit a home run during the last inning, and suddenly they were scared. Again, the ball sailed into David's outstretched glove. Jeremy sighed and held his position through two more throws.

He spun the bat towards his dugout and turned to David as he jogged away. "Pansy!"

David glared. He held up his glove to shield the obscene gesture he made.

Jeremy waited on first base as one of their rookies stepped up to the plate. An inside ball whistled past the man's bat. Jeremy groaned. David threw the ball back to Toby. This was murder.

The crowd hooted. Sarah sat on the edge of her seat, knee bouncing up and down. Maggie held her hand over her mouth. No doubt rooting for David.

"Strike three! Out!"

Jeremy hung his head. Time to change over. David neared him. Payback time. He stuck out his foot. David stumbled but then righted himself.

"Oh, you'll pay for that."

Jeremy smirked. "See you back on the plate."

David glared at him and hurried to his team's dugout.

Baers threw him his glove as he rolled his batting helmet into the hole. "You trying to pick a fight, Jer?"

He pulled his hat low over his eyes as he followed Baers onto the field. "No. Not really. Make him mad, and he'll screw up. Two more innings. We got this one."

Jeremy paused at the mound where Dillon stood, chalking his hands. "When David comes up, right and low, then a change up, then right and high."

"He'll miss?"

"Most times. It's the change up that throws him off."

Dillon nodded as Jeremy rushed to second base. The umpire called for the first batter.

Toby sauntered to the plate. Within moments, the first hit sounded through the night. A high pop fly to left field where Markston caught it. One down, two more to go.

Jeremy grinned as David stepped up. His brother rotated the cap until the bill pointed backwards and slammed the batting helmet down. He pointed the bat in Jeremy's direction.

The man actually dared to pull a Babe Ruth. Dillon let go with the first throw. David's bat soared above it, tipping the ball into the left foul line. Jeremy grimaced. His brother was getting better at those right and lows.

The change up sailed passed without a hitch. David snarled and backed out of the batter's box. He tapped his cleats with the bat, looked at the spectators, and then returned to the plate.

Jeremy risked a glance. Sure enough, Maggie half stood, hand over mouth.

Dillon's pitch soared through the air. David's bat met it with a thwack. Jeremy cursed and ducked as the white ball whistled inches above him. His blasted brother nearly took off his head.

Jeremy stretched out with a foot tagging the base, waiting for Baers to pitch the ball in. David's thundering feet reached his ears. The ground vibrated.

Baers scooped the ball off the ground and side-armed it to Jeremy. The softball smacked into his gloved palm. He whirled, brushed his brother across the shoulders with the glove, and leapt out of the way as David's body slid across the base.

Dust flew into the air.

Jeremy landed on his feet. David's hand on the base halted his slide, and he rose to his feet. Both of them turned to the umpire.

The umpire pumped his arm down. "Out!"

"What?" David stepped up to the umpire as he dusted off his uniform. "You got eyes? I was safe. Touched the base before he touched me."

Thomas Dearborn hurried down the lane. "David!"

"Just back off." Jeremy placed a hand on David's chest. His brother didn't need to get thrown out of the game.

David knocked Jeremy's hand off. "You back off."

The umpire rose to his full five feet eight inches. "My call. I saw his tag. You're out." He stood nose to chest to David. "Accept it, or you're out of the game."

Heartbeats passed. Thomas slid between the umpire and David. "Let it go, David. It was a good call."

David's eyes went from the little man, to Jeremy, to his chief. He pushed past Thomas. "Fine. Lousy ump."

He rammed his shoulder against Jeremy's as he stalked past. Jeremy rolled his eyes and threw the ball to Dillon. The umpire backed up to his spot.

Stupid brother was going to get himself thrown out of the game. Figured. Sam came up to bat, and Jeremy stood through one more out. Maybe they would actually win this game.

He shuffled down the dugout's steps and collapsed on the bench. His cold bottle of water greeted him. The liquid washed the dry dust down his throat.

"Jeremy." Sarah's voice called to him.

He smiled at her and pushed himself up to meet her at the end of the dugout. She threaded her fingers through the fencing.

"Nice play." Her smile outshone the lights.

He laughed. "I thought so. See the Babe Ruth he pulled?"

"Yeah. And it went exactly where he said it would go."

"Nearly took my head off." He downed another swig of his water.

Laughter danced in her eyes. "Oh, I wish we had instant replay. You should have seen yourself. I thought your eyes were going to pop out."

Jeremy shook his head. "You rooting for him?"

"No, baby. The Polecats always have my loyalty. But Maggie is going crazy. She's Demons all the way." She pressed her face to the fence. "Kiss?"

So much like high school. He leaned down. His lips grazed hers through the diamond opening of the chain link.

"Jeremy! Man, save it for later." Baers hitched a thumb towards Captain Conners. "There's a change in the line up. Felts hurt his ankle, and Smith had a toilet emergency. Conners needs you on deck."

Jeremy smiled at Sarah. He claimed one more quick peck. "See ya, honeybee."

"Jock." Her giggle followed him as he hurried away.

Baers handed him his batting helmet and bat. Jeremy stepped out on deck as Markston swung and missed.

"Strike two!"

Jeremy hooked the bat over his shoulder and watched the stands. Sarah returned to her seat by Maggie. She looked up and gave a small wave. He smiled. Man, this felt too much like high school.

The metal ring of the bat as it met the ball shattered the night air. The ball soared into the air over deep center. Markston half ran, half skipped towards first as the ball arced and then plummeted to the ground. It landed near the fence. As two of the firemen raced towards it, Markston flew around the bases. He rounded second as the ball shot to third. A dust cloud flew into the air as Markston slid into third base.

Jeremy held his breath. Oh, man, he had to be safe. The dust settled. The umpire spread out his arms.

"Safe!"

Jeremy whooped. "Yes!"

If he could get Markston home, then the game would be theirs. He hurried to the batting box and tapped home plate.

David huffed behind his mask. "Not going to make it."

"Just squat there. I don't plan on you catching Toby's pitches."

"Hold!" David held out his hand.

Jeremy blew out an irritated breath. He backed up as the umpire dusted off the plate. Again. Once through, Jeremy settled back into his stance.

Before Toby wound up for his pitch, David stood. "Time." He backed up and showed his glove to the umpire.

Jeremy narrowed his eyes as David worked at the glove, tightening the laces with his teeth. He smirked at Jeremy and then squatted.

"You're such a jerk."

"Takes one to know one." David smacked his leg with his glove. "That was a bad call earlier."

Jeremy stepped back out of the box. Two could play that game. He thumped his shoes, ignoring his brother's scathing glares. The umpire pointed to the plate.

"Batter up."

Jeremy stepped forward and brought his bat into position. Toby pitched. The ball hurled towards him. He swung. Too late. The bat vibrated as it connected with the ball and sent it over the right side fence.

"Foul! Strike one!"

Jeremy brought the bat to his shoulder. "Told you. Not going to get the chance to catch them."

Another slap against his shin. He lowered his bat and tapped David's chest guard. "Stop being a jerk."

David jumped to his feet, knocking his mask off his head. "I ain't being the jerk. You want a go, old man?"

Jeremy met his brother, stepping closer until they were practically nose to nose. "Play ball, David."

The umpire pushed at them. "Break it off or you're out. Both of you." He bent and brushed at the plate as David retrieved his mask.

David glared one more time at Jeremy and settled the mask back onto his face. Jeremy shook his head.

"Play ball!"

Once again, Jeremy settled into position. Toby grunted as the pitch spliced through the air. Jeremy swung and grimaced as the ball soared into a high fly, landing midway between first base and home plate. Well outside the line.

"Foul! Strike two."

David drove a fist into his glove. "That's two strikes."

"And none for you." Jeremy snarled as David whacked his leg with the glove. He whirled around and smacked David's mask with the bat. "Cut that out."

David jumped to his feet and ripped the bat from Jeremy's hands. Jeremy made a grab at it, but David chucked it to the side. The umpire backed up a few feet and stood with his hands propped on his hips, shaking his head.

"You are such a jerk, David." Jeremy pushed past his brother to retrieve the bat, but David's hand latched onto the back of his shirt and yanked. The jarring thud of landing on the ground drove the breath from his lungs.

Anger flooded his mind. Jeremy kicked and swiped at David's feet, knocking them aside. His brother hit hard, sending up a small plume of dust. Jeremy rolled to his feet just as a fist pummeled into his side. He grimaced. An oath spilled from his lips.

The town had waited for the yearly game fight. Might as well give it to them. Jeremy lashed out with another kick. His foot met the back of David's knee, sending him once again into the dirt. He pounced onto his brother's back and forced David's face into the coarse, red soil.

"You're a–" The curse cut short as Jeremy pressed David's mouth further into the dirt. David mumbled curses through the soil that coated his face.

Might as well make that mouth just as filthy as the words that came out.

An elbow rammed his stomach. Jeremy rolled off his brother. Before David gained his footing, hands latched onto Jeremy's arms and pulled him away. Firemen pulled at David, who bucked against them. Toby wrapped his arm into a choke hold around David.

Jeremy grinned, tasting blood in his mouth. Another split lip.

The umpire glared at them both. "You're out of here!"

The crowd cheered. Jeremy shook his head. Whatever they thought, he and David didn't do this for their benefit. Pure anger poured from his brother's eyes as his team dragged him towards the dugout. Jeremy allowed his own teammates to herd him away.

Conners met him at the steps. "Thanks a lot, Boyette. Better be glad we were already up by one." He gave Jeremy one last, hard look and jerked his thumb to the deck. "Baers, you're up. Boyette's out, so you gotta take his place."

Jeremy hobbled to the corner of the bench and collapsed, ignoring the harsh stares of his teammates. He didn't mean to get so riled at his brother, but the man could try the patience of Job.

Maggie watched David as he sat with his back against the dugout's fence, packing his bat bag. She admired his muscles as they rippled along his forearms. The overhead lights silhouetted his strong jaw line and angular nose when he turned his head.

Maggie sneaked up behind him, reached through the chain link, and thumped an ear.

He whirled. The anger that flashed died a quick death. A smile lit his dirty face. Sweat ran in little, red rivers along the side of his temples.

"Maggie!"

"Hey, handsome." She gripped the chain link and smiled at him as his fingers folded over hers. "So, I didn't think it would be you and Jeremy doing the yearly game fight. What gives?"

He shook his head. "Doesn't matter. Look, I was about to leave and head home to clean up. Meet me at the gates?"

She searched his eyes. Something dangerous swam beneath them. Something cold and hungry. "Okay."

He turned and zipped his bag. "Let me tell the guys, and I'll be right over."

Maggie pushed away from the dugout as he walked over to his teammates. She hurried to the gates. Most of the people still watched the game, but she didn't need to see the last inning. Jasper City Polecats were going to win this year.

She nodded a greeting to a couple walking past and carrying heavily laden bags. Most of the vendors left earlier in the evening. Now only couples strolled the well-traveled path, enjoying the night air. She bumped into Officer Darryl.

He smiled as he steadied her. "Hi, Miss Maggie. Enjoying the game?"

"Oh, yeah." She motioned at the ball field across the park. "Looks like the Polecats have it this year. Jeremy was thrown out, by the way."

The older man laughed, his paunch shaking above his belt. "Figured as much. Guess that means he'll be on duty earlier than expected."

"He's working tonight?" She fell in step beside him.

"He switched with Benson Myers. You heard about Benson's wife?" He waved towards a crowd of teenagers huddled at one of the food carts.

"No. Don't tell me, she went into labor?"

"Twins."

Maggie clapped her hands together. "That's great. I need to make sure I send a card. Benita always came to the shop every week." She spotted David heading her way. "Take care, Officer Darryl. And go catch the rest of the game."

He dipped his head her way. "Good night, Miss Maggie."

As he veered away from her, an arm snaked around her waist. A deep, velvet voice tickled her ear. "Leave you alone for a few minutes, and other men are accosting you."

She plowed a fist into David's shoulder. "Silly. Officer Darryl was just telling me about Benson's wife. She had twins. Isn't that great?"

"Heaven help them." He guided her through the gates, his hand resting on the small of her back.

Heat radiated from his palm, spreading across her lower back. She peered up at him. In the dark, his eyes seemed to glow with an inner fire. Something in the set of his face created a cold lump within her stomach.

He stopped beside his motorcycle. His hand left her back as he straddled the seat and turned to her, helmet in hand. "Here."

She held the helmet. "What?"

Was he wanting something? Needing her to do something?

"Put it on. Take a ride with me."

His eyes bored into her heart. She swallowed. A ruthlessness rose to the surface of his face. She shook her head as she stepped closer. "I can't tonight, David."

He accepted the helmet back from her with a scowl. "Why not? We've been trying to make plans to go out, but nothing ever comes of it. Tonight's as good a time as any."

Maggie took a deep breath. Oh, how she wanted this, but right now, he scared her.

"David." She touched his cheek and stroked the coarse beginning of whiskers along his jaw. Even with a layer of red dust, even with a faint undercurrent of anger, his face captivated her. "It's late. Why not stop by my place tomorrow, and we'll listen to my records?"

He smiled slightly. "What if I want more? Tell you what. Why don't you come with me tonight? We'll listen to them together, just you and me, tonight. All night?"

He snagged her belt loop and reeled her closer. She stumbled across the rocks in the lot. Her hands splayed across his chest. His hand traveled over her shoulder and up her neck, heat trailing in its wake.

Her fingers dug into his muscles. "No. I can't do that, David."

His eyes clouded over. Good gracious, he was changing before her. A part of her melted at the wildness that he exhibited. Oh boy, she needed help in staying strong.

"Can't or won't?" His fingers wrapped in her hair, forcing her head down. His lips met hers in a crushing kiss.

She whimpered. Everything inside turned to pudding. Her hands curled around his head. Oh, let it happen. She couldn't hold back any longer.

A truck backfired. Maggie jumped. She pushed against him as she sent a quick thank-you heavenward. This would have been a huge mistake.

"David."

"Just a backfire. Come on, hop on." His green eyes burned.

She stepped back. Her hand still held his. When did she grab it? "I can't. I'm sorry."

He stared at her for a moment and then pulled away and started his bike. Every emotion fled from his face with each rev of the motor. "Fine. I'll call you tomorrow."

Maggie held a hand over her fluttering heart. Something was so wrong with this. What changed? "I can call you later tonight."

He shook his head and then slammed the helmet down onto it, the strap dangling below his chin. "No need. I won't be home until late. See ya, Margaret Allison." He gave her one last hard look and then backed away.

She blinked against the spray of rocks from the motorcycle's tires. Tears pricked her eyelids. What had just happened? What was wrong with David? Was the change in him because she wouldn't stay the night with him? She took a deep breath.

"You're a big girl, Maggie." She kicked a rock with a foot and frowned. The man could make her all gooey inside and then, in a flash, turn cold like an arctic iceberg.

"Maggie! There you are." Sarah's voice shouted from the gates. Dennis and Sophie trailed behind her, laughing.

She heaved another sigh and slapped at a mosquito that buzzed her neck. Her fingers caressed the spot where David's fingers had been. The heat from his touch still lingered, even though a cold wind blew across the parking lot.

Oh, Lord, be with him tonight. Something beyond her understanding churned within him.

CHAPTER 13

D avid revved the Harley even higher. Reckless? Who cared? The wind rushed past him. His initial anger rode its wake. Jeremy caused this. Whether that was an exaggeration or not, he didn't care. Maggie was the problem too. Maggie with her beguiling eyes and long, soft tresses. He didn't need either of them.

His arms strained to control the bike as he flew around the curve. The Mudslide was half a mile down the road. His body craved its namesake drink. How many days had he denied himself a taste? Too many. Now, thanks to a brother and a woman, he was only yards away from paying Jim Beam a call.

Gravel kicked up as he rode the bike into the parking lot. Here on the edge of town, everything had a different feel. Sunset came sooner. The hush of night fell quicker.

David dismounted and noticed Sam's truck. He grinned. Alright, things were better. Drinking buddies were here. He hurried to the door. Inside the not-at-all-swanky bar, cigarette smoke hung like a thin veil in the air. The proprietors had an old style jukebox in the corner, and it played a Hank Williams Jr. song. He grimaced. Surely there was more than country on that box.

At some of the tables, men, faces savaged by booze and time, laughed and drank with women sporting caked-on make-up.

In dark corners, loners with haunted looks sipped drinks. Then there were people like him. They joked, laughed, and played pool. Here for a good time.

He stopped at the bar. "Sandy, give me a Mississippi Mudslide with a Jim chaser."

He needed his elixir of forgetfulness. Sandy placed the small drink in front of him, and he downed it in two gulps. He didn't know which went to his head first, the vodka or the Kahlua. The shot glass of Jim Beam, smooth, velvet liquid, flowed into his body. He laid the bills on the bar and threaded his way through the tables. Sam and Toby circled the pool table, throwing the balls out of the pockets and onto the table's top. They looked up and shouted.

"David, man! You made it."

David removed his jacket and flung it over a nearby stool. "Only live once, right?"

"Yeah, right." Sam handed him the pool stick.

Toby laughed and racked the balls. "She turned you down, didn't she?"

"Shut up. Here." He gave Sam twenty bucks. "Get us some beer. Make it good." David took the blue chalk cube and rubbed the cue tip. "My break?"

Toby held out his hands. "Go for it."

Anger, hurt, betrayal, and shame all wrapped in a neat little wad traveled down David's arm and into the pool stick. With a loud crack, the balls scattered across the green felt. Three stripes and a solid flew in the pockets.

"Stripes." How fitting.

On his next shot, the thirteen ball missed by an inch, and he stood away from the table as Toby gauged his own move. Sam returned with the beer.

David smiled. The mellow taste of the lager filled his mouth. Sweet nectar. Before long the buzz would be there. That comfortable old friend.

Within minutes, he and Toby had the table down to just the eight ball. Toby knocked it into the side pocket, and another game began.

An hour and four beers later, with a crowd ringing their table, David tapped the corner pocket with his stick. "Twelve ball, corner."

"Long shot, David." Sam leaned against his stick. He nudged Toby, who stood, droopy-eyed, by the wall. "Toby, wake up, man. It'll be your turn soon."

David grinned and leaned down to line up his shot.

The stick slid smoothly through his fingers and connected with the cue ball. It rolled down the length of the table, tapped the twelve ball lightly against the side, and the purple striped ball fell into the pocket. Now the eight ball taunted him.

The crowd clapped. David looked up. A dark-haired temptress along the edge of the crowd, her tongue playing with the straw in her drink, stared at him. She gave a small wink in his direction. He smiled. Her attire left nothing to the imagination. Her shirt, little more than a bandana, clung to her. She wore shorts that would have put Daisy Duke's to shame.

"David! You going to shoot or drool over her, man?"

David rapped Sam on his side with the stick. "Eight ball, side pocket."

"No way."

A soft voice added to theirs. "Side bet? You buy a round of drinks? Something to make it fun?"

David and Sam turned to the woman. Even the half-drunk Toby lifted his head. She wove her way to them, teetering on extremely high heels. A hint of musk, a pleasant and heady perfume, floated through the air and tickled David's nose. She stopped short of their side of the table.

"Deal." Without a thought the words left his mouth. "I miss, I buy."

Sam shook his head and backed up to give David room. "You're an idiot."

"Well, either way, I'll still get what I want." He gave the woman, and her not-so-hidden promises, one last look and then bent down. To do this shot, he needed to bank the cue ball. The stick angled ever so slightly, and David aimed at the top right of the ball.

Maybe it was the beer. Maybe it was the intoxicating perfume. Maybe he just didn't care if he lost, but the cue ball banked the far side, came back toward him, and tapped the eight ball. The lone black ball stopped on the edge of the side pocket.

Sam hooted and took the easy shot. The ball fell into the side pocket.

The crowd laughed, clapped, and started to disperse. The woman grazed her eyes over David and sashayed back to the bar.

Sam laid the stick on the table. "I think I need to get Toby home."

David punched Toby in the shoulder. The burly man barely opened his eyes and let out a belch. "Need help?" he asked Sam.

"Nah. Used to it, man." Sam grabbed one of Toby's arms and slung it over his shoulder.

Ignoring Sam's comment, David shrugged on his jacket and took Toby's other arm. Together they hoisted the man to his feet.

"Yo, dudes. Wha' ya doin'?" Toby shuffled his feet in step with theirs.

"Takin' you home, man."

"Who 'on?"

"Y'all did." David dragged Toby through the bar. "Supposed to buy drinks, but looks like it's a rain check for y'all."

"Should be a rain check for you." Sam kicked the door open with his booted foot.

Together they half dragged, half carried the drunken Toby to Sam's truck. David grabbed the door handle and opened the side door. It was harder hoisting Toby into the truck than dragging him out of the bar. Toby groaned and curled up in the seat.

"I'll see you 'morrow."

"I meant it, David. You're wasted, man."

David spread his hands opened. "Four beers ain't nothing. 'Sides–" He looked at the door. The dark beauty leaned against the frame. "–I got a promise to collect."

"Like I said. Idiot." Sam jumped into his truck. "See ya later, man. Stay safe."

David slapped the hood as he walked by, trying to keep his feet from stumbling, and threw a wave. "See ya."

The woman pushed away from the door frame as he approached. The perfume seemed stronger and her eyes, darker. There were promises hidden in there. Her lilting voice, smooth as Jim Beam, met him. "Buy that drink now?"

David wrapped his arm about her waist and pulled her to him. "What would you like?" He led her to the bar, arm still around her, thumb stroking the bare skin.

He sat down, and she perched next to him, her long legs crossed. David touched her bare knee, caressing the soft skin. She didn't slap him away.

She leaned forward, and David glimpsed her body underneath that itsy-bitsy fabric. "How strong are you?"

"Hmm?" He tore his gaze away from her chest. "How strong you need me to be?"

She smiled. Her teeth gleamed as she spoke. Vampire. One bite on the neck, that was all. He would want that. "There's a drink that I like. You want to know the name?"

"What?" He leaned in closer. "Something exotic?" He traced her collarbone with a fingertip. She didn't push his hand away. Her head arched back a little, and he nuzzled her neck. Her fingers ran back and forth across his chest. The manicured nails dug in with each pass.

"Something strong." She pulled back and rapped her knuckles on the bar top. Sandy moseyed over. "Four Spreaders."

David chuckled. "I know that drink. Bring it on, baby." A hot thirst dried his mouth as the drinks were poured, equal parts rum, tequila, gin, and vodka.

Their glasses clinked and in one gulp, the fiery hot liquid slid down his throat. His head exploded in a clouded daze. His face flushed. His body melted. Man, that stuff hit hard.

David smiled. "Tell me your name."

"Tammy." Her voice slurred the words, or was that his hearing? She leaned closer, and David felt the heat from her body.

He half stood and pulled her closer. "One more, yeah?"

"Well, I ordered four. It gets me going."

"I bet." David handed her the drink, and he downed another. He welcomed the sensation. Dante's inferno. His descent into sin and pleasure was forthcoming. Her arms snaked around his neck.

"I tol' you it gets me goin'." Her slurred words barely registered.

David fell into her dark eyes and their forbidden delights. No quitting now. Her red lips parted. Someone had changed the songs on the jukebox, and he dimly acknowledged the new song, the J. Geils Band singing *Rage in the Cage*. Yeah, that was him tonight, a rage rearing to be loosed.

His lips barely touched hers. Soon he'd have–

A hand landed on his shoulder and propelled him back. He crashed into the stools.

A gravelly voice echoed in the bar. "Tammy!"

David staggered against the effects of the push and the booze, aware of people standing and leaving. Sandy pulled out his cell phone.

"I ain't yours anymore, Roger." She swayed on her heels and gripped the bar for support.

David pushed one of the stools out of the way. No one was going to deny him his pleasure tonight. He'd had enough of that. He sidled between the bearded, tattooed man and Tammy. The guy was a bulky mass of fat and muscle. Tammy pressed herself against David's back, her hands clutching at his biceps through his jacket.

"Go away. Woman says she don't want ya." David stood nose to chin with the man, daring him.

"Out of my way, little man. She belongs to me. She leaves, you don't get messed up." He pressed himself closer.

David pushed back and shrugged off Tammy's hands. "She ain't goin'."

"Listen. She's my woman. I say she leaves. And you get to live."

Tammy pressed against him, her hands grabbing his back pockets. David smiled. "And I said she don't wanna go."

The tattooed man stepped forward, fist cocked. Her hands left his body.

"No. I'll go." Tammy slid from behind him.

David laughed. Did she think he was stupid? She gave up way too easily. He turned, grabbed her wrist, and yanked his wallet from her closed fist.

"No country bumpkin here, darlin'." He slipped the wallet into his jacket pocket.

She glared at him. He snarled. Did she think she would get away from him? He grabbed a handful of her hair and yanked. His lips met her mouth in a rough kiss. Like he said, no one was going to deny him his pleasure.

A fist slammed into him and sent him into the bar. The edge struck him above his kidneys. David whirled. Tammy fled out the door, and the tattooed man heaved another strike at him. David dodged. With a maniacal laugh, he grabbed a mug from the bar and slammed it across the man's face. Like a bull, Roger shrugged it off and glared at David.

Not good. David reached down, pulled out his pocket knife and flicked open the blade. They circled once, and David motioned to him. "Let's go, wimpy boy."

It started. He jumped back from the fist and slashed with his knife, feeling it slice through the skin. Then a vise grip latched onto his wrist and the knife hit the floor. David flew through the air. He lost his breath as he landed on a table. He rolled off and faced Roger again. The guy's booted foot sent the knife skittering along the boards and out of sight.

"Lost your toy, little boy."

David snarled and sent a kick into that fat gut, feeling his foot sink between the folds. Pleasure at seeing the man double over coursed through David's body. He drove his knee up. Cartilage crunched as it connected with the man's nose. David's elbow came down onto the neck. Then he was flying again. His head hit the support beam, and stars flashed before him.

A lead block drove itself into his stomach. Rancid tobacco breath hit him in the face. David spat at Roger and lashed out with his head, connecting with a brick wall of flesh. Both of them dropped to the floor. Oh, that was stupid.

David staggered up and landed a fist into the guy's face. Blood spurted. A glancing blow struck David across the temple, and he stumbled back a little. He wasn't going down that easy. He felt blood dribble from his own nose and swiped at it.

The man's breathing was heavy, but he roared and charged. David grabbed a chair and swung. His shoulders vibrated as it slammed into Roger's chest. Then David was on the floor. He clawed away and stood. Roger advanced on him, and David tackled him. Both of them hit the floor, and he took his chance to drive his fist into that bearded face. Once. Twice. Then an anvil had him sliding under a table.

David enjoyed the mayhem. Come what may. This was better than false promises. Rage fueled him.

———————

"J forty-nine, we got a report of a disturbance at Mudslide Bar on Donaldson Road." Dispatch broke Jeremy's silent contemplation of his brother as he patrolled his route. So many things did not add up.

He grabbed his mike. "Copy that, dispatch. Radio J forty-three. Probably another bar fight."

"Copy, forty-nine."

Jeremy hit his lights and drove through a red light. And here he thought tonight was going to be quiet. Within minutes, he arrived at The Mudslide. Baers pulled in right behind him.

He greeted the big man as he climbed out of the car. "Same old stuff. I hate this kind of night."

Baers grunted and shrugged into his vest. "You're telling me. Festival night, what did you expect? At least most already left the bar."

People milled outside, drinks and beers in hand, as they waited for Jeremy and Baers to approach. Crashes sounded from inside as they got closer. Glass shattered, and a foul curse echoed.

Baers chuckled. "I think that would be physically impossible."

Jeremy removed his baton. He reached for the door when someone in the crowd moved, and the gleaming red of a Harley caught his eye. His eyes narrowed, and he nudged Baers. "We got trouble. David's in there."

Baers grimaced. "Want me to call Markston in?"

A bottle crashed through the busted window, narrowly missing Jeremy's head, and David's voice followed. How many curses could his brother string together? "No. Not enough time. I'll take David down."

Baers grabbed the door and threw it open. The aftermath of a bomb greeted them. Tables were overturned, bar stools lay on their sides, some shattered. A spider-webbed pattern cracked the glass.

Eagles' *Witchy Woman* played in contradiction to the scene. The only participants to the bomb aftermath party were David, jacket torn and hanging from his shoulders, and a large, tattooed man. Blood dripped from their faces. Grime clung to their clothes.

Jeremy winced as he watched his brother crash into the wall behind the bar. He and Baers hurried inside. Baers bee-lined for the other guy. David popped up with a baseball bat in his hands, vaulted the bar, and swung at the man. The guy ducked, and the bat splintered against the bar's edge.

Tattoo man dove at David. Baers reached the man, threw him against the bar, and pinned his arms. Jeremy grabbed David's shoulder before his brother could deliver another swing. He whirled David around, ducked his punch, and grabbed his brother's wrist. The shattered bat clattered to the floor.

He forced David's arm up behind his back and pushed him down onto the floor with his other hand on the back of David's neck.

David cried out and delivered a kick to Jeremy's shins as he went down. Jeremy lost his grip as his brother bounced away.

David hurled a curse and dove.

Jeremy took the hit and wrapped his arms around David's waist as his brother tackled him to the peanut strewn floor. Nut shells crunched underneath him and dug into his neck, but he didn't let go. Punches to his side connected against his vest. He grabbed David around the neck and pulled him over onto his back. Now elbows jabbed down upon him. Jeremy managed to throw a leg over David's and rolled over, pinning David underneath him, his knee digging into David's kidney.

David's breath, vile and drenched in alcohol, stirred the shells and sent them skittering away. Jeremy yanked David's arms behind him and slapped the cuffs on. He felt the bunched muscles underneath him relax.

He let up from his hold and slid to the side. David flipped over and aimed a scissor kick at his head. Jeremy ducked. Blasted viper.

Shells dug into his knees. He pulled out his baton, but his brother suddenly stopped and rolled over to his side. Jeremy sighed in relief and leaned over him. David moaned quietly. Tears ran down David's nose and dotted the floor.

What made him stop?

He scooted closer to his brother, careful of another viper attack, and rested a hand on David's head. David didn't move.

"Got him, Jer?"

Jeremy glanced at Baers. He had the tattooed guy standing, cuffed, and pressed against one of the support beams of the building. "Yeah. Go ahead and take him to the car. I'll wait."

Baers nodded and prodded the man out the door. Jeremy returned his gaze to his brother lying next to him, drunk, broken, and vulnerable. "What happened to you, David?"

Jeremy brought his clenched hand to his mouth and took a deep breath. He fought for control as his body shook. He tried to push his anger aside. Somewhere inside him was that cold void he needed.

David turned his face further into the peanut shells, his chest heaving. When Baers returned, he helped Jeremy lift his brother to his feet. David remained silent, head down. Whatever his brother was thinking, Jeremy didn't care to know. Right now, he had to do his job. Not worry about his little brother.

Of the people who milled outside earlier, few remained to watch the show. The bar manager, his balding head glistening in the blue light from the cars, yelled to everyone that the bar was closed for the night.

Baers opened the back door of Jeremy's squad car. David collapsed on the seat. He refused to meet Jeremy's eyes.

Baers turned to Jeremy. "You going to book him?"

"I should." He motioned to the bar manager. "Mr. James, come here, please."

Mr. James approached. "Jeremy, you should know that there was a woman involved."

Baers pulled out his notebook. "Describe her."

"Small build, black hair, scantily dressed. Her heels were red, I think. She came on pretty strong to David. Then the big guy there came in. Yelled at her. Next thing I know, he and David were tied into each other. She high-tailed it out of there."

Jeremy pointed to the man who scowled at them from the back of Baers' car. "You seen him before?"

"No. He just came in while David was at the bar."

"How long was David here?"

"About two hours or so. He and his buddies were playing pool. The woman was there. Then Sam and Toby left. David came back inside, and Sandy poured them some drinks."

Baers closed his notebook and looked at Mr. James. "You may press formal charges tomorrow morning."

Mr. James regarded Jeremy and peeked inside the squad car at David, curled up on the seat. "I should, but I won't." He turned back to Jeremy. "Your brother needs help."

Jeremy shook his head. He wasn't getting in on this, no way. What his brother needed was another beating.

Mr. James' hand rested on Jeremy's arm. "I've known you and your brother since y'all were little tykes. Something is eating at your brother, and the bottle ain't gonna help him."

Jeremy looked away from the man's stare. Sometimes he hated living in a small town. Too many people knew you. Knew your business. "I ain't my brother's keeper, Mr. James."

The man shrugged and turned to walk away. He took a couple of steps and glanced back at Jeremy. "If I press charges, you know David will probably have to do time. But if he agrees to rebuild what he broke, I'll forget the whole thing." He shuffled toward the bar, calling back over his shoulder, "I'll keep his bike safe till he repairs my bar."

If he agrees to rebuild what he broke? Now, that was a double whammy. He leaned against the car, heard a soft moan from the seat, and prayed to God that David didn't puke back there.

Jeremy looked at Baers. "What do you think?"

Baers, arms crossed, shrugged. "The man's right. Throw him in the cell for the night, let him sleep it off."

Jeremy sighed, pushed away from the car, and scowled at Baers, at his brother, at the bar. "Absolutely unbelievable." He rounded the car and jerked open the door. "Take that scumbag in and book him for destruction of property and run for priors."

"What are you going to do with David?"

Jeremy hesitated and refused to look back at his brother. "Throw him in the cell and let him sleep it off. I'll pick him up in the morning."

"Then?"

"I'll take care of him, one way or another." Jeremy slid into the seat and slammed his door shut. He grabbed his mike and called in. "Dispatch, J forty-nine 10-24 and en route to the station."

He revved his motor and tore out of the parking lot. His anger had no focus. It bounced from his drunken brother in the backseat, to his situation at the moment, to the truth he would have to reveal to his family, to the reason this all started in the first place which came right back to his drunken brother in the backseat.

Jeremy cursed and drove.

CHAPTER 14

Morning hit him like a sledgehammer. David clutched at his stomach and rolled over. His matted eyes refused to open fully. His head pounded through the cobwebs. He managed to push to his feet and stumble to the sink. His fingers fumbled with the knob, but finally cold water splashed down into the metal basin.

He dunked his head under the flow and rinsed the foulness out of his mouth. His stomach heaved, but he fought it back. He reached for the towel hanging on the holder. It wasn't there. He froze.

Oh, man. He turned and surveyed his surroundings. Cot. Metal sink. Metal toilet. Bars. He wiped his face with his grimy shirt tail, made use of the toilet, and lowered his aching body to the mattress, back against the wall.

Events from last night resurfaced. The pleasure seeking. The pain. The fight. The booze. His brother's face. He brought his knees up and propped his forehead on crossed arms. Shame oozed over him. Now Jeremy knew his evil secret.

His stomach turned. His head thumped. A rattle at the cell door brought his head up. He stared at the familiar face. Jeremy waited for Markston to insert the key and slide the door open.

"Thanks," Jeremy said to the officer.

"No problem. Captain said to go out the side door. More privacy."

David watched wide-eyed, or at least as wide-eyed as he could get. They weren't going to charge him? Jeremy propped against the bars, his ankles crossed, and regarded David for long seconds.

David snarled, "Just get it over with."

Jeremy sighed and stepped into the cell, gloved hand outstretched. "Come on. Let's get you out of here."

David shrugged off his brother's offer of help and stumbled to his feet. His head swirled about, the room tumbled, and he tipped over with it.

Jeremy's hands grabbed him and righted his body. "Come on, stop being a stubborn jackass. Let me at least help you out to the car."

David lost his willpower to fight. Again, shame descended on him. Together they stumbled out into the bright morning light. David groaned and covered his eyes. Why did God have to be so cruel? Why couldn't it have been a cloudy day?

Jeremy fumbled with the car's passenger door. David eased inside. He pulled off his jacket and threw it onto the back seat. The foul odor of his shirt wafted up to his nose, and he fought another wave of nausea.

The driver's door opened. Jeremy slid into the seat. He started the car, and the air conditioner blasted cold air. David sighed and relaxed. That helped.

"Here. Change your shirt."

David looked down at the shirt Jeremy threw in his lap. It was a plain white t-shirt, and it was clean. David peeled off his dirty one, grimaced at the smell of his body, and pulled the clean one on. This was just wrong. He felt too dirty to wear something so clean.

Jeremy handed him a pair of sunglasses, and without a word, David slid them on. Better and better. Now he could hide behind the dark lenses. Keep the world out.

Jeremy started to back up, but slammed the car back into park. David looked over at him. His brother stared straight ahead, muscles working in his jaw.

"How long?"

"What?" He turned his gaze out the passenger window and brought his hands to his stomach. It was flipping on him again.

"You know what I mean. How long have you been like this?" Jeremy rested his hands on the steering wheel. "Baers ran you. You had two DUIs in St. Louis, David."

David sunk into his seat. His stomach knotted and unknotted. His heart slammed against him. "Two and a half years."

Jeremy sighed and shut his eyes.

How many times was his brother going to do that? Sighing was worse than yelling, than beating the ever-loving . . . His thoughts faltered. Jeremy was disappointed in him. He pitied him.

David snarled and turned on his brother. "I don't–"

Jeremy's hand lashed out and slammed David against the car door. The quickness of Jeremy's strike left him speechless.

"Just shut up. I don't want to hear it. No excuses. No nothing." Jeremy rammed the gear into reverse and peeled out of the parking spot. The car jostled to an abrupt stop, and then they were moving forward.

David sunk further down into his seat. Now that they were moving, even the cold air blasting on him didn't make his stomach stop quivering.

"And I will knock your head in if you puke in Sarah's car."

David closed his eyes and leaned against the head rest. Let the world fall in on him. Let him die now.

Jeremy drove in silence. The drone of the air conditioner filled the car. David contemplated turning on the radio, but his head couldn't take another verbal lash. Better to let Jeremy cool a bit.

David looked out the window. This wasn't the way to his apartment. Within a few moments, Jack's Express Café loomed before him. He didn't want people around him, and his brother just brought him to the middle of the square. Jeremy shut off the car, got out, and slammed the door.

Pain from the jolt stabbed him through his head. Jeremy could wait forever out there in the sun. He was not getting out of the car. The door jerked open, and Jeremy leaned against the car's frame.

He spoke slowly. A muscle twitched at his jaw. "You can buck up and get out, or I can drag you out and taser your sorry butt."

David got out.

He kept his hands close to his convulsing stomach. He glanced around and sought out Maggie's shop. She would be there tomorrow, pricing items, selling clothes. Happy little shop day.

He grimaced as Jeremy jabbed him between his shoulder blades and sent him staggering forward.

"Walk."

David walked.

The bell above the door jingled. Jeremy nudged him farther in, this time with a gentler push. Smells assaulted him. Bacon, sausage, eggs, and coffee. Oh, Lord, help him. He couldn't fight it this time. He turned and rushed toward the restroom, ignoring the looks from a couple of Sunday morning patrons.

He shoved at the door, fell to his knees in the first stall, and vomited stomach acid into the toilet. The sunglasses clattered to the floor as his stomach convulsed and heaved. Tears blurred his vision, and spittle hung in strands from his lips.

The door creaked open. Water ran in one of the sinks. His stomach dry heaved again.

A wet brown paper towel slapped against his mouth. Jeremy knelt behind him and pulled him back into his arms. David leaned his back against his brother's chest and gulped in air. The towel mopped his face.

"Stop." David grabbed the towel. "I can do it. I'm not a baby."

Jeremy grabbed him under his arms. David stood on wobbly knees and nonexistent feet. He staggered to the sink. His forearms against the cool porcelain held him upright.

His brother never said a word. He just turned on the water and helped David wash his face. He gave him back the sunglasses, held the door open, and led him to a booth in the back corner of the cafe.

David eased his sore and sick body down onto the soft, blue vinyl cushion. It wasn't a waitress who came to the booth to take the order. Jack Niemeyer approached.

"Morning, Jer. What'll it be?"

"Two coffees. Extra strong this morning, Jack. Bacon, eggs, and gravy biscuits for me. Soft scrambled eggs and toast for David."

Jack nodded. "I'll see to it. Rough night?"

Jack's gaze burned him, but he refused to look up. His brother's pity was one thing, but someone else's was another.

"Yeah. You can say that."

David ignored his brother and the silence that loomed between them. He pinched the bridge of his nose. Pressure pushed at his eyes.

The bell jingled again, and Jack's voice greeted another customer. The cafe's sounds mingled. The cash register pinged, silverware clattered, indistinct voices murmured. The sounds collided with the drumming pulse inside his head. He had to get out!

David pushed up out of the booth, but Jeremy's hands clamped down on his wrists, forcing him back into the booth. "Sit."

His hands balled underneath his brother's, but he sat. Jeremy let go. Two mugs of coffee appeared. When did Jack arrive?

Jack placed a small coffee pot at the edge of the table. "Here's the carafe. Looks like your brother could use it."

David jerked his head up, and the retort on the tip of his tongue slid back down his throat. Jack's face didn't show him pity. It didn't show him disappointment. It showed understanding.

He swallowed past the lump. "Thanks."

Jack nodded and spoke to Jeremy. "Your plates will be out soon. Let me know if there is anything else you need, okay?"

David's hand shook as he brought the coffee to his lips. The liquid was hot, but not too hot that he couldn't swallow. He grimaced. The drink could stand without a cup. He forced another swallow down.

He had to admit, it did help. His stomach slowly uncoiled itself. His headache receded a bit at a time. When their plates arrived, little was said as they ate.

Jeremy shoveled food into his mouth, while David took small bites. Fear of his stomach rebelling and puking up egg kept him eating at a slower pace. After a while, he drained his coffee cup and pushed away his plate.

Jeremy never said a word other than to thank Jack for the breakfast and ask for more coffee. Another small pot of brew appeared. Inquisition time arrived.

His brother set his cup down and propped on his elbows. His blue eyes pierced him. "When did you realize you had a problem?"

David sighed and leaned back. "After my second DUI. I tried to quit."

"David, you and I both know you can't do this on your own."

"Why do you think I came back?" David clenched and un-clenched his hands as they rested on the table. "I knew if I stayed in St. Louis, I would lose myself. Or worse, kill someone the next time."

Jeremy shook his head. "Just coming back home doesn't help you. You need to talk it out, go to meetings. Get professional help."

David threw a hard curse at his brother.

Jeremy smirked. "I wouldn't enjoy it, little brother. And frankly, neither would you."

David snarled. "If I get professional help, I will be suspended from the job."

"Thomas knows?"

David pushed at his saucer. "I think he suspects, but I haven't been drunk, per se, until last night."

Jeremy poured some more coffee into their cups. "What threw you over the edge last night?"

"You really want to know?" David gave a harsh laugh. "You, dear brother. You and your sanctimonious attitude."

A small bit of glee blossomed within him as Jeremy choked on his coffee.

"What?"

"You have to be so much better. Obey the rules. Be a pillar of goodness. Jeremy the brave, Jeremy the great. Jeremy the hero." David clamped his mouth shut. He spoke too much. Revealed too much.

"I didn't ask for the award, David." Jeremy glanced around him, his jaw at work again.

David half wished his brother would clamp his jaw so tight it would never open again. "You sure didn't refuse it. An award for something you didn't do."

"Why should I refuse it? I've worked hard for it. I spent two years helping the detectives with that case. But you wouldn't know that, would you?" Jeremy shook his head. "It's been three years since you left. You came back, but you aren't the same. You're an alcoholic. You're a womanizer. Seriously? You would rather hole up with some tramp? What about Maggie? Did you think about her?"

David stood. He fought the impulse to throw the coffee in his brother's face. Instead he leaned down and whispered. "Better to be a whoremonger and alcoholic than a coward and a liar."

He left Jeremy sitting there with a shocked expression. Yeah. Let him feel shocked that someone would tell him the truth. As he pushed out of the café, his stomach tried to revolt against the food. A part of him whispered that what he said wasn't true, and he knew it. David pushed that thought away.

He stopped short on the sidewalk and closed his eyes. Just great.

Jeremy drove him here. He didn't have a ride. He lived at least five miles away from downtown. Better start walking now. He burrowed his hands into his pockets and turned. Jeremy stood there, leaning against the parking meter.

Jeremy walked to the car and opened the passenger door. Again, shame descended upon him. David ignored his brother, slid into the car, and pulled the door closed.

Jeremy rounded the vehicle and settled into the driver's seat. David couldn't look at him. Half of him wanted to apologize for the words, guilt eating at him, and the other half wanted to hurl more curses at him.

In silence, Jeremy drove David across town to the small apartment building. He pulled into the parking garage.

David didn't move. What more could be said? What more could be done?

Jeremy removed his gloves and threw them on the dashboard. About time he removed those gloves. Then he reached into the back and grabbed David's filthy jacket and shirt.

"Look. Right now isn't a good time to talk. You're angry. I'm sure as–" Jeremy stopped and sighed. "Just go sleep. I'll be here later this afternoon. Church lets out soon."

"What?" David sneered at his brother. What was he planning? He didn't need anyone.

"You don't have many choices right now. I will be here to help you pack. You're moving back in with Mom and Dad. And you will tell them that you are an alcoholic, and you need help."

Jeremy turned his gaze to him, and David clamped his mouth shut against the curse and retort. His brother's eyes were a hard, steely blue.

"If you don't want my help, then you will need Dad's. Look, just go. Get inside. Right now I can't stand the sight of you. And to think I skipped church for you."

Pain hit David. He blinked. Never had his brother rejected him. Was this how it felt when he said it to Jeremy? He always had his brother, didn't he?

His heart closed in on itself. Fine. He could be that way, if he wanted. No one needed Jeremy, especially David.

"Fine."

His brother passed him his clothes. David snatched them from Jeremy's hand, and the pink, puckered scars along his brother's palm stared up at him. Old burn scars.

CHAPTER 15

David stood by the living room window, looking out across the front yard. A breeze blew loose a few leaves from the massive oak tree guarding the driveway. They followed the breeze and came to rest against the windshield of Marty's Navigator.

Jeremy had called them. Family intervention time. David frowned. The last family intervention had been five years ago when Darlene suffered a bad bout of depression. His gaze focused on the reflections in the window.

His mom set a tray of drinks on the coffee table. Marty and Darlene sat on the couch, waiting. Sarah sat in the big easy chair–his chair–legs crossed, her foot bouncing up and down in the air. Dad and Jeremy were somewhere out back. At times he could hear them arguing.

His mom moved. She watched him, brow furrowed. He'd disappointed her again.

He shoved clenched fists into his front pockets. Why couldn't his brother just leave well enough alone? He would have been fine at his apartment. Instead, Jeremy forced him to come here. A faint pain flared in his wrist where Jeremy had twisted his arm to make him get into the truck.

The back door slammed. David stared at the reflection of Jeremy as he stomped his way into the living room and plopped down on the sofa across from Marty and Darlene. His dad glared at Jeremy for a moment before turning his eyes in David's direction.

"Son, come sit down."

David refused to budge. He didn't want to do this. He didn't want to see their faces as he bared his sins.

His heart clenched, strangling the air from his lungs. It was better if he left. He bolted from the window, heading for the door, but ran into Marty's large form. His dad stood and barred his way to the kitchen and its back door escape.

Marty's gentle hand landed on his arm. "Come on. Sit down."

His choices were gone. Poof. Up in smoke.

Eyes downcast, he eased into the wingback that his mom loved. Stiff and overstuffed. Fitting. Stiff as a corpse and over-stuffed with anger and sin. Yeah. That was him.

"David?" His mom's voice broke through his thoughts. "You need some tea?"

His voice cracked. "No."

He leaned forward and propped his elbows on his knees, hiding his face in his hands. He couldn't do this. His shame was too great. What would they think of him? They would despise him, cast him away.

The rustle of thin pages dominated the room. His dad's voice resonated as words from the Bible surrounded them. "Come to Me, all you who labor and are heavy laden, and I will give you rest. Take My yoke upon you and learn from Me, for I am gentle and lowly in heart, and you will find rest for your souls. For My yoke is easy and My burden is light."

Dad's hand, strong and gentle, landed on his shoulder, squeezing it. "Lord, you tell us to cast our burdens upon thee. Today we come to you for David's sake. Help us understand this heavy burden my son carries. Help him to open up to us and to you. Guide us through this time of conflict. In your name we pray. Amen."

Amens flitted across the room.

David remained silent. His throat refused to allow the word to escape. A knot lodged midway, and no amount of swallowing would push it down.

His dad pulled up a chair from the dining room and sat beside him.

"David? Honey, we're here for you." His mom's soft voice drifted to him. "You want to tell us?"

He shook his head. His stomach flipped over inside. Something wet hit his hands. He brought his hands away from his face. Perfect. Tears. That was all he needed now. He rocked forward and pressed his forehead against clenched fists.

His dad's hand landed on his shoulder again. He stopped rocking. No matter what they wanted, he would not look up.

Jeremy cleared his throat. "I'll start, Mom."

Oh, yeah. Jeremy the Good. His dad's hand painfully squeezed his shoulder.

"We've been seeing the signs, but none of us recognized them. To put it simply, last night David was involved in a drunken bar fight. I threw him in a cell to sleep it off and had Baers run David's name through the system. It came back citing two DUIs in St. Louis. I asked him this morning how long he's been like this. He said two and half years."

His mom gasped.

"David?" His dad's hand moved to the back of his neck.

"What?" He forced the word out past a dry mouth. Wet eyes, but a dry mouth. How ironic.

"You need to tell us."

He started rocking again, pressing his fists against his eyes. Pain shot through his head. So much better than the pain in his heart. So much better than the turmoil that clenched his gut.

Soft hands grabbed his fists and forced them down. Darlene knelt in front of him. Her green eyes, bright with unshed tears, implored him.

"It's okay. You can tell us, little brother."

He shook his head. "I can't. I hate . . . I hate myself for being like this."

Her hand cupped his face. "No matter how hard it is to say it, you must."

"I can't look at you. Any of you. I don't want to see your revulsion at what I've become. What I've done."

One hand squeezed his neck. Another patted his hands. Would they still love him enough to touch him after they heard him speak?

David risked a glance at his mom. She sat beside Jeremy, her hand clasped in his. Another wave of anger rolled through him and just as quickly disappeared.

He nodded. "I have to, don't I?"

His dad's hand rubbed his neck. "Yes, Son."

David nodded again. Darlene leaned back and held both of his hands in hers. He raised his head and studied the wall across from him, his eyes traveling over the TV, the shelves of movies, and finally resting on the waterfall painting on the wall. *Living Waters* was the name of that lithograph. How he wished he could bask in that cool, refreshing water right now.

He pushed the words across his lips with a leaden tongue. "When I left, after–" his breath hitched. Darlene's hands tightened on his. "After Rebecca died, I thought moving away would help. But I found myself . . . I stopped going to church. Stopped talking to God. I . . ." He pushed Darlene away, jumped up, and retreated to the window. His hand flattened against the cool glass. "I started partying. It felt good. A couple of nights here. A couple of nights there."

He rested his head against his hand. The words, once started, wouldn't stop. "I found myself drinking. At first, it was just on weekends while out and about with the guys. Then I was having a drink every other night. Soon, it was every day."

Marty's hand touched his shoulder. David looked up at his brother-in-law. A small smile touched the man's ruddy face. "Come sit down."

He allowed Marty to lead him back to the chair. "It wasn't just the drinking. I–" His stomach threatened to revolt. He buried his hands in his hair, digging his fingernails in his scalp. "I . . . can't. I'm sorry. I can't say it."

Tears threatened to spill. He clamped his mouth shut. Oh, why? Why did he have to say it? Why couldn't it stay buried within?

His mom, with Sarah by her side, knelt in front of him. Marty's hand rested on Darlene's shoulder. Jeremy's hand rested on his mom's shoulder. Darlene and his mom each grabbed a hand, holding it. His dad reached over the back of the chair and settled his hands on David's shoulders.

David took a shaky, deep breath. "I started sleeping around. I don't even remember her name. I was drunk; she was drunk. I ran a red light. My first DUI. Five months later I was with . . . I think her name was Amber—or Ashley? Anyway, we were on the interstate coming back from the downtown clubs. I was lucky that I knew the patrol officer. My second DUI, and he helped me get off with only a fine. I knew then it was bad. If I stayed, no amount of pull would get me off. I could easily kill someone next time because I couldn't stop drinking.

"I still can't. I want it all the time." Tears coursed down his cheeks. He rocked forward. "I want to stop. I came home so I could stop . . ." He hung his head. He had to say it. "I'm . . . I'm an—"

He tore his hands away from his mom and Darlene. His fingernails bit into his palms. "I'm an alcoholic. And—" He looked at Jeremy. His eyes were impassive. "I need help."

———————

Jeremy heard Darlene draw in a shaky breath. "That's the first step, David. We're here for you."

David searched their eyes. His mom and Darlene cried. Marty pressed his lips together, chin quivering, and rubbed David's shoulder. David turned his gaze to Jeremy.

Jeremy stared back, cold and distrustful. David had bared his soul, yes, but Jeremy should have known that David wouldn't tell it all. The rest of the story floated there in his eyes.

David swiped at his tears and looked away. Jeremy scowled. His brother was a fine actor.

Darlene turned to their mom. "Marty and I will go to his apartment and finish collecting his things. Marty, you can discuss the situation with the landlord?"

"I can. No need to worry about that."

Mom perched on the arm of the chair, teetering on the skinny edge. Her arm looped over David's shoulders. "It'll be better for you here, sweetheart. We'll help you through this."

Jeremy shook his head. He opened his mouth, but his dad glared him into silence.

Pity David. Pamper David. Did they not realize they'd just been played by a player? He rose from the couch and stalked to the kitchen. Maybe what David said was true. Maybe he did want help, but his brother played on their sympathies to throw them off the trail.

He paced the kitchen, rubbing at his neck. He sent up a prayer. Help him stay calm. Help him keep his anger at bay. Curse the devil sneaking up on him like this.

"Jeremy?" His dad rounded the corner. "You okay?"

"No, Dad. No, I'm not." He pointed a finger at the living room where his family stood huddled around David. "You see that, but yet don't see. He's playing y'all for fools. He didn't tell you everything."

His dad's eyes flared. "He will in time. This is only a first step for him. It's going to be a long road ahead for your brother, and he's going to need everyone's help."

Jeremy stopped pacing. He raised his eyes to the fluorescent lights in the kitchen and traced their casing. He swallowed and took a deep breath. "I need a smoke."

"Not in here, you don't."

"I know that." His shoulders slumped, and he brought his eyes back to his dad. "You heard him say that he slept around. He would have done the same last night. He was getting cozy with some floozy at the bar."

"Which would have been the alcohol talking, not him." His dad sighed. "Whatever he's done, we can't hold that against him."

Jeremy huffed and started pacing again. Couldn't they see? His dumb—

He stopped and leaned his arms against the bar. "What about Maggie? I won't allow him to play with her heart. Sarah's cousin is too vulnerable for him to mess around with."

Sarah's voice spoke from around the corner. "Maggie's not a little girl, Jeremy. She's not Sophie. She can decide for herself what to do with David. I believe they're both good for each other." She walked into the kitchen and stood beside him. "Let them take care of themselves. No reason for us to interfere."

"Sarah, honey," Jeremy took her hands in his, "he's playing everyone for a fool. You think he wants to stop drinking or whoring around?"

His dad's voice bellowed. "Yes. He does. And don't you dare condemn him for his actions. No sin is above another."

Jeremy flushed under his father's angry gaze. He raised his lips in a snarl and shook his head. "Fine. If y'all want to believe him, go ahead." He looked up and met David's eyes.

His brother stood at the entrance. His face, void of all color save the bruises from last night, stared at him. David's chest heaved a couple of times.

"I'm not my brother's keeper, Dad." Jeremy watched the pain shoot through David's eyes before a burning anger replaced it.

"Y'all might believe him. But I won't until I actually see him trying."

"That's fine, big brother." Sarah and his dad whirled around at David's voice. "Be a doubting Thomas all you want to. I don't need you, anyway." He turned away and approached the bar. "Dad, I need my truck keys. I'm heading over to Bro. Johnny's."

His dad reached into the rosy, glass fruit bowl that held everything but fruit. The keys jangled as he held them out.

"Thank you. I've got my phone." He turned but then stopped.

Jeremy met his scathing look with one of his own. He knew his brother better than the family did. How many secrets bound them together? His brother would screw up big time one of these days.

Anger mingled with pain in David's eyes before he turned to the hat tree and grabbed a baseball cap. The door shut quietly as he left.

Jeremy sighed as the rumble of David's rattletrap thundered away.

"Sit."

"What?" Jeremy narrowed his eyes at his dad. Sarah pushed at him.

He sat on the bar stool.

His dad placed his Bible on the bar and opened it. "I know you don't think you need to be your brother's keeper, but I want you to listen to a couple of stories. We'll start with Cain and Abel, then Jacob and Esau, and then Joseph."

"I know those stories, Dad." Jeremy started to stand, but Sarah pushed him back down.

"Jeremy, you're angry with David. You need to handle it so we can all help him." She sat beside him and grabbed his hand. "Go ahead, Dad."

Jeremy dropped his head to the bar. Kill him now. He was way too old for Bible school.

———————————

"Miss Maggie, I can't find the ball anywhere." Poppy stuck her head around the corner of the kitchen.

Maggie retrieved another bowl from the dishwasher and placed it in the cabinet. "Did you look outside near the gnomes?"

Poppy ran to her side. Her eyes nearly popped out of her head from her wide-eyed expression. "Miss Maggie, you know I don't go near those things. They stare at me."

Maggie laughed and shut the dishwasher. She draped the hand towel over the sink's edge. "Go on outside, and I'll be out in a minute to help you. And make sure you feed and water the cats."

"Okay." The little girl sprinted out of the kitchen. The screen door clanged closed.

Maggie rubbed at the back of her neck, trying to work out the tension. Her muscles refused to unknot. One horrible night thinking about that bad boy brother, and look what she had to deal with. Muscles that refused to loosen. And why, oh why, did she always gravitate to the men with bad boy attitudes?

She collected the magazines off the table and dumped them in the wicker basket by the couch. Poppy loved looking at the fashion magazines.

Oh, what she would give for just a small amount of time to herself. After picking up Poppy this morning, she had been on the move nonstop, but at least it kept her mind off David. She growled. Almost kept her mind off David. There she went again, thinking of him.

"Oh, flipping monkey tails." She stuffed the throw blanket back into its corner on the couch to hide the rip Samson put there. She really needed to get that cat de-clawed.

Poppy flew into the living room. "I found it, Miss Maggie. Papa Johnny said to look on the carport, and there it was. Ready to go out yet?"

"In a moment, Poppy. Let me straighten the house. You can help by taking yours and Papa Johnny's shoes and putting them in the shoe box by the door."

"Okay."

Maggie smiled as Poppy picked up her father's shoes, holding them away from her with a forefinger and thumb while pinching her nose with her other hand. She didn't blame Poppy in the slightest. Her father's garden shoes were rough on the nose. She did it herself whenever Dad wasn't around.

Maggie stacked the devotional books on the coffee table and replaced her father's ministry Bible, reinserting the bookmark. She stood and looked around. "Well, Poppy, I think we finished the chores. What say we head on out to the koi pond?"

"But, I thought we were going to play ball?"

Maggie sighed. "Okay. I just thought we could relax a little around the pond, tease the fish, and all."

Poppy's eyes lit up. "Tease the fish?"

"Oh, yeah." Maggie walked to the china cabinet that dominated the living room's corner. She opened the bottom drawer and pulled out a small bag of fish food pellets. "You drop these in a little at a time around the pond and watch the fish swim in circles. It's quite funny when you get them to go under the little waterfall."

Poppy clapped her hands together. "Yeah, let's do that, please?"

Maggie shut the cabinet's door as the doorbell rang. She frowned. She hadn't heard a vehicle approach. "Go on out back while I see who's here."

As Poppy hurried to the backyard, the doorbell chimed one more time. Maggie pulled the heavy steel door open.

She blinked. David stood there, the storm door propped open against his back. His eyes widened slightly before looking down at the steps. "Maggie."

She tamped down her joy at seeing him. He didn't deserve that from her. Wariness flowed through her heart. A coldness rolled off him. She saw a bitterness in his stance.

"David," she stood to the side, "come in." Daggum her courteous nature. It was part and parcel of being a preacher's daughter.

He slid past her and into the living room. She eased the door closed and turned to him. His arms were crossed, hands clenched. He avoided looking at her.

"Is there—"

"I came here—"

They stopped and smiled. He raised his head. She held back the gasp as she studied the red bruises along his jaw and left eye. A shallow cut trailed along his left jaw line. Stubble covered his face. She stepped forward. Pain hit her in the gut when he took a slight step to the right and away from her.

He looked away. His voice sounded as though he had gargled with sand when he spoke. "I came to see if Bro. Johnny had time to talk with me."

"Okay. Dad's out back. I'll go get him." She motioned at the couch. "Have a seat." Again her confounded courteous nature.

He perched gingerly on the edge of the couch as if every movement caused him pain.

"Do you need a drink?"

A flash of an emotion–fear? longing?–flew across his face; then it was gone. He shook his head. "Not right now. I . . . I'm not thirsty for anything yet."

He kept his eyes averted from her. She nodded and gave him a last look. His hands were once again clenched, and he rocked slightly. Her heart melted into a glob of hurt and compassion.

Why couldn't she stay angry at the man?

She started to reach out to touch him but instead withdrew and hurried out of the room. Whatever had happened and whatever consumed him, he needed her father right now, not her.

The back door squeaked as she pushed it open. Her father sat at the patio table, leg crossed over his knee and his phone plastered to his ear. She stepped closer.

"–yes, I understand. I'll take care of him, don't worry . . . We'll help him through this, Dean. Trust in the Lord." He smiled and then chuckled. "I know you do, Dean. Hold on a moment."

Her dad dropped the phone a few inches from his mouth. "Maggie? Is he here?"

Good gracious, what was going on here? She pointed to the house. "Yeah, if you mean David. He's parked on the couch, waiting for you."

Her dad put the phone back to his ear. "He's here, Dean. I'll call you when he leaves . . . Okay. Bye." He stood and turned to her.

"Dad? What's going on?" She spied Poppy near the pond, poking the water with a blade of sage grass. Her world whirled about in her mind. Two people she loved here. Both crying out.

"Apparently, David is having some problems. You know I can't tell you, honey, but give him time with me. He'll come around and let you know."

His hand patted her upper arm before he started walking to the parsonage. She hurried to him. "Dad!"

He stopped as she grabbed his hand. "Yes?"

"Tell him, let him know . . . that I lov– care. No matter what's going on, I'm here for him. I don't want him to think that I might not be." She let go of his hand as he nodded and disappeared into the house.

What would happen now? How could she help him?

Her questions went unanswered. No sudden insight. No sudden proclamation. Just Poppy's giggle as she teased the goldfish. Maggie stuffed her hands, and the fish food bag, into her pockets and kicked at a pebble as she trudged to Poppy. She eased down to the ground, her legs bent to the side.

Sun blazed off the red hair as Poppy looked up. "Who came?"

"David."

"Mr. David is here?" Poppy hopped up, casting her sage grass away.

Maggie snagged the girl's shirt and halted her flight. "Not now. He needs to talk to Papa Johnny, okay? We'll see him before he leaves."

Poppy slumped and then sank cross-legged on the edge of the small pond. "Oh, okay, then. Maybe after Papa Johnny gets through?"

"Maybe. Here." Maggie opened the bag and pulled out a pellet. "Take one at a time and drop it along the edge, leading the fish to the waterfall."

She smiled as the girl led the fish in a circle until one swam under the waterfall, only to be pushed to the other side of the pond. The girl's high-pitched giggle warmed Maggie's heart, erasing some of the hurt. She shielded her eyes against the sun and glanced back at the house. Her love was in there, and she saw his pain. But he didn't ask for her. What could be so terrible that he couldn't tell her?

She glanced up at the sky and sent up another prayer before returning to Poppy's fish adventure.

———

David's knee bounced as he sat on the edge of the couch. He didn't expect Maggie to answer the door. Stupid. She lived here. Of course she would answer. A part of him had hoped she would, but the other part wished it had been Bro. Johnny. It would have made things simpler.

He scrubbed at his face and winced. Agony shot behind his eyes. His whole body was a mess of bruises. His gut wrenched painfully from hunger. The thought of food made it flip over. He pressed his hands together and held them to his lips. Which was better, hunger pains or nausea?

A bump against his foot brought his gaze down to the floor.

"You must be Sorta." He picked up the small kitten that Maggie had told him about. It nosed his hand and curled into a ball within his palm. The kitten's purr rumbled against him.

He absently stroked the kitten as his eyes traveled the ceiling, finding patterns and faint faces in the sheetrock crackling.

"David?"

He whipped his head around, wincing again, and started to rise as Bro. Johnny walked in. The kitten dug its claws into his arm in protest.

Bro. Johnny waved him back down on the couch. "Don't get up." He settled in the chair near the couch and leaned his elbows on his knees. "Shall we begin?"

David laughed. "You don't waste time, do you?"

He set the kitten back on the floor, and it shot across the room to fight the dust motes streaming in from the window.

"Why should I spend time on pleasantries when one of my flock is in pain and turmoil?" Bro. Johnny smiled. He reached forward and pulled a big Bible towards him and then handed David a small, thin pamphlet. "Your father called. He didn't give me details, but he said that you needed help with an addiction."

David's face flamed. Shame flowed through his veins as he played with the pages of the devotional book. "It's bad. I've tried to stop, but it keeps getting stronger, worse." He jumped up and started pacing. His hand rubbed at his neck, squeezing, releasing. Bile threatened to rise up his throat. "I . . . I don't know how to say it. Jeremy called intervention time at Mom and Dad's. I broke.

"Do you know how awful that feels? Breaking and crying in front of your family?" Anger rose from the pit of his gut.

He held a hand out at Bro. Johnny. "I can't control anything anymore!"

"And that is where we will start." Bro. Johnny's soft voice halted David's pacing.

He dropped his hands to his sides and stuffed them in his pockets. "What do you mean?"

"You believe that you have to be in control. You alone. That's the first hurdle we will have to overcome. When we, as God's children, try to control our lives, our destiny, our decisions, we will ultimately fail." Bro. Johnny flipped through some pages, searching the lines of words. "When do you pray? When do you talk to the Lord?"

David shrugged. He sighed and collapsed on the couch, leaning his head back against the top edge. Such a short couch. "I stopped. I was angry. God let Rebecca die. I lost so much that night." His voice broke.

He searched out more faces in the ceiling. There was one. An old man with a beard. "I . . . I cursed Him. Cursed Jeremy because he didn't try. But–"

He sniffed. Why were the words so hard? There was another face. Little girl with a big grin. "But I saw scars on his hands this morning. And now, I wonder. Did he try? Those were burn scars."

He slanted his eyes over to the preacher. Bro. Johnny leaned back in his chair, Bible resting on his leg, ankle crossed over knee. He held a finger near his lips, listening.

"Don't stop. Tell me what you feel, David. I do not judge you. Man will sin and will fall. Jesus gives us the grace to move forward and to learn from our mistakes, helping us and picking us up."

David took a deep breath. "I hate saying it. It makes me sound so vile . . . so ugly."

"Sin is ugly, but when we cast it off, it can't stain us. Do you know why?"

"Because we are washed in His blood."

"Do you believe that?"

A tear traveled down David's face. "I do."

"Then speak everything out loud."

Another face. A glaring, deformed face with jagged teeth. He blinked. His eyes sought out a different pattern. A face with big cheeks and wide smile. A goofy face. A small smile pulled at his mouth. "I drink. I'm an alcoholic. I want it all the time. Even tried to quit, but I couldn't. Last night, I tried . . . oh, man. You're her father!"

"I'm your pastor. Right now that's all I am."

David sat up, ending his search for faces in the ceiling. He stared at the floor, tracing the black lines in the hardwood. The words rushed past. "I tried to get her to go home with me, to sleep with me. She refused. I went to a bar. Got drunk. Something with a woman, but it's all hazy. Got into a fight. Spent the night in jail. And then intervention time with the family." He took a shaky breath. "I had two DUIs in St. Louis. And the bad thing is, I don't care. I honestly don't care. I want to lose myself in the drink."

Bro. Johnny cleared his throat. "I have to ask, did you have sex with the woman?"

David glanced at him. "No! I thank God that I didn't–"

"Don't do that." Bro. Johnny's stare pierced him. "Don't thank God if you don't mean it. Are you using it as an expression or truly thanking Him?" David looked away. "Your heart isn't right, David."

He flared his nostrils. "Ain't right? I came here for help, to talk, not to be put down!"

Bro. Johnny's hand latched onto his arm, holding him in his seat. "Listen to yourself. One statement, and anger takes control. Where would you go now, if you left?"

David sank against the cushions. He swallowed against the lump in his throat. Where would he go? The answer stared at him, glaring and mocking him from the darkest part of his mind. "I would go . . . go get a drink. Drown the pain."

"Exactly. Do you want to be a slave, David?"

He raised his eyes back to Bro. Johnny and took a real, long look at the man. Maggie's father. His preacher. Cobalt eyes that should have been cool, twinkled in a face that enjoyed the sun. Wrinkles surrounded the eyes and lined his forehead. He almost laughed at the freckles that covered the man's cheeks. So much like Maggie's. A trimmed, salt-and-pepper beard lined his jaw. It was a face that loved everyone. A face that commanded attention. A father's face.

David swallowed. Bro. Johnny was so much like his own father. "No, sir. I don't."

"Well, you are. It's obvious that you have a problem, and you've allowed alcohol to be your master. In order to change, you must decide that you do not want to be a slave to it any longer. The only real way to defeat it is to become a slave to Christ. Where alcohol as your master offers death, despair, and guilt, Christ offers grace, mercy, freedom, and love. The alcohol's master is Satan, who is weak compared to the strength of Christ. Which master will you choose, David?"

David hid his face in his hands, tears pooling in his palms. He rocked forward.

"Let's read. John chapter eight, verses thirty-four to thirty-six. Jesus answered them, 'Most assuredly, I say to you, whoever commits sin is a slave of sin. And a slave does not abide in the house forever, but a son abides forever. Therefore if the Son makes you free, you shall be free indeed.'"

David wrapped his arms over his head. Tears coursed down his face and hit the hardwood.

Bro. Johnny's arm reached around his shoulders. "So, I ask again, which master will you choose?"

"I want freedom. I want Jesus back."

Bro. Johnny squeezed his neck. "Jesus never left. He is waiting for you to return."

David raised his head. What a sight he must look. Red eyes, red bruises, whiskers covering his jaw, and snotty nose. He pulled a handkerchief from his back pocket and rubbed at his nose. One of the old-fashioned teachings that stuck with him. He almost snorted at the errant thought.

"What do I do now?"

"You," Bro. Johnny pointed at the book, "read that every day. Let it speak to you. Follow along with the Bible. Each morning, open to Proverbs. One chapter for every day. And I want you to be here once during the week. I know your schedule will keep you working odd days and sporadically, but on a free day, stop by. You and I have a lot of work to do."

David stood. He tried to smile. "You don't look at me like I'm pond scum."

"If I did that, David, I would have to look at myself the same way." He stood and placed a hand on David's shoulder. "And the next step will be to go out that back door, apologize to my daughter, ask for forgiveness, and start anew."

An invisible anvil slammed the breath out of him. "She'll hate me."

"I know my daughter better than you right now. She'd never condemn you. But speaking as her father, I will bust you over the head if you hurt her again." The cobalt eyes turned cool.

David nodded and averted his eyes. "Yes, sir."

"Good. Now I have things to get in town. Tell Maggie I'll be back by dinnertime." Bro. Johnny propelled him across the kitchen and to the back door. "Go."

The screen door squeaked. His day went from horrible, to terrifying, to upside down, to calm, and now back to horrifying. It was amazing that he was still sane.

———————

He didn't deserve her, but here she was, lying next to him, holding his hand. On the other side, Poppy shifted. The trampoline bounced slightly.

She giggled. "If I do this," she pushed with her foot, making the trampoline sway up and down, "it makes the stars all jiggly."

"And makes my stomach all jumpy. No bouncing, please, Poppy." Maggie raised up on an elbow and peered over David's chest. "Here, come lay between us."

David grimaced as her little body slithered over his and wiggled between him and Maggie. She wormed her way into the small space. The trampoline bounced again as she plopped back and continued gazing at the stars.

He looked over at Maggie and smiled, their intertwined fingers resting above Poppy's head. "Thank you."

Maggie blinked. The reflection of the stars twinkled in her eyes. "For what?"

"For forgiving me and giving me a second chance." He turned to his side, sending Poppy giggling as the trampoline danced underneath them.

"You jiggled the stars, Mr. David." A yawn escaped her.

Maggie continued staring at him for a moment before she spoke. "I . . . you deserve a second chance. Everyone does." She smiled. The soft look in her eyes sent a warm, fuzzy feeling through his gut. "Thank you for telling me the truth. I know it had to have been hard."

David sighed. He laid his head back on the black rubber. "It was very hard, love. But it's so easy to talk to you." Her fingers tightened in his. His heart thudded.

It was so easy. She had sent Poppy on an errand, and he had poured out his sins while sitting on a stump in the backyard. She threw no angry or ugly words at him. Tears pricked her eyes, but she had brushed them away and rushed into his arms. He gazed at the stars. He didn't deserve her. Not at all.

A streak flew across the sky, burning a white path.

"Look! A falling star!" Poppy pointed and bounced the trampoline. "Make a wish, make a wish!"

David's eyes met Maggie's. She smiled at him. "I did, Poppy. I did."

Poppy flopped over on her stomach, bouncing the trampoline so hard that their hands came apart. "What did you wish? You can tell falling star wishes. They'll still come true. You just can't tell birthday candle wishes."

David laughed and brushed a strand of bangs off her fore-head. "And you know this how?"

"Really, Mr. David. Everyone knows that." She rolled her eyes at him.

"Yeah, David." Maggie rolled over onto her elbows. "Everyone knows that."

He grinned. Gals were ganging up on him. "Maybe girls do, but us guys, we don't care about such silly things."

Poppy gasped and poked him in the side. He laughed. Maggie nodded at Poppy, and the little redhead prodded him again. He grabbed his side, laughing. Shame on Maggie for telling his little flower he was ticklish. Poppy squealed and pounced. Their bodies flopped around on the bouncing trampoline as he pushed the skinny, little hands off his side and dodged Maggie's searching fingers.

"You have to tell your wish, Mr. David. Promise?"

Wicked girls. He laughed and nodded. "Okay, okay. But you first, little flower."

She brightened at his nickname for her.

He stretched out his arm, and she nestled against him. Maggie fought the bouncing trampoline as she scooted closer to them. Her head came to a rest on his arm as Poppy moved her head to his chest.

He sighed. This was what it was supposed to be like. This was what he almost had. He fought down that thought and the anger that rode with it. That was the past. This was his future. Here. At this moment. Here with his girls.

"I wished," Poppy's whisper drifted across them, "that I could have lots of nights like this. What did you wish, Mr. David?"

He stroked her hair with his free hand, smoothing the errant wisps. "I wished . . ." He looked at Maggie. She watched him with a half smile on her beautiful lips. ". . . same as you, little flower. More nights with my favorite girls."

Poppy's arm tightened around him. "Miss Maggie?"

Maggie draped her arm across Poppy. "Me? I wished for someone to tell me what happened to my gnomes."

David returned his gaze to the stars. Oh, boy. He was definitely in for it now.

"Mr. David moved them."

"Oh, little flower, you weren't supposed to tell."

Maggie rose to her elbow. Her eyes gleamed as she stared down at him, one brow arched. "Uh huh. Where are they?"

Poppy rolled over. She pressed her back against his side. "He put them under the hedge bushes."

"Really?"

David grimaced. "Yeah."

"Whatever for?" Her eyes widened so fast, they nearly shot her eyebrows into her hairline.

"Um." Poppy elbowed him. "You tell her."

He pushed back at her. "It was your idea."

"I ain't telling. I didn't do it. You did. You just asked me where a good spot would be."

Maggie drummed her fingers along his arm. "Well, why?"

He sighed, and he and Poppy spoke at the same time. "They stared at me."

CHAPTER 16

The tool box clattered as David pushed it across the bed of his truck and strapped it down. He pulled off his work gloves and threw them into the cab. Even with that protection, small blisters had formed on his palms.

He eased his body onto the seat and opened his checkbook. This was going to hurt. A wry chuckle escaped him. Penitence for being an idiot. He scribbled his signature and tore the slip out of the book.

A flash of red caught his attention. Mr. James pushed the Harley toward him.

"She's a beauty, David. You did good work on her."

"Thanks, Mr. James." David held the check out as the bar manager lowered the kickstand. "Here's the money for the windows and mirrors."

"I thank you." The older man tucked the check in his breast pocket. "Those tables and chairs you brought are nice. You make them?"

"No, sir. Found them at a yard sale last week. Did make the stools, though." He smiled and perched on the lowered tailgate. "If someone else acts stupid like I did, those stools should withstand the onslaught."

Mr. James laughed. "Well, you did great work. What about the flooring? You and that man really tore up my boards."

Heat rose up David's neck. "The installers should be out tomorrow to do the measurements. Should be installed in a few days. I got it covered."

The man nodded. "Well, let me help get her up in the truck."

David slipped off the tailgate and dragged the ramp out of the bed. He and Mr. James pushed the bike into the truck. As Mr. James slid the ramp back into the bed, David hopped up and secured the tie-straps over the bike. He finally got her back and wasn't going to take the chance of something happening to her.

He gave the straps one last tug and jumped down.

Mr. James thumped his shoulder as David slammed the tailgate shut. "Come have a drink."

David arched his brow. A drink? Man, he needed one—that was for sure. He followed the older man. Mr. James pointed to the steps of the porch.

"Have a seat. I'll bring it out."

David sank down on the roughhewn boards and wiped his hands on his jeans. The sun beat down on him. His shirt stuck to him. After four hours of heavy labor, he definitely could use a cold beer.

"So, tell me, young man," Mr. James let the door slam behind him, "how's the help coming along?"

Water droplets dripped off the cold can. David pursed his lips and then chuckled and accepted the can of root beer. "Guess this'll be the only kind of beer I'll ever get from now on."

The old coot smiled and flashed the gap in his front teeth. "You better believe it. A man falls like you did, and he should never have the thing that made him fall in the first place. That's what makes the man. Whether he can walk away or whether he gives in."

The pop-hiss from the can sliced into the silence of The Mudslide's parking lot. David chugged a long drink. The vanilla taste of the soda refreshed him. He could get used to this eventually, although it did nothing to quiet the longing for a really good, ice-cold beer.

"So, I'll ask again. How's the help coming along?"

David shrugged. "Okay enough. Family and Bro. Johnny are trying to help me. Staying back at Dad's again. Jeremy keeps a close eye on me, like the good big brother he is." The bitterness in his voice left an odd taste, so he swallowed another hit of root beer. "Bro. Johnny also has me reading in this little devotional of his."

He rolled the can between his palms. The cold and smooth surface soothed his blistered skin. "I won't lie to you, Mr. James, I hate being watched. Every move I make is catalogued, summarized, and judged."

Mr. James huffed, took out a handkerchief from his pocket, and wiped the sweat from his exposed head. "It'll seem that way at first, son. But it isn't. There's two types of men I see come to my bar. Those who enjoy a nice beer or whiskey and then go home. Then there's those who try to drown themselves, thinking that the alcohol will erase their troubles. And it will for a while . . . until you wake up the next day."

David avoided his gaze. An ant traversed across the white rock gravel, scurrying away on its mission. His eyes followed it as the man continued. "Like I told Jeremy that night, I've known you since y'all were little tykes. I seen you two grow up and become fine men. Your daddy did good on raising his two boys. But–"

Silence reigned for a few moments. David looked up at the old man. No. Not old. Just old eyes. Mr. James had to be about the same age as David's dad.

Scarred and callused hands busied themselves rolling a cigarette. He scratched a match and lit the rolled tobacco before turning back to David.

"But with you, you took your pain and doubled it."

David nodded. Same ole song and dance. He watched a car zip down the highway. There was nothing to say. Mr. James and everyone else could talk until there was no air left in the world, and they still would not get it.

"You might believe that no one understands, young David."

David closed his eyes. Science fiction come to life. How was everyone reading his thoughts?

Mr. James blew a cloud of smoke. "I've seen it many times. You have a blessing, though."

"How so?" David forced down the lump in his throat with the last swallow of root beer.

"You have family. You have friends. Without them, you would never be able to make it. Don't fight against your family's help. Not everyone has that."

The man's words drove a spike into him. His nostrils flared. He stood and threw his empty can in Mr. James' blue recycle bin by the steps. "I'm aware, Mr. James, that not everyone in this world has family to fall back upon."

He stalked to the truck and opened the passenger door. One too many talks. He didn't need another lecture. "I've got something for you."

David handed a silver aluminum bat to the bar manager. "To replace the one I busted."

Mr. James grinned around his half-smoked cigarette. "Thank ya. It's a nice one."

"My bat from high school. Last game when I hit the grand slam."

"I remember that night." Mr. James propped the bat on his shoulder. "Jeremy couldn't stop talking about it all night. Brought his buddies here that night and gave a toast to you. Bragged how you upped the ante and busted his record."

The sly dog was determined to remind him of his brother. David closed his eyes against the small amount of pride that rose from somewhere deep down. His brother had been proud of him.

The wind picked up. Dust blew across his face. David sighed and slammed the truck door. He knew there was a reason why he drank. To bury those memories and the ones that they inevitably led to.

Mr. James slapped his shoulder and interrupted his thoughts. "See ya around, young man, but you are no longer welcome here in my bar." He looked up at the sky. "You better get, though. Looks to be a storm coming in."

Yeah, he wasn't kidding.

"Well, thanks for the lecture, Mr. James." David rounded his truck. "And call me if the installer doesn't make it out here."

"Will do. And David?"

David arched his brow as he slid onto the seat. Mr. James leaned against the passenger door. "Remember what I said about family. They'll be there for you."

A blast rattled the window panes. David leapt from the bed and yanked on his pants. What the–?

He stood, shoes in hand, in his bedroom. He hurried to the window and looked out. A flash of lightning lit up the sky, followed by the crash of thunder. He wiped the sweat off his lip. His chest heaved from a heavy sigh. The shaking wouldn't stop. He pressed his fist against his mouth and bit his knuckles.

It wasn't an explosion.

It wasn't the car.

David melted against the side of the bed, knees pulled to his chin. Like the rain that ran down his window, tears ran down his face. It had been months since a thunderstorm caused him to dream about that night. An onslaught of feelings launched their barrage at him. When would the dreams stop? How could he still miss Rebecca? If he missed Rebecca, then how could his heart long for Maggie? The pain of that question gnawed his gut.

He chucked his shoes across the room. His hands scrubbed his face, erasing the tears. Something else was needed to push this aside. He hadn't touched a drink in the week since he had arrived back at his parents' house, but he wasn't stupid. At the very back of one of the kitchen cabinets, the least used in the entire house, he had stashed some Grey Goose. In case that was found, he had a fifth of Glen Livet on top of the cabinets hidden behind the lip.

David rose from his position and eased his door open. It creaked softly. He froze. There was no movement. He tiptoed down the hall, keeping to the wall to avoid stepping on any loose boards.

The carpeted stairs muffled his steps, and David slid around the corner into the kitchen. He paused. A sound reached his ears, something upstairs maybe, but the silent call of the drink was louder.

He slinked around the bar, knelt down, and opened the cabinet. His mom's food processor, an old blender, and Tupperware items rattled as he reached past. His hand met only the back wall of the cabinet. A curse flew from his mouth, and David fell to his knees and pushed the appliances out of the way. There was no Grey Goose bottle. Did he put it somewhere else?

David pulled the next cabinet open and cast the pots to the floor. No bottle. The next one only revealed cleaning items. He pushed across the floor on his knees and practically ripped the next door off its hinges. Nothing but casserole dishes and pie pans. It had to be somewhere. He needed it.

He surveyed the empty cabinets in the dim glow of the security lights outside. Fine. Then he'd just settle for the whiskey. He hopped up on the counter and reached above the sink. His fingers found nothing.

Another curse flew from his lips. Maybe it just slid down a little. He reached further down and smiled as his hand encountered the smooth feel of the bottle. He gripped it tightly and eased down off the counter. Yeah. Outsmarted them this time. He risked turning on the sink light. The little fluorescent bulb flickered. David looked at the green bottle in his hands and then smashed it into the sink.

Glass shattered, but there was no liquid in it.

He whirled, vile curses spewing from him. Somewhere he was sure he used God's name.

How could they? He needed the drink. He needed to wash it all away!

The lights above him blasted to life, and he jumped when he heard his father's voice.

"Son?"

David bit back a sob. His hands clenched and unclenched. Tears burned his face. What a mess he stood in. What a mess he must look. But they had to understand. They just had to. He needed that drink. It was the only thing that would take all the pain away.

His dad walked into the kitchen, sidestepped a mixing bowl, and set a frosted bottle of Grey Goose on the bar. "You were looking for this?"

Like a zombie in a movie, David felt his feet walk to the bar, saw his shaky hand reach and grip the bottle, and felt his mouth water at the thought of the taste. His dad took the bottle from him. He whipped his head up to shout a curse, but he stopped when his dad placed a drinking glass down in front of him.

David swallowed hard as he watched the clear liquid splash into the glass, but his dad was pouring too much.

"Wait. That's enough." His voice croaked, dry and raspy. Thirst gnawed at him.

Dad's eyes were fathomless. His face expressionless. The liquid still poured until it reached below the rim. "Is it? That's what you tore the kitchen up for, isn't it?"

His voice didn't rise one octave; nevertheless, David shrank away. He backpedaled until his back pressed against the sink. His dad held the glass out to him. The liquid danced and shimmered, calling out to him.

Taste me. Savor me.

"Take it, Son, and be damned."

David craved it, but why did his father curse him for his need?

Didn't he crave his father's love more than the drink? The question entered his mind, and David couldn't push it aside.

"If you drink it, your life will be over. You will not stay here any longer. You will be a part of the world. If you drink this and give in to its pleasure, you will lose yourself, your soul. Is that what you want?" His father pressed the glass into David's hand. He grabbed David's other hand and wrapped it around the glass.

Yeah. Sweet feel of vodka. The pain will be gone tonight. But what about tomorrow? David stopped the glass at his lips as the thought came to him. Tomorrow it will be the same, pain and anger. When will it end?

When you drown it in forgetfulness.

David tipped the glass. The liquid touched his lips, and it burned. It burned as if he were thrown into hell itself. Where was the sweet touch he savored? It wasn't supposed to burn. Yes. It always burned. His soul burned.

He paused and pulled the glass away. His father reflected in the vodka. David raised his head and gazed into his eyes. Love pooled in their depths, and David saw his reflection stare back. A crazed man looking for his next fix, his next liquid sin. A man who lost his way, who fumbled, not seeing, and cursing the dark.

The glass slid from his hands and crashed against the tile, vodka pooling against the broken shards. The glass was broken. He was broken.

He landed on his knees and pressed his face against the cool tile. "Oh, God, forgive me. Dad, help me."

His dad's arms wrapped around him, and together they rocked back and forth. Tears poured from David's eyes and heart. The craving still lashed at him, but it was no more than the soft rain that lashed against the house, an annoying gnat of a thought that could be crushed on a whim.

The sound of soft-soled house slippers reached him. He dared not look up. He didn't want to see the disappointment in his mother's eyes. She knelt down, her rubber ducky nightdress coming into view. Her soft, cool fingers brushed against his hot brow. David broke down again. Quiet sobs racked his body.

How could they love him? How could they stand him?

"Because you are our son."

Did he ask out loud? He didn't know. He knew only that his mother's voice was a sweet balm upon his heart. She pulled him into a tight embrace, his head resting on her bosom like a child being rocked to sleep. His father's hands rested upon his head.

He heard soft prayers being whispered, and a gentle hush fell over him. His craving abated, but his shame still covered him.

═══════════

His gut clenched. David ran a finger under the waistband of his jeans, relieving some of the pressure against his abdomen. It had to be nervousness.

He had to relax. Maggie was at the shop. This was his day off. It was only a meeting with Bro. Johnny. Nothing catastrophic.

Tufts of lavender plants dotted the sidewalk. He navigated the gray, concrete slabs. His stomach flipped against his backbone again. He couldn't do this.

The sun mocked him with its bright and cheerful presence. A cool breeze blew, alleviating some of the heat on his face. Sweat traveled down his back. His t-shirt clung to him. Tomorrow would be better. He whirled around as the front door opened.

"David, good morning."

David's shoulders sagged. He took a deep breath before turning to face the preacher. "Morning, Bro. Johnny."

"Walk with me."

The man descended the steps. Apparently, he expected David to obey. David rolled his shoulders forward. The muscles creaked and joints popped as he followed Bro. Johnny across the thick grass toward the church. He fell into step with the preacher.

"I'm glad you decided to come today."

David stuffed his hands into his pockets. He pursed his lips. "Dad call you?"

"Yes." Bro. Johnny veered from the path leading to the church and headed toward the fence that surrounded the cemetery. "But don't fault your father. He's very worried about you."

"I know." They reached the black wrought iron. David leaned his forearms against the top railing and clasped his shaky hands. "He call this morning or last night?"

"This morning, right before you got here. You had a bad night?"

Bro. Johnny mimicked David's stance. He looked over at David and then gazed across the landscape peppered with headstones and statues.

"Very bad." David hung his head and stared at his shoes, scuffed and worn. "I really don't know how to handle this."

"You are taking the right steps now." Bro. Johnny met his gaze. "Talk to me."

David sighed. Every fiber within him revolted at the idea of revealing his latest sin. He steeled himself. His hands clamped onto the rail for support. "I can't seem to handle thunderstorms very well. Last night, thunder woke me, and for a split second I was back there. At the car wreck. I . . . thought it was Rebecca's car." He cleared his throat. He couldn't believe he was going to ask this. "Tell me, how can I miss Rebecca and still love her without feeling guilty? Feels like I'm cheating on Maggie. I can't straighten out these feelings."

"David, listen to me on this. Maggie knows that Rebecca was the love of your life. She knows that you still have that love for her. Even though you love Maggie with the same amount of love you have for Rebecca, she knows that Rebecca will always be a part of you." Bro. Johnny hooked an elbow over the fence. "God made us capable of loving many people at once. When the Holy Spirit resides in us, we will have big hearts. Hearts able to hold all that in."

David leaned his back against the fence and crossed his ankles. "At times, I feel like I am doing an injustice to Maggie for harboring feelings towards Rebecca. Sometimes I feel like I am disrespecting Rebecca's memory for loving Maggie."

"Rebecca is dead. In all sense of the matter, she was your wife, even though you were not officially married. You treated her with respect and love; she honored you. There is a reason the vows say 'til death do us part.' We become free to love again." He nudged David toward the wrought iron table that sat near one of the oak trees. "Have a seat and tell me about your night."

David eased into the hard, iron chair. He leaned his head back as he crossed an ankle over his knee. "I needed a drink."

"Or so you thought."

"Or so I thought." How humbling to have to tell someone about his fall. His horrible night, his horrible soul naked in the sun. "I had hidden some bottles in the house. I needed them. Practically destroyed Mom's kitchen until I discovered the liquor wasn't there." He sighed and met Bro. Johnny's eyes. "I needed that drink to wash everything away. The horrible memories, the guilt . . . the pain. It hurts all the time."

Bro. Johnny reached into his shirt pocket and pulled out a small, brown Bible. The edges curled from apparent use and a corner frayed. "I received this little New Testament from a friend thirty years ago. It was the turning point in my life. At a time when things threatened to crash down upon me." He placed the Bible on the table and pushed it across to David. "Open to Proverbs twenty and start reading."

David lifted the Bible. So small in his hands. His fingers trembled as he turned to the Book of Proverbs. "Wine is a mocker, strong drink is a brawler, and whosoever is led astray by it is not wise." His voice broke.

He threw the Bible down on the table and jumped up. Such a small book, but it packed a wallop against his chest. David stumbled away. Tears hindered his vision.

How could words printed thousands of years ago talk about him? How? He held a fist over his heart. It hurt him as it pounded against his sternum.

His hand lashed out and splayed against the nearest tree. He looked around. Back in the pastoral yard. At his feet the gnomes grinned at him. He turned away from their knowing eyes and sank to the ground. Acorns dug into his bottom as he pulled his knees up and lowered his head.

Bro. Johnny's loafers, shiny and pristine, stopped in his field of vision. David refused to look up.

"David, God's words will speak to us all. We just need to listen."

"How could those sentences describe me so well? It's not possible."

"With God all things are possible." Bro. Johnny lowered himself beside David and leaned against the tree. "You are not the only man to succumb to the lure of alcohol. And every one of them was like you. You drink. You fight. You are fast to anger. This is not what God wants of his children."

David raised his head. Pressure pounded against his skull. "I tried. I really did, but I never told anyone the whole story. Never even told God."

"But He knew already."

"I know." He closed his eyes against the pain, the hurt. The memory flooded his mind. The fire consumed his life, everything he desired and loved. "I'm afraid to speak the secret. No one knows."

"And this drew you to drinking." Bro. Johnny passed the Bible to David. "Tell me, did you read your Proverbs today?"

David snorted. "No. I also failed in that."

"David, everyone fails and falls. Stop your self-loathing and self-pity, and read. Right now."

David flinched at the sharpness of his tone but opened to his required reading. "Dishonest scales are an abomination to the Lord, but a just weight is His delight. When pride comes, then comes shame; but with the humble is wisdom. . . ."

He ignored the sun beating against his back and on his head. Sweat mingled with tears, but he kept reading. It had been a long time since he heard God's voice. He had almost forgotten how it sounded.

CHAPTER 17

David pushed against the charred door. It fell to the side, sending showers of sparks flying as it hit the floor. Somewhere beyond the flames, he could hear the constant beep of the PASS device.

"Toby, over here."

Together, they shoved past the furniture slowly being consumed by the licking flames. David, with his hand on Toby's shoulder, followed further into the smoky room. The beeps sounded louder.

"Here!"

Jason's voice, laced with pain, came from the right corner of the room. They pushed an easy chair out of the way. Jason, on his side, pulled off his mask and gripped his left knee. Lying beside him was part of a ceiling rafter.

"Stupid board fell on me. Twisted my knee." He grimaced as he tried to move.

"Take him, Toby." David pulled Jason to his feet.

Toby's arm snaked around Jason's chest, and they hobbled out through the burning room.

"Command, found him. Need EMS standing by."

"Roger that. Be advised . . ."

David's radio crackled. "Command, say again. I did not read." He smacked his radio. At the same time a beam from the far side of the room crashed into the window. Fed with fresh oxygen, the fire leapt to life.

"David! Look out!"

Toby's voice was lost in the uproar of flames. David fell to his knees and shielded his face against the sudden onslaught of heat. The flames rolled over him and toward the window.

"Go. Get him out!" David got to his feet and hunched over, avoiding the fire eating away at the ceiling. "I'm right behind you!"

Toby led the limping Jason through the smoke and toward the door where helping hands would be waiting.

Fire consumed the house. The flames ate their way toward David as he made his way through the hallway. He felt that he had always walked through hell, and it never had scared him, but this fire was different.

It licked and caressed the walls and ceiling, determined to consume it all. Just steps away loomed the door. Toby and Jason's backs had disappeared through the smoke. It swirled, but before David took a step, a sudden roar filled the hallway.

A blast of extreme heat hit him full force in his chest. He flew back, landing hard on his side. He struggled to his feet, only to have one collapse beneath him, and the other to fall through the floorboards.

The uproar of the fire drowned his scream. Above him, boards and chunks of sheetrock slammed down. Boxes fell from the attic. White and black smoke wafted around him.

He clawed at the floorboards and managed to pull his leg out of the hole. The fire rushed and danced above. Even through his gloves, the heat from the downed board seared through. He dragged himself away from the hole and reached for his radio. Pieces dangled from its clip.

Oh, great. David tried to regain his footing. Pain shot through his leg. He bit back his curse as he fell to his side.

Around him, hell grew and turned its eyes on him. For the first time, fear touched him.

He twisted and pulled his tank off his back to read the gauge. Not much left. This was his third time in, and his tank was running dry.

Not that it would do much good, anyway. A crack ran the length of his mask. The smells of burning wood, carpet, and other materials entered his nostrils.

A rafter above crashed into the floor and fell through. Definitely needed to get out. The hallway was not safe. He used his one good leg and scooted down the hallway. He paused outside a bedroom door. His broken mask clattered to the floor as he flipped it off his head.

With his teeth, he pulled off a glove and felt the door. No heat. He struggled with the glove. It refused to slide back on his hand. He used it and gripped the door knob. The door swung inside. Thick smoke billowed down the hallway, drawn to the fresh air. He coughed and dragged himself inside the untouched master bedroom.

Sanctuary, for the moment. He shoved the door closed and looked around the room through watery eyes. If he could get to the window, he could get out of this devil's den. He reached around him.

Where was his mask? David looked around on the floor. Great. He had left it in the hall. He hesitated. Maybe he could make it back through the doorway to get it.

A sudden crack dominated the unearthly silence of the room.

A part of the ceiling fell down. He ducked flying debris. Heat flooded the room as the fire from the attic fell through. Hell's flames blocked his way to safety.

But it no longer mattered.

The fire was unimportant as it smiled, slowly creeping its way to him. In the deafening laughter of the fire, a steady rhythmic beeping marched along with his heartbeat. That was a new one—the fire beating out a high-pitched tempo.

Strength melted from his body. He lay among the debris and watched the flames creep closer to claim him. Pain streaked through his leg. His mind focused on the dancing flames. Smoke lulled him to sleep. His eyes blinked lower and lower.

"Too many regrets." His voice rasped in his throat as he spoke to the fire. He tried to draw in a deep breath. His chest shuddered from the painful, hacking cough. "Should have told the truth."

Maggie. Her name entered his mind. His floating pink angel. The flames grew taller. "I should have told her."

He tried to raise a hand of defiance to the flames, but his arm refused to budge. Did someone spill glue? Why was he stuck to the floor? Through the haze, heat battered him, and calmness and peace settled around his heart.

It wasn't a bad way to die. He would be unconscious before he felt the flames burn him. Too bad he didn't get a chance to have a last meal. A good slice of steak, medium rare, loaded baked potato. Scratch that. Make it an apple pie and maybe a chocolate shake. Yeah, something sweet. Like Maggie.

A white light hit him in the face. Huh, so that part of death was true.

"We found him!"

Well, that declaration didn't fit with the program.

Rough hands rolled him over. The pain in his ankle shot through his leg. Off the floor he rose. Was he floating?

No. There were feet under his head. And a hand with no glove. Wait, that was his hand. Someone carried him. So, he wasn't dead yet.

Smoke and flames swirled. Voices shouted. Then bright light. He hit the ground hard.

"Get those turnouts off!"

Hands pulled at his clothes. He fought against them.

His jacket pulled at him and then disappeared, and his pants and boots slid off him. White light hit his eyes again.

"Pupils are dilated. Crank the oxygen. Full."

What? A mask slipped over his face, and some of the haze receded, but his body still refused to properly obey him. Jeremy's face blurred in front of him.

"Hey, little brother. You'll be okay." Jeremy's face came closer.

David reached out to his brother. "I'm naked, and no one bought me dinner first."

Jeremy laughed, and his hand rested lightly on David's face. "No. You're not. We just had to remove the turnouts."

David patted at his brother's tactical vest. A cough racked his chest.

"You know," Jeremy shook his head, "you are one lucky man."

David smiled and tried to push the mask aside. "No. I'm—"

"Don't try to talk. Let the oxygen work." Jeremy disappeared from his vision.

He stared at the sky above. The haziness receded a little. Apparently, he wasn't going to die today. Wasn't that good? Another cough ripped through his dry throat. Oh, man, he needed a drink. He smiled through one more cough as paramedics loaded him into the ambulance.

He craved water. That was a first.

"So, weren't you scared?" Maggie dipped her hand into the water, letting the current flow through her fingers. "I mean, you were trapped. Sounds almost like something out of a movie."

David settled the oars on the bottom of the rowboat as they lazily drifted across the small pond behind his parents' house. He shrugged. "Yes and no."

"That isn't an answer." She scooted to the seat in front of him and sat with her back to him. He bent down and wrapped his arms around her, holding her as his chin rested on top of her head. His heart thudded against her back. She stroked his clasped hands and relaxed against him. "Either you were or you weren't."

His breath stirred her hair as he spoke. "At first I was. Thought I was going to die. That's the second time I felt that. Once at the river, and now the fire. All I could think was that I never did tell the whole truth. Then, I felt peace inside me."

Maggie tried to turn around to face him, but his arms clamped tighter, holding her still. He stretched out his leg with the ankle brace. His lips tickled her ear. "Don't turn around. I'll never be able to tell you if you look at me."

Fear settled into her heart. What could be so bad that he had to hide from her as he spoke? He laid his cheek against hers. Hot skin against her cool skin. She nodded. "Okay. Go ahead, then. What do you mean, the whole truth?"

"Before I do, can you tell me something?"

She nodded again. A cloud moved in front of the sun. Gray light settled over the pond. The birds quieted. "Yes."

"Did you mean it when you told your father to tell me that you would always be here for me?"

"Oh, David." She pulled his arms tighter around her as she pressed her head against his. She could do this. "Always."

A deep sigh shuddered inside his chest and rattled against her back.

"I've kept a secret for three years now. And your father said I will have to release it to be released from the alcohol." He cleared his throat. "Two weeks before the wedding, Rebecca found out . . ." His fingers drummed against her hands.

Long moments passed. Maggie waited. Found out what? She swallowed. She could guess the answer to that.

His breathing grew heavy, and a wet drop hit her shoulder. She reached behind her and found his cheek. Tears slicked it. She caressed him. "Go ahead, sweetie. You'll feel better. Just say it. In a rush. It's the best way."

He nodded. His voice rasped in her ear. "She found out she was six weeks pregnant . . ." His chest shook, but he continued.

"We decided not to tell anyone, least of all her parents. Pass it off as a honeymoon baby. No one would know."

Knowing what it might have been was one thing, but actually hearing it was another. Maggie's heart broke. Tears fell from her eyes. He didn't fight her as she gently turned around on the bench to face him.

"My child died, Maggie! Rebecca and my child." He hid his face behind his hands. His body shuddered.

She didn't know what to say. To have lived with that pain. The torture that he put himself through. Her brows drew together. No matter what, he needed her.

She grabbed his hands and pulled them away from his face. Tears enhanced his eyes, darkening the lashes. "Come here."

With slow movements so the boat wouldn't tip over, she knelt in front of him and brought his head to her chest. His arms encircled her, holding on for life. She laid her cheek against his head, the hair tickling her nose.

He needed another haircut. She buried her fingers in the long strands and kissed his head. Her David. So much hurt and pain consumed him. She looked heavenward. Oh, please let him find peace. Let him see that someone loved him.

"It ate at me."

"It will when you keep it to yourself, love. David, look at me." She pushed him away.

He lifted his face to hers. His finger reached out and traced her lips. "You don't think badly of me?"

"Oh, sweetie, no." She captured his hand in hers and kissed his fingertips. Tears slid down the side of her face. "You grieved for Rebecca, but you never allowed yourself to grieve for your child. It's time. You need to let go of the pain. Let God heal you, love."

Fresh tears pooled in his eyes before, one by one, they trickled down his cheeks and over the faint bruises. "You're too good for me."

"Shh. No such thing. We were brought together for a reason. Now, cry to your heart's content. Let the pain go." She pulled him to her again and held him. Her arms held him against her chest. His body shuddered with each wave of pain.

Time slowed.

The sun broke through. Its bright rays played against the water, glinting into her eyes. Ducks in the distance glided towards them, calling out in greeting.

His shudders slowed until they stopped completely. Her shirt stuck to her chest, wet and hot. He sniffed.

"They want bread." David pulled away. He swiped at his cheeks and gave her a trembling smile. "Mom's been feeding them."

"And that's why you brought the stale crackers along?"

"Well, if I didn't, they wouldn't leave us alone."

Maggie laughed. "You did it because you like feeding them."

He ducked his head as a blush colored the tips of his ears. "Don't tell Mom. I enjoy giving her a hard time about the quackers."

She brushed a thumb across his cheek, wiping away a trail of wetness. A softness dominated his eyes now. "Better?"

"I am now." He captured her hand and held it, threading his fingers through hers. "I . . ."

Maggie placed a hand on his mouth. "Shh."

He tensed for a second as her hand left his mouth and her lips met his, but he sighed and relaxed. His lips moved with hers in a gentle, soft kiss. The first one they shared since he left the festival.

She smiled against him, her hands still looped around his neck. "Let's feed the ducks before they climb into the boat."

———————

Jeremy waved to Maggie as she drove away. A clatter echoed from the garage. He stepped over Fat Tom and spied David in the corner, head buried under the hood of his Fastback.

"You think you'll get it running?"

David's head popped up and whacked the hood. He grimaced and threw him a hard look. "Eventually. What's up? You checking up on me?"

"That. Plus, Sarah asked me to drop off some stuff for Mom. Scrapbooking things." He jerked his thumb over his shoulder in the direction Maggie took. "You and Maggie good now?"

"Not that it's any of your business, but yeah. We worked it out." David reached for the bottled water and took a swig. He sighed and returned to the motor. "She had to go check on Mrs. Axelbury at the store."

Jeremy stepped up to the car. The oppressive heat in the garage prickled his skin. His department hadn't released the summer uniforms, and rolling up the sleeves didn't help one bit. He picked at his uniform and pulled it away. "Anyway, I was heading in to work and thought I would see how things were going with you."

David sighed. "I'm fine. I won't lie and say that I don't crave a drink. I do. All the time."

"Dad said you had a bad night the other week."

A scowl marred David's face as he took another drink from the water bottle. "Did he? Should have known he would tell you."

Jeremy leaned his hip against the side of the black car. "He called Darlene too. For prayer, stupid. Not to gossip."

He hopped away as David swung a greasy wrench at him. "David."

"Jeremy." A malicious smile flitted across David's face and disappeared, but a hard look still gleamed in his brother's eyes.

"I'm heading into work. Don't mess with the uniform, man. We've got inspection today."

David snorted and resumed his engine work. "Well, be a good boy and head on to work."

"You're really out of sorts today." Jeremy arched his shoulders in an attempt to loosen the plastered shirt off his back. David's water bottle sparkled in the sunlight and overhead lights. "Why didn't you just push the car outside to work?"

"Shade in here."

Jeremy picked up the bottle. He frowned. "It's not cold. Whatdja do? Just get it from the pantry?"

"Mom didn't have any cold ones, but that's fine with me. Learned to drink what I could get." He made a grab for it.

Jeremy pulled away from his greasy hand. "Hold up. It's hot. Just want a drink."

As he unscrewed the top, David gritted his teeth.

"There's a cold one inside. I put them in earlier. Go get one."

"Nah. Just need a swallow is all." Jeremy lifted the bottle. David's hand closed over it just as the hot, burning liquid coursed down his throat. Jeremy gasped and ripped the bottle from his brother's hand. He slapped his palm against his brother's chest. "Vodka!"

David closed his eyes. "I just needed a small drink. To calm my nerves. That is all."

Jeremy closed his fist over David's shirt and pulled him closer. "You can't have any drink whatsoever. Don't you understand that?"

David slapped at his hands, knocking them loose. He made a grab at the bottle, but Jeremy threw it across the garage and into the driveway.

"You—"

A fist slammed into his face.

Jeremy fell against the concrete floor. Just when his lip had healed. He spat a mouthful of blood to the floor. David strode across the garage toward the bottle.

Jeremy jumped up, grabbed his brother by the back of his shirt, and hurled him into the wall. He pressed David against it, his arm across his throat. "You are so dumb. How are you going to quit if you keep slipping in drinks?"

"I can. I need it every once in a while."

"You idiot."

Jeremy doubled over as a knee rammed into his stomach. David's fist slammed across his cheek.

David sprinted over him, but Jeremy grabbed his brother's leg and sent him sprawling over the floor. He jumped to his feet and approached David, who staggered to stand.

Jeremy cut his brother's curse short with a quick jab to the face. David rolled with the punch and delivered a wicked blow into his side.

Jeremy grappled with David, each trying to find a good hit. Jeremy took another blow to the side. He snarled and sent David stumbling into the driveway with a push.

David clenched his fists and glared as he approached.

"Stop it, David." Jeremy stood his ground. He winced. It was going to hurt taking his brother down this time.

David swung a right hook at him. Jeremy blocked him and grunted as David's left connected with his ribs. He ducked another swing and delivered his own blow against his brother's ribs.

David fell to the side, holding his ribs. Yeah, not completely healed yet. Jeremy grabbed David's shirt and rammed his knee into his brother's face. He snarled. His stupid brother needed to be taught a lesson, one way or another.

David grabbed his leg. His breath left him as he landed on his back.

A fist hammered down on him. Jeremy took a blow to the chin, parried another, and then captured his brother's fist in his hand. He jacked a leg up into David's back and sent him into the ground behind his head.

He rolled over and pinned David down, his legs holding David's down. He had almost two inches on his brother, and he'd use every last one to keep the hothead under control. David's head banged against the hard ground as Jeremy plowed his fist into his face. His knuckle opened a cut on his brother's face. Then he was on the ground.

Jeremy bounded up to leap back at his brother and faltered midstep. His father stood there. Red anger flushed his dad's face. David gingerly picked himself up from the ground. He spat a wad of blood from his mouth.

"What is going on?" Dad's bellow scattered the birds from the oak tree. He moved to stand between them. His arms splayed to his sides at chest level, keeping them away from each other. "Jeremy?"

"He's drinking again."

"You–" David leapt for him, but his dad's hand held him back.

Dad pulled David closer. David grabbed at his father's hand and looked away. "That true?"

"Big deal. I watered down the vodka." David sagged against the hold on his shirt.

Jeremy snarled. "You idiot. It's still alcohol."

His dad's hand slammed into his chest and hauled him closer. "You, shut up. Alcohol addiction isn't easy."

He pushed at them. They stumbled back. "David, Jeremy, with me."

Jeremy looked at his brother as he skirted a wide path around him and followed their dad. His dad found the bottle, half empty on the driveway. He picked it up and handed it to Jeremy.

"What do you want me to do with this?"

Dad faced him. No emotion showed. A coldness from his eyes raked over him. "You will hold it." He turned to David, who stood well behind them. "And you, where are the rest of them?"

David glared at Jeremy and then limped forward, hands in pockets.

"Jeremy."

He glared at David's back and followed, pouring out the watered-down vodka as he went. Dumb-headed brother.

Always causing trouble. David stopped in the corner of the garage and pulled a bottle out of the small toolbox. He handed it to their dad. Jeremy accepted it when it was passed his way.

Without a sound, Jeremy followed David around the house as he went to the old grill. Another bottle of liquor was passed to him. Jeremy raised an eyebrow at the label. José Cuervo. Good tequila.

Soon, four hiding places later and with Jeremy's arms laden with bottles of liquor, David turned and shrugged. "That's all."

Dad narrowed his eyes for a moment and then turned to Jeremy. "I want you to carry your brother's burden to the laundry room. There you will hold them until he empties every last one."

Their dad walked past the hedgerow. Jeremy turned his gaze to David. His brother stared back through a dust-covered face.

The bottles stacked in his arms were at risk of falling to the ground. They needed to get this over with so he could clean up and get to work. "After you, dear brother."

David scowled. Jeremy followed him through the patio door, past the kitchen, and into the laundry room. Jeremy started to put the bottles on the counter, but his mom's voice spoke from the kitchen.

"Your dad just called from the pond. He said that you had to hold them. You cannot put them on the counter."

She peeked around the door jamb. "And David, you have to pour each of them out. Go ahead."

"You're watching?"

She shook her head. "No. It's for you two to do alone." Her eyes traveled from one to the other. "Remember when you two used to fight growing up? So many fistfights, until one day, your dad sat you down and explained the role of brothers." She smiled softly. "I love you two, but y'all are really trying my patience. You need to find your peace or I swear, I will take you to task."

Jeremy hid his smile. His little mamma whooping up on them drew a reluctant smile. He glanced up at David, who pressed his lips tightly together. A faint dimple in his cheek was the only indication that he was hiding his own amusement.

David met his eyes. Jeremy couldn't help it. He smiled and then started laughing. David joined in.

His mom glared at them. "Men!"

She stomped off. "And make sure you wash it out of the sink. I won't have my laundry room smelling like a brewery."

They chorused. "Yes, ma'am."

David drew in a breath. "Guess I should get started?"

Jeremy stepped closer to his brother and the sink. Dad and his lessons. First the Bible school lesson and now this. He nodded at the far right bottle of Bacardi. "Take the rum. It's about to fall, and then we'd be sweeping and mopping. I don't know about you, but I really don't want to add housework to the list."

David drew the bottle from the pile and twisted off the top. He upended it. The brown liquid splashed into the sink. "Neither do I." He threw the empty bottle into the trash can.

Jeremy nodded to the tequila bottle. "That's the next one."

David pulled it out of his arms. "I'm sorry. I really am trying."

Jeremy heaved a sigh. "I believe you. Just don't mess up again. You can do this. Okay?"

His brother's back tensed as he poured the drink down the drain. "I hear you."

Jeremy handed him a bottle of Glen Livet. His brother sure had expensive tastes. He gazed at David as he opened the bottle and pulled the cork. David might have heard, but did he listen?

He looked at his arms, holding his brother's liquor bottles. He heard his father's lesson. Apparently he was to be his brother's keeper. Just great. Just absolutely great.

CHAPTER 18

"We're leaving now, Son." David's dad pulled open the door and regarded David while he sat in the easy chair, reading a magazine.

"Okay, Dad." He didn't look up from the page.

"Enjoy your day off, sweetheart." His mom kissed the top of his head.

David smiled up at her. "Oh, I will. I shall enjoy my time away from fire, smoke, car wrecks, and washing trucks." He patted her hand. "Don't worry about me, Mom. I'm okay today."

She smiled, but the worry still lingered in her eyes.

"Come on, Leigh."

His mom shuffled out, carrying a large bag filled with scrapbooking material for his sister, and his dad stared at him.

David smiled and poured all the charm he could muster into his expression. It had to reach his eyes. "Have fun at Darlene's."

"Want us to bring you anything?"

David shook his head. "Nah. I'm good. I'll fix a sandwich or something. I just plan to sit back and relax today, maybe go fishing. Heading to the pool later with Maggie."

"Okay. Love you, Son. Call us if you need us." With one last look, his dad closed the door.

David waited until he heard the motor of their car start and the crunch of the gravel. His magazine hit the floor as he hurried to the window. The sheer curtains in the living room billowed slightly from a breeze. His parents' car disappeared around the curve, and he counted out one full minute–just in case Dad fully read him. No car came back.

The longing called out even louder, and he wouldn't be able to hold out much longer. Shame knocked at him, but he pushed it away and turned his back. Not this time.

He was smarter now. He had been more careful about where he stashed his bottles. His mom and dad still searched periodically in the house for any of his drinks.

He whistled as he turned and walked out the back door. Plenty of time for a quick drink before Maggie came to get him for their date at the pool. Fat Tom hopped up on the wrought iron patio table and gazed at him through slitted eyes. David narrowed his eyes at the feline. Dumb cat acted as though he could read David's mind.

David ignored him and trotted to the storage building, the grass cool under his bare feet. He pushed open the door. The ladder hung on its hooks along the side wall, and he wrestled it down. It left marks along the floor and in the dirt as he dragged it out and around the back of the building.

Pieces of black shingles broke off as he leaned the ladder against the wall. He shook the ladder once to settle and balance the feet and then climbed. The bottle gleamed under a few leaves. David knocked the leaves away and grabbed the bottle with his right hand.

A grin stretched its way across his face. Talk about being in the gutter. He climbed down, bottle safely gripped in his hand.

His chaise lounge sat at the water's bank, and David walked to it, his opened shirt flapping out behind him. He fought the impulse to look over his shoulder. No reason to feel guilty. No one else was there.

The chair creaked slightly as he settled onto it. It was still early morning, and the sun hadn't popped over the trees yet. Quiet permeated the small pond. Even the pesky mockingbirds were not around. He heard a quack. There they were. His mom's ducks regarded him with doleful eyes and swam past, quacking at each other.

His gaze returned to the bottle in his hands. He got it. Now to drink some of it. His hands shook as he peeled the label off the top. Just a small drink. One little swallow and then back into hiding.

The clear bottle glinted at him, and David brought it to his lips. His hand shook harder.

He hung his head. What was he doing? He couldn't have a drink. Not now. He had been dry for two weeks. He promised his parents—and Maggie. She would be here later. He couldn't disappoint her.

But hadn't he been disappointed before and lived through it? Yeah. Better to quench that small thirst than to waste his energy fighting it. Save his energy for his time with Maggie. Maggie and her little pink one-piece. Besides, what they didn't know wouldn't hurt them. Buck up!

The pungent sweet smell of the rum reached him. David closed his eyes and inhaled. Such a soothing aroma.

The liquid shot straight into his bloodstream. A small bit dribbled down his chin. Oh, how he missed that feeling. That buzz. He wiped off the drop and took another sip. It wasn't as smooth as Jim Beam or vodka, but it felt good.

The ducks paddled by again, and David raised the bottle to them. "Hey, duckies. Here's to us."

The bottle reached his lips one more time, and David took a longer drink from it, reveling in the burn that coursed down his throat. Burning was better than feeling empty.

———————

Maggie pulled her truck into the driveway and turned off the motor. She grabbed her bag and hopped out. If David didn't want to answer his phone, then she would come early. He probably fell asleep again, but he had promised her a day at the pool, and she came to collect. She checked her watch. It was only two o'clock; surely he would be up by now.

Fat Tom was stretched out on the steps, and Maggie hopped over him.

"You're so lazy, pretty boy." He rolled over and answered her with a meow.

She bent down and ruffled his belly fur. He purred and licked her hand. With a laugh, she stood. She raised the clown door knocker. It fell with a bang. She waited a few seconds and did it again. Still no answer.

"Think he is still asleep, Fat Tom?" She tried the door. It was unlocked. She pushed it opened. Silence greeted her. "Hello?"

Her voice echoed back to her. Hmm. She ventured in and closed the door behind her. "Hello? David?"

She climbed the stairs, glancing at the pictures as she went. One of the pictures showed David and Jeremy hanging from a tree branch. They appeared to be yelling, while Darlene stood under them with a water hose. It was one of those rare captive moments in life where the camera caught the love and laughter and froze it in time. She smiled. David was a cute child.

She saw more portraits. Graduation from high school. One of Jeremy graduating the police academy. Another of David graduating the state fire academy. She paused over that one, taking in the sternness of his face. Hopeful, daring, and so young, wearing his turnouts. Her finger slid over the photo and stopped at his eyes. There was a dreamer's look in him. A look that was now missing.

Maggie sighed and turned away. She'd bring that dreamer's look back to him. She searched the rooms and found his bedroom empty, the bed covers disheveled, and clothes strewn about the floor. Typical.

She bounded down the stairs and into the kitchen. David's phone was on the bar. She picked it up. Three missed calls from her, plus her four text messages. Maybe he was at the pond and lost track of time. Fishing did that to him. She dropped her bag on the bar.

The patio door easily slid open under her hand, and she stepped out. Fat Tom had made his way to the back and now waited for her.

"Do you know where he is, Tom?" Like a cat would know. Cats weren't like dogs, but Fat Tom held his tail in the air and trotted toward the pond. Maggie followed. Her steps faltered when she stepped past the hedgerow.

David laid in the chaise lounge, hand hung to the side, and a bottle on the ground.

"Oh, David."

His legs hung off the sides, his shirt bared his chest, and his head was on his shoulder. The sun beat down upon him, his face and chest already reddened from its rays. She shook him, but he wouldn't rouse.

"David?" She cupped his face in her hands. "David? Wake up, sweetie."

Even in his sleep, his brow furrowed as if he was having an argument or had heavy thoughts on his mind. She leaned closer. The sweet alcohol smell hung heavy on his breath. Did he drink the whole bottle? She let go of him and picked up the bottle of Rum 151. Only a few drops remained.

Maggie sunk to her knees beside him. How could he be so stupid? He was doing so well, why now? No point to wondering about that. Her father's words entered her head: "Addiction is hard. It's a tough battle to fight."

She sighed. "What's done is done, love."

The passed out man snored in response.

She stood, leaned down, and kissed his forehead. He needed to be inside and out of the sun. She grabbed her phone to call Dean, but then she paused. She couldn't do this to David. It would shame him to no end. Maggie bit her lip. Her dad? No. Not yet.

She glanced around, thinking. David shifted slightly. A small snore came from him.

She brushed a lock of hair away from his eyes. Her sweet David. Bound in chains that she would never be able to understand. She traveled a slippery slope with him, but she wouldn't abandon him. Maggie tipped her head back and breathed deep. How bad would it get before it was over? How far would he fall before he would be able to stand again?

She knew then who to call and dialed her phone.

"Hello?"

"Sarah. I need to talk to Jeremy." Maggie reached over and pulled David's shirt closed. The less sun beating down on his red chest the better.

"He's asleep. Is it important?"

"Yeah. I need his help with David."

She heard Sarah's sigh on the other end. "I won't even ask. Let me wake him. Hold on."

Maggie waited. The sun beat down on her back, and she craved a cold can of cola. If she craved her soda this much, how big was David's craving for alcohol? It must be a demon of unfathomable depths.

"Maggie?" Jeremy's voice sounded hoarse with sleep. "What's going on?"

"I came to get David to go to the pool. I found him at the pond, passed out. I can't move him, Jeremy. But we've got to get him indoors before you have a lobster for a brother."

Jeremy's sigh was heavy. He sounded exhausted from last night's shift, and now this. "How much? Do you know?"

Maggie picked up the bottle. The glass reflected the sun's heavy rays. "A whole bottle of Rum 151."

"Oh, help the idiot." She imagined Jeremy pinching the bridge of his nose. "He's lucky to be in nothing but a sleep. Are you sure it was the whole bottle?"

"No. It was on the ground when I got here. I guess it could have spilled out. But he drank enough to put himself in a coma."

"Fine. I'll be there in about ten."

"Should I call your dad?"

"No. Let me handle it." A click came across the line, and Maggie closed her phone.

She needed to call one more person. She dialed again. The voice of experience and love answered. "Hello?"

"Dad?"

"Maggie, what's up? I thought you were going to the pool this afternoon with David."

"That was the plan."

"What happened?"

She looked over at him. His face should have been soft with sleep. "I came over, but David fell again."

"How bad?"

"Pretty bad. Rum 151. I don't know if he drank the whole bottle or not, but he's passed out on a chaise lounge at the pond. I'm staying with him. Jeremy's coming over to help. Dean and Leigh are at Darlene's. I was wondering . . ."

"Go on, love." Her father. She could always depend on him.

"David's gonna need a lot of help. He was doing so well this last week, but, Daddy, he's fighting against devils that I can't understand." Her voice broke. Until now she had been strong, but now it crashed down on her.

Her father was silent for a second. "When he wakes, bring him here."

She passed a hand under her nose. "You know he's going to feel shame and guilt when he wakes up. He needs our help."

"Easy, sweetheart. Hush. I'll be ready. We will all help him. Okay? I'll call Miss Phyllis–"

"Don't tell her!"

"Maggie, I will just say he needs everyone's prayers because he is going through a rough spot. It will help to have the prayer chain started."

"Thank you, Daddy." She wiped the tears off her cheeks.

"You're welcome, sweetie. David is a fine man. And every-one loves him." She heard a rustle at his end and pictured him with his opened Bible. "Just let me know when."

"Okay. I love you."

"Love you too, Maggie."

She closed her phone and turned to look at the man who had claimed her heart. He still slept, his mouth agape and soft snores escaping. She sighed and waited for his brother to arrive.

———————

Jeremy slammed the truck into park and hopped out. His feet skidded across the gravel. Even with sunglasses on, the sun pierced his eyes. Anger boiled within him. Again his brother had the audacity to up the ante, and this time Maggie got to see the extent of his fall. His stupid, idiotic, selfish brother.

He stomped around the house, absently giving Fat Tom a greeting. His feet, fueled by anger, hit the grass in heavy steps. Leave it to David to destroy his sleep. A yawn escaped him as he passed by the hedgerow.

Maggie was sitting on the chaise lounge beside his brother. Her knee bounced in nervous energy. She leapt to her feet and ran to him.

"Jeremy!" Her arms pulled him into a quick hug. Then she was pulling him down to the bank. "Thank goodness you're finally here. We've got to get him into the house."

"I know." Jeremy paused at the chaise lounge and gazed down at David. She was right. His brother was slowly de-evolving into a lobster. Part of him wanted to leave David out here in the sun, let him become a mass of sun blisters. Jeremy sighed. Apparently, this was part of the job description of being his brother's keeper.

He squatted and took David's arms. With a quick roll, he had David on his shoulders in a fireman's carry. Sheesh, he was heavy.

Maggie hurried ahead of him, and Jeremy grunted as he started toward the house. David's weight made it difficult to climb the slight rise to the backyard that now seemed an endless green–a scene from the proverbial nightmare. Jeremy snorted. He had his nightmare on his back.

"Maggie, get the door."

He slid past her through the opened patio doors and into the cool interior of the home.

"On the couch?"

"No. Just help me up the steps, and we'll put him on his bed." Jeremy turned to the stairs. "Keep your hands on him to keep him from falling off me."

With Maggie's hands supporting David, Jeremy lumbered up the stairs and prayed a quick thanks that David's room was the first one on the right. Maggie reached past him and pushed open the door. Jeremy sneered at the messy room. How fitting. He turned and, with no finesse, dumped his brother on the bed and then sighed in relief. David's body bounced a little as it hit the rumpled covers.

Maggie slipped a pillow under David's head, pulled his arms up onto the mattress, and straightened his legs. "Did you have to be so rough putting him in bed?"

"Relax. He didn't feel it." Jeremy pushed aside David's legs and sat on the edge, flexing his shoulders. "Besides, your boyfriend there was heavy. Better on the bed than the floor."

Maggie pushed aside David's shirt. "Could you remove his shirt while I go downstairs? I have some aloe vera I can put on his sunburn."

Jeremy rolled his eyes. His brother drank himself into a stupor, and now he gets pampered. Just absolutely great. "Sure."

She disappeared from the room, and Jeremy turned back to his brother. David still snored gently. Anger burst forth. Jeremy fought the urge to smack his brother in the head and to close his fist around that red throat. He clenched his fists and hung his head. "Oh, Lord, quiet my anger."

He would not be a "Cain" to his brother, no matter how much David ticked him off.

Jeremy laid a shaky hand on David's head, feeling the heat of his sunburned face. "Lord, be with my brother. Help me to help him. I don't know the anguish he feels or the temptation of alcohol that drives him, but let him know, dear Lord, that I am with him. Let him see that I and the rest of the family still love him. In your holy name, dear Jesus, amen."

Maggie stood at the doorway to David's room. Jeremy had finished his prayer and was removing David's shirt. She leaned her head against the doorjamb and offered a quick and silent prayer of her own for the brothers. Like two circling rams, they kept butting heads.

She cleared her throat as she entered the room. Jeremy looked up. Dried streaks stained his cheeks. "I got the stuff. Let's get it on him."

Jeremy shook his head, his face impassive. "You do it. I'll be downstairs." He yawned and cast a last look at his brother before leaving the room.

Maggie eased herself down on the bed. David had shifted slightly. She scooted up, finding a more comfortable position. Upending the bottle of aloe vera, she squeezed a small glob out and dabbed a little along his cheeks, nose, and forehead. He didn't move or flinch in his drunken sleep.

She squeezed some more out of the bottle, and with her hands full of the goo, she smeared it across his reddened chest. The small triangle of light colored hair on his chest tickled her fingers. Maggie took another glob of gel and smoothed it down his stomach, careful not to rub too hard. She smiled.

Maybe if he were ten years younger, his stomach would be sporting a six pack, but weeks of his mother's cooking had added some padding to that hard abdomen. Around his navel, a diamond patch of hair covered that flaming sun tattoo. Maggie traced it with her fingernail. Just like him, blazing and wild.

Snap out of it. She shook her head and leaned down to kiss his temple. "Yeah, too bad you're asleep and out of it. I'm playing doctor with you." With a quick peck to his face, Maggie rose off the bed and placed the bottle on the nightstand. She wiped her hands on her shirt. Ugh. Sticky stuff.

Maggie eased downstairs and peeked into the living room. Jeremy sprawled along the couch, pillow over his face, snoring. She blew out her breath. In a house with two sound-asleep brothers. She shrugged and grabbed a cold can of cola from the refrigerator and her book from her bag that she had left on the bar.

She reentered David's room, found him exactly as she left him, and settled down in the easy chair by the window. So much for her pool day. With a sigh, she opened her Nicholas Sparks book.

———————

Some giant monster banged against his brain worse than ever before. He groaned and rolled over, catching himself before he hit the floor. Another groan escaped him. Khaki walls greeted him. What? Confusion hit him, not to mention another wave of sickness.

He pushed himself to a sitting position, and his stomach clenched. When did he come to the house? Where the heck was his shirt? The world spun when he stood, and everything went hazy. Again his stomach clenched, and it rose with a vengeance.

He stumbled out of his room and across the hall to the bathroom. David fell to his knees. Vile liquid spewed into the bowl. His stomach heaved again. Tears blurred his vision, and spittle hung from his mouth. Why did he do this to himself? He lowered his head to his clasped hands. Why did he fail himself?

He gasped when the towel touched his face. David jerked around and found his angel kneeling on the bathroom floor with him.

"It'll be okay, David."

"Wha—"

"Shh."

His stomach heaved. Again he hung his head over the toilet. More, and hopefully the last, of his stomach's contents left his body. His arms shook. His body trembled. He fumbled for the handle, and the sound of the flushing water flooded his head with needle sharp pain.

The cold towel touched his face again and wiped at his mouth and eyes. His strength gave out. He collapsed to the floor, curling around his aching stomach.

Maggie's hands pulled at him. He crawled forward a bit. His head found her lap, and there he lay. Spent, defiled, and once again broken. Too weak for tears. Too weary for lies. Too sick to face his sin.

His angel stroked his face and neck with a cold cloth, caressed his quivering body with a soft hand. She made no comment, made no move other than keeping the cloth on his face and neck, brushing his hair back, or caressing his shoulders.

Time passed. Finally, David's stomach stopped clenching into hard knots.

"Is he through?"

David shut his eyes against his brother's voice.

"Yeah. Think so."

"Here. Have him drink this."

He felt water droplets hit him on the neck and turned his aching head. The bottle glistened in the bathroom's light. Who turned on the lights? Water drew tiny rivulets along the label. This was a thirst that was not a sin. Maggie passed the bottled water over his head and placed it into his hand.

"Let's try sitting up, okay?"

Her small hands pushed at him. David managed to sit himself upright, knees up and arms propped on them. He hung his head between them, the blood pounding and whooshing in his ears. Another wave of nausea plowed into him.

"Don't give in. Slow breaths." Maggie pressed herself against his bare back, cradling him, holding him. "That's it. Slow. Deep. Out."

He listened to her voice. Slow. Deep. Out. The wave of sickness passed, and he raised his head.

The top to the bottle proved difficult, but he got it off and took a small sip. He swished the water around, turned his head and spat it out into the toilet. Her hands reached around his chest and held him. He felt her cheek against his shoulder blades as he took another small sip. It soothed his parched throat.

"How long was I out?" His voice rasped and grated. He took another sip to smooth it over.

"Long enough to burn. Jeremy brought you inside." Her voice was soft, hesitant.

Shame ate him. Guilt that she had to see him like this. He didn't want to look at her, see her disappointment. Know her disgust with him. How could she not be disgusted with him? He disgusted himself. Muscles bunched in his shoulders and arms. Anger rose. He was a complete failure.

"Shh." Maggie's voice cooed at him. "Stop thinking, love. Calm down."

She leaned against him, her arms holding him tight, her head pressed to the side of his.

"It'll be okay. One fall. That's all it was."

His chin trembled. "I failed. I always will." He gritted his teeth. Let the anger stay. It was better. Let him wallow in his failure.

"Calm down, love." Her hand left his chest and stroked his temple, brushing his hair away. "Calm down. I'm here for you."

David shook his head. "You shouldn't be. I should be more for you. I don't deserve you." He pressed his fists against the ache in his head.

"Do you think anyone deserves those who love us?" She scooted around to face him. He turned away. He couldn't look into those angelic eyes. "David?"

She cupped his face, guiding him to look at her. Backlit against the light, her hair glowed in a halo around her face. Her blue eyes shone brightly with unshed tears. Freckles played across her nose and forehead. Those freckles that captivated him. Those lips he traced with his fingertips the other night.

Tears fell and ran down his face when he blinked. "I failed you, Maggie. I failed everyone."

"Oh, David. We didn't expect you to do this in one week or even in three. We know there will be times when you will fall." She pulled him to her, cradling his head against her chest. "We all fall. But Jesus picks us back up, love. Jesus, and family."

He wrapped his arms around her waist, holding on for dear life. If he let go, he would disappear forever down into the swirling black void. She was the voice of reason in his hell of a life. The angel of salvation and love. Never had anyone ever understood him so completely.

Really? He answered his own question. There was one person who made all things right. Made everyone whole. His hold on Maggie tightened.

Her arms cradled him, her heart beat in time with his. Slowly, the calming presence of peace filtered into his body. Time stood still, and everything quieted. Only he and Maggie were there, held in each other's embrace. He wanted to stay that way forever.

But as with everything in life, it didn't last. Jeremy cleared his throat.

"Maggie, go downstairs. I'll take over from here."

His life buoy in an ocean of uncertainty pulled away from him. "You think he'll be okay?"

"Yeah. He's going to be sick for a while. He's pretty messed up right now."

David snarled. "He can hear, you know. He isn't deaf, just fighting a wicked hangover."

Oh, that was stupid. Pain rocketed through his head again.

"Shh." Maggie held his head to her, her hands stroking his hair. "Let Jeremy help you, love. I'll go get you some aspirin, okay?"

"Don't have a choice, do I?"

Jeremy reached past him and pulled Maggie to her feet. "Go on. Now."

She eased past. David heard the door click shut. He felt Jeremy squat down behind him.

"Get it over with, whatever you plan to do. I–"

His stomach heaved again, and David hurled himself at the toilet. Whatever he was going to say left him, along with everything else.

How many times was this going to happen? He had nothing left inside.

David sank to the floor again, cool tile against his hot skin. He groaned.

"Come on, little brother. Let's get you bathed and clean."

Shame kept him on the floor. He refused to look at Jeremy. Another moan escaped him. "Leave me, okay? Just go."

Jeremy's hands grabbed him roughly under the arms and lifted him to a sitting position. David leaned back against the tub and looked up into his brother's eyes. There was no anger this time. Not even pity. That surprised him.

"I can't do that. Like Maggie said, you can't expect to beat this in just a couple of weeks, nor beat it alone. Come on, buck up." Jeremy reached past him and turned on the shower.

David groaned and covered his head with his arms. The water's tempo drove spikes through his skull. He allowed Jeremy to pull him to his feet and push him into the tub. Lukewarm water splattered against his hot skin. His stomach rolled, and a spasm gripped it. When he swayed, Jeremy's hand lashed out through the shower curtain and steadied him. Slowly, the sick feeling passed, and David held his face up to the water's stream.

"You're good?"

David grunted.

"I left a towel on the sink. Be right outside if you need me."

The door closed. David was alone. He fumbled with his shorts and pushed them off. Water ran over him, washing away the clammy film on his body. If only the film on his soul could be washed away as easily. A black haze filtered through his vision, and David leaned his head against the cool fiberglass wall until it receded. He stood under the stream, battling nausea and his own shame until the water ran cold.

———

Jeremy entered the kitchen. Maggie had filled a glass with orange juice and had some bread ready in the toaster. He shuffled to the bar and leaned against it. Weariness ate at his bones. His eyes hurt, and that old familiar pain drummed its way back into his head.

He scrubbed at his face with his hands and sighed. Mom and Dad would be home soon. Then they would know. His brother didn't need that this time.

Maggie looked up from buttering the toast. "I'll take him to Dad's. That way no one will know, okay?"

Not only did she have the compassion of an angel, but apparently the woman could read minds too. "Yeah, that would be good."

"Will he be fine in the shower?"

Jeremy shrugged. "Either he will get clean or drown. I'm betting on the former." He pushed away from the bar and crossed to the patio door. He needed a cigarette.

He slid open the door and leaned against its frame. The pack in his pocket was almost depleted. He would need to stop at the store and get some more. Jeremy shook one out and slipped it between his lips. The taste of the tobacco soothed him. He lit it with his Zippo lighter.

A ring of smoke floated across the patio as he exhaled. His nerves began to calm down. He felt Maggie's presence and looked over at her as he inhaled another dose.

"It's pretty bad for him, isn't it?" She stared out across the yard, eyes distant.

"Yeah." Jeremy hunched his shoulders and drew another drag into his lungs. Bad was an understatement. "For an alcoholic, the lure of a drink will eat at him. It's an addiction that is hard to control. Just takes time."

Maggie leaned her head against the opposite frame and sighed. "Like smoking?"

Jeremy coughed mid drag. "What?"

Her blue, innocent looking eyes turned on him and traveled down to his hand. "If alcohol is a craving, and David feels like he can't live without it, then what is smoking? You crave the nicotine. David is killing himself with booze. You're killing yourself with tobacco. You two are so much alike."

Jeremy stood mouth gaped open as she walked back to the bar. His eyes narrowed, and he returned his gaze to the backyard. He was quitting; David was not. That was the difference. He put the cigarette to his lips and paused. He was such a hypocrite.

Infuriating woman! How did she do that? Jeremy felt the pull of the cigarette in his hand. If this was hard for him, Lord only knew how hard it was for David. Jeremy growled.

"We'll do it together, little brother."

He flicked his barely smoked cigarette to the patio concrete and ground it to death with his boot heel. Lord, help his family. He amended his prayer. Lord, help the idiotic criminals if he got his hands on them before he kicked his habit.

He heard Maggie's soft voice and turned to find David easing himself onto a bar stool, a shirt in hand. His brother was in bad shape. His face was drawn, and dark circles ringed his eyes. For a man who was a lump of lead earlier, he was looking like a small breeze could break him in two. David struggled with his shirt as Maggie fixed his food.

Jeremy slid the patio door closed and went to help his brother slip into his blue Hawaiian shirt. He snatched the garment from David's hands and held it open as David slid his arms through the sleeves. "Well, you are contrasting nicely. Put on a pair of white shorts, and you would be quite patriotic."

Maggie pushed the orange juice closer. "Did you put the aloe on?"

"Yeah." David took a sip, and his body melted into a slump. "I found it."

Jeremy sat beside him and slapped him on the shoulder, taking perverted pleasure in seeing David wince. "Now that you are up and about, after you eat, you are going to see Bro. Johnny."

David nibbled his toast, not saying a word. Finally, some humility from the man. He was too tired for this today. Jeremy looked at Maggie and pushed away from the bar. "I'm heading back home. Call me if you need me, but I pray to God you don't have to."

David ignored Jeremy's pointed stare.

Maggie nodded. "I will, but we'll be okay. Thank you, Jeremy."

He nodded and waited, but David just chewed in silence. Yeah, it would be too much to hope for an apology or thank you this soon. He gave David a heartless smile and slapped him one last time across the chest. "See you, little brother."

CHAPTER 19

David turned the ignition. Nothing. He caressed the dashboard. Come on, baby. He turned it again, and the Mustang answered with a purr of the engine and a billow of black smoke.

"Rough morning, huh, baby?" David inspected the inside of his car. He was sure he got all the trash out yesterday. Better check the glove box. One hit on the button, and it fell forward. David paused. The bottle glinted at him, beckoning. His breath caught in his chest, and his mouth watered.

He hadn't touched a drop in two weeks. The stores, the shelves, the billboards, they all mocked him. Even the ads in the magazines. He ignored their callings. His finger fondled the smooth glass, and slowly he brought it out of its cave and into the light.

He'd forgotten that he'd hidden the fifth of Smirnoff. His hands shook as he peeled at the cap. Just one taste. It wouldn't hurt. David broke the seal and removed the metal cap. The scent reached his nose, and David frowned. It didn't smell the same.

He stared at the label. He couldn't do this. Not to Maggie. Not to himself. He recapped it and held it away from him. It still called to him. He'd make it hush.

He hopped out of the car. The trash can stood at the corner. A couple of plastic bags full of nuts and bolts lay in the corner on top of a toolbox. David dumped one of the bags into the box, slipped his vodka bottle into the bag, and threw it into the trash can. No one needed to know that he found the vodka.

He passed the test, didn't he? He threw it away. David slid back into the seat and searched his glove box for anything else. All clear except for an old pack of Big Red gum. Paper rattled as he pulled the hardened piece out of the package and slammed the glove box shut. There was no heat to the gum. He grimaced as he tried to chew it. How old was that stuff?

He twisted around and backed the black Mustang out onto the driveway. The rocks crunched as he drove slowly to the front door. She stood there waiting, his vision in pink. His floating cotton candy delight.

David stopped the car, hopped out, and rounded to the passenger side. With a flourish, he opened the door and bowed. "Milady, your black vintage chariot awaits."

Maggie smiled. She didn't immediately get into the car; instead, she ran a hand over the top. "She's marvelous, David."

"And so are you. Hop in. Let's go."

Maggie turned to him and leaned against the opened door. Her bright baby blues twinkled as she stared up at him. "Always in a rush."

David dropped a small kiss on the tip of her nose. "I am this time. Come on, hop in."

She lowered herself into the seat, smoothing her sundress down over her knees. David closed the door and ran to his side. His surprise for her was going to be great. As he slid in, he spied her rummaging in the glove box. Good thing he found the bottle first. Her hands pulled out the gum.

"Is this any good?" The piece she pulled out broke and cracked in her hands.

David spat his wad out the window. "No."

Her laughter filled the car as he pulled away from the house. She shut the glove box, turning to him. "So. Where we going? You owe it to tell me."

"Surprise, darling." He looked over at her. "You look great, by the way."

"Thank you. You're handsome yourself." She leaned closer. "Tell me, please. I dressed up for you. Wore this pink dress, pink polka-dotted headband, and pink shoes because they're your favorites."

"Surprise. And I really like you in that outfit. Makes me think of cotton candy."

She punched his shoulder. "And you look like a secret agent man, just country style. No black slacks?"

David glanced down at his dark denim pants, black boots, and white shirt. "What's wrong with this?"

Her voice purred in his ear. "Nothing. Makes you look . . . stunning."

David stopped the car at the intersection and breathed again. He shot her a sideways glance. "That wasn't what you were thinking."

"No. But it'll have to do. Unless you tell me where we're going." The little pink pixie dared to tease him.

David leaned over and pulled her closer, inhaling her scent. His lips barely grazed hers as he spoke. "No."

She caressed his cheek and kissed him quickly. "Fine, Mr. Mysterious."

He smiled, shifted the gears, and drove straight on. "You really hate surprises, don't you?"

"No. Not really. I hate the suspense." She settled back into her seat.

"Well, this one you will like. Been planning it for days now."

"Cool." She reached for the radio. "Does it work?"

"Only AM."

He drove down the narrow road. The gravel road was just ahead, right past the stop sign. Maggie would love it. And he had it all set up. Umbrella, blanket, and cooler. Just a private, little picnic by the creek.

David dropped his hand back to the steering wheel and stopped the car at the sign. Maggie tuned and turned the knob, smiling at the info stations and talk stations. Didn't she realize that was all AM practically consisted of? He smiled at her persistence and batted her hand away from the radio to turn it off.

"There's nothing on AM, honey."

He shifted in his seat and checked both ways. Nothing was coming. He hit the blinker and started his left turn toward paradise.

Maggie screamed his name. A curse flew from his lips. The truck roared down upon them. His foot hit the gas pedal. The Fastback jumped and came to a rest at the side of the road. It rocked as the truck barreled past.

David slumped against the steering wheel. "That was close."

Maggie's hand gripped his forearm. Her chest heaved. "Way too close. I thought it was going to hit us."

David blew out his breath. "So did I. Stupid idiot." He reached into his back pocket, pulled out his phone, and dialed.

"Who are you calling?"

"Joe at the highway department. Let him know that there's a reckless driver out here— Joe! . . . yeah, man, I used your extension. Shouldn't have given it to me, dude . . . ha! Look, there's a reckless trucker on Middleton. Black semi cab, no trailer. I was making the turn on River Creek, and the idiot about plowed into me and Maggie . . . Sure. Okay. Bye."

David pocketed the phone. Maggie stared at him. He cocked his head. "What?"

"Nothing." She grinned and leaned toward him. "I like how you get all self-assured and in control. True boss man."

He laughed. Tension from the near miss melted away. "And you're being silly." His lips almost touched hers when his phone cackled at him. He sighed as he retrieved the phone. He'd chuck the thing in the river if someone called while he and Maggie were on their picnic.

Maggie arched her brow. "Seriously? Joker from Batman?"

"Yeah. Jeremy's ringtone." He flipped open his phone. "Jeremy?"

"David, get to the Littleton house. There's a fire. Just called it in. Entrapment."

David snapped the phone closed, chucked it in Maggie's lap, and peeled out onto the road. "Hold on, baby. We gotta get to Poppy's house."

Her eyes widened, fear etching itself across her face. "Why? What's happening? Is Poppy okay?"

David shook his head. His knuckles whitened as he gripped the steering wheel. "Fire."

Maggie blanched. Her hands flew to her mouth. "Poppy?"

"I don't know, baby. We'll get there. Just hold on." He shifted the car into a higher gear and floored the pedal.

He risked a glance at Maggie. With eyes closed, tears coursed down her face, fingers pressed to lips that moved silently. His heart wrenched at the sight. The car swerved dangerously onto Main Street.

Rage boiled within him. They couldn't lose Poppy. Not after he fell in love with her and Maggie.

The car squealed around the turn off Main Street and onto Thomas Drive. David cursed the traffic light up ahead as it switched to yellow.

"Hold on!" He hit the gas and took the left turn as the light turned red. Angry honks followed him. Who cared? Nothing was going to stop them from getting to Poppy.

Ahead, Engines One and Two had hoses out. B-shift's captain hurried about as they ripped open side panels. David slammed on the brakes and jumped out.

Maggie followed. He vaguely acknowledged Jeremy as his brother wrapped his arms around Maggie, halting her run.

David ran to Engine One. "Tony?"

The captain turned to him. "David. Thank God! Suit up. I need men in the house."

David yanked a bag out of a side panel. He dumped the turnouts out as Tony pulled an air pack, still talking. "Two of us are on light duty. Chief's on his way. I've four full-times and three rookies."

The suspenders on the pants snapped against David's shoulders.

Tony continued. "Engine Three is out for repairs. Classic case of being under budgeted, man. Pencil-neck mayor."

David hooked his jacket closed, slipped on his gloves and helmet. "Let's go." He spotted a rookie suiting up. "You, come on. You're with me."

Tony helped him shrug into his air pack while hurrying to the house. The heat from the fire beat at them. Glass broke to his left. The guys had a hose going. David thumbed his mike and nodded to Tony. He pulled his mask over his face. The respirator hissed.

"Going in."

Tony's voice crackled over his earpiece. "Fire's in the right of the house. Smoke is thick, boys, so stay alert."

"Copy." David stooped and entered. He shook his head. Just like a training day, thick smoke hung in the air, allowing only three feet of visibility.

The rookie laid his hand on David's shoulder. Together, they step-shuffled their way into the living room.

David touched the arm of a ratty couch. The fabric stuck to his glove. "Smoldering. Let's see if we can find them. Tony? The little girl and anyone else?"

"The grandmother. Neighbors saw them earlier."

David pushed ahead. They should be easy to find in this small house. He keyed his mike open. "Rook, down the hallway."

"Wait. I think I see an arm."

David turned and strained to see through the fire. The smoke swirled and revealed a flash of pale skin. Old woman hands. Maybe Poppy would be with her. The rookie took a step as a faint sound reached David.

He snatched the man's jacket. "Hold up." David cocked his head. Down the hallway. A faint scratching. A small yell. "This way. Poppy is down the hall."

The rookie shook his head, his eyes glaring at him. "There's a body there. We grab the closest, man."

David grabbed the man's jacket and hauled him closer, masks touching. "We don't know if she is alive, but Poppy is. Follow me."

"Look, man, you grab her. I'll take the grandmother." He started to step forward.

"Never leave your partner." David thumped the rookie's mask and yanked him down the hall. "Follow or find another job. Grab your ax."

He touched the wall to his right. Heat emanated from the paneling. He touched it farther down. No heat. Yet. The smoke cleared somewhat, giving him a look at their surroundings. Short hallway. Three doors.

The rookie felt the door to his left. "Hot."

David nodded. He touched the door next to him. No heat. He banged on it. "Poppy?" A faint cry sounded from the room. "This one."

"Command, victim one. Room on right, behind kitchen." He pushed against the warped door. "Rook, hit it."

He stepped back as the rookie took an axe to the cheap, wooden door. Smoke billowed into the slashes as the ax bit and shredded the barrier. David kicked at the remaining splinters.

"Poppy!" His muffled voice in the tiny, smoke-filled bathroom was met with silence. He snatched the shower curtain back.

Her small form curled into a fetal position within the tub, a wet towel over her head. His smart girl. He scooped her up as his partner called it in to command.

They entered the hallway. Smoke hindered their vision. "Where's the line?"

"I got it." The rookie tugged the line as David pressed his shoulder against the man's back, following him through the black cloud.

David stumbled over a warped floorboard. He cursed the house. They should have been out by now.

Bright sunshine shot through his mask. David tripped over the sidewalk and rushed to the engines. Behind him the flames rolled out of the house, determined to capture their prey.

He ripped his mask from his head as he collapsed onto the ground with Poppy in his arms, covering her small body with his. The heat flowed over them. He pushed to his knees and looked down at Poppy.

No. No. No.

Her tiny chest wasn't rising.

―――――

Maggie waited and waited. David had disappeared into the house. Her David. Her Poppy. Jeremy's arms held her upright. Her knees had long ago turned to gelatin.

She prayed through her tears, mumbling through her hands. "Please, please, let them live. Please, please."

How long had it been? David went in moments ago. Voices split the air. Poppy was found. Grandmother in the living room.

She faltered forward a step. Jeremy's hand clamped on her forearm.

"Stay back."

She didn't want to. Fire shot through the kitchen's roof. Her eyes followed it as it traveled along the roof. Where were they? They had to be on their way out.

A yell penetrated the chaos. Flames shot from the living room's window. That hated duct-taped window.

"They're coming out!"

Maggie wrenched her arm from Jeremy's grasp as one of the firemen and David stumbled out. They ran to the engines. Behind them a tremendous roar filled the air.

Tony yelled out from one of the engines. "Flashover!"

Firemen ducked back. David fell to the ground with Poppy shielded in his arms. Maggie kicked off her heels and ran to them. Clammy hands clutched at her heart. Terror clamped her stomach. Jeremy shouted to her, but she couldn't stop. Not when David cried out, screaming Poppy's name.

His helmet rolled away as he leaned over Poppy. Maggie stumbled. She wrapped her arms around her middle as her body shook. Poppy's red hair shone against the sparse grass of the yard. Her face, pale and covered in soot, fell limply to the side.

All she could do was watch. Watch as David bent and breathed into Poppy. He checked for breath, and then he breathed again. His sweaty hair clung to his head as he bent, breathed, checked, and breathed again.

She sank to her knees. "Please, oh, please!"

Paramedics rushed by her. Jeremy's arms held her. When did he get here behind her?

"Poppy!" The anguish in David's voice broke her heart. It competed with the roar of the fire as it engulfed the derelict house.

She pushed Jeremy away and crawled beside Poppy, the grass hot against her bare knees. "Wake up, baby! Poppy!"

Jeremy dragged her to her feet as David compressed the little girl's chest.

"Please, God!" Maggie beat against Jeremy's chest with her fists. Poppy's skin turned gray, her lips blue. "Please, don't take her!"

A small cough.

Her legs gave out. "Oh, thank you, Jesus! Thank you."

The paramedics strapped a mask over Poppy's face. They moved quickly, strapping Poppy onto the backboard. David looked up from his kneeling position. Black rivers trailed his face.

He rose and helped to lift Poppy onto the gurney. The paramedics wheeled Poppy away.

David staggered to her. The smells of smoke, sweat, and water surrounded him. "Maggie."

She grabbed his face, looking into his eyes. Her head spun. Thoughts swirled, and fear beat a rhythm. He was okay, solid. Alive. "She's okay?"

He nodded. His gloved hands grabbed hers and pushed. "She's breathing. Go. Go with her."

Like she needed any urging. He stood there, Jeremy beside him, as she ran to the ambulance. One of the paramedics held out a hand and pulled her up.

"Strap in."

She plopped down on the foam bench. The doors shut as the paramedic in the back with her hooked an IV to Poppy's small body. The oxygen hissed through the mask. She leaned over Poppy and stroked her hair as she whispered a prayer.

"Please show me that she'll be okay."

Poppy's eyes fluttered opened. She gazed at Maggie for a second before they closed again.

Maggie hung her head and cried.

CHAPTER 20

D avid shut the lid to the trunk. His picnic spot now sat barren. He leaned against the side of the car and gazed at the river. The setting sun reflected an orange array of light onto the water.

Quiet, so strong it was almost palatable, dominated the area. This would have been a perfect day. It would have been the beginning of a new life. At least he had hoped.

Strange how things could change the course of a life. Never in a million years, no, make that a bajillion, would he have believed he would have another chance at a family of his own.

He pulled out his phone. Marty answered on the second ring.

"David, you okay? Darlene just told me about Poppy."

He stuffed his free hand in his pocket. "Yeah. As well as expected. Look, I'm calling for a favor. I know you don't personally handle them, but Jackson does. Can you make sure that DHS doesn't whisk Poppy away?"

Marty laughed softly. "You're a step behind, brother. Jeremy and Darlene have already been up here. I've got Jackson working on it now. Don't worry."

"How you doing it?"

"Asking for temporary custody. Listing Maggie as guardian. We got enough to show that Maggie has been a stable force in Poppy's life. You let my firm handle the legalities. You go take care of your girls."

David smiled at Marty's statement. "I will. Bye."

He closed his phone and turned as a patrol car pulled in behind him. Jeremy climbed out. His eyes sought David's.

"Hey. Thought I would find you here. Always been your spot."

David turned back to the river as Jeremy joined him at the car. The wind picked up and scattered loose grass around them. "Had to think."

Jeremy propped a hip against the trunk. "Everyone's at the hospital."

"I know. I talked to Maggie earlier. She's staying the night." David laid his head back on the car's roof. With the day winding down, his muscles protested at every move. "I really need a drink."

"I don't doubt it. But . . ."

"But I won't. Don't worry. I really am trying, big brother." David closed his eyes. "It's so hard to ignore it, especially when something like this happens."

A familiar scratch rasped from Jeremy's direction. David held out his hand without looking at his brother. "Give. You promised you would quit."

David faced him when he didn't reply. Jeremy placed the cigarette in his mouth and inhaled. "I am. Gotta calm my nerves."

"Stub it out. If you go back to smoking, I go back to drinking."

"My smoking isn't hurting others—"

David ripped the cigarette from Jeremy's mouth and crushed it into the ground. "Dare you to make a move. One call," he held up his phone, "and Sarah will be here. Want to explain that to her?"

Jeremy scowled and hurled a hard curse his way.

David smiled. "I seem to remember saying the same to you not too long ago."

He resumed his diligent watch of the river as Jeremy chuckled. Some ducks quacked by, arguing with each other. More grass whipped around their ankles.

Jeremy leaned against the car beside him. "Something's on your mind, more than Poppy. Care to tell? Time was, you used to be able to talk to me."

. "Things change, Jer."

Lots of things changed. Him. His brother. His life. His problem was not knowing where that change was taking him. Have faith, Bro. Johnny had said.

"Some things always do. Some things never." Jeremy pulled out a small package of gum. He took one out and offered the pack to David.

David chose a piece. "I know. Like my job."

"How so?" Jeremy stuffed the gum package into the side pocket of his pants.

David sighed and leaned his back against the car top again. "I broke protocol, Jeremy. First victim in, first victim out. Instead, I ordered the rookie to follow me. I could hear Poppy."

Silence stretched for a few moments. "I don't blame you, David. I would've done the same."

David huffed and chewed his gum. "Thing is, I didn't know if Poppy's grandmother was alive or not. Frankly, didn't care. My only concern was to get to Poppy." He pushed off the car and stalked to the edge of the river bank. Jeremy followed. "Thomas reprimanded me. Violation of protocol and abuse of command."

Jeremy stood to his side. Silent.

How many times in the past did his brother seek him out, finding David standing on the river's edge? Jeremy always knew when he needed to talk. When he needed to release whatever had bothered him.

"Her grandmother died during the flashover. Maybe before then. Who knows? I should have allowed the rookie to take Poppy's grandmother out, but instead, I made him follow me. 'Never leave your partner.'" David heaved a sigh. "Thomas assured me that it was a hard decision to make."

"What decision?"

David scuffed at a lump of flattened grass where the blanket had been. "Apparently, he knew that I had a problem. He was just waiting to see if I would come clean. And I did. I told him I'm getting help from family and Bro. Johnny." He faced Jeremy. "So on top of the violations, he and I agreed that with my frame of mind, not knowing if I would fall again or not, that I didn't need to be in a command position. I've been moved to Fire Prevention and Safety Officer, plus Training Officer. Can still fight the fires, but no command."

Jeremy fidgeted with his pocket. "That's an eight-to-fiver?"

"Yup." David smiled and moseyed back to his car. "I think it will work out for the best. Less stress."

His brother stopped him before he opened the driver door. "Anything else you need to talk about?"

David paused. Jeremy's hand rested lightly on his forearm. A hint of the pink scars peeked from underneath the thumb. No. He didn't have anything else to say.

"Not yet." He shrugged off Jeremy's hand. "Someday, maybe."

Jeremy nodded. "Whatever you say, little brother. Heading to the hospital?"

"Yeah." He slid into the seat but paused before closing the door. "Hey, Jer?"

Jeremy arched a brow at him.

"Thanks for finding me."

A smile crept across Jeremy's face. "Not a problem, David. Not a problem."

━━━━━━

The harsh lighting in the hospital's hall gleamed off the commercial tile. The highly polished floor reflected his boots with each step.

He hated hospitals. Their incessant beeps, loud intercom blares, and muted conversations. David rounded the last corner. At least this floor stayed relatively quiet.

David pushed open the door and peered inside the small room. The air nebulizer on Poppy's face wheezed in greeting. No TV. No movement. The lamp above the bed cast a small glow onto the little girl and the woman who lay by her side.

Maggie glanced up as the door clicked shut and rose slightly. Her eyes lit up, going from a bright blue to dark sapphires. She put a finger to her lips. "She's sleeping. She'd been asking for you."

David bent down and placed a kiss on the top of Maggie's head. "Had a meeting with Thomas and then drove out to the river to think."

A frown creased her forehead. She glanced at his hands and back to his face, worry clouding her eyes.

He smiled. "No. I didn't have a drink. Jeremy showed up." He reached down and brushed a lock of red hair from Poppy's face. "How is she?"

Maggie resumed her reclining position by Poppy. "She might be able to go home tomorrow. Smoke inhalation. She'll be on the nebulizer for a couple of weeks." Maggie looked at him again. Tears glistened. "You saved her, David."

He rounded the bed. It sank slightly as he eased down on the other side of Poppy. It was a narrow fit, but he managed to balance himself on the edge, one foot hooked over Maggie's leg. His fingers sought her hand above Poppy's head. With his head pillowed on his arm, he gazed into Maggie's face.

"I love her. I would never let anything happen to her." He stared at Maggie. Her face softened as she watched him. Never did he believe this would happen to him again. "I love you."

A tear escaped and ran down her chin. Her lips parted. "Oh, David, I love you, too."

"I love you both." They looked down at Poppy, who stared up at them through sleepy eyes. "Are you going to kiss? Because if you are, I need to know so I can hide my eyes."

Maggie blushed. David hooked his arm around Poppy's waist and dropped a small kiss on her forehead, his chin bumping against her breathing mask. "How you feeling, little flower?"

"Weird." She patted clumsily at the mask. "Like Darth Vader."

Maggie laughed and scooted further down the bed. "At least you don't look like Vader."

"Yeah, that's a plus." David shifted. "Here, let me get up so you'll have more room."

Fear leapt into Poppy's eyes. "No!" She clamped onto his arm, wheezing. "Stay. Or the fire will get me. The fire won't get me if you're here."

David's heart collapsed. "Poppy, baby, there's no fire." He held her close. Her pulse beat wildly against his hand. "Shh. I'll stay, though. Okay? Through the night."

"Maggie?"

"Me too, sweetheart." She reached below and pulled up a blanket from the foot of the bed.

David helped her settle the blanket over them. "See? We'll sleep right here with you."

"Promise you won't leave me?"

"Promise."

Maggie nodded in agreement.

Slowly, Poppy relaxed against the pillow. She watched them through heavy-lidded eyes as the nebulizer wheezed, lulling David into a comfortable doze. Maggie's thumb caressed his hand. His arm grew numb, but he dared not shift again. Poppy's fingernails had already laid claim to the skin.

Poppy's voice brought him back around. "You know what?"

He yawned. "What, little flower?"

"I think there was more room on the trampoline."

Maggie giggled. Poppy smiled at them and then giggled too. David shook his head.

"If y'all are going to giggle like little girls, I'm leaving."

They looked at each other and then smiled at him. He closed his eyes. "But you're right, there was more room."

The sound of Poppy's small laughter lifted his spirits. A thought rose from deep inside. He desired this. The image of Maggie and Poppy by his side for years to come.

Their soft conversation lulled him into a deeper sleep, his arm still draped over Poppy, hand resting in Maggie's.

Maybe things weren't going to be so bad, after all.

CHAPTER 21

David stepped out onto the narrow dirt path of the cemetery. Grass grew sparsely in between the tracks, and he followed it past the few cars that lined the side. Josephine Littleton had few friends. Most of the people here were from church and were here for the little girl who stole their hearts. The little girl who stole his heart.

His eyes sought out Maggie. Dressed in gray, she picked her way carefully across the green landscaping. Poppy, in the black and white checkered dress, clung to her hand. That must've been Poppy's only dress. Poor Poppy. Her red hair, pulled back into a ponytail, glistened brightly in the sun. David looked up through his shades. The sun shone for Josephine's funeral. It rained at Rebecca's.

David wove his way through the headstones and caught up with the crowd as they slowly walked to the gravesite. There was no tent. No carpeting. No chairs. Bare minimum.

Maggie stopped at the head of the brown casket, near an arrangement of ugly red and yellow carnations. She looked up as David approached. So many emotions ran through her mind. Relief, indecision, longing, and love.

David stepped up to her and held out his arms. Without hesitation, she buried herself in his chest. With his right hand, he pulled Poppy close to him, her little arms encircling his waist and holding on for dear life. His two ladies.

"I didn't think you were coming." Her voice was muffled against his starched shirt.

"I almost didn't. It's hard being here." He held her as people gathered around the casket. Under his hand, he felt Poppy's skinny frame shake. He pulled her closer.

Bro. Johnny stepped up. David kissed the top of Maggie's head, and they separated, keeping Poppy between them, holding the thin child together.

Bro. Johnny's voice rumbled over the brown casket. "The Lord is my shepherd; I shall not want. . . ."

—————

Afterwards, David walked with Maggie and Poppy as they followed the other church members. Poppy plodded along, head down. She stopped suddenly and pulled at his hand. He turned to her as she wiggled out of Maggie's grasp.

"Poppy?"

Her blue eyes, overrun with tears, looked up into his. "What's going to happen to me? Are they going to take me away?"

Her question caught him off guard. Why would she think that?

Maggie fell to her knees and gathered the little girl into her arms. "Oh, baby, no. No. You will stay with me for awhile."

"And then what?" Poppy pushed out of Maggie's arms and backed up a step. "I don't have anyone no more."

"Poppy!" Maggie lunged to catch the fleeing girl, her hands grasping air instead.

David grabbed Maggie's arm as Poppy ran toward the grove of trees in the distance. "Stop. Let me get her."

He left Maggie standing there. Bro. Johnny hurried toward her.

That child was fast!

He jogged, eating up the distance between them. David swept Poppy into his arms within a few seconds. Her little body twisted and bucked against him, but he held her to his chest. She cried and tried to bite him. Little minx. He clamped her tighter against him. Her hair tickled his nose.

"Hush, little flower. Hush." He cooed at her.

Sobs and hiccups racked her body. David knelt down to the ground, cradling her. He rubbed his cheek against her hair. The scent of honeysuckle rose from the red strands. She had used Maggie's shampoo.

He had no idea how long they stayed there holding on to each other, but the water from the well-manicured lawn seeped into his slacks, and Poppy no longer cried. She grasped his arm in a vise grip, her head buried in the crook of his elbow like a frightened kitten.

With a hiccup, she gazed up at him through tear-laden eyelashes. "Maggie won't leave me?"

"No. She won't leave you." David smoothed her bangs away from her eyes. "And I won't, either."

Poppy hiccupped. "I miss Grandmamma. How do I love Maggie if I still love Grandmamma and wish I was with her?"

The question hit him hard. How could he explain that? He rose to his feet and pulled her close. How do you explain death and life to a hurting child? His gaze drifted to the other side of the cemetery. Oh, man, this was going to be difficult.

"Let me show you something, Poppy."

He rose to his feet, tucked her hand into his, and turned to gaze back at Maggie. She stood with her father under a big oak tree, watching. David held up a hand and then pulled Poppy farther into the cemetery. Five rows over, by the angel statue. Rebecca's parents spared no expense.

Poppy gazed at the angel who stood with open arms above the rose granite headstone. "Who's this?"

David knelt to one knee and brushed a few leaves off the top. He only visited once after the funeral but never gained the courage to do so again. Poppy still stared at him. He pulled her down onto his knee and pointed at the words. "Read."

A child's curiosity never failed. "Rebecca May Jo . . . Johan . . ."

"Johansen."

"Johansen. April eighteenth, nineteen seventy-seven. May twentieth, two thousand eight. Beloved daughter and beautiful . . . beautiful what?"

"Fiancée."

"What's that?"

"That means a woman who is promised to be married to a man." David wrapped his arms around Poppy. "She was promised to me."

Poppy looked at him and then turned her gaze back to where Maggie stood waiting. "I don't understand."

He reached out and traced Rebecca's name with a finger. "Rebecca and I were to marry three years ago. She died in a

354   *Mississippi Nights*

car crash. I miss her, Poppy. But that doesn't mean I can't love Maggie." He placed a kiss on her temple. "Or you."

She ran her hand over the stone and the foot of the angel. "You still love Rebecca?"

"Yes. I will always have a spot here," he tapped his chest over his heart, "for Rebecca. Just like you will always have a spot here," he covered her heart with his hand, "for your grand-mamma. But our hearts are big, and we can love other people."

Poppy didn't say anything. She sniffed once and then buried her head into his neck. "Will Maggie be mad that I ran?"

"No, little flower. Never."

"Does she know that you still love Rebecca?"

David took a deep breath. Oh, man. "Yes. And she knows I love her. Rebecca is my past, Poppy. Maggie is my future. Do you understand?"

Her nod brushed her escaping hair across his nose. "I think so. You can love Rebecca like a . . . like a memory?"

"Yes. Like a memory." He laid his cheek against her soft head and gazed at the headstone with Poppy. Like a memory. He felt no pain, only bittersweet memories of sunshine and happiness. How different his life was then compared to now. Now he had two women in his life. His cotton candy girl and his little flower. And he wouldn't change it for the world.

CHAPTER 22

"It's huge!" Poppy stood on the deck as the pontoon boat bobbed in the water beside her. Her huge blue eyes took in the sight of Pick Wick Lake.

"That it is." David picked her up and handed her to Jeremy, who helped her onto the boat. "It's a big part of the river. See across to the other side? That's part of Alabama. If you go up-river, you'll be in Tennessee."

He laughed as she knelt on the cushioned seat, still staring out at the expanse of water. "Wow. Will I get to see?"

"Oh, yeah. We'll check out the lock dam later. You can watch one of the barges go through, how's that?"

Poppy bounced in her seat. "Awesome sauce!"

"Awesome sauce, indeed, Poppy."

"Untie us, David." Jeremy sat at the wheel as Sarah busied herself securing the coolers and baskets. "Sure you don't want to ride with us?"

"What? And miss the fun?" He shook his head and untied the line from the mooring cleat. "I didn't borrow the Jet Ski from Toby for nothing. Maggie and I'll catch up."

Dennis stood at the back of the pontoon, so David threw the second line to his nephew.

"Okay. We'll be in Indian Creek."

"See ya, Mr. David!" Poppy's wide-mouth grin outshone the sun.

Sophie plopped down next to her, and the two waved as they slowly rode out of the marina. A blue heron flew by to land on the stone breaker wall, and Poppy's squeal ricocheted off the water.

David gave them one last wave as Jeremy gunned the boat, and it shot off into the open lake. This was good. Being here would keep the girl from moping about. Finally, she would realize she was a part of them, a part of the family.

He shaded his eyes against the glare of the sun off the water. The boat disappeared around the bend, past the gnarled tree that stood in front of the motel.

A slight tremor moved through the floating pier. He turned his head with a smile. Maggie and her pink one-piece walked toward him. Her life jacket dangled from her fingers. He smiled. Should have known she would buy a pink one, and neon pink at that.

She looked around. "They took off already?"

"Yeah. The kids were hopping around, eager to go. Sarah and Jeremy were having a hard time controlling them. Hopefully Darlene and Marty will make it back from the rental with the second boat." He hooked his arm around her waist. The Jet Ski sat at the corner of the pier, waiting. "They went to Indian Creek. You want to join them, or what?"

Maggie smiled. "Depends on what the 'or what' is." She handed him his sunglasses and then slipped into her jacket. "Next time, remember them."

"Yes, ma'am." He slipped the glasses on and sighed in relief. "That's better. Well, my dear, your watery chariot awaits."

He pulled the Jet Ski closer and hopped on, one foot holding it closer to the pier. Maggie dug her fingers into his shoulder as she slid onto the seat behind him. Her arms clasped tightly around his stomach, and his body tightened in response.

On the air, her cotton candy scent mixed with the fresh breeze and the water. Intoxicating. Thank goodness there were no dead fish floating today. He snickered.

"What's so funny?"

He bent forward and unlashed the line holding the Jet Ski. "Nothing. Just a wayward thought."

"So, tell me."

David shook his head as he started the motor. Her fingers poked him, and he nearly leapt off the seat and into the water. Evil woman.

"Okay! Just don't tickle, please." He looked over his shoulder at her. "I'm just glad that you don't have to compete with the smell of dead fish."

Maggie laughed. "You are so weird."

"But you love me."

She kissed his shoulder and then pressed her cheek against it. "Drive on, Lord of the Jet Ski."

"Yes, ma'am."

He revved the vehicle, ignored the No Wake sign, and shot out of the marina. Maggie's laughter rippled over him. The wind rushed past them and whipped at their bodies. He sliced the Jet Ski through the waves, water spraying them.

Maggie yelled above the sound of the motor. "Where we going?"

"Alabama!"

"What?"

David pointed across the lake. "Corner of Alabama. In that cove."

He spied a Bayliner cruising and veered toward it. "But first . . ."

The wake offered its tempting waves. Maggie's gleeful shout echoed as they jumped the rolls of water. He turned sharply and rode in for another pass.

Freedom. He laughed. Excitement and freedom from his days, from his cravings.

Maggie held on for dear life, her fingers latched onto his vest. They soared into the air for the final jump. He turned the Jet Ski around. The children on the boat waved and shouted. Maggie waved back as he rode away, searching for more.

"Why didn't we follow them?"

"Rude to do so. Ride a few and then move on." He spotted a barge. "Those are fun, but only to cool off. Waves aren't so high."

Maggie scooted closer. "Let's do it. I'm getting baked sitting here."

David laughed and took off across the lake again. "Yes, ma'am."

———————

Jeremy leaned back in the chair and propped his feet on the corner of the dash. He sighed as he watched the scene before him. The boys had jumped into the water. They splashed and tried to coax Poppy to jump in.

"No way. That's deep. It probably has big fish in there. And they'll eat my legs off."

Marty Jr. laughed and splashed a handful of water up at her. "There's only strands of weeds floating around. See?" He threw a long, green strand of duckweed at Poppy. It plopped against her legs.

She squealed and slapped at it. "Gross!"

Jeremy laughed. "Marty, cut it out."

Dennis swam toward him. "Oh, Dad, we're just funning her."

"No throwing weeds at her, though."

"Fine, Dad." He turned to Poppy. "Sorry, Pop."

Marty smiled. "Yeah, sorry, Pop. I didn't–" he thrashed around. "Wait. Dennis, there's something in here!"

Jeremy shook his head at the boys. Should've known they would torment the poor girl. Poppy leaned over the edge, her eyes nearly ready to pop out of her skull.

"What?" Dennis whirled, sending a spray of water over the girl. She didn't flinch, intent on discovering what they were yelping about. "What was that? It just swam past me."

Poppy's lips trembled. "I told you. Get out of the water. The fish will bite your legs off."

Dennis started swimming toward the boat.

"Hurry, Dennis!" Marty thrashed. "It's got me. Pop–"

Poppy started screaming as Marty went under. "Mr. Jeremy, Mr. Jeremy, the fish ate Marty!" Tears streamed from her eyes as she scuttled away from the edge.

Sarah glanced at him from the front as she handed the fishing rod back to Sophie. "Jeremy."

"Fine." He stood. Time to end the torture. "Poppy, they're just messing around."

"But he went under. Look!" She grabbed his hand. "See!" She led him to the gate and peered over the side of the boat.

Dennis slapped the water's surface. Marty popped up and sent a wave of water cascading over Poppy. The boys hooted and swam towards the back.

Poppy sputtered. Her face flamed. "Stupid boys! I'll get you back!"

"You can try, Pop-tart." Dennis cackled.

Jeremy chuckled. "Ignore them, Poppy. Just ignore them."

She glared at him. "You're just a man. You're on their side." She crossed her arms, gave him a hearty huff, and stalked to the front of the boat.

Sophie smiled and gave her a hug when she sat on the small deck. "Catch a fish. Then when Daddy fillets it, you can put the guts in their shoes."

Poppy's reply was lost as Jeremy turned his attention to his wife. Sarah punched his shoulder. "That was mean. Letting the boys pick on her so."

"Ah, she's needs it. Besides, she enjoyed it."

"She's got a temper, Jer. Those boys better watch out."

He arched a brow at her as he joined her under the canopy. "What can she do? Have to catch a fish to put the guts in a shoe."

"David's been teaching her."

"Oh boy." He glanced at the boys. They had their heads together, conspiring. "I can't wait to see what she plans."

"Hey, Mom!" Sophie stood up and waved. "It's Aunt Darlene and Uncle David!"

Sarah turned to the kids behind her. "Boys! You better head in, David's coming."

They quickly swam to the boat. Their laughter mingled with Sophie's. He turned to Sarah. "You do have the towels and food in something waterproof, right?"

She sighed. "Yup. Sophie, you and Poppy stand behind the gate, honey."

The girls closed the gate and knelt on the side seats, shielding their eyes from the sun.

Poppy looked at Sophie. "What's happening?"

Sophie smiled at her and then returned to watching the others approach.

Jeremy shook his head. "He's coming in fast. Showing off for Maggie."

"And for Poppy." Sarah grabbed his arm and ducked her head closer to him. "Oh, I hate it when he does this."

Jeremy chuckled.

David rode circles around Marty Sr. and Darlene's boat, jumping and splicing the waves. The roar of the Jet Ski's motor increased. His smile flashed across his tanned face. Maggie's smile matched his.

"Maggie's just as crazy." Jeremy cringed as his brother rode the Jet Ski full throttle at the boat.

Poppy's hand flew to her mouth. "He's gonna crash!"

Jeremy slipped on his sunglasses, stretched his arms out along the seat, and smiled. He loved this part.

David veered sharply, sending a tall wave of water cascading over the deck of the boat. Jeremy gasped as the cold water hit him. Sarah yelped. Dennis and Marty shouted at David as he rode away.

Jeremy wiped at his face as Sophie laughed.

She pointed at Poppy. "Oh, Poppy!"

Poppy placed her hands on her little hips and turned to face Jeremy. A big clump of weeds hung over her head and down her face. "That's it. This means war."

David reclined in the side seat of the pontoon. The sun beat on his face and legs, drying his soaked shorts and hair.

"You're going to get burned, you know."

David cracked his eyes open and peered at his brother. "Yup. Maybe."

He raised his head. The pontoons had been lashed together and beached on the small island in the middle of the lake. The kids' laughter bounced through the trees and off the water as they looked for mussel shells along its shore.

"Marty's got the grill going." Jeremy sat opposite of him, arms stretched out to the side, ankle over knee. "Don't know about you, but I'm famished."

"Yup." David laid himself down on the seat, one leg bent. "Water'll do that to ya."

"This was a great idea that Maggie had. Good for Poppy, although I have to warn you. She's after revenge."

David turned his gaze to Jeremy. "Really? For what?"

"The ski splash."

"Oh." David laughed. His little flower couldn't stay mad at him for long. Besides, he taught her everything she knew, anyway. "Well, I figured if I took her for a ride on the ski, then maybe she'll forget about that."

Jeremy snorted. "Oh, I doubt it. She's a spitfire."

"That she is." David stood and looked at the island. The wind picked up and cooled his hot skin.

Maggie sat at a stone picnic table with Darlene and Sarah. She threw her head back and laughed at something. A faint trickle of her soft laughter reached him. He took a deep breath.

This was so perfect. Seeing her with his family. He looked at Jeremy. "Can I ask you something?"

Jeremy nodded. "Anything, but I prefer it under the canopy. Whether you like to burn or not, I, on the other hand, definitely have an aversion to it."

David chuckled and followed his brother. He perched on the top of the seat in the corner. His gaze traveled over the water. Another barge across the river slowly floated past.

"Well?"

"It's about Maggie." David dropped his gaze to his clasped hands. "And about me."

He blew out a breath. It was hard, trying to talk to his brother again. But he missed him. Missed the conversations and the talks.

David cleared his throat. "I wanted to know what you thought about me asking Maggie to marry me."

Jeremy grinned. "You should know the answer to that."

David shrugged. "I wanted to hear it from you. I mean, I'm a recovering alcoholic. Maggie is gaining custody of Poppy. I don't want to jeopardize that."

Jeremy moved to sit on the top of the seat beside him. "I think it's a great idea. It's obvious you love her. And we all know she loves you. As for how it will affect Poppy . . ." Jeremy looked at him, studying him. "You are wonderful for the girl. And she has helped you in more ways than one, David."

David looked away. A lump formed in his throat. "Yeah. She has."

"I know you love that little girl. So do we." Jeremy spoke softly. "You never told me everything, David."

The change in topic threw him off balance. He jerked his gaze back to Jeremy.

Now it was Jeremy's turn to look away. "I know things will never be like they were before. But I think we can make it work. Think you will ever learn to trust me again?"

David shrugged. "I want to. I'm not ready to tell you . . ." He pressed his lips together.

"Not ready to tell me that one last thing?"

"Yeah."

Jeremy nodded and stood. David reached out and stopped him with a hand on Jeremy's arm. "Wait. There is one thing I need to tell you."

Jeremy's cool gray eyes met his. "Go on."

"I'm sorry. I blamed you for so many things. I had forgiven you for all the harsh things that were said before I left. Do you think—can you forgive me in return?"

David frowned. Where did that come from? He was only going to say he was sorry. But a part of him, the anger, the frustration, the rage, floated away as it rode the wake of his words. Another taste of freedom.

Jeremy clapped his hand on David's shoulder. "Did that long ago, little brother." He smiled. "Come on, let's go eat."

David smiled. When did their roles change over? It used to be him who ran from the emotional scenes. He hopped off the boat and splashed down into the shallow water as Poppy came running to him.

"Look! I got all kinds of trumpet shells. See?" Her eyes sparkled as she held out her handful of the small, spiral mussel shells.

David ruffled her hair. "Those are beautiful, little flower. Come on. Let's go show Maggie."

He put his arm over her shoulders as they stepped across the shale-coated bank. David met Jeremy's eyes and smiled. His brother was right. He and Poppy did wonders for each other.

———————

Maggie gasped as the Jet Ski banked sharply. They were so close to the water, she could have reached out and scooped up a handful. The Jet Ski broke the tranquility of the cove, rippling its dark, gray water.

David cut the motor. Silence descended. Only the lapping of the waves against the thick weed-covered banks kept them company. She gazed over his shoulder. The corner of the cove hid most of the lake, muffling the sounds of boats and people.

"It's beautiful here. So calm."

David nodded. "Think you can slide on around here in front? I'll let you ride us back."

"Really?" Maggie let go of his vest. His hands grabbed her leg, helping her slide around him. She giggled as she settled into the seat. "I'm backwards. I don't think I can drive like this."

He stopped her with a hand on her waist as she tried to turn around. "Hold up. I'll help you, but stay like this for a moment."

She arched her brow at him. "You planning some monkey business?"

He grinned as his ears turned pink. "I promised you weeks ago that I wouldn't force the issue with you."

Maggie resettled in the seat. The hair on his legs tickled hers as she dangling her legs back over his. "Okay then. What's up? Oh, I know what you want."

"Yeah? What's that?" He leaned closer.

"You want to take this opportunity for smooching." She sidled closer to him and wrapped her arms about his neck. "We haven't had a chance at all today."

His eyes darkened as he looked at her. White teeth peeked from between his parted lips. "That's true."

His mouth closed around hers. Maggie melted into him. He still tasted of cherry cola that he drank earlier at lunch. She broke away and gasped. "You kiss way too good for my health, Mr. David Boyette."

He smiled. "Same goes for you, Miss Maggie Goddard." His hand smoothed back her wet hair. "Can I ask you something?"

She captured his hand and kissed his fingertips. He bit at the inside of his lip as he waited for her answer. Way too handsome for her peace of mind. "Anything."

"It's really important. I mean, extremely."

Now what? She doubted she could handle another emergency. Finally a calm, stress-free time in life, and she didn't want it to cave in on her.

She took a deep breath. "Okay?"

He fiddled with his pocket. The sound of Velcro separating pierced the still air. "I found something not too long ago, and I really wanted your opinion on it."

"Oh, is that all?" She fanned her face. He was such a silly goose. "I thought to myself, 'oh, boy, now what emergency is rising?'"

David laughed. He opened a small, hinged box and presented it to her. Her breath caught. The pink opal sparkled against the silver filigree band. Oh, the sneaky devil.

"Maggie, marry me, please."

She clapped her hand over her heart in a vain effort to calm its erratic beat. Thoughts flew out of her head. Her mind grasped futilely to gain at least some idea, anything to be able to talk.

A worried expression crossed his face. "Maggie?"

Her mouth opened, and she squeaked. She pressed her fingers to her lips as a tear rolled down her face. Well, if she couldn't say it, she'd show it.

She grabbed his face and planted the biggest kiss she could muster. Every bit of longing, happiness, and love flowed from her and into the touch of their lips.

When she pulled back, he sat with closed eyes, face still tilted toward her, and with a bemused expression.

He swallowed and licked his lips. "That was a yes?"

Maggie laughed and threw her arms around him, kissing him again.

"Yes, silly! Yes!" Her shout echoed, scaring birds from the trees.

David visibly sighed. He smiled and pulled the ring from the box. His hand shook slightly as he slipped it onto her finger. "Thank goodness, because I was about to die of fright for a second there."

She cut off his words with another kiss and then leaned her forehead against his. "And I couldn't speak for a second there because you made me so happy."

"I do have one more thing to ask."

"Oh? What's that?"

His face flooded red. He closed his eyes. "Can we have the wedding soon? Your kisses are killing me, baby."

CHAPTER 23

David jumped and spilled his coffee on the counter when his phone vibrated. One of these days, he was sure to have a heart attack from that. He reached into his front pocket and pulled it out. It was early for her to call.

"Hello, beautiful."

"David! Dad's in Memphis. No one else is here. You gotta help . . ."

He set his cup down. Apprehension rippled through him. "Maggie, what's wrong?"

Her words tumbled through the phone. "She left a note, but she's gone. I thought she was in bed when I went to take a shower. I can't believe I'm such a bad mother. How could I let her run away? I don't know what—"

"Maggie!" He shouted over her words. "Calm down! Tell me—"

"—I'm almost there."

There? Where there? David rushed to the front door and threw it open. Sure enough, her truck barreled down the driveway.

Rocks flew as she skidded to a stop. The driver's door practically flew off its hinges. She rocketed from the cab. David pocketed his phone and hurried toward her. It would have been comical if she had not been so upset. She still cried into the phone as she ran to him.

". . . it was her pillow and not her. I can't—"

David snatched the phone from her hands and crushed her body into his. Words continued pouring from her, her fists wringing his undershirt. "Poppy said I couldn't love her anymore, and I don't know what to do. I can't find her."

The door behind him opened. His dad stood there, pulling his suspenders up on his shoulders. "David, what's going on?"

"Your guess is as good as mine. She's not making much sense at the moment." He pushed Maggie away and held her at arm's length. Tears streaked her face. Her eyes gleamed like polished sapphires. Her chin trembled with each breath. "Calm down, Maggie. Tell me, slowly, what happened."

Her hands fluttered as she spoke. "I woke up. I thought Poppy was still in bed. I checked, I mean I really checked. I thought it was her. I can't believe I'm a bad mother already. I only went to take a shower." Tears flooded again. Her chest heaved, and she collapsed against him. She pulled a paper from her shorts' pocket. "Here." She shoved it into his face.

He passed the note behind him. "Dad, read it please." David held her racking, sobbing body as tight as he could with the other arm. She slowly fell to her knees, and he sank with her.

Dad took the paper. Mom arrived on the scene and rushed to their side. David gently rocked Maggie as her sobs subsided. Her misery and pain stabbed deep into him. It killed him to see her this way.

His dad's voice rose above Maggie's wails. "Dear Maggie, I know that you can't love me since David is going to marry you now. I think it is better if I find a new home. Please don't worry about me. Take care of Sorta and make sure Samson doesn't bite her. Tell David that I love him but that I know he can't love both of us. I'll be sure to write. Poppy."

Maggie pressed herself harder against his chest. Tears soaked him. Her body shook, and she burrowed herself deeper into his arms.

His dad looked down at Maggie. "When did you find this?"

"A . . . inutes . . . go."

At his dad's confused expression, David translated. "She said a few minutes ago." He slowly brushed back her tangled hair. His hand rubbed circles around her back before gently pushing her back so that he could look into her eyes. "Listen, she couldn't have gotten far. We'll find her."

Nothing but sobs came out. How many tears did she have? His poor baby was a walking hydrant. He placed a hand on her head and pulled her to him once more. Her hair, still wet from her shower, clung to his cheek. Her arms latched around his waist.

"Come on. Buck up a little. We can't find her like this."

Maggie nodded, but David felt new wet patches form against his stomach. His mom knelt down beside them.

"Here, Son, let me have her. Y'all go get our little girl." His mom gently pulled at Maggie and coaxed her to her feet.

Sputtering and sobbing, Maggie stumbled inside with his mom. David rose to his feet. His dad stood holding the letter out to him. He took the note and read. She had used Maggie's sparkly pink pen.

His heart slammed against him. Air left his lungs. He wavered as he read Poppy's pretty handwriting. His finger traced the letters. So many times he had helped her with her penmanship. Sitting on the small living room floor, using the old coffee table as a desk. Maggie watching them from the kitchen. His hand shook. His little flower had left them.

His dad laid a hand on his shoulder. "Careful, Son. Let's get the family together. We'll all find her."

A tear splashed down on the note, and David realized his face was wet. He folded the note and stuck it in his back pocket. "I . . ." He cleared his throat and fought the lump down. "I'll call Jeremy. You call Darlene."

He scrubbed at his face. His hands shook harder as he tried to press the speed dial on his phone. He managed to hit the four button. As he waited for Jeremy to answer, he walked off down the driveway. Gravel skittered beneath his sandals.

"David?"

"Jer. Poppy's gone. Maggie came over. Poppy left a note. She's disappeared." Saying the words, David felt like Maggie. His body trembled. His gut clenched. Tears threatened to flood. He leaned his hand against the old oak tree. "We need everyone to help find her."

"We'll be there in a few minutes."

No questions. No hesitation. David closed his phone. His brother was coming.

His family was coming.

Minutes seemed like eternity as they stretched. His heart hammered at him again. There was no way his ribs were going to retain its furious beats. Dad's hand massaged his shoulder, and the wild jackrabbit leaping around inside him calmed down.

He brought his head up at the sound of a deep rumble. Jeremy's F-250 screamed around the corner and braked, sending a white cloud billowing past. Sarah's car careened past them to the house. She leapt out, threw a wave, and ran into the house, Sophie right behind her.

Jeremy hopped out with Dennis. They flattened themselves against the truck as Marty Sr.'s Navigator pulled into the driveway. Darlene flew out of the SUV and ran to the house.

Both of the Martys emerged.   Marty Sr.'s voice rumbled. "How we doing this?"

Jeremy pointed at Dennis. "You take Dennis and Marty. Check out the downtown area; then, branch off into the mall. David and I will take the outer highway close to Maggie's. Dad, you take Mom and check the church, the cemetery, and the playgrounds."

The front door slammed. Maggie ran toward David. The impact of her body catapulting into his almost knocked him down.

"Sarah, Sophie, and I are going to check the riverside and make our way down to Arkabutla," Maggie told him. "Poppy's always talked about having a camping trip down there."

David's hands wrapped around Maggie's face, and he looked deep into her eyes. "Are you okay?"

She nodded, pressing her lips together. "I am now. Family's here."

He lowered his forehead to hers. Cool skin against hot. "Yeah. They are. Go. Jeremy and I will check the highways." He tasted salty tears as he covered her lips in a quick kiss. Then she was gone, running back toward Sarah's car.

Jeremy slapped David's shoulder as he passed. "Come on. Every second counts, little brother."

Jeremy's truck roared to life as David slid into the seat. They left the rest of the family scattering for their own vehicles.

Poor Poppy. Feeling alone. Feeling unloved. Feeling like he once felt.

He lowered his head into his hands and scrubbed at his hair. Fingernails dug into his scalp. His heart lurched within him. Tears boiled inside. He needed to control himself.

"Don't hold it back, little brother." Jeremy's hand slid across his shoulder, squeezing it. "Talk to me."

David shook his head. "Go to Maggie's cottage. Let's check the riverbank. Poppy and I walk the banks a lot."

"Sure thing."

Within minutes, they arrived at Maggie's. David jumped out and raced to the backyard. The little wooden pier was empty. He took the left trail with Jeremy on his heels.

"Poppy!" His voice echoed in the woods and off the river. No reply came. No Poppy.

Jeremy grabbed his arm and pulled him to a stop. "Let's look elsewhere. She wouldn't go this deep into the woods."

David nodded dumbly and followed his brother back to the backyard. She had to be somewhere. Oh, please, lead them to where she was.

His breath hitched.

His knees buckled.

David sunk to the ground. His mind whirled—his family, his girl. Everything and nothing cascaded through him.

He knelt on the hard rocks in the dirt. They dug into his knees. His heart ached.

He stretched out his hands. His head bowed. Smooth dirt caressed his forehead. Now he knew how King David felt. He could feel his soul ripping apart, and for the first time in so many years, he cried out with his whole heart.

The words would not come, but God knew his heart. He had to know his heart. Oh, please, keep her safe. Don't let another be taken from him. Keep her wrapped in your loving arms. Protect her. Help them find her.

His hands formed fists around the small rocks, squeezing them until they cut into his palms. "Don't abandon me, please." He breathed the words, the dirt stirring underneath his lips. "Don't take another away, please. Guide us to her. Oh, God, forgive me. I've wronged you. Don't let my sin harm her."

"God doesn't work like that, little brother."

Jeremy knelt beside him. No touch upon his head or shoulder this time. No other words spoken by him. His comforting presence bolstered David's resolve.

David closed his eyes. A feeling of peace washed over him, urging him to speak again. He opened his mouth, tasting dirt against his lips.

"I ran from you, Father, but you would not let me go. I hated you, Father, but you would not stop loving me. Now, I am back in your arms, and I beg your forgiveness. My child is gone. Please help me find her. Don't let her repeat my mistake. I cannot do this without you. I see that now. I am yours. Oh, Lord, I am yours!" A sob became his amen. Tears fell and created small puddles of wet dirt. The rocks in his hands were a lifeline thrown to him. Eternity passed. Time never existed.

Jeremy's hand was feather light as it rested on his shoulder. Strength and calmness entered his body. David looked up. It was all different. He couldn't name it. He couldn't place his finger on it. But somehow, his world was different.

His brother grabbed him under his arms, and he stumbled to his feet. Smalls bits of gravel clung to his hands, and he flicked them off, wincing at the burning sensation. Deep cuts from the gravel criss-crossed his palms. There would be scars, but those were just physical.

He breathed in deep. His emotional scars were gone.

Jeremy's hand left, leaving a cold void on his arm. His voice sounded strangled as he spoke. "Come on. Let's try the highway. She might be along one of them."

David slipped into the cab as Jeremy started the engine. Jeremy took a right turn onto the highway.

David looked out the windshield. The dark gray highway zoomed under them. Trees flew past. A flock of birds weaved through the blue sky. How bright everything seemed in the morning sun.

"Talk to me. What did you mean by 'don't take another away'?" The words were hesitant, as if he already knew the answer.

David opened his hands and stared at the red cuts. How easy it came to speak to God. How difficult it was to speak to his brother.

Jeremy touched his shoulder and then replaced his hand on the steering wheel. Out of the corner of his eye, David watched Jeremy rub at his mouth with his left hand. Patiently waiting.

Silence stretched. The highway loomed before them. His future stretched before him. He had to only reach for it.

"I can't lose her, Jeremy." The words fell out before he could stop them. He paused. He didn't want to stop them this time. "Maggie and I love her too much. Anything can happen to her."

"We'll find her, David. We will. Have faith." Jeremy took a left, leading away from the church. "She couldn't have gone far."

David clutched at his stomach. Fear gnawed him. Fire burned inside, licking at his soul. The urge for a drink grabbed at him. He pushed the thought aside, but it refused to go away. Fire needed fuel. He refused to give it fuel. He had to tell his brother.

"I can't lose another one, Jeremy. Not another child. That's what I meant earlier." The words rushed past his lips, unburdened. He kept his eyes trained on the floorboard.

Again time suspended itself as Jeremy drove down the highway.

Tears dropped, hitting his clenched fists as he glanced at his brother. Three and half years of holding the secret inside. "Rebecca was pregnant."

Jeremy swallowed hard. "No one knew?"

David shook his head. "No."

"Honeymoon baby story?"

"Yeah." David dropped his gaze to his hands again. "And now Poppy will be taken away. I can't lose another child, Jeremy. I can't."

His chest heaved. Sobs, held in check, racked his body, shaking it and rattling his bones. He denied the fire its fuel, but the sobs continued. He buried his head and wrapped his arms around it. He gave in. Whoever said "the truth will set you free" ought to be shot. Telling the truth hurt. Painfully hurt.

Jeremy's hand gripped the back of his neck and squeezed. "For three years you held this inside?"

"I did." David rocked his body, willing the sobs to quit. "I'm sorry. For everything." He raised his head and stared at the Ford logo on the glove compartment. "I . . . "

He faltered. A sigh escaped.

"I'm sorry too." Jeremy's hand fell away.

David looked over at him. Jeremy sat ramrod straight, staring ahead.

"You didn't do anything. I'm the one who was a jerk, an—"

"Yeah." Jeremy cut him off. "And so was I. You needed me. I wasn't there. I didn't even try to understand. I didn't want to understand."

"And I should have tried to talk to you. I had to blame someone. I blamed God, but the pain was still there, so I blamed you—"

"But—"

"I—"

David and Jeremy glanced at each other as their words overlapped. A grin stretched across their faces. David laughed and looked away at the empty highway. He wiped at his eyes with a thumb.

"We good, little brother?"

David nodded. "We're good."

"Then let's go find our baby girl, shall we?" Jeremy drove.

The image of a little redhead leaning over the newspaper and asking about the casinos and if they were like the Old West ones popped into David's mind. That was three weeks ago when they were at Pick Wick. His breath caught. Could she actually be going there?

"Jeremy, I know where to find her. Head for sixty-one."

"Tunica?"

David laughed. He ran a hand over his mouth. "Yeah. She's heading to the casinos. Don't ask."

Jeremy shook his head and turned at the next road.

David sat back. There was an urgency within him, but no fire. Fear wanted to rear its head, but he turned away. There was nothing to fear anymore.

"I think I see a little redhead." Jeremy slowed and pulled to the side.

Up ahead, Poppy, wearing her black and white checkered dress, struggled with a small suitcase, dragging it behind her. It fell to the side, and she kicked it.

David pursed his lips. "Well, I do believe she's in a foul mood."

Jeremy laughed. "Good luck."

Poppy looked up. She scowled when she saw Jeremy's truck. With a determined look, she picked up her suitcase, turned, and staggered farther down the side of the road.

Jeremy shook his head again. "Well, I don't think she's going to give in easily."

David opened the door and hopped out. "No one can withstand the Boyette brothers. Come on, let's go get her."

His legs ate up the graveled roadside. Poppy huffed and puffed. The suitcase had to be heavy, but she was relentless. David smiled. The girl was just like the family.

"Poppy!" David called out to her, but she sped up and dodged an anthill. She stumbled. The suitcase fell to the ground and spilled open.

With a cry, she threw herself down on the rocks and started piling the clothes and books back into the case. David eased himself down beside her and placed his hand on hers. "Poppy?"

She snarled at him and jerked away. "Go away."

"I can't. Not without you."

She pulled her knees to her chest and wrapped her arms around them. "I can do this on my own. Maggie has you now; she don't need me."

David reached for her, but she recoiled. That hurt. He let his hand fall back to the suitcase. His brows creased. "That's not true. She needs you. I need you."

Forget it. He didn't care if she bit, clawed, or bucked. He pulled at her, fighting against her flailing limbs.

"Stop it. I'll call the police! I mean it!"

David chuckled as Jeremy knelt down in front of them. "Police is already here, little flower." He held her tight, smoothing back her hair. The scent of honeysuckle rose up from her silken strands. "Shh. Relax."

She wailed, her body doubling over. Then she reared back, her head banging against his mouth. "But no one wants me. No one loves me!"

"Not true!" David turned her around, forcing her to look at him. He had to get this into her stubborn, red head. He grabbed her face and held it. "I love you! You're my girl."

"Not true!" She echoed his words. "If you love Maggie, then you don't have room for me. I know you lied. A heart can't love more than one. You don't even love your brother!"

If words were hammers. His chest crumbled in on itself as her onslaught bashed into him. In his foolishness, he almost destroyed an innocent.

He wrapped his arms around her and crushed her to him, pressing his lips against the top of her head. Tears rolled down his face.

He could only whisper. "I'm sorry, Poppy. Believe me when I say that I love you."

She shook her head. "No one can love me."

Jeremy reached out and rubbed her back as he moved closer to them. "Poppy, love, everyone loves you."

Her little hands pushed at David, and he allowed her to turn her head towards Jeremy. Dried streaks lined his face. How many tears were going to flow today?

She stared at Jeremy. Then turned to him. "Really?"

David kissed her forehead. "Really."

Confusion sketched itself across her face. "But you hate your brother, don't you?"

"No, little flower." David lowered his head to hers. Her hair tickled his nostrils. Jeremy placed a hand on his back and one on Poppy's. David looked up and met Jeremy's eyes. "I love my brother. It's just taken me a while to realize that."

Her arms circled his waist. Above them, the sun brightened. David's heart brightened with it. He cleared his voice. Enough of this. "Come on. No time for soap operas. Maggie is waiting."

Jeremy's hands fell away. He turned to reload her suitcase. Poppy pulled away and tried to smile. "She won't be mad?"

"No. She will be overjoyed to have you back." He tweaked her nose. "You ready?"

Poppy nodded and allowed Jeremy to help her to her feet.

David heaved a sigh and jumped up, slapping and clutching at his pants leg. "Thank you. Because I think an ant just crawled up my pants."

Poppy's laugh echoed down the open highway. She threw herself back into his arms, and David held her, laughing with her. He had his girl back.

EPILOGUE

David thumped his fist against his thigh. His stomach rolled. His head threatened to explode. He pressed a hand against his chest, willing his heart to slow down.

Sheesh, he was nervous. He fell back into the metal chair and bowed his head. He needed peace. He needed calm.

"I don't think I have ever seen you so jittery."

David looked up and smiled at Jeremy. "Yeah, I know."

Jeremy walked to the full length mirror and fingered his boutonnière and then rubbed his hand over his shaved head. "This from a man who will jump into a raging fire."

"Well, a fire you can beat down. This–" David waved his hand toward the area beyond the room's door, "this is another matter. This is something totally different. And strange."

"It is different and strange. But, it's unbelievably wonderful." Jeremy tweaked the pink rose one last time, straightened the pink cummerbund, and scowled. "What other concessions did you have to make? Pink on a man."

David rose and stood beside his brother, gazing into the mirror. Twin shaved heads. Black suits with pink roses and pink cummerbunds. "Real men wear pink, dude."

"Keep lying to yourself, little brother." Jeremy ran his hand over his head again. "Can't believe I shaved my head too. You're the one who lost the bet."

"You did it so I wouldn't look too much like a fool up there."

Jeremy chuckled. "Yeah. What are brothers for, right?"

"I think that is definitely on the list." David reached around Jeremy and retied the bowtie. "I swear, you never get this right."

"Well, I haven't worn one since my own wedding; what do you expect?"

"There." David stepped back and brushed at his suit. "How do I look?"

Jeremy smiled. He stepped up and brushed at the black sateen lapels. "Amazing. So, what did she agree to, for you to wear pink?"

David felt his ears burn. "Something black, lacy, and barely there."

"With feathers?"

David nodded. "And music."

A rap came from the door. Their dad poked his head in. "They're ready. Time to go."

"Okay. Just a minute, Dad." David turned to Jeremy. "Thanks."

"For what?"

"For everything. Being there before and being here now. I don't think I would be able to stand up there without collapsing if I didn't have you beside me."

Jeremy placed his hand behind David's head, and their foreheads touched. "Think nothing of it. Prayer?"

David nodded. He clasped the back of his brother's head as Jeremy spoke.

"Lord, bless this union today. Let it be the first of many happy times. Grace us with your presence and love. In Jesus' name, amen."

"Amen." David broke contact with Jeremy and brushed at his eye. "I swear, I think wearing pink turns me into a pansy."

Jeremy slapped the back of his head. "Told you. Come on."

They left the small room. David took a deep breath and blew it out. It was only a small ceremony. It was only a new life. His head tingled, and everything went light.

Jeremy's hand clasped his shoulder. "Buck up, man. If you faint at your own wedding, you'll never live it down."

David nodded. "I can do this. It's only a wedding, right?"

Jeremy laughed. "Don't let Maggie hear you say that. Only a wedding?"

He smiled and followed Jeremy out into the sanctuary. Only a wedding. Only a second chance was more like it.

God had given him another chance at love. He wasn't going to let it go this time. Second chances only come once.

For more information about
D. M. Webb
&
Mississippi Nights
please visit:

www.dmwebb.com
dmwebb42@gmail.com
www.dmwebb-writebyfaith.blogspot.com

For more information about
AMBASSADOR INTERNATIONAL
please visit:

www.ambassador-international.com
@AmbassadorIntl
www.facebook.com/AmbassadorIntl